Juvenal

Decimi Junii Juvenalis Satirae XIII.

Thirteen satires of Juvenal

Juvenal

Decimi Junii Juvenalis Satirae XIII.
Thirteen satires of Juvenal

ISBN/EAN: 9783337382001

Printed in Europe, USA, Canada, Australia, Japan

Cover: Foto ©Andreas Hilbeck / pixelio.de

More available books at **www.hansebooks.com**

DECIMI JUNII JUVENALIS SATIRAE XIII

THIRTEEN SATIRES OF JUVENAL

WITH NOTES AND INTRODUCTION

BY

G. A. SIMCOX, M.A.

FELLOW OF QUEEN'S COLLEGE OXFORD

SECOND EDITION, REVISED AND ENLARGED

JOHN ALLYN

BROMFIELD STREET, BOSTON

1873

PREFACE TO THE SECOND EDITION.

IN the first edition I confined myself almost exclusively to such annotations as a reader of Juvenal's own day might have required, if very stupid and not very ignorant. Even from this point of view the commentary should have been fuller than it was then, perhaps than it is now. In the present edition I have tried to give just enough information about the proper names mentioned in Juvenal (when anything is known) to save beginners the trouble of a search in Dr Smith's valuable dictionaries, which every schoolboy can hardly be expected to possess, though they ought to be in every school library. It was beyond both my ambition and my power to add anything to the illustrative materials which have been accumulated already. Fortunately it lay more within the scope of the *Catena Classicorum* to try to disengage the exegetical results on which Mr Mayor's magnificent series of parallel passages seem to converge. His edition would leave no room for mine if schoolboys and undergraduates liked their work well enough to linger over it. The personal and subjective character of Mr Macleane's edition seems at first obtrusive; in time his manliness becomes attractive; at last his independence becomes suggestive. Second thoughts have convinced me that he

b 2

was right in more than one passage, especially on questions of punctuation where in the first instance I had followed Mayor. Wherever the text was simply a matter of manuscript authority, I have been glad to give Jahn's without discussion; where the various readings affected the sense or had a character of their own, it seemed better to choose for myself and to give my reasons: there is always something irritating about an edition which indicates a variety of reading without giving a clue to the editor's principle of selection.

Juvenal is a writer in whom every attentive reader may hope to discover something fresh, while every reader whose vigilance has not been chastened into sagacity must expect sometimes to discover more than is there; but in dealing with Juvenal it is safest to err on the side of excess. In a highly literary age artificial connexions and effects occur more readily than natural; a writer can hardly employ an expression which does not imply a train of half-forgotten thought. The chronology of Juvenal's life and writings suggested in the Introduction, which has been materially expanded, is of course very precarious; but it seems to rest upon facts which have still to find their place in a really adequate conception of his system of satirical allusion.

Three satires have been altogether omitted as not required in University Examinations, which proceed on the creditable hypothesis that all candidates for a pass or honours either possess or cultivate the temper to which such reading is as painful as it ought to be.

INTRODUCTION.

ABOUT the life of Juvenal only three things can be said to be known;—that he was the heir of a wealthy freedman; that he practised declamation till middle life, when he found out his talent for declamatory satire; and, lastly, that he was banished to a frontier command, as a punishment for affronting an actor. Cf. VII. 88—92.

It is more than probable, from the Fifteenth Satire, that Egypt was the scene of his banishment, in which case the *Scotti*, mentioned in the fifth and sixth of the seven lives, printed by Jahn, must either be a copyist's blunder, founded on *Coptos*, or a false inference from XIV. 193. Some have conjectured, from the great variety of emperors specified as having sacrificed the poet to the vanity of a discreditable favourite, that the whole story is a fiction, based on the satirical allusion to Paris, in the Seventh Satire, and the expressions in the Fifteenth, which imply a personal acquaintance with Egypt. This is supported by the observation, that Paris was put to death by Domitian, A.D. 83, while no Junius was consul till A.D. 84. We have no right to reject the story of the exile, supported as it is by Sidonius Apollinaris, who refers to it (IX. 266) as the established belief of the fifth century; and the chronological difficulty about its cause may perhaps be removed by observing, that all the lives but one treat the emperor as the offended party, and that three state expressly that it was only on their republication that the lines on Paris gave offence. Domitian was quite capable of resenting the imputation of conferring military commands at the suggestion of an actor, especially when the actor's influence had been removed; nor would his resentment be lessened if Juvenal had deliberately republished, with an application to his own reign, what had been originally directed against the earlier Paris, the favourite of Nero. A wider question suggests itself here. Did Juvenal begin to write under Nero, and to publish under Domitian, while the revised edition of his works was interrupted by death, perhaps in Trajan's reign?

That some such revised edition was attempted is probable, from the statement of one old biographer, that a considerable interval elapsed between the original composition of the lines on Paris, and their reappearance in the Seventh Satire; from the remark of another, that he enlarged (*ampliavit*) his satires in exile; and from the curious circumstance that there are MSS. in which the Sixteenth Satire, a mere fragment is placed before the Fifteenth. Obviously, copyists must have changed the order which Juvenal intended, in order that all the satires might appear to be finished, except the last; perhaps also those who doubted the genuineness of the fragment may have wished to propagate their suspicions by relegating it to a sort of Appendix. If Juvenal was in the habit of retouching his compositions, it is obviously unsafe to infer the date of a satire from single lines; for in such a laboured style innumerable additions and insertions would be possible, which would improve the brilliancy of the general effect, without impairing its unity. Hence we cannot build much upon the following list of passages.

In I. 47, VIII. 120, Juvenal mentions the exile and rapacity of Marius Priscus, who was condemned for oppression in proconsular Africa, A.D. 100, which is the latest date that we can fix with certainty.

In VI. 502, there is an allusion to the successive layers of curls, which cannot be traced on the imperial busts, our only authority, higher than the reign of Trajan; but (*ib.* 385) a musician is mentioned, who was already famous when Martial published his Fourth Book, comparatively early under Domitian.

In XII. 80, there is an allusion to the inner basin of the *Portus Augusti*, which was not completed, according to the Scholia, till Trajan, though the general construction of the harbour was due to Claudius; and the Scholiast may have confused the harbour at Centum Cellae, now Civita Vecchia, with that at Portus.

Moreover, as the information about Trajan is introduced to give an erroneous sense to *rursum*, we are scarcely bound to believe that the *interiora—tuti stagna sinus* had been enclosed as a separate basin when Juvenal wrote.

In VIII. 51, there is an ambiguous passage, that would suit the latter part of Trajan's reign, or the early part of Vespasian's, almost equally well or ill. The reference to the eagles, which control the conquered Batavian, would be most in place immediately after the revolt of Civilis. On the other hand, Vespasian never sent an expedition to the Euphrates; and it would be an unpleasant inaccuracy to couple the achievements of Cerealis and Corbulo: unless, indeed, Juvenal may mean to refer to the danger of the eastern frontier, in the troubles after Nero's death. On the whole, the earlier date seems best; as to mention nothing further than the Euphrates would have been a very poor compliment to Trajan, if his reign was intended.

In XIII. 27, there is a yet more ambiguous appeal to the age of a friend, who was sixty years old when Juvenal wrote, and was born when Fonteius was consul. This excites our hopes of being able to fix the date of at least one whole satire; but unfortunately one Fonteius was consul A.D. 12, another A.D. 59, yet another A.D. 67. Lipsius and Professor Ramsay prefer the earliest date; most other authorities adopt the second.

In XV. 27, we have to choose in the same way between one Junius, who was consul A.D. 84; another, who was consul A.D. 119; and a Juncus whose other names may have been Sextus Julius, who was consul on the ides of October A.D.

127, as is proved by an inscription found in Sardinia, published by the Archæological Society of Rome, Vol. VI. p. 231: it is a grant of citizenship to those who had served 26 years in the fleet of Ravenna and to their families, and is dated by the year of Hadrian's reign and by the consulship of Juncus and Severus.

The first date is objected to, because Paris was dead, and because a Juvenal was resident in Rome, and intimate with Martial, when the latter published his Seventh Book (circa A. D. 93). The first objection is answered above. In reply to the second, it would be sufficient to say that there is no reason for supposing that the exile lasted longer than six months, the usual period for which such commands were conferred; though it is hardly necessary to identify the friend of Martial with the Satirist.

It seems at first sight as if there could be little doubt about the date of the Fourth Satire: we assume that it must have been written after Domitian's death, while Crispinus was still alive to insult respectable opinion. On reflection perhaps we shall see reason to qualify both these assumptions. It is really as hard to apply the wonderfully spirited opening of the Satire to a favourite who had fallen as to a favourite who was dead. Taking the first twenty or thirty lines alone as they stand, we should certainly suppose that they were the introduction to a very audacious lampoon on a reigning sovereign and on a favourite still in power. We really do not know enough to set aside this *prima facie* probability; moreover the main incident of the poem is of a kind which a satirist might certainly be expected to seize while it was fresh instead of waiting for twelve years till the scandal had got cold. There is no reason to put the council of the Turbot later than 89 A. D., which is the latest point at which we can suppose that Cornelius Fuscus, the prae-torian prefect, was alive in Italy to attend it. There is much that is tempting in the supposition that the first draft of the Fourth Satire is Juvenal's revenge on his return from his Egyptian exile. Such a lampoon might have had a clandestine circulation when Domitian had left for the Dacian frontier, if not before, and the burlesque epic solemnity of 37 sqq. would be all the more amusing applied to a living contemporary. On the other hand, the present form of the Satire may be later than the death of Crispinus. The last five lines which imply the death of Domitian might be detached; but it is hardly possible to mutilate the description of the *proceres*, and this as we have it must be later than 95 A.D., the date of the execution of the younger Acilius Glabrio, only a year at most before the death of Domitian. It is difficult to fix the date at which Domitian made himself conspicuous as the guardian of the morals of the vestals; we may assume that they were made aware of their liabilities as soon as he did so: the first two victims of the pontifex maximus were allowed to kill themselves above ground, the third was put to death with the antiquarian formalities, A.D. 89 or 91.

The only indication of the date of the Fifth Satire is to be found in vv. 107—110, which must belong to the generation after Nero; but too much weight must not be given to them, as 106—113 might be removed without injury, perhaps with advantage, as an unnecessary after-thought of the poet, who was afraid that he had not brought out his real opinion of Virro.

The date of the Seventh Satire must be determined by our selection of the Caesar who is hailed at the beginning as the solitary patron of the Muses. It is scarcely necessary to exclude Hadrian, on the ground that Trajan had done nothing to afflict the Nine; for the contrast is not between the liberality of one emperor and the illiberality of another, but between imperial patronage and public indifference. On the other hand, there is nothing in the satire that can be construed into a reference to what had passed under Trajan, or was passing under Hadrian, whereas the allusions to Domitian's reign are frequent.

We have references to the poverty of Saleius satirized by Martial (IV. 3. 6), to the recitations of Statius, which probably began with the First Book of the Thebaid (which is said to have been completed A.D. 94, after twelve years' labour); and the mention of his Agave proves that the Paris of the completed satire must be Domitian's favourite. In spite of this, however, most editors waver between Trajan and Hadrian, inclining to the former, though it would be much more reasonable to treat Trajan's reign than Domitian's as a period of literary decline. The Scholiast, who did not share their zeal for the purity and independence of Juvenal's literary conscience, says, with naïve absurdity, "Neronem palpat."

It is chiefly in the First and Eighth Satires that we find plausible grounds for suspecting allusions to the reign of Nero, which have furnished such a plentiful harvest of conjectures to annotators, from the Scholiast downwards. Madvig (in his Opuscula Academica, I. 29—63, II. 167—205) has effectually refuted the excesses of this tradition; but he has not condescended to examine whether it is wholly destitute of foundation.

Of course, every one would admit that a note like this on I. 59, "*Qui bona. prae.: propter equos hoc dicit et Neronem tangit,*" is a mere conjecture, neither very acute, nor very probable; but notes like those on I. 33—35, seem to embody in a blundering way a real ancient tradition. The reader shall judge :—"*Delator amici. Heliodorum significat delatorem . . . . Heliodorum dicit Stoicum philosophum, qui L. Junium Silanum, discipulum suum, cum argueretur conjurationis, inficiatum domesticam delationem etiam testimonio oppressit. Alii filosophum Trajani dicunt, qui Baream senatorem detulit et damnavit. Nonnulli Demetrium causidicum dicunt, qui multos Neroni detulit. Soranum Baream Celer filosophus, magister ipsius, scelere delationis occidit, et ipse postea sub Vespasiano ob hoc ipsum, Musonio Rufo accusante, damnatus est. . . . . Massa morio fuisse dicitur et Carus nanus, Latinus vero actor mimicus. Hi omnes Neronis fuerunt liberti et deliciae Augusti. Latinus autem mimus quasi conscius adulterii Messalinae uxori Neronis, ab ipso occisus est. Massa autem et Carus Heliodoro deferente occisi sunt: cujus futuram delationem ita timebant ut ei munera darent."* Here the sentence about Trajan's philosopher, who denounced and condemned the noble Barea, is an obvious confusion due to the fact that, while Barea suffered under Nero, the annotator supposed for the moment that Juvenal was satirizing the reign of Trajan. Again, when we are told that Messalina was the wife of Nero, it is more than doubtful whether we are to give the deponent credit for remembering that Nero was one of the surnames of Claudius; nor is it certain that the statement that Massa and Carus fell under the accusation of Heliodorus is more than an inference from the description in the text of their trembling homage to the great unknown of Juvenal.

When we turn to Valla's excerpts from Probus, we find at once a confirmation of our belief that most of the statements quoted above represent the tradition of a period when many authorities now lost were accessible, and an explanation of the blunder about Trajan's philosopher, which Valla himself repeats. According to Probus, Heliodorus was the *delator*, and the error, (corrected in the above citation, on the authority of Lipsius,) which substituted Licinium Syllanum for L. Junium Silanum, must be at least as old as his time. He adds that Massa, the fool, and Carus, the dwarf, both belonged to Trajan, while he implies quite correctly that Messalina was the wife of Claudius, though he does not ask himself how the same favourite could be an object of terror to members of Trajan's household, and to a victim of Claudius, or even Nero, who certainly *may* have taken a fancy to avenge his stepfather's dishonour.

It is probable that Probus was perplexed by what is certainly difficult to explain,—the mention of a favourite of Nero, and a corrupt governor under Trajan, in the same satire. Probus dilutes the difficulty by multiplying allusions to Trajan, as well as to Nero, without inquiring whether Trajan was a contemporary of Tigellinus. The moderns, at any rate, since Madvig, have generally cut the knot by supposing that the mention of Marius definitely fixes the date of the whole satire, and that Juvenal was indulging in a rather flat mystification, when he introduced an imaginary Mentor to warn him of the danger of denouncing Tigellinus, and propitiates his phantom monitor by a promise only to attack the dead. For if Tigellinus is merely the disguise of another reigning favourite, it would be necessary to prove, in the first place, that Trajan had a favourite who had power to persecute; and impossible to prove, in the second place, that any danger of the kind, which may have existed, could be avoided by only admitting names whose owners had departed; for Tigellinus had been dead nearly forty years; and the warning implies that his name was a transparent pseudonym for some well-known character, whom Juvenal's public were certain to recognize as the evil genius of Trajan. If we suppose that the real Tigellinus was meant, the allusion to Crispinus, in v. 27, is no objection to the theory that most of the satire was written under Nero, who raised Crispinus to the Senate, according to Probus, though his fortune culminated under Domitian.

The date of the Eighth Satire is yet more ambiguous. Besides the allusions already discussed to the Euphrates and the eagles which control the Batavian, we read (167—171) how Lateranus goes to drink in the tavern and feed with its greasy napkins, though he is of age for the wars of Armenia and Syria, for the defence of the river Danube and the river Rhine; old enough, in fact, to guarantee the security of Nero. Further on, at v. 193, the author speaks of his contemporaries as selling themselves to the stage and the arena, without a Nero to compel them; and at v. 221, we are informed that the musical tastes of Nero were the worst atrocity which called for the righteous vengeance of Vindex and Galba. Of course these last lines must have been written after Nero's death; and they explain the ambiguity of v. 198, where *citharaedo principe*, &c. must mean *after* an emperor had taken to music; what wonder that the nobility took to pantomime? for *nullo cogente Nerone* must be taken as a proof that the shameful devotion of men of rank to the stage was an effect which had

survived its cause. Some old copyists seem to have felt
citharaedo principe as a difficulty after Nero's death; hence
the gloss *natus*, which has replaced *mimus* in most MSS. It
remains to explain the allusion to Lateranus, as of age to
defend Nero, and the address to Rubellius Plautus or Blandus.
In the first place, we may observe that the general and shameless relaxation of manners suits better with the age of Nero·
than with that of Domitian, the reviver of the censorship; in
the second place, Lateranus must obviously be a contemporary
of Nero; in the third place, it is exceedingly improbable that
the younger Blandus (if there ever was one) could be the child
of an imperial mother; because if Plautus, like his father, had
married into the imperial family, Tacitus would have mentioned
it as an additional reason for the jealousy of Nero; and it is
not likely that Juvenal would have confounded Plautus with
his son. It would be less violent to suppose that Juvenal
wrote *Plaute* under Nero, having taken offence at the seclusion,
which Tacitus and his class admired, and afterwards, when
preparing his satires for publication, decided on altering an
obsolete apostrophe, but forgot to change the circumstances
when he altered the name. If this hypothesis seems com--
plicated, it must be remembered that *all* the MSS. have *Blande*
or *Plance*, while *Plaute* rests only on the high authority of
Lipsius; that the hero of the second Dunciad, in addition to
his own sins, has to endure much inappropriate invective due
to the peculiar dulness of the hero of the first; and that what
was possible to Pope in an elaborate work, was not impossible
to Juvenal in a passing digression.

One piece of evidence still remains for notice,—the allusions
in Martial to a Juvenal with whom he lived on terms of
affectionate familiarity at Rome, when he published his Seventh
Book (where the twenty-fourth epigram is addressed to Juvenal,
and the ninety-first alludes to him), and who was still presumably at Rome as a restless suitor for preferment in the
beginning of Trajan's reign, while Martial, having given up
the struggle, was enjoying the repose of his native Bilbilis

(Mart. XII. 18. I). As none of these epigrams contain any allusion to our Juvenal's career as a satirist, as the gentlemanly mendicancy implied in the latest epigram is incompatible with the statement of the biographers that he could go on with the study of declamation for amusement till middle life, and with his own allusions to a modest competence, and as Juvenal himself says nothing of Martial, I am inclined to believe that there were two Juvenals who lived at Rome in the time of Martial.

On the whole, therefore, it is not impossible that Juvenal was born about 20 or 30 A.D., and lived into Trajan's reign, which would make him seventy or eighty years old at the condemnation of Marius Priscus,—the one date we are able to fix with confidence in the whole of Juvenal's life. He began to write in the last years of Nero, and probably had prepared most of the materials which he finally placed in the First and Eighth Satires, and the rough draughts of others, before he published the little *jeu d'esprit* on the actor Paris. Perhaps also it would follow that the comparative repose and elevation of Satires x.—xiv. are due rather to the tranquillising influence of the reigns of Vespasian and Titus than to the mellowing influence of advancing years. Before A.D. 84, he had poems enough completed to be published, with the enlarged version of Satire vii., now pointed against the favourite of Domitian, who had just been sacrificed to the jealousy of his master. In that year he was banished to Egypt, probably for six months, and there witnessed the savage outbreak of fanaticism which is recorded in the Fifteenth Satire. He returned to Rome in a state of suppressed indignation against the tyrant who had appropriated a doubtful compliment to a fallen favourite as a reflection on his own good government, while he had entirely disregarded the decorous homage to himself, with which the satire opens. He was able to take a full revenge after Domitian's death, by the publication of the Fourth Satire in its present form. The additions, on this hypothesis, must be taken as a proof that, like Landor, Juvenal retained his energy as well as his malice late; for he must have been nearly seventy, and may have been nearly eighty when Domitian died. His own death, if he began to write in middle life under Nero, must be placed early in Trajan's reign, and this would account for the remarkable absence of all distinct allusion to Trajan's victories, which would have been quite in place in the Eighth Satire, or in the Fourteenth, where, on the contrary, he implies (v. 193) that frontier hostilities of the most paltry kind afford the only chance of military distinction. Nor is it likely that he undertook any fresh satire under Trajan, except perhaps the Sixteenth, which would suit very well with a time when a little military insolence was the most serious evil which a satirist with failing powers could select for attack. If the fragment be the prologue to a satire on military corruption and maladministration, its date would naturally be carried back to the time of Domitian's efforts to ingratiate himself with the soldiery, which began with the German campaign, 84 A.D.

From this sketch it appears that Juvenal must have been from five-and-twenty to thirty years in writing sixteen satires, one a fragment; and the difficulty is not greatly diminished if we take the second Junius and Fonteius; for even then his literary activity must be made to extend from the death of Domitian to at least 120 A.D. Nor can we assume that Juvenal wrote slowly because he wrote in a laboured style; for Statius, whose style is far more laboured, has left it on record that he finished poems as long as most of Juvenal's satires in two or three days. Of course it is possible to find a reason for many delays in the evidence, external and internal, that Juvenal's satires passed through much in the way of revision and expansion. Maternus (Tac. de Orat. III. 2, 3) could recite a tragedy on Cato one day, and the next sit down to consider how many of Cato's tirades or epigrams (it is distressing not to know which) should be transferred to Thyestes; but Maternus was almost as exceptional as Southey, who finished one epic over night and wrote a hundred lines of another before breakfast the next morning. There are tempers to which it is easier to put aside what has to be altered for weeks, which grow into months. As tempers vary and our knowledge of Juvenal's is likely to remain imperfect, it is safest to re- member the busy idleness in which a Roman gentleman passed his life at the capital, and the lazy leisure of the country holidays, which is indicated by Horace's Epistles, and the Eleventh Satire of Juvenal, and to conclude that the main business of Juvenal's life was to live, and that his satires were only occasional ebullitions of an indignation, not without in- tervals and consolations. "*Facit indignatio versum*" is his own motto; and indignation is not a permanent motive for exertion, since it is generally mixed with contempt; for there cannot be a better excuse for indolence than scorn of the only activity in which it is possible to take part. Our own Gifford was often invoked to lash the vices and follies of the age, but sensibly concluded that it was not worth while to be always in hot water for the sake of an age which needed so much lashing.

The writings of a satirist may easily leave us in doubt as to the events of his life: it is not certain that they will impress us with the character of the writer, or even that they will be, so far as they go, a trustworthy representation of his habitual self. We may reckon with more confidence upon finding traces of his personal ideas which are often distinctive, even when the character is commonplace; we may be sure of getting a tolerably complete view of the points at which life bore hardly upon the class and the generation which the satirist represents.

It is hardly fanciful to trace in Juvenal the last protest of the Marian democracy against the imperial system, as we trace in Tacitus the protest of the expiring aristocracy of Sulla, rather than of the effete oligarchy of Scaurus: like Sulla, Tacitus desired that the Senate should be an open corporation rather than a close one; like Sulla, he believed that the Senate ought to be in a position to govern the Roman Empire; unlike Sulla, he felt that the dignity of the order and the security of its individual members was the end, and the prosperity of the empire the means. After all there is little reason for surprise that the antagonisms which produced the empire should have lived on under it. The power of the emperors rested upon opinion no less than upon force; or rather, the convictions and interests of the military force of the State made it necessary that there should be an emperor. Among other causes, public opinion had considerable influence in deciding who the emperor should be; it had certainly a paramount influence in deciding how long any particular emperor should reign. Conspiracies always began in the camp or the palace against an emperor whom opinion had condemned; and it is characteristic of the difference between ancient and modern society, we may add, between Roman and Byzantine society, that when an emperor had once become a mark for conspiracies, one conspiracy or other was sure to succeed at last. The first Cæsar certainly gave unnecessary offence to the prejudices of the nobility. Octavian, Claudius, and Vespasian, though deferential in externals, kept the balance substantially even. Tiberius and Domitian, while they decimated the aristocracy, leant steadily in the direction of privilege; the despotism of Caius was demagogic that it might be levelling; the despotism of Nero was levelling that it might be demagogic. It is a proof of the intensity of the storms which agitated the last century of the republic, that their after gusts could sway the course of the empire. Upon the whole, the nobility had weathered the gale; from the time of Gaius Gracchus to the time of Publius Clodius and Gaius Curio, there had been a constant struggle, not only to introduce new principles of government, but to raise a new class to power to carry out those principles. The principles triumphed with the first Cæsar; all the Cæsars continued to watch over their development with a solicitude, seldom unintelligent, and scarcely ever relaxed. But the second Cæsar had decided that the triumph of the principles of the democracy should be as little of a triumph as possible for the democratic party; and certainly should not be a triumph over the nobility. Instead of sweeping the privileged classes away to make room for the reign of the people, a ladder was set up by which the most enterprising, who were seldom the most self-respecting of the people, could climb to a level with the privileged classes.

By the time of Juvenal the educated section of the Roman *bourgeoisie* had discovered that *la carrière ouverte aux talents,* so far as it was not a scramble in the mire, practically resolved itself into a lottery with many blanks and few prizes. Under the republic it was impossible for a member of the lower middle class to rise very high, except in the army, and even there the difficulties were very great; but for a man whose ambition was moderate, there were many more opportunities of making money both under the shadow of the aristocracy, and at their expense, than under the early empire. The centralisation of provincial patronage, though a gain to individuals, was of itself a loss to the class. Then the corporations of *publicani,* which had practically kept the administration of the revenue in their own hands, lost their freedom of action when they came into contact with imperial procurators. They tended more and more to give way to great contractors who had friends at court. Nor had the bar as a profession for the middle classes deteriorated less than the administration of the provinces, whether in partnership or in rivalry with the nobility. In the days of Cicero the professional accuser was still tolerated; he had a large range of crimes to prosecute, he had a large range of courts in which to prosecute; as there was no public officer to supply his place, it was even recognised that he had an useful function in the State. It was felt indeed that the orator who only appeared for the defence in criminal cases had chosen the higher walk in his profession, for the obvious reason that he retained a hold upon his clients, which made him of consequence in the State; while the accuser had nothing more to look forward to when he had gained his conviction and pocketed his fee. Still some respectability was reflected even upon him by the circumstance that there were occasions in the life of every ambitious man that made it worth his while to prosecute, if only that he might measure his strength against some personage of established reputation. Besides, civil relations were less regular and less definite than they became after the legislation of Augustus, and interests of all kind came more frequently into collision. Under the empire all this was changed: the political rewards of the bar were curtailed; its honourable influence in politics was all but destroyed. Those who prosecuted occasionally for ambition, and those who prosecuted habitually as a trade, found themselves merged in an odious class whose only function seemed to be the invention of pretexts for delivering all who had anything to lose to the capricious greed and cruelty of the government. And though subserviency to the government was odious, its favour came to appear the surest, if not the only road to influence and authority over the courts, while the importance of the courts was upon the decline. In the time of Cicero the pleader who led the courts could banter the jurist upon his unfruitful learning and unmeaning technicalities. Under the empire the position of the pleader was lowered, and that of the legal writer was raised by other causes, and especially by the tendency to refer every case, when possible, to the emperor for a decision on the merits. Meanwhile the ordinary barrister was obliged to keep up the show of political influence after he had ceased to desire the reality, and to make a pretence of having clients, in order, if possible, to attract customers; and this perversity of their position made it harder for them really to succeed by the transparent fiction that they had succeeded.

Lastly, the Roman middle class had experienced a loss in Juvenal's day which was almost heavier than the deterioration of careers which had never led the *tenuiores civium* to independence as a body. The nobles had discovered that they had no use for clients. The same change took place in England at the beginning of the seventeenth century, and is bewailed in the well-known ballads of the Old English Gentleman and the Young English Gentleman. The cause of the change was the same at Rome as in England, the administration had become too strong for the aristocracy.

Under the republic a respectable Roman, who was not rich, expected to be kept from want and even from discomfort by the liberality of one who was, simply in exchange for his services as gentleman in waiting and for keeping his vote and interest for what little they might be worth at the service of his patron. In this he was seldom disappointed even though he might not have the intelligence to make himself conspicuously useful nor the ambition to rise very high. The system had attained its fullest development towards the close of the republic, when the great position of individual aristocrats was sufficient in itself to constitute a danger to the aristocracy; nor did it show signs of decline during the early days of the empire. While those who had co-operated in its establishment had still to be rewarded, and those who might have disturbed it had still to be conciliated, the old and new aristocracy had undiminished patronage to bestow, and they bestowed it in the accustomed channels. Even when the empire had declared war upon the senate, there were nobles who speculated upon the reversion of the empire, there were others who plumed themselves on an influence which was almost an authority at court; to the first class it was essential, to the second it was convenient to be at the head of a large body of attached dependants. It is doubtful how long the system would have lasted if the privileges of the prætorians had attracted them to the side of the senate, in the first century instead of the third, when we find them arrayed with the senate and the equestrian order against Aurelian. Even then those nobles whose ambition remained within the bounds of loyalty might have discovered that influence was only valuable over those whose discontent might be formidable. As it was it soon became clear that the emperor was not only too strong for the senate but was always appointed by the army. Then the nobles' temper finally changed: they saw that clients of the old type were an useless expense, and, what they felt almost as much, an useless fatigue. Greek freedmen and Greek sycophants were more subservient and more amusing and helped a nobleman to spend his money more comfortably. Still their goodnatured vanity continued to expose them for more than two centuries longer to the importunities of dependants whom they did not want. The only difference was, that in the time of Ammianus Marcellinus the genteel mendicant generally came with an introduction from the provinces to the nobles who scarcely read anything but Juvenal's satires upon their ancestors whom they resembled so exactly.

If the destitution of the *bourgeoisie* did not increase after Juvenal's day it had already reached a sufficiently alarming point. Rome was full of educated loafers, men with the tastes, the education, often the capacities, though seldom the pedigrees of gentlemen, all without a career, all in search of promotion. Some of them had inherited a competence, some were often puzzled to know where to find a dinner. None of them had occupations, hopes, interests, or duties. Some of them succeeded in begging cheap privileges like the *jus trium liberorum*, which enabled them to struggle on till better times came; others gave up the struggle and went back to their country towns which they had really never had a substantial reason for quitting. They had come to Rome to get an education, and they stayed in Rome because their education would be useless anywhere else, long after they had discovered that it was useless there. Juvenal belonged to the least unprosperous section of the class, which was not the least discontented. When a man begins to find himself at a loss for a dinner he naturally finds plenty of defects in the order of things which left him without one. But even when his indignation is fresh a chance dinner will suppress it for the day, and, in process of time, the need of a dinner will suppress all wishes and feelings beyond itself. The tribunes of the proletariate are seldom proletarians; and Bohemians are seldom able to maintain their testimony against the oppressions of Bohemia up to the venerable age of eighty. Because Juvenal was well to do he was all the fitter to represent the grievances of the gregarious idlers who loitered away dreamy days between the baths and the forum, and scarcely ever felt life worth living except while the excitement of the circus roused them for a moment from their apathetic unrest.

In reading Tacitus we are never allowed for an instant to escape from the impression that the tyranny of the imperial government was the crying evil of the age and the parent of all the rest; in the letters of Pliny (though he represents perhaps a later period than Juvenal) we see something of the bright side of that part of Roman society to which imperial tyranny was the one flaw in an universe otherwise admirable. But Juvenal and his class had grievances that they felt far more than the caprice of the emperor; whom they were probably always prepared to flatter and inclined to libel (if that were not impossible). Their great grievance was that they were scandalised to see worse men better off than-themselves, they were outraged by the crowds of *nouveaux riches* and treasured the stories against each (sometimes, e.g. at I. 46, 47, it strikes us that the stories may not impossibly have had two sides), they fumed at the luxury which they were not invited to share, they consoled themselves by accumulating all the instances of ignoble vanity, of mad craving after paltry distinction, of sordid debauchery which dishonoured the new patrician of degenerate Rome. The eighth satire is one long commentary on the impotence of the class whose oppressive pretensions still kept new men in the shade; it carries us back to the days of Nævius when the Metelli were elected to the consulate in their cradles. The second is a stinging invective on the indescribable vices of a class whose chosen hero was the emperor Otho, because his momentary energy and the careless gallantry of his end seemed to be a pledge to them that they had not unmanned themselves by profligacy which he had exceeded. They might quote the austere Tacitus and the complaisant Martial in support of their homage to their favourite; but he made no impression whatever on the sturdy puritanism of Juvenal. The third and fifth satires are directed at least as much against the heartlessness and the ruffianly insolence of the great as against the defective police of Rome or the snobbish appetites of the diner out, or against the smooth servility of foreigners. We seem to trace in Juvenal vestiges of another grievance which afflicted *Romanos rerum dominos gentemque togatam* as soon as Claudius and Nero had decided that the empire should be cosmopolitan. Not only did it become possible for foreigners to succeed almost as well as natives where success depended upon merit, to succeed better where success depended upon favour; but as there are passages in Horace which suggest without proving that the Romans were beginning to carry on an active trade between the Levant and Rome, so there are passages in Juvenal which suggest that this trade was passing back into the hands of the Levantines.

Of course the indictment of the 'have nots' against the 'haves' never varies much in its nature, and is always only too well supported by facts. The class of which Juvenal chose to be the organ is always bitter against men of assured position; but the organ of their bitterness is generally without an echo; the expression of their discontent is generally stifled by the certainty that it will be met by the conspiracy of silence; it could not be stifled in Rome, and, to that extent, we are warranted in concluding that Rome was worse than London.

As Juvenal's class was proud of its nationality it had naturally no sympathy with the cosmopolitan philosophy of Stoicism; in this Juvenal resembles Tacitus: the grievance of the satirist was that his order could not profit by the world, the grievance of the historian was that his order could not govern the world: neither of them was inclined to accept the doctrine that the world was not made for individuals or for classes, but that these were produced by the order of the world and for the order of the world. Yet both Tacitus and Juvenal owe much to Stoicism: the taste for sonorous morality was sufficiently strong in both to make them eager to avail themselves of as much of its conclusions as could be separated from its premisses. To Tacitus Stoicism commended itself as the system which Helvidius had studied *quo firmior adversus fortuita rempublicam capesseret* (Hist. IV. 5). But it is certain from more than one passage that he had succeeded in arranging his own life without the support of convictions though not without the stimulus of ideas. As these ideas were mostly borrowed from the Porch, it would be possible for a careless reader to class him among the disciples of Zeno. It would be hard to make the same mistake about Juvenal: there is indeed one satire, the fifteenth, where he appeals to Stoicism with as much respect as a satirist can appeal to any authority; there are others, like the fourth and tenth, where he uses Stoical ideas without anything approaching to a disclaimer of the authority of the reigning philosophy: though even in the tenth the distinction between true and false goods, upon which the whole satire turns, is really Socratic rather than Stoical: in fact the distinction between real and apparent prosperity vanishes as soon as it has been laid down that everything external is ideally indifferent. Moreover, there are passages like III. 116 sq., XIII. 120 sq., where the writer shows an unmistakeable animus against Stoicism, or at least against Stoics. One cannot tell how far he may have been disgusted by the inconsistencies of individuals, and there is no doubt that such scandals were very gross, and far from rare; but, in fact, their pretensions were intolerable to all but those who felt that they too were philosophers; their demands upon human nature were too severe for any man to accept honestly who was not heartily in earnest about his own character, a subject which seldom interests a satirist.

Another point in which Juvenal and Tacitus in the main coincide is their indignation against the *delatores;* a pest which has had its analogues under every tyranny. At Rome it assumed a peculiar form owing to several circumstances, of which the most important were the hypocrisy of the Caesars in retaining the forms of a republic and the absence of any system of state police. The tyranny of a bad emperor was irresistible, but it was far from being omnipresent: the government of the senate and the equestrian order had proved itself inadequate to embrace the vast and complex interests of the Roman world: this conviction had helped to reconcile those who were not personally interested in the success of Julius or Octavian to the necessity of seeing the control of the world deputed to a single governor. But though the centralised administration justified their confidence by its superior efficiency, though at the end of the first century much had been accomplished both in the interest of the government and of the governed, the task was immense, and it may be doubted whether the government of Diocletian had overtaken its immensity; it is certain that the government of Domitian had not. There were still multitudes of questions which were decided by the courts or by the senate almost without interference from the prince, and within this extensive though diminishing arena it was still possible for politicians to win an influence that was almost independent of the favour of the emperor. It was possible for an individual to confer so many obligations that men shrank from voting against his opinion in the senate and against his clients in the courts : though this did not protect him from the necessity of giving in his adhesion to each successive government, it made it worth the while of every successive government to defer to him on condition that he should give it his hearty support. It may be doubted whether any government which disposed of so much patronage as the early emperors was so unfettered by routine in selecting the objects of its favour : even Nero had not a court, Domitian had hardly favourites, and a share of this patronage was within the reach of any citizen who could make it worth the emperor's while to court him. Nor was this all : a Vibius Crispus or a Marcellus Eprius (Tac. *de Oratoribus*, VIII. 3) could extend the influence to which he owed the friendship of Caesar by an ostentation of that friendship : men shrank from offending the intimate of the Palace, if they did not shrink from disobliging a man who had obliged them, or their colleagues whom he had obliged. All this together made up the position which Tacitus and his contemporaries designate by the comprehensive term *potentia*. And *potentia* was not to be had for nothing; it was necessary to take the side of the prince heartily, for he almost always felt himself isolated, and distrusted everybody, even those who professed attachment and aspired to his intimacy. During the first century of our era few men at Rome acquired or retained power in the state without having denounced disaffection to the person of the emperor. Such denunciations became necessary as a pledge of loyalty after a man had risen, they were convenient while a man was rising: under the conditions of the Roman state it was useful to an ambitious politician to be loved, it was essential to be feared: by obliging one man he commonly disobliged another; by ruining one man he terrorised all. Nor does Tacitus leave an attentive reader under the impression that these denunciations were exactly frivolous. The Roman criminal law was terribly elastic: Law is never precise except when it is interpreted by courts with a continuous tradition, and when offences are punished with sufficient certainty to remove the motive for capricious and exemplary severity. The sweeping ferocity of Roman legislation under the late Republic and the early Empire was natural to inexperienced reformers who could not count upon their zeal being seconded by the steady activity of the courts. Almost as many were condemned under the empire for offences against morality and religion as for attempts against the security or the dignity of the emperor. To take one instance out of many, there is not really any better reason for doubting that Barea and his daughter had been guilty of a capital crime than for supposing they deserved to be put to death. Yet though the law was vague and comprehensive it seems probable that, except when Tiberius proscribed all who had made the mistake of courting Sejanus, a quiet man who made no enemies and who did not care to criticise the government was practically safe below the rank of senator, and a prudent man incurred little danger even there. Under almost every emperor the government felt itself too insecure to tolerate disaffection; the political classes insisted on keeping up the habit of treating almost every emperor as an usurper, and speak-

ing and acting as if they were living under a provisional government. There were men who made a trade of detecting and
denouncing disaffection; sometimes, though very rarely, they
descended to the arts of the modern informer: those who
were independent of the trade did not always disdain to
take advantage of the imprudence of a personal enemy to
revenge a private grudge, by denouncing their antagonist on
any charge that would bring his fate to be determined by a
sovereign, who was always under the temptation to strengthen
his position by terrorising the aristocracy. Undoubtedly Tacitus was right in assuming that in every old society a wise
administration will have to wink at profligacy, and that no
administration, which is not strong enough to tolerate any
amount of disaffection which stops short at overt acts, can ever
be otherwise than mischievous and tyrannical. At the same
time it is to be remembered that what Tacitus complained of
was after all only this, that the law was put in force against his
order. He never forgives a senator who could separate his
own interests from those of the senate: his ideal was that the
nobles should hold together in order to govern when a good
prince reigned and to set limits to the tyranny of a bad emperor.
This explains a difference between his judgment and Juvenal's
on individuals like Messalinus Cotta, Seneca, Piso, and Vibius
Crispus. They were all bountiful or at least goodnatured,
therefore Juvenal respected them; they were all *potentes*,
therefore Tacitus distrusted them. Seneca escapes best; it
was ungracious to attack the memory of a victim of Nero,
but all Tacitus' praise is for the genius, not for the virtue,
of the philosopher; he writes upon principles which pre-
clude the question how far such intense and genuine ethical
fervour could atone for political compliances. Piso was guilty
of a desire to reign, and Tacitus will not decide whether he
owed his reputation to his virtues or to vices which produced
the same effects. Vibius Crispus he seems to admit was generally respected as an able and distinguished man, though the
historian belonged to a set of purists who refused him their

esteem. Cotta seems to have been honestly in favour of a strict and severe system of administration; but only a system of consistent tolerance and mutual support could have enabled the senate to hold its own against Tiberius—and Cotta is condemned accordingly. Juvenal does not differ from Tacitus in his judgment on the rank and file of the *delatores*, who owed their influence exclusively to their activity in providing the government with victims. Their activity in reality pressed quite as severely on the *bourgeoisie* as on the aristocracy. Not improbably the government of a Domitian shed less blood for its own protection in all the Roman empire than many of the mediæval tyrannies of Italy, and those not the worst, shed in a single year. A large and active class of informers was hardly required to provide for all the executions that we have reason to suspect. But the exchequer which had to provide so many largesses for spendthrift nobles, for men of letters *en disponibilité*, for the populace of the capital, always required to be replenished; and the *delatores* made it their business to replenish it. The rights of the *fiscus* were as extensive and undefined as the majesty of the emperor who represented the state : it might almost be said that the means for enforcing them were as inadequate. A single *advocatus fisci* here and there who might be seduced or intimidated was not enough to enforce the multiplicity of claims which the inventive ingenuity of the crown lawyers had revived or established *a priori*. The result was that even in the fourth century there were great numbers of respectable people in the habitual enjoyment of what might be plausibly represented as due to the emperor. These were imperfectly reassured when a well-intentioned sovereign decreed that the informers should be punished if they prosecuted without the sanction of the *advocatus fisci*, though of course it was possible for private persons to ascertain the instructions and to calculate the action of a known and responsible official. Under Domitian and other emperors who, as Domitian himself observed, encouraged informers by neglecting to discourage them, it was impossible for a senator to feel that his property was his own, it was impossible for the class which stood below the senators to count upon receiving the legacies which might be left them, when Caesar administered to the estate of every man who had ever been heard to say that Caesar would be his heir. We are left to form our opinion of the rapacity of the imperial government from a good deal of general declamation and from one or two specific instances, doubtless taken from extreme cases. It is probable that the material loss was not what the Romans chafed at most; both Roman commoners and Roman nobles when they spoke of liberty meant what they said: the sense of having a master was far more galling to them than the sense of not having power to influence public affairs, and the rapacity of the *fiscus* did more than any thing else to bring home to them the insufferable fact, that they had a master who was steadily concentrating all the resources of the state under the control of his single will.

When we turn from the grievances of Juvenal to his ideas we find him even more reactionary than Tacitus, more sincere, and more uncompromising in his regrets for the simplicity of the past. This is one proof among many that the side of democracy is not necessarily the side of progress. As a matter of fact cosmopolitan civilisation was introduced at Rome by a section of the aristocracy, of which the elder Africanus was the first representative, and Sulla and Lucullus among the last. In politics they endeavoured to mediate between the democrats and the oligarchy, or at least to keep themselves aloof from the excesses of both: their ideas of culture excited as much opposition from the conservative jealousy of the poor as from the conservative frugality of the rich. The first proved, as might be expected, the more durable obstacle of the two. Juvenal railed heartily against tortoiseshell sofas while Tacitus complacently bewailed the impossibility of suppressing luxury. In general it may be said that Juvenal is one of the satirists who endeavour to combat vice by consecrating prejudice. He is of the family of Aristophanes and Moliere, not of Lucian and Erasmus, of Rabelais and Voltaire. It may be reckoned either as his merit

that he attacked little which was really valuable, or as his
misfortune that his time presented nothing valuable to be
attacked; it is certain that no satirist had fewer such attacks to
answer for. Lucian and Voltaire did their best to propagate
what serious thinkers of every school might combine to stig-
matise as infidelity. Aristophanes contributed directly to the
condemnation of Socrates; in the latter part of his career his
protest against sophistical refinements subsided into an excuse
for self-complacent brutality. Moliere devoted one of his best
comedies to the sanctity of passing conventionalities; another
to the indelibility of social distinctions; another to the utter
ineptitude of female culture. Juvenal to be sure does object
to a woman having an opinion on the comparative merits of
Homer and Virgil, but he objects not because her opinion
is certain to be ridiculous, but because she is certain to annoy
her husband with it. And he is more consistent as well as more
moderate than Moliere: he pines for the good old times before
the importation of hexameters: he regrets the obsolete life of the
Sabine farmer, when the men of the family worked all day in the
fields, and came home to a huge bowl of porridge, while the
women kept their hands coarse and their hearts clean by spin-
ning; and every body was convinced, without quite knowing
what purple was, that it was something wicked and outlandish.

It is curious that the universal empire of Rome should
have failed so completely to produce anything like a cosmopolitan culture. As long as Rome remained the capital both the
emperors and the aristocracy continued to oscillate between
a provincial affectation of native simplicity and a childish ostentation of foreign graces. Nero's passion for personal display
had carried him far beyond Greek precedent, and such prece-
dents as he had dated from the days when Greek civilisation
was still shut up within the narrow limits of civic life, which
might excuse a man for showing off his accomplishments to
his neighbours, before Philip had reproached Alexander for
playing the lyre too well for a king. Even after that time
young men of good position still acted in the Atellan farces

at Rome. It is hardly probable that actors were deprived of their civil rights till the time of the Punic wars. The severity of Roman manners did not reach its highest point until the new aristocracy had become sufficiently powerful to impose its family traditions upon public opinion. Possibly if Juvenal had gone far enough back in his search for the good old times he would have escaped from much of his Puritanism. But it is an extenuation of his narrowness that the incapacity for understanding that accomplishments from driving upwards could be practised with simplicity and decorum, for grace or for pleasure, not for parade, was not only his defect but the defect of all Roman society. But though the conditions of the society in which he lives may condemn a writer to choose between two unsatisfactory standards, it does not follow that the fervour of Juvenal's denunciations proves nothing against the clearness of his personal insight. All fervour on such subjects is unintelligent, because it is misplaced; all standards upon such matters are really provisional, though they serve to protect a temper of self-respect and self-restraint which possesses a permanent value. There have been countries where a nobleman who respected himself would not dream of trying to make a reputation by his poetry: it is said that Lady Byron expected her husband as a part of his reformation to leave off his 'silly habit of writing verses.' In Spain the nobles took a pride in their dexterity in bull-fights, and a Roman noble required at least as much skill to succeed as a *bestiarius*. We should be shocked ourselves if a member of our aristocracy were to sing in public except for a charity; but we should see no objection to his rowing in a public race, or belonging to a four-in-hand club, while to an American, the field-sports, on which we pride ourselves, appear as barbarous as boxing.

Fervour on these subjects has other disadvantages beside the certainty of becoming grotesque when it comes before an audience of another period and another race. It effectually excludes geniality. Plautus shares the fundamental conception of Juvenal, that life ought to be in the main a round of

somewhat prosaic duties relieved at rare intervals by somewhat
dull festivity. Yet Plautus succeeds in being thoroughly genial:
he laughs without a touch of Juvenal's ferocity at the follies of
the world: at bottom he regards enjoyment as synonymous
with profligacy, but though his standard of profligacy is hardly
reasonable he regards profligacy with tolerance as a folly not as
a crime. Even in Juvenal the relish for innocent pleasures
was not wholly extinct; we can trace its remains in the casual
wish that the fountain of Egeria had been left in its primæval
simplicity, in the invitation to Persius to come to an early
dinner at twelve and hear Homer and Virgil—a form of dissipation, in Juvenal's judgment, too exciting to be indulged in
often. Perhaps the clearest trace of all is the pretty and sympa-
thetic description of the slave-boy who does not like being
taken away from his kids to wait at table. Still it may be
said that the honest man, who is the ideal of most satirists,
is seldom so unattractive as he appears in Juvenal. His
austerity indeed is so impracticable as to betray him into
unreality. If in order to be virtuous it is necessary to be dull
with the dulness of three centuries ago, it becomes necessary,
in order to make existence endurable, that excesses should be
permitted, not to say encouraged, in the young. For instance,
in the Eighth Satire, where the tone is intended to be lofty,
after the indictment against Lateranus is complete, an advocate
is introduced to plead in extenuation, that everybody does the
same when young; whereto Juvenal only ventures to reply,
that Lateranus is old enough to know better. In the Eleventh
Satire, where the tone is intended to be genial, he says it is
quite proper for young men to take their mistresses to the
circus in their finery, and talk loud, and bet high; for himself
he prefers to sun himself in a corner where he can get rid of his
toga. His ideal was hardly one to inspire the sustained enthusiasm or the tranquil assurance which would have guaranteed
the consistency of his moral tone. As it is we find him at one
moment lashing himself into a tempest of indignation that a
nobleman should actually put the drag on his own carriage

with his own hands; at another, recounting the deepest moral
degradation as coolly as an election commissioner, who enjoys
the exposure of a corruption which he honestly intends to suppress. In the Ninth Satire particularly the tone of bantering
irony is almost as disgusting as the subject; the Sixth is *less*
offensive, but the writer is obviously determined to extract the
maximum of amusement from the painful subject of marriage,
which he regards from the old Roman point of view as a necessary evil or rather a disagreeable duty, which it is Quixotic to
undertake to perform for the public benefit, and childish to
assume with any hope of personal satisfaction. Accordingly he
proceeds with a little passion, a great deal of verve supported
by a great deal of gusto, to catalogue all the grievances of
husbands, who are never secure against being taken to task
for solecisms when alive, or against having their children murdered by their own mother after their death. The Second
Satire is written in what may fairly be called a tone of honest
indignation, though we should suspect the sincerity of most
writers who put a witty denunciation of loose men into the
mouth of a loose woman.

Both Persius and Horace are really more cheerful as
well as more sincere. Their satire is not a protest against the
hardships of life, it is not the organ of the grievances of a discontented class; the world would suit them well enough if it
could only become a little more reasonable for its own benefit,
not for theirs. Horace perhaps found its folly such good fun
that he had hardly charity enough to wish it wiser, and Persius
was too good a Stoic to be annoyed by the general unwisdom
except so far as it presented a temptation to himself. So far as
they have a serious purpose (and Persius is very serious) they
preach where Juvenal denounces. It was impossible for them
to stop short, like Juvenal, with a catalogue of vicious habits to
be abandoned, of virtuous practices to be renewed; their conception of virtue, without being precisely higher than his, was
at any rate more inward and more free. They did little perhaps to raise the conception of character, but they succeeded

in keeping before themselves and others the principle that the formation of character is the end of conduct and our main concern in life. Even Horace, with all his indolent and ostentatious indecision between rival schools of philosophy, never wavers in the conviction that salvation is to be found in the true philosophy, and if this is unattainable, in the search for it. His attitude was like the attitude of many in our day towards theology; he felt himself elevated and strengthened by the endeavour to live in the presence of the highest problems, though he neither expected nor greatly cared to solve them. He outlived his poetical ambition, he outlived the hope that his faults would wear away under the influence of time and friendly advice and his own vigilance. And there is something pathetic in the gentle compunction with which he speaks of the self-indulgence which he shared with so many, and of the incurable inconstancy of purpose which had struck him from the first as the great enemy to reason and to peace of mind. But a wise man is seldom impatient with any one whom he wishes to improve even when it is too late for much improvement, and Horace was patient with himself and with the world, and was able to derive amusement to the last from both. One catches an echo of Horace in the *causeries* and 'Roundabout papers' of our own day; in the fierce sermons of the sixteenth and seventeenth centuries we still trace the working of the bitter leaven of Juvenal.

Nothing came amiss to Horace, from the intellectual interests of the society which Maecenas gathered round him as missionaries of culture, to the comical discomforts of the journey to Brundisium, from the popular follies which he was content to ridicule and share, to the ludicrous aspects of Stoicism, which was too useful an auxiliary to be discarded, and too grotesque and formal to be respected. Even Persius, with all his gravity and his pathetic anxiety for self-improvement, has a strong sense of the propriety of enjoying life, and even of exhibiting gladiators as often as the emperor thought proper to gazette a victory. The same frank, almost buoyant realism asserts itself at the end of two of the severest Satires, by a sort of tribute to the coarse, robust, healthy animalism of the average centurion, who is alive without the law, and can venture to ask whether it is worth while to miss one's breakfast to be like Arcesilas and the musty Solons of the Porch, and even to bid for a hundred starveling Greeks at a penny a piece; though Persius is firmly convinced all the while that nothing but the teaching of those despised Greeks can save his fashionable contemporaries from the bondage of feverish desire, and the ruinous consciousness of growing degradation. Nor is Persius less humorous when he refuses to sell his private laugh, mere nothing as it is, for Labeo's Iliad, or any other man's, and owns, naïvely, that though he is not indifferent to praise, he cannot write for it only or chiefly, in times when everything is praised, from the rough heavy work of old Accius to the trifles of men who dictate smooth emptiness as they loll on citron couches, and pronounce the Aeneid inflated and obsolete. It would be absurd, of course, to attempt to set Persius above Juvenal. We may infer, from the complimentary exhortation put into the mouth of Cornutus (v. vv. 14, 15), that it was his ambition to found upon Horace a style of reater finish and condensation; and he corrected himself into obscurity in the attempt. His knowledge of life was exceedingly limited, and hence he is constantly enforcing monotonous commonplaces by borrowed illustrations, in which there is nothing fresh, except the shy youthful fervour of the dutiful boy—for he remained a boy to the last, though he was nearly thirty before he died on the Riviera—who describes himself as *petulanti splene cachinno*, and yet repeats the morose formulae which he had learnt from Cornutus, just as poor Maurice de Guérin repeated the austere ultramontanism of De Lamennais. Still, this single element of interest, combined with the literary honesty which kept Persius from writing any thing which was not a part of his permanent consciousness, makes him improve upon every reading, which is more than can be said of Juvenal, who writes as if he thought and felt

d 2

little in the intervals of writing. The same might perhaps be said of Aristophanes, but there is a tone of hilarity and animal spirits about the old Attic Comedy, which springs from the contagion of a crowd and the merriment of a holiday, while in Roman Satire, where this element of gaiety is missing, the author is always in danger of lapsing into stiff morality, or crabbed invective, and never succeeds for long in maintaining himself in the genial position of Aristophanes, who, though often coarse, and almost always narrow, has the great gift of sitting loose to his own beliefs. He is never reduced, like Juvenal, to such sorry devices, in order to raise a laugh, as appeals under protest to a mythology which he and his audience disbelieve; for he possesses a far more piquant resource in the outrageous parodies which he executes on a mythology which he is sincerely resolved to defend. In a parabasis of Aristophanes, we feel the merriment of the citizen, as well as the anxiety and ambition of the author; in a Satire of Juvenal, disappointed ambition is the only visible motive of a poet who wishes us to laugh, because he is long past laughing.

It is to the credit of Juvenal that he should have preferred to consider himself as the successor of Lucilius, rather than as the latest imitator of the Old Attic comedy. It is characteristic of Roman culture that Horace and Persius, rather than plead guilty to the charge of having borrowed nothing from Greece, should have chosen to represent themselves as continuators of Aristophanes. It is characteristic of Roman society that the *satura* of Ennius should have given way to the *satura* of Lucilius. The former seems really to have been analogous to the old comedy; we cannot doubt that in the hands of Ennius it tended to become a reproduction of Greek models, nor can we doubt that Lucilius, though he was a literary innovator, and introduced a kind of poem for which there was no Greek precedent, inspired himself as much as possible from Greek sources. In this way it is possible to account at once for the well-known judgment of Quinctilian, that, in Satire at any rate, Roman literature was independent, and for the pretension of Horace to be throughout a polished plagiarist. The habit of personal lampoons seems to have been common to both Greeks and Romans. It is possible, that in the original comic chorus, which resumed its native freedom in the parabasis, individuals had the opportunity of distinguishing themselves by telling impromptus; while it is certain that the Romans retained to a late period the capacity of joining extempore in a metrical expression of humorous contempt. But among the Greeks, the element of the chorus, which was capable of musical and poetical ornament, was the one selected for cultivation; the time came when the moody and unsocial Roman, in the solitude which succeeded the festival, worked up all that he had said, and all that he had wished to say, and all that he meant to say, when another festival gave new occasion for license, till at last the result had outgrown such informal opportunities of publication, and the satirist had to recite his lucubrations to a select audience, and confide the manuscript to a circle which at first was probably still narrower.

But even if we still possessed all the lost works of Ennius, Lucilius, and Varro, it is possible that we should hardly feel safe in forming a very definite theory of the origin of Roman satire. It would be difficult to be positive about the beginnings of our own literature, unless we were able to ascend above Chaucer and Gower. We are on firmer ground when we endeavour to trace the development of Roman satire between Horace and his two successors. It is a proof of the growing unreality, the mechanical sequacity of post-Augustan poetry, that both Persius and Juvenal follow Horace in affecting alarm at the consequences of their own freedom. The secluded life of Persius makes the affectation peculiarly offensive in his case; but both he and Juvenal are equally faulty in forgetting that Horace did not deprecate hostility till he had done something to deserve it; and reserved his hesitations and apologies for the introduction of his Second Book, which shows signs of serious precaution in the care with which the poet contrives to make himself the butt, or a butt of his own satire. Horace would certainly have smiled at the servility of his imitators; one of whom deprecated a persecution which he never did anything to provoke, and anticipated, with a comic mixture of vanity and cowardice, the martyrdom which he was never to undergo, while the other published his exaggerated terrors after he had experienced how little a Satirist had to fear, even from a tyrannical emperor. Again, Horace's mentor is carefully individualized by a certain dogmatic dulness and oracular vapidity, while both Persius and Juvenal are content to ventriloquize through a colourless puppet, who might be made to say one thing as well as another. Yet it cannot be doubted that both Persius and Juvenal tried intelligently to improve upon Horace.

If one were to endeavour to select the gravest fault of Horace's Satires, probably a sort of pointless garrulity would occur at once to most of his readers. His good things are embedded in a torrent of commonplace, which, doubtless, catches the tone of well-bred conversation very well, as he is rather fond of boasting; but this only proves that the ordinary conversation of the very best society will not bear to be reproduced at length. In addition to something which is almost tediousness, we miss the half ideal medium, which any tolerable system of conventional poetic diction secures, even when it is as unreal as Juvenal's, who often trusts to unintelligent reminiscences of Horace, for the names of hostile tribes on the Roman frontier, and for the *status* of Roman families. Juvenal is never incomplete, he is never abrupt, he has an habitual sense of what is due to the finish and dignity of literature. He is one of the smoothest and clearest of writers; and this is probably what Acron means when he speaks of his "suavity," which he contrasts with the "asperity" of Lucilius. It is easy to believe that there was a freshness and a raciness about Lucilius that made his jolting and disjointed invectives interesting reading to people who read much. Acron praises Horace for combining this "asperity" with the "suavity" of Juvenal.

He is certainly more spontaneous than Juvenal, and he cannot have been so rough as Lucilius. But it is harder to determine what is the precise bearing of the judgments of the ancients upon one another, than to decide for ourselves in which of his characteristics Juvenal and Persius were content to resemble Horace, in what directions they sought a remedy for the short-comings of their model. One contrast, indeed, is the result of a difference, not in their aims, but in their circumstances: Horace, writing in the first instance for a limited circle, abounds with allusions to persons whose names have been preserved by him alone; Juvenal's butts recur far more constantly, and contain a far larger proportion of public historical characters, while Persius, who lived out of the world, draws his illustration almost exclusively from literature. Subject to this limitation Persius endeavoured to preserve the structure of the Horatian Satire, with its free range of topics, its arbitrary changes from exhortation to anecdote and dialogue, its frank appropriation of old literary effects, while he added the concentrated vigour and the definite purpose in which his master seemed deficient. Juvenal, on the contrary, simplifies the whole, while he developes the parts. He rejects all direct quotation as likely to disgust a jaded audience, and seeks the necessary interest in emphasis rather than in condensation. The machinery of dialogue is very much reduced in extent, and care is taken that the reader shall never be puzzled by the way in which it is employed. In Horace we are often perplexed how much space to assign to each of the imaginary speakers; in Juvenal this question is less perplexing, or rather less important; he prefers to soften his transitions rather than to mark the limits of his snatches of imaginary conversation. We might say perhaps that there is almost the same proportion between the dramatic element in Juvenal and the dramatic element in Horace, as there is between Aristotle's method of discussing an ἀπορία and the method of one of Plato's dialogues. In Plato and Horace the dramatic form exists for its own artistic value, and in Horace its artistic value is not always great; in Juvenal the discussion tends to become what it is in Aristotle, an impersonal vehicle of thought, which is occasionally more convenient than direct exposition. But Juvenal's favourite method is straightforward declamation, which is kept down by irony to the level of satire. One artifice of his irony, which distinguishes him from both his Roman predecessors, is the habit of introducing a low word in a sonorous passage. Neither Horace nor Persius has any aversion for the *mot propre;* but their style is homogeneous, whether it sinks or rises with the subject. Most of the instances of Juvenal's ostentatious homeliness have been pointed out as they occur in the notes. This is the place to add a few words on another characteristic of Juvenal's manner of work, which a modern reader would hardly venture to detect without the support of ancient tradition. When we have reason to believe that Juvenal enlarged his Satire, it is natural to ask if it is possible to discover the joins, and this gives an interest to passages which otherwise we might pass over *sicco pede.* There is hardly evidence to decide whether Juvenal took a description of a shipwreck from his portfolio and cut it in half to insert a catalogue of the property which Catullus sacrificed when he wanted to utilize an old copy of verses for the Twelfth Satire. It is possible that vv. 13—20 in the Third Satire were written in the MS. order, and that the writer intended to leave them as they stood. If these passages stood alone it might be hardly worth while to mention the guess, but the question has a bearing on the most considerable difficulty which exists with reference to the text of Juvenal.

There are many lines in Juvenal which are or which may be spurious, and all the suspected lines belong in some sense to one common type. They all have something of an explanatory character, as if the reader could not be trusted to fill up the author's outline, or to carry on his thought, as if what had gone before had always to be resumed, and as if what was to come had always to be introduced. All might be confidently rejected if they occurred in the text of a condensed and fastidious author like Persius; in a writer so vigorous and yet so prolix as Juvenal, it is possible to defend most of them as at worst pardonable redundancies, it would be easy to defend all of them as belonging to alternative drafts of the passages in which they occur, between which the writer never decided.

Most of them make perfectly good sense where they stand, and are supported by all the ancient authorities. Others are omitted by several MSS., and one or two interrupt the connexion wherever they can be placed. The first fact proves at most that they displeased ancient critics as well as modern ; the second would be decisive if there were not reason to believe that Juvenal never finished the revision of his satires.

The introductory satire is naturally polished with most care, and there only one critic has been found to suspect one line (v. 157), which is so difficult that his suspicion is likely to be more popular than it deserves.

In the Third Satire Jahn condemns v. 104[1], against the MSS. and John of Salisbury; Heinrich and Pinzger condemn v. 113 as an unnecessary explanation ; for the same reason, if the MSS. were few or worthless, vv. 49, 50, might be eliminated ; Heinecke condemns v. 281.

In the Fourth Satire nobody condemns any thing.

In the Fifth, Heinrich rejects the end of v. 9, and the beginning of v. 10, and the whole of v. 66. Pinzger had anticipated his dislike of v. 51 ; but the latter critic defends v. 91, though omitted by Pithou's MS. and condemned by Weber, Heinrich, Jahn,—who also condemns v. 140, I suppose for reasons of taste which would justify Heinecke's rejection of vv. 146—148.

In the Seventh, Jahn, Pinzger, and Heinrich condemn v. 15, which contains an unusual quantity; Jahn alters v. 50 to suit his rejection of v. 51 ; Heinrich condemns vv. 138 and 181 ; Valla condemned vv. 240, 241.

---

[1] Whenever nothing is said to the contrary, the MSS. are unanimous in favour of the verse attacked.

In the Eighth, most MSS., but not the best, omit v. 7 (*see note*): v. 78 might be omitted as a question of taste, on the same principle as all editors omit *Gutta cavat lapidem, consumitur anulus usu,* which occurs in the Dresden MS. after XIII. 18: vv. 111, 112, are in all the MSS.; but they are so flat that Jahn and Manso wish to leave them out altogether, while Heinrich and Heinecke more plausibly treat *unicus* as a gloss on *unus,* and go straight on to *Despicias tu.* Jahn and Lachmann condemn v. 124; Ruperti, v. 194, and is followed by Heinrich in his condemnation of v. 202.

In the Tenth, Ruperti condemns v. 37, Pinzger v. 148; Heinrich condemns v. 189, but not v. 187.

In the Eleventh, at v. 30, Heinecke wishes to read *vel sacri in parte senatus Esse velis, seu tu magno discrimine causam Protegere affectas, &c.,* striking out two lines, which are a tasteless display of cheap reading. Heinrich condemns vv. 63 and 99, in which last he is followed by Jahn: v. 108 is omitted by Heinrich and several MSS., and condemned by Jahn: vv. 165, 166, are also omitted by several MSS., and condemned, perhaps justly, by Heinrich, Pinzger and Jahn: as the Scholium in several MSS., which gives them, "*Hi duo versus et in aliis reperti sunt,*" makes it not improbable that they are a marginal quotation, which different copyists foisted into the text at different places. Heinrich condemns v. 182, but not v. 208.

In the Twelfth, v. 36 is condemned by Heinrich; vv. 51, 52, by Bentley, Pinzger, Heinrich, Jahn.

In the Thirteenth, Heinrich is alone in condemning v. 166.

In the Fourteenth, v. 229 interrupts the grammatical sequence, is omitted in six MSS., and condemned by Ruperti, Heinrich, Jahn; but it seems more likely that Juvenal left it, than that an interpolator introduced it.

In the Fifteenth, Ruperti condemns v. 34. Francke, who wants to show that he wishes disinterestedly to purify Juvenal's text as well as to prove that he was never in Egypt, omits from *summus utrimque* in v. 35, to *sed* in v. 38, as well as the longer passage from *horrida sane* in v. 44, to *titubantibus* in

v. 48. The last omission is approved by G. Hermann, and of course by Heinrich. Francke also condemns vv. 97, 98, which are too bad for any interpolator who knew, what Juvenal did not when he wrote them, what was coming next. Orelli and Francke show their taste by omitting from *Elemento* in v. 86 to *reor* in v. 87, and from *nec enim* in v. 107 to *putant* in v. 108, respectively.

In the Sixteenth Satire, nobody condemns any thing, though some condemn every thing. It is fortunate that these questions may be answered one way or another without affecting our judgement of Juvenal's meaning, without materially affecting our judgement of his literary form; for, as we have seen, they must be answered, if at all, with little help from external evidence.

The principal manuscript authority for the text of Juvenal is at present inaccessible, and our knowledge of it depends chiefly on Pithou's collation in the sixteenth century, when it was at Buda; it is now said to be at Monte Pessulo. It is very carelessly written, as are the ancient Scholia, which seem to rank next in the confidence of the best editors. Here are a few readings from Pithou's MS., which I have sometimes cited in the notes as P., taken from the First Satire alone :—

v. 35. *Quem Massa tim etque munere palpat*, for *Quem Massa timet, quem munere palpat.*

v. 38. *Nontib . .* with two letters erased, for *noctibus.*

v. 53. *Audio medeas*, for *Aut Diomedeas.*

v. 85. *Votum ira voluptas*, for *votum timor ira voluptas.*

v. 102. *Prior inquit et ego adsum* for *Prior inquit ego adsum.*

v. 106. *Purpurae* for *purpura*, to the destruction of the metre.

The Scholia have the look of being copied from notes carelessly made from dictation, for where Juvenal's words are given they are frequently spelt phonetically, so as to represent a later pronunciation.

Our instances shall be taken from the Seventh Satire: on
v. 2 we have the note *Camenas. tacentibus poetis*—where the
lecturer must have meant to explain *tristes*, while the scholar
took down the least important part of the heading. In the
same way in v. 7, *Clio* heads the following note—*id est osti-
arius vel custos atriensis.* Here the explanation is so curtailed
as to be grammatically incomplete; but this might be due to
a wish for brevity. When, however, we see that the pupil
has only taken down the last word of the clause (*migraret
in atria Clio*), which the lecturer recalled for comment, we
are inclined to set down the mutilated form of the note to
the hurry of dictation. Here is a stronger instance of the
same kind, from the note on v. 83: "*Promisitque D. T. Letam.
Ideo quia libenter audiebat. Est enim et ipsud poema delectabile
et ipse dicitur bonam vocem habuisse,*" when the annotator
obviously did not know whether the lecturer was explaining *laetam* or *tanta dulcedine captos*, and accordingly tried to
put down both.

Rather higher up we have a confusion of another kind on
v. 73, *Pignerat Atreus. fenerator. id est, qui Atreum scribit et ut
sumptus habeat res suas pignori dat;* where the first part of the
note is a perverse explanation of the single word *Atreus*, and
the second a perfectly correct paraphrase on the whole line.
On v. 80 we read, *Marmoreis et Serrano. Nomina sunt poetarum pauperum. At Serrano vas fictile in quo At. Serranus
solebat manducare. Saleio ut mendico. Catilum fictilem in quo
ea quae salsa sunt apponuntur.* This note embodies both the
forms of confusion which arise respectively from inaccuracy
in taking down the master's words, and from mixing up two
distinct explanations. Valla's quotation from Probus throws
some light on the source of the latter ambiguity. *Nomina
fuisse poetarum Probus putat, alii "sarrhaeno," ut idem ait, et
"saleio" vasa accipiunt fictilia; juniores vero "salino" legunt et
"sarrano," ut, per vas in quo sal componitur, quaeque vilissima
intelligamus.* The same satire supplies a fair crop of mere
clerical errors, such as would arise from a careless attempt to

follow dictation : e.g. at v. 60 we have *magne* for *magnae*, at
v. 82 *amice* for *amicae*, at v. 208 *spirandisque* for *spirantisque*
or *spirantesque*, at v. 231 *ut legat storias* for *ut legat historias*,
just as in a note on Sat. I. 1, which gives something like a life
of Juvenal, the line that caused his banishment is quoted as
follows, *Quod non dant proceres dabit strio.* As these Scholia are
found in two MSS. at least, which often differ widely in their
readings, it seems likely that our present copies are derived
from an archetype annotated from dictation when Juvenal was
still regularly taught in schools. It is even possible that the
same MS. may have contained the annotations of successive
generations of pagan and Christian teachers, for besides the
incongruous explanations quoted above, there is a note on
XIV. 102, which implies that Tacitus is the only authority
accessible on the subject of Moses, while a note two lines
further on explains *Quaesitum ad fontem* of holy baptism.
But all speculations of this kind are most uncertain, for in
the absence of independent external evidence it is impossible
to limit the number of hypotheses which may be constructed
to meet the limited facts. Still there can be little doubt
that, in one form or another, the Scholia do contain the re-
siduum of the old grammatical tradition, and this gives an
authority to their readings, and even their interpretations,
which is certainly not due to the intelligence of those who
have transmitted them to us, for Probus had access to many
authorities now lost, though he may not always have used
them critically.

The authority of Pithou's MS. seems to rest largely on the
frequency of its blunders and the originality of its spelling,
which together seem to prove that any good reading which it
contains must rest wholly on its intermittent fidelity to a very
ancient text. All the other MSS. are in C. F. Hermann's
judgment "*multiplici veteris correctoris licentia deformata.*"
Perhaps the corrector may have been Niceus, who, as we
learn from one of Jahn's MSS., read and emended the first
book at any rate, at Rome, in the house of M. Servius (pro-

bably the commentator on Virgil). It may be well to exhibit some specimens of this "*licentia*," taken chiefly, though not exclusively, from the old corrector of Pithou's MS., who wished to bring his copy into respectable conformity to the common type. In this endeavour he sometimes effaced the original reading entirely, sometimes he left it legible besides his own correction, so that it might perhaps be possible to ascertain, if the MS. were now accessible, whether it was corrected by two different hands, or whether the difference in the style of the corrections is due to the fact that the same owner went through the MS. twice, possibly with different authorities.

In III. 13, P. had *pres[e]ntius* from a reminiscence of Virgil, who is fond of *praesens* in this sense, Ec. I. 42, Georg. I. 10, II. 126, while the corrector and the other MSS. have *praestantius*. In III. 21, P. had *h* with two other letters erased to make room for *ic*, perhaps because P.'s original had forgotten the *hic* at v. 16, and wished to substitute "*his*." At v. 29, P. and the Scholia give *Artorius*, most other MSS. read *Arturius*, and several have *Arturi* to match at v. 212, which certainly looks like patching; on the other hand, P. and the Scholia have *municipales* at v. 34, which the corrector and the interpolated MSS. give correctly. Two lines further on, the corrector deliberately gives the difficult reading *vulgus quem lubet* (unless he intended to write *vulgi*), while P. had the easy reading *vulgus quum jubet*, and other MSS. endeavour to meet the difficulty by reading *vulgi*. Again at v. 218, the corrector alters the easy reading *Haec Asianorum*, which is found in P. and the Scholia, into the difficult *fecasianorum*, which the other MSS. give with trifling variations, so that it seems that here at least P.'s archetype deliberately altered the text to remove a difficulty.

In XI. 38, P. had most probably *culina*, like two other MSS., while the corrector and the majority of MSS. read *crumina* or *crumena*. At XI. 91, P. has *postremo*, the majority have a false and obvious correction, *rigidique*. v. 128, P. has *vires*, the majority have *bilis*, which being coarser, is not less likely to be genuine. At XII. 92, the corrector and all the other MSS. but one have *operatur festa;* P. or his original did not see that *Janua* was the nominative, and so introduced an impossible plural to agree with *festa*. At XIII. 28, P. has *nunc*, which is flat, but needs no explanation, and looks like a correction of the difficult *nona*, which is supported by the variant *nova*, though this last must be later than *nunc*, as dating from an age when prosody was forgotten. At v. 208 P. has *saeva voluntas*, probably an inaccurate reproduction of *scaeva voluntas*, which is a perverse attempt to improve on *sola*, the reading of the great majority of MSS. Lastly, P. has not retained the original order of xv. and xvi., and its reading *Junco* at xv. 27, looks very like an attempt to improve metre at the expense of history.

Though these instances may tend in some measure to prove that P.'s archetype was not written with uniform fidelity, I have not the least wish to set aside the judgment of such scholars as Jahn or C. F. Hermann on its general superiority. Perhaps it would be too much to say that the defects of Pithou's MS. illustrate the uncertainty of the guidance which the best scholars are compelled to trust, and that C. F. Hermann's old corrector may sometimes have had better materials than his critic.

D. JUNII JUVENALIS

SATIRARUM

LIBER PRIMUS.

SATIRA I.

SEMPER ego auditor tantum? nunquamne reponam,
Vexatus toties rauci Theseide Cordi?
Impune ergo mihi recitaverit ille togatas,
Hic elegos? impune diem consumserit ingens
Telephus, aut summi plena jam margine libri   5

1 reponam] May be future or subjunctive. I prefer the latter. "Am I never to reply?" if so, *impune recitaverit*, "Is he not to be punished for having recited?" Any way the passage shews the very close affinity of the future tense to the subjunctive mood.

2 toties] It lasted so many recitations.—*Cordi*, a stock character in Valgius, Virgil, Juvenal, and Martial. According to the Scholiast, he is spoken of as a contemporary in Valgius's lost elegies.

3 togatas] Sc. fabulas. The characters wore the *toga*, while in regular comedies they wore the Greek *pallium*: the best known writer was Afranius. Dicitur Afrani toga convenisse Menandro, Hor. *Ep.* ii. 1. 57. According to Seneca, *Ep.* 8. § 4, they stood half-way between tragedies and comedies. Horace, *A. P.* 286, speaks of them as shewing a laudable spirit of literary enterprise.

When one considers the immense naïveté of Plautus and the way in which he overloads his subject with morality, we may infer that where the support and restraint of Greek traditions were to a certain extent removed, there would be much dull preaching and little dramatic interest. Horace in the passage quoted gives the judgment of wholesale acquirers of antiquity.

5 Telephus] A king of Mysia wounded by the spear of Achilles and healed by its rust. He figured in a play of Euripides now lost with a piquant display of ostentatious poverty and fluent sophistry. He and Orestes are subjects of tragedy: the epics of the day are characterized, fr. 6—12.

summi] As the margin (the feminine is found also in Licinius, Macer, Rabirius, and Vitruvius) at the end of the roll is full already, the poet writes on the back *too*, and

S. J.   1

Scriptus et in tergo, nec dum finitus, Orestes?

Nota magis nulli domus est sua, quam mihi lucus
Martis et Aeoliis vicinum rupibus antrum
Vulcani. Quid agant venti, quas torqueat umbras
Aeacus, unde alius furtivae devehat aurum   10
Pelliculae, quantas jaculetur Monychus ornos,
Frontonis platani convulsaque marmora clamant
Semper, et assiduo ruptae lectore columnae.
Exspectes eadem a summo minimoque poeta.
Et nos ergo manum ferulae subduximus, et nos   15
Consilium dedimus Sullae, privatus ut altum

has not done yet: *et*, even when out of its usual place, generally goes with the word which comes *after* it.

7 lucus Martis] "In quo Ilia peperit," Schol., would occur in a poem on Romulus: the rest, as far as *Aeacus*, suggests a 'rifacimento' of the Odyssey. *Alius* must be taken as indicating a transition to another legendary cycle, otherwise we might place the grove in Colchos, according to another guess of the Scholiast, and refer the rocks of Aeolus, in the modern Stromboli, and cave of Vulcan, in the modern Vulcano, to the Argonautic legend, on the authority of Ap. Rhodius (iv. 761).

11 quantas] The poetasters refine upon Ovid : "insani dejectam viribus Austri Forte trabem nactus." *Monychus* = Mononychus, a centaur.

12 Frontonis] Pliny (*Ep.* ii. 11, § 3) praises the oratory of one Fronto Catius, who may have bequeathed to P. Cornelius Fronto, the tutor of M. Aurelius, the *horti Maecenatiani*, on the strength of which he claimed connexion with Horace.

marmora] Mayor seems to take this of marble panels round the walls, shaken by the shouts of the audience, which is hardly consistent

with *platani;* Macleane, of the marble pillars, which makes *columnae* tautological. One is tempted to think of marble statues, cf. xiii. 115: as if the poet's friends told him his stirring verse was enough to make stones cry out, while Juvenal implies that they echoed the noise he made, which was enough to shake them on their pedestals.

13 assiduo ruptae lectore] Mayor follows Hand in thinking that the omission of *ab* marks the absence of voluntary agency. Hand admits that the omission only occurs in the poets and later prose writers, where it can be explained by metrical convenience, or a passion for brevity. Here we might explain the words as an ablative absolute, because there is a reader always leaning against them, because readers give them no rest; cf. viii. 137, hebetes lasso lictore secures.

15 ergo] This is to be taken in connection with the preceding line. All poets treat the same subjects; well, I am qualified to treat them too, inf. 19 *tamen* serves to contrast *hoc* with *eadem*.

16 dedimus] "We *have* given," is a present qualification for writing. *Dormiret*, the result contemplated, is naturally in the past, as the advice must have been decided on long ago. Cf. vii. 161; x. 167. Boys

Dormiret. Stulta est clementia, quum tot ubique
Vatibus occurras, periturae parcere chartae.
  Cur tamen hoc potius libeat decurrere campo,
Per quem magnus equos Auruncae flexit alumnus,   20
Si vacat et placidi rationem admittitis, edam.
Quum tener uxorem ducat spado, Maevia Tuscum
Figat aprum et nuda teneat venabula mamma;
Patricios omnes opibus quum provocet unus,
Quo tondente gravis juveni mihi barba sonabat;   25
Quum pars Niliacae plebis, quum verna Canopi
Crispinus, Tyrias humero revocante lacernas,
Ventilet aestivum digitis sudantibus aurum,
Nec sufferre queat majoris pondera gemmae:
Difficile est satiram non scribere. Nam quis iniquae   30
Tam patiens urbis, tam ferreus, ut teneat se,
Causidici nova quum veniat lectica Mathonis,
Plena ipso; post hunc magni delator amici,
Et cito rapturus de nobilitate comesa

began their rhetorical education with political *suasoriae*, and went on to legal *controversiae*.

 20 Auruncae] Suessa Aurunca, where Lucilius was born.

 23] Practising as a ' bestiaria,' in the costume of an Amazon. This profession, and that of gladiator, was opened to women under Nero, and closed to them by Severus.

 25] Repeated (x. 226).

 26 Canopi] Canopus was to Alexandria what Greenwich and Rotherhithe are to London, a town of sailors and their parasites, sometimes visited by pleasure-seekers from the capital, cf. xv. 46 n.

 27 Crispinus] A favourite of Domitian, flattered by Martial, cf. iv. 24. According to the Scholiast he was raised to the senate by Nero, it would be natural however to take the next line as an allusion to his *equestrian* rank, cf. vii. 89, Semen-

stri vatum digitos circumligat auro.

 28] His fingers sweat under his light summer ring of plain gold. At the same time it probably refers to a personal peculiarity: the least thing made him perspire because he took no exercise, cf. iv. 108 n.

 29 majoris gemmae] A gem of any size.

 32 Causidici—Mathonis] Matho is a bankrupt (vii. 129); a braggart (xi. 34); and a standing butt of Martial. *Causidicus* is a mere hack pleader in Cicero, who wrote when advocates were still patrons, not mere servants of their clients. Tr. When councillor Matho comes by in his new litter, and his worship fills it. As it was not usual for two people to ride in a litter, *ipso* must be a sneer at Matho's dignity and cannot be taken as emphasising *plena* which is a sneer at his size.

 34 rapturus de nobilitate comesa]

Quod superest; quem Massa timet, quem munere palpat   35
Carus, et a trepido Thymele submissa Latino;
Quum te submoveant qui testamenta merentur
Noctibus, in coelum quos evehit optima summi
Nunc via processus, vetulae vesica beatae?
Unciolam Proculeius habet, sed Gillo deuncem,   40
Partes quisque suas ad mensuram inguinis heres.
Accipiat sane mercedem sanguinis et sic
Palleat, ut nudis pressit qui calcibus anguem,
Aut Lugdunensem rhetor dicturus ad aram!

Quid referam, quanta siccum jecur ardeat ira,   45
Quum populum gregibus comitum premat hic spoliator
Pupilli prostantis?   Et hic damnatus inani
Judicio (quid enim salvis infamia nummis?)
Exsul ab octava Marius bibit et fruitur Dis
Iratis: at tu victrix provincia ploras!   50

"Ready to clutch, ere long, at the remains of the nobility whom all devour." He means their persons, not their property. Merivale, viii. 158, identifies the *delator* with Memmius Regulus, consul A.D. 63. The Scholiast says he is Heliodorus, who is otherwise unknown, unless he could be identified with Helius, under Nero; he says that others referred to P. Egnatius Celer, iii. 116 n, others to a certain Demetrius a *causidicus* like Matho; he had read of a Latinus, put to death by Nero as an accomplice of Messalina. Another Latinus was a mime under Domitian, flattered by Martial. Massa was already mischievous, A.D. 70, when he betrayed Piso, and was formidable under Domitian. Carus had only one victory to boast of when Agricola died, A.D. 93.

40] Gillo is *heres ex deunce;* Proculeius *ex unciolâ*, a paltry twelfth.

43] In Homer *Il.* iii. 33—35 we have the paleness of a man who

sees a snake, in Virgil *Aen.* ii. 379 the alarm of a man who has trodden upon a snake, the bare feet are Juvenal's own.

44] Where the unsuccessful competitors in the literary contests instituted by Caligula had to provide prizes for their betters, and the worst had to efface their own compositions.

47 **inani**] When the prosecution undertook, as in the case of Marius, to recover to the amount of 700 sestertia unlawfully received from definite persons on definite grounds; it is probable that the actual proceeds of all his extortions were far larger.

48 **infamia**] Which made a *rich* man *intestabilis.*

49 **Exsul ab octava**] He would have had to wait for the ninth at Rome. Cf. viii. 120.

50 **victrix**] Because the Africans, thanks to the exertions of Pliny and Tacitus, secured his condemnation. *ploras* because they were left impoverished.

Haec ego non credam Venusina digna lucerna?
Haec ego non agitem? Sed quid magis Heracleas
Aut Diomedeas aut mugitum Labyrinthi,
Et mare percussum puero fabrumque volantem,
Quum leno accipiat moechi bona, si capiendi   55
Jus nullum uxori, doctus spectare lacunar,
Doctus et ad calicem vigilanti stertere naso;
Quum fas esse putet curam sperare cohortis,
Qui bona donavit praesepibus et caret omni
Majorum censu, dum pervolat axe citato   60
Flaminiam puer: Automedon nam lora tenebat
Ipse, lacernatae quum se jactaret amicae?
Nonne libet medio ceras implere capaces

51 **Venusina digna lucerna**]
Worthy of lucubrations in the style
of Horace. Cf.:

"Arateis multum vigilata lucernis
Carmina." (Meyer, *Antholog.*
76.)

52 **Sed quid magis**, &c.] Probably
to complete the sentence we should
supply Sed quid magis [dignum
credam, num] Heracleas. Heraclea
from Heracles, Diomedea from Diomedes, and like Odyssea from Odys-
seus, whence our Odyssey or, better,
Odyssee.

54 **puero**] *May be* the dative
after 'percussum:' when the dative
is used after a passive verb, except
for metrical convenience, the act accomplished is regarded not only as
proceeding from the agent, but as
affecting him; so here, "the sea
which the boy found he had
struck."

55 **leno**] The husband may be
heres ex asse, if the 'lex Voconia' excludes the woman; probably as the
Lex Papia Poppæa removed this
disqualification in the case of women
who had borne a certain number of
children, the whole means "the husband will take the bequests the wife

earns, unless she has fathered bas-
tards enough upon him to be able to
take them herself."

56 **spectare lacunar**] As if in
thought.

57] See sup. 6, note.

58 He expects a new start, as
praefectus cohortis sociorum; a
farmer's son would begin as centurion. Cf. Ut locupletem aquilam
tibi sexagesimus annus Conferat
(xiv. 197).

59—62] lit. "who has made the
stables a present of his property,
and finds himself without a penny
of the money of his family, through
bowling along the Flaminian road
like a servant (or while still a boy):
for he used to hold the reins himself
when he shewed himself off to his
mistress who wore a man's cloak for
the drive." *Automedon*, he plays
Automedon to her Achilles, hence
puer and *lacernatae ipse*, when
stimulated by her presence; at other
times we are to suppose that he was
content to be driven by a servant of
his own.

63 **medio quadrivio**] The man is
too eager to wait till he gets out of
the noise and bustle of the crossing.

Quadrivio : quum jam sexta cervice feratur
Hinc atque inde patens ac nuda paene cathedra, 65
Et multum referens de Maecenate supino,
Signator falso, qui se lautum atque beatum
Exiguis tabulis et gemma fecerat uda ;
Occurrit matrona potens, quae molle Calenum
Porrectura viro miscet sitiente rubetam, 70
Instituitque rudes melior Locusta propinquas
Per famam et populum nigros efferre maritos ?
   Aude aliquid brevibus Gyaris et carcere dignum,
Si vis esse aliquis ! Probitas laudatur et alget.
Criminibus debent hortos, praetoria, mensas, 75
Argentum vetus et stantem extra pocula caprum.

64 jam sexta] Soon he may ride in an octophorus, as he does already in a hexaphorus. Were the bearers ranged abreast before and behind, so that the width of the litter increased with every pair of bearers?

65 nuda paene cathedra] So like a woman as to enjoy the impropriety of exposure. In the 'sella' you sat, in the 'lectica' you lay at length, in the 'cathedra' (which was all but appropriated to women) you were able to loll.

66.] Reminding you strongly of the way in which Maecenas used to sprawl. The line will be more piquant if we suppose that the fellow had flatterers who compared him to Maecenas, and that Juvenal pretends to see the resemblance so far as it is not flattering.

67 Signator] A forger of attestations. Probably here he forges the will, as well as witnesses it, as his fortune and gentility (*lautum*) cost a small pair of tablets, as well as the trouble of damping his ring, to get a clean impression.

70—72.] When her husband is thirsty, and she has to hand him some mild wine, she puts the bramble frog in, and teaches her country

cousins to brave the public voice and eye (*per famam et populum*), as they bury their husbands, whose faces were blackened with poison.

71 Locusta] A Gaulish woman, helped to remove Claudius and Britannicus, and was sacrificed by Galba, with other creatures of Nero. *Melior*, because it was more respectable to have dealings with a lady of position than with a Gallic adventuress.

73 Gyaris] Now Chiura or Jura, sometimes reckoned with the Cyclades, sometimes with the Sporades.

75 praetoria] A very curious word for palace, the place where a grandee took up his abode, fixed his *head-quarters* in the country; it occurs again perhaps with a slightly different shade of meaning (x. 161), where see note. *Mensas*, the tables of choice wood.

76 Argentum vetus] Pliny, *H.N.* xxxiii. 55, speaks of the higher kinds of *coelatura* as obsolete. *Stantem extra pocula caprum.* Probably the famous original of the bowl given to Martial (viii. 51) with Love riding on a he-goat.

Quem patitur dormire nurus corruptor avarae,
Quem sponsae turpes et praetextatus adulter?
Si natura negat, facit indignatio versum,
Qualemcumque potest, quales ego vel Cluvienus.   80
    Ex quo Deucalion, nimbis tollentibus aequor,
Navigio montem ascendit sortesque poposcit,
Paulatimque anima caluerunt mollia saxa,
Et maribus nudas ostendit Pyrrha puellas,
Quidquid agunt homines, votum, timor, ira, voluptas,   85
Gaudia, discursus, nostri est farrago libelli.
Et quando uberior vitiorum copia? quando
Major avaritiae patuit sinus? alea quando
Hos animos? Neque enim loculis cómitantibus itur
Ad casum tabulae, posita sed luditur arca.   90
Proelia quanta illic dispensatore videbis
Armigero? Simplexne furor sestertia centum
Perdere et horrenti tunicam non reddere servo?
Quis totidem erexit villas, quis fercula septem
Secreto coenavit avus? Nunc sportula primo   95

78] They commit adultery before they are well married with boys in petticoats.

79 Si]=εἴπερ. If, as I assume.

81 tollentibus aequor] The whole surface was raised at once.

82 sortes] An Italian way of divination. Cf. Sortes Praenestinae. Here an oracle in general. So viii. 110, the rapacious governor carries off the very Lares, though they were only worshipped in Italy and in Roman colonies.

83 caluerunt mollia] 'Mollia' is proleptic, softened as they warmed, warmed till they were softened.

88 sinus] Cf. Cic. Verr. ii. § 134, "Avaritia . . . hiante."

89] When was gambling so spirited? For this elliptical form, cf. "Ag. Hos Scyrus animos? Pyrrh. Scelere quae fratrum caret" (Sen.

Troad. 340).

90 arca] The strong box contrasted with 'sacculus' (xi. 26), here with the ivory case, loculi, for money and jewels.

91 dispensatore] Cashier and paymaster (vii. 219).

92 Simplex] A man must be mad twice over to throw away 800l., and not find his slave the clothes he has a right to.

94 fercula septem] Augustus only had three courses or trays as a rule; so also Pertinax till his accession. Coena=κοινή, according to Plutarch; coesna, according to Donaldson, from 'cum' and 'edo.' Both etymologies assume the common orthography which is now generally condemned.

95 primo limine] He will not let you an inch into his house.

Limine parva sedet, turbae rapienda togatae.
Ille tamen faciem prius inspicit et trepidat, ne
Suppositus venias ac falso nomine poscas.
Agnitus accipies; jubet a praecone vocari
Ipsos Trojugenas; nam vexant limen et ipsi   100
Nobiscum. "Da praetori, da deinde tribuno.
Sed libertinus prior est." "Prior," inquit, "ego adsum:
Cur timeam, dubitemve locum defendere, quamvis
Natus ad Euphraten, molles quod in aure fenestrae
Arguerint, licet ipse negem? sed quinque tabernae   105
Quadringenta parant. Quid confert purpura major
Optandum, si Laurenti custodit in agro
Conductas Corvinus oves? ego possideo plus
Pallante et Licinis." Exspectent ergo tribuni;
Vincant divitiae, sacro nec cedat honori,   110
Nuper in hanc urbem pedibus qui venerat albis:

97—102] The patron (ille) does not trust to your giving a name on the list which is in the hands of his paymaster, you may be personating some one who, you happen to know, is absent, he makes the *praeco* (he is a 'rex' himself and keeps a herald) call the list over and watches himself to identify each applicant as he answers. Even nobles with pedigrees as old as Troy submit to this humiliation; and though they take precedence of you, a Syrian freedman [? a perfumer] takes precedence of them.

104 **molles—fenestrae**] The marks of the heavy earring he had worn till he became a Roman citizen and abandoned such things to women.

105] "My income from five shops is equal to the 'census equester.'"

106—108] "With such an income I am as good as a senator, and need not wish to be one; why, Corvinus has to take other people's sheep to graze on his land at Lau-rentium, and as we may say look after them himself, while I may be richer than any freedman." Laurentium was a great grazing country. Corvinus is probably the great-grandson of the patron of Tibullus: in A.D. 59 he was consul with Nero, who assigned him a pension of 500 *sestertia* a year, a larger income than the freedman's after all. *Conductas pascit, i. q. pascendas conducit.*

109 **Pallas**] A freedman of Claudius, by whose interest his brother Felix was made procurator of Judea. Licinus, a freedman of C. Julius Caesar, made a fortune by plundering Gaul. Horace mentions a barber of the name (*A. P.* 301), to whom the Scholiast refers (sup. 25). If he is right, both are mentioned here; but Mayor and Macleane duly notice that *Licinis* for 'a Licinus' is a common construction, though it is more natural to say, "More than Pallas and the Licini," than "More than Pallas and a Licinus."

111] Newly imported slaves had their feet chalked; perhaps that they

Quandoquidem inter nos sanctissima divitiarum
Majestas : etsi, fünesta Pecunia, templo
Nondum habitas, nullas nummorum ereximus aras,
Ut colitur Pax atque Fides, Victoria, Virtus,   115
Quaeque salutato crepitat Concordia nido.
    Sed quum summus honor finito computet anno,
Sportula quid referat, quantum rationibus addat :
Quid facient comites, quibus hinc toga, calceus hinc est
Et panis fumusque domi? Densissima centum   120
Quadrantes lectica petit, sequiturque maritum
Languida vel praegnans et circumducitur uxor.
Hic petit absenti, nota jam callidus arte,
Ostendens vacuam et clausam pro conjuge sellam.
" Galla mea est," inquit; " Citius dimitte : moraris."   125
" Profer, Galla, caput."   " Noli vexare, quiescit."
    Ipse dies pulchro distinguitur ordine rerum :
Sportula, deinde forum, jurisque peritus Apollo

might be traced if they ran away;
perhaps that their feet might not
dirty the *catasta*.

113] According to St Augustine
(*De Civ. Dei* iv. 21—24; vii. 11, 12),
who probably got his information
from Varro, Pecunia was a goddess.
Juvenal does not mean to say that
she was not, only that she had not a
temple like the other deified abstrac-
tions; most of those he mentions
were among the best known public
buildings at Rome; the Temple of
Concord, erected by Livia as a thank-
offering for her happy marriage with
Augustus, was one of the finest buildings in Rome ; the next line is probably a sneer at the careless way in
which it was kept.

116] The goddess, that is to say
her storks, twitter when worshippers
salute their nest.

117, 118] It is to be remembered, that a grandee would know
more rich parvenus, and get over
the ground faster than those who

needed the dole.

119 **toga, calceus**] Which they
might dispense with, but for their
attendance on the great.

120 **densissima lectica**] " Carriage
company," as we say, and in great
numbers ; the *comites* would have to
walk.

121—127] If a man's wife has a
family claim, she is dragged round
too : the officials are up to the dodge
of continuing the claim after her
death by exhibiting her empty chair.

128 **Sportula**] It is clear that
there were afternoon doles of money,
—" Balnea post decimam lasso cen-
tumve petantur Quadrantes" (Martial x. 70. 13),—of food (Juv. iii.
249).   On the other hand, the praetor's train (x. 45, 46) have received
their dole for the day before the
show; and the description above
(95 sqq.) implies an actual distribu-
tion. Bekker and Mayor can hardly
be right in making the word here
mean the invitation to the evening

Atque triumphales, inter quas ausus habere
Nescio quis titulos Aegyptius atque Arabarches,   130
Cujus ad effigiem non tantum meiere fas est.
Vestibulis abeunt veteres lassique clientes,
Votaque deponunt : quanquam longissima coenae
Spes homini : caulis miseris atque ignis emendus.
Optima silvarum interea pelagique vorabit   135
Rex horum, vacuisque toris tantum ipse jacebit.
Nam de tot pulchris et latis orbibus et tam
Antiquis una comedunt patrimonia mensa.
Nullus jam parasitus erit : sed quis feret istas

sportula; if the invitation were given, and dishonoured (inf. 133), Juvenal would have made a point of this, and instead of complaining that they had to buy their dinner, he would have said that they had nothing to buy it with.

Apollo] The group of Apollo and Marsyas "in foro Augusti." Hence *juris peritus.* It was made of ivory. Cf. Hor. I. *Sat.* ix. fin.: "Sic me servavit Apollo," after the bore has been carried off into court; and for Marsyas (*ib.* ii. 119 sqq.) : "Deinde eo dormitum, non solicitus, mihi quod cras Surgendum sit mane, obeundus Marsya, qui se Vultum ferre negat noviorum posse minoris." He is glad that he has not to rise early to pay his court, and keep an appointment in the city, where the men on 'Change are such harpies that their shy looks flog Marsyas over again.

129 triumphales] "*Statuas* scilicet."

130 Arabarches] "Egypt under the Empire was divided into three districts—(ἐπιστρατηγίαι) Upper Egypt (Thebais), Middle Egypt (Heptanomis), and Lower Egypt. Each of these was governed by an ἐπιστράτηγος, who united in himself all civil and military authority. The ἐπιστράτηγος of Thebais also bore the title ἀραβάρχης." [As Berenice

and Myos Hormos, the harbours for the Red Sea traffic, whence caravans brought the goods over to Coptus to be re-shipped on the Nile, were in his government, it was natural that he should have the management of all Roman relations with the Arabian coast.] "The Egyptian is the same person as the Arabarch," Mayor. The title was ridiculous, since the days of Pompeius (Cic. *ad Att.* i. 17), who had brought it home from the East in company with too many others.

131 n. t. m.] sed etiam cacare.

132 veteres] As they have danced attendance on him so many years, and followed him so far that very day, they think he might invite them to dine at his own table now and then; he owes them something beyond the dole which they share with a crowd of strangers every morning.

134 caulis] So Persius' notion of comfort (vi. 69), "Nunc, nunc impensius unge, Unge puer caules."

136.] With all his tables (probably of citron, from three to four feet wide, or rather under, and costing 8000*l.* apiece and upwards), he finds one quite room enough to eat up an heritage upon.—*Antiquis,* cf. "Mensa — per multas elegantium dominorum successiones civitati nota" (Sen. *de Tranq. An.* I, § 4).

Luxuriae sordes? Quanta est gula, quae sibi totos   140
Ponit apros, animal propter convivia natum !
Poena tamen praesens, quum tu deponis amictus
Turgidus et crudum pavonem in balnea portas.
Hinc subitae mortes atque intestata senectus.
It nova, nec tristis, per cunctas fabula coenas,   145
Ducitur iratis plaudendum funus amicis.

Nil erit ulterius, quod nostris moribus addat
Posteritas; eadem cupient facientque minores;
Omne in praecipiti vitium stetit. Utere velis,
Totos pande sinus. Dicas hic forsitan, "Unde   150
Ingenium par materiae? unde illa priorum
Scribendi, quodcumque animo flagrante liberet,
Simplicitas, cujus non audeo dicere nomen?
'Quid refert dictis ignoscat Mucius an non?'
Pone Tigellinum: taeda lucebis in illa,   155

144—147] He has had plenty of time to make a will, and remember his friends, but he has not done so; so they come to scoff at his funeral, and the town laughs at their indignation.

subitae] An old man who over-ate himself every day, and went straight into a hot bath, would very likely bring on apoplexy.

153 **Simplicitas**] This is almost an instance of παρὰ προσδοκίαν: after *unde illa priorum* we might have had *libertas* at once, and after the clause with *scribendi* we expect it still, though a very fastidious reader might think it awkward after *liberet*. Instead, we have *simplicitas*, which serves to identify the quality, which the writer does not venture to designate by its proper name. Of course, it is possible to make the quotation begin at *cujus*, and if we had the complete works of Lucilius, we might find that it was right, though *a priori* hardly likely.

154] In the person of Lucilius.

"Secuit Lucilius urbem, Te Lupe, te Muci" (Pers. i. 114).

155—159 **Tigellinum**] Perhaps proverbially a modern favourite, if the whole Satire was written under Trajan. I follow Madvig and Mayor in restoring the MS. reading *deducit*, which has been corrected by copyists, who did not know or believe that *quae* could be supplied from *qua* as the *nom*. Cf. "Quibusque fuisset minima cum corporibus contagio seseque ab iis semper sevocassent" (Cic. *Tusc.* i. § 72). "Quibus pecunias imperasset neque contulissent" (*Hist. Bell. Alex.* 56). If these passages be relevant, as is possible, though the construction in them is much neater and clearer, the whole will mean (a) "We shall see you shining in the torch where people burn, standing smoking with a stake through their necks, while the dripping from the torch draws a broad furrow in the sand." There is no evidence that these victims were *defossi*, which would have made the

Qua stantes ardent, qui fixo gutture fumant,
Et latum media sulcum deducit arena."
Qui dedit ergo tribus patruis aconita, vehatur
Pensilibus plumis, atque illinc despiciat nos?
"Quum veniet contra, digito compesce labellum: 160
Accusator erit, qui verbum dixerit, Hic est.
Securus licet Aeneam Rutulumque ferocem
Committas; nulli gravis est percussus Achilles,
Aut multum quaesitus Hylas urnamque sequutus.
Ense velut stricto quoties Lucilius ardens   165
Infremuit, rubet auditor, cui frigida mens est
Criminibus; tacita sudant praecordia culpa.
Inde irae et lacrimae. Tecum prius ergo voluta
Haec animo ante tubas: galeatum sero duelli
Poenitet."—Experiar, quid concedatur in illos,   170
Quorum Flaminia tegitur cinis atque Latina.

stake unnecessary, and wasted half the illumination; and if there were, it would be curious to say a thing draws a furrow, when you mean that it is the occasion of digging a ditch. If not, we must read *deducis*, which may mean either (β) "You *will* be burnt, and *are* wasting your labour on a grand scale;" cf. vii. 48, 49, "Tenuique in pulvere sulcos Ducimus et sterili littus versamus aratro:" or (γ) "You *will* be burnt, and even now *are* being drawn through the sand to execution," which interpretation seems rather forcible-feeble; it is also possible to defend (α) as an interpretation, with a slightly different construction, supplying *ea* from the sentence instead of *quae* from *qua*; perhaps it may be added, that *media* makes (β) a shade more probable, as it is more absurd to plough the middle than the edge of the desert.

161] Mayor, "*accusator erit* [ejus] qui verbum dixerit, ' hic est,'" quot-

ing three passages, where no other antecedent is possible, and where a similar ellipse is therefore certain; here *accusator* ought to be the antecedent; if so, "He'll treat you as an accuser, if you so much as say, That's he."

164] "Or Hylas, who went down after his urn, and was sought so long."

169 **ante tubas**] "Cur ante tubam timor occupat artus?" (Virg. *Aen.* xi. 424). The metaphor is still kept up from *ense* (*sup.* 165).

171] **Flaminia—Latina**] These roads are probably selected because Paris was buried on one, Domitian on the other. We cannot infer from this passage that Juvenal had never attacked contemporaries: the first Satire in its present form was manifestly intended as an introduction to a series of satires collected after the individuals satirised were dead and gone.

SATIRA III.

QUAMVIS digressu veteris confusus amici,
Laudo tamen, vacuis quod sedem figere Cumis
Destinet atque unum civem donare Sibyllae.
Janua Baiarum est et gratum litus amoeni
Secessus. Ego vel Prochytam praepono Suburae.   5
Nam quid tam miserum, tam solum vidimus, ut non
Deterius credas horrere incendia, lapsus
Tectorum assiduos ac mille pericula saevae
Urbis, et Augusto recitantes mense poetas?
Sed dum tota domus reda componitur una,   10

2 vacuis] Empty, as appears from *unum civem donare Sibyllae;* but we have "Sed vacuum Tibur placet aut imbelle Tarentum" (Hor. *Ep.* i. 7, 45), where it means leisurely:— "quieta Cyme" (Stat. *Silv.* iv. 3. 65).

4 Janua Baiarum est] So called as the point to which Domitian carried his new branch of the Via Appia, to meet the local roads of the district of Baiae.

5 Ego vel Prochytam praepono Suburae] Juvenal names Prochyta, a bare volcanic island then uncultivated, as the most unattractive place in the neighbourhood of Cumae, and the Subura as the part of Rome where a poor Roman would naturally have to live. Cf. xi. 51: "Esquilias a ferventi migrare Subura."

6 miserum] Implies the absence of the comforts of civilisation, *solum* the absence of the pleasure of society.

9 Augusto recitantes mense poetas] They are dangerous, as they make you hear them in crowded rooms, in the hottest part of the holidays, when you have no excuse for refusing, if in town.

10 componitur] We should say, "While the household was being packed up"—speaking from the point of time at which we *are;* the Romans say, "While it is being packed up" from the point at which the subject of the principal verb *was.* Cf. xiv. 94, 95:

"Totam hanc turbavit filius amens,
  Dum meliore novas attollit marmore villas."

In general, however, a continuous process, or state contemporary with a single determinate fact, seems to be in the present; while if the contemporary event be equally continuous, it attracts the clause with *dum* into the past tense; so, "Dum Sulla in aliis rebus erat occupatus, erant qui suis vulneribus mederentur" (Cic. *Rosc. Am.* 32).

Substitit ad veteres arcus madidamque Capenam.
(16) In vallem Egeriae descendimus et speluncas
Dissimiles veris. Quanto praestantius esset
Numen aquae, viridi si margine clauderet undas
Herba, nec ingenuum violarent marmora tophum !   15
(12) Hic, ubi nocturnae Numa constituebat amicae,
Nunc sacri fontis nemus et delubra locantur
Judaeis: quorum cophinus foenumque supellex;
Omnis enim populo mercedem pendere jussa est
Arbor, et ejectis mendicat silva Camenis.   20
Hic tunc Umbricius, "Quando artibus," inquit, "honestis
Nullus in urbe locus, nulla emolumenta laborum,
Res hodie minor est, here quam fuit, atque eadem cras
Deteret exiguis aliquid: proponimus illuc
Ire, fatigatas ubi Daedalus exuit alas,   25
Dum nova canities, dum prima et recta senectus,

11 madidam] From the aqueduct, a branch over the aqua Martia, which ran over the porta Capena.

12—20] The order in the margin is that of the MSS., the order of the text is Jahn's, and is a decided improvement; cf. xii. 32, for another instance of what looks like a tendency to write passages for their own sake, and to piece them together afterwards.

13 praestantius] P. seems to have read *praesentius*, as the corrector has erased a letter, and written 'praestantius;' if 'praesentius' had been right, it would most likely have been quoted by Servius, to illustrate the passages in Virgil, which suggested it to a solitary interpolator, who was followed by an ignorant copyist.

16 constituebat] Made assignations.

17] They ran up hovels in the grove, and put up lean-to sheds against the chapels, and perhaps bivouacked under the porticos.

18 cophinus] There was a festival of the Cophinus among the Jews. "Ordinis res est ut Aegyptius Pharao incedat cum diademate Israelita cum cophino" (Sidon. *Ep.* vii. 6); it very likely grew out of a ceremony enjoined at the presentation of firstfruits (*Deut.* xxvi.), here it simply means that the Jews are very poor and live like Gypsies, they carry a truss of hay for a shake-down and a basket for broken victuals.

20 mendicat silva] The wood is said to do what its tenants do, cf. "crepitat Concordia" i. 116.

23 here] "In here neque E plane neque I auditur" (Quint. i. 4, § 8). "Here, nunc E litera terminamus; at veterum comicorum adhuc libris invenio 'heri ad me venit,' quod idem in epistolis Augusti quas sua manu scripsit aut emendavit deprehenditur" (Id. i. 7, § 22). Augustus inclined to phonetic spelling (Suet. *Oct.* 88).

24 Deteret] "Will wear something from its small remainder tomorrow;" *proponimus* begins the apodosis.

Dum superest Lachesi quod torqueat; et pedibus me
Porto meis, nullo dextram subeunte bacillo.
Cedamus patria : vivant Artorius istic
Et Catulus ; maneant qui nigrum in candida -vertunt,   30
Quis facile est eadem conducere, flumina, portus,
Siccandam eluviem, portandum ad busta cadaver,
Et praebere caput domina venale sub hasta.
Quondam hi cornicines et municipalis arenae
Perpetui comites, notaeque per oppida buccae—   35
Munera nunc edunt et, verso pollice, vulgus
Quum jubet, occidunt populariter : inde reversi
Conducunt foricas : et cur non omnia ? quum sint

30 maneant—vertunt] This general aptitude of turning foul fair is illustrated by a double catalogue of things which others can do, 31—38 ; and of things which the speaker cannot do, 41—47.

32 Siccandam eluviem] In which convicts were employed whom the contractors would have to superintend. The attraction was the chance of 'finds.'

portandum ad busta cadaver] Probably means that the man joins a company which farmed the funeral 'properties' kept at the temple of Libitina, and contracted· for conducting funerals.

33] "At the risk of being sold as slaves in case of default." So the Scholiast ; and I believe he is right. Most say, " To act as auctioneers ;" but the auctioneer did not supply the slaves. Moreover this view is against the symmetry of the construction, which is preserved if we suppose that *praebere* corresponds to *conducere* as effect to cause, while· it is violated by putting *praebere* in a row with the many accusatives which *conducere* governs. The *hasta*, probably a symbol of the *comitia centuriata*, or military assembly, was also set up in the court of the *centumviri*, and is here called *domina*, as a pur-

chase in an auction gave *dominium.*

34—36] "Formerly these people were horn-blowers, and went their rounds with the country circus, till every country town knew their puffed cheeks." (Cf. however xi. 33, 34: Dic tibi quis sis Orator vehemens an Curtius et Matho buccae. The same sense is not impossible here.) "They give the shows now ; and, when the mob bid them, turn up their thumbs to do a little killing for popularity." *Vulgus quum jubet* is P.'s reading, which makes *occidunt* rather awkward, for want of a definite object ; all the other MSS. have *libet*, and most of them *quem*, and I suspect they are right—"Kill whom it likes the mob ;" but the accusative after 'libet,' as an unusual construction, suggested the alternative conjectures *vulgi* and *jubet*; while 'quum' for 'quem' is· due to pure stupidity and laziness. If *vulgi* is read, it will mean, "When the mob turn up their thumbs, have the most. expensive gladiators killed for· popularity." The Editor gave effect to the wishes of the mob, just as at concerts there is generally some one to give a formal decision upon *encores.*

38—40] Why should they not

Quales ex humili magna ad fastigia rerum
Extollit, quoties voluit Fortuna jocari.   40
Quid Romae faciam? Mentiri nescio; librum,
Si malus est, nequeo laudare et poscere; motus
Astrorum ignoro; funus promittere patris
Nec volo, nec possum; ranarum viscera nunquam
Inspexi. Ferre ad nuptam quae mittit adulter,   45
Quae mandat, norunt alii: me nemo ministro
Fur erit, atque ideo nulli comes exeo, tanquam
Mancus et exstinctae corpus non utile dextrae.
Quis nunc diligitur, nisi conscius, et cuï fervens
Aestuat occultis animus semperque tacendis?   50
Nil tibi se debere putat, nil conferet unquam,
Participem qui te secreti fecit honesti:
Carus ërit Verri, qui Verrem tempore, quo vult,
Accusare potest. Tanti tibi non sit opaci
Omnis arena Tagi quodque in mare volvitur aurum,   55
Ut somno careas ponendaque praemia sumas
Tristis et a magno semper timearis amico!
    Quae nunc divitibus gens acceptissima nostris
Et quos praecipue fugiam, properabo fateri,
Nec pudor obstabit. Non possum ferre, Quirites,   60

combine incongruities, since they are fortune's favourites, who exhibits her caprice in them?

42 **laudare**] After the public recital. *Poscere*, for private perusal.

44, 45 **ranarum viscera nunquam inspexi**] Ostensibly as an 'aruspex,' really as a poisoner.

45, 46 **quae mittit**] Letters and presents. — *Quae mandat*, messages.

47 **nulli comes exeo**] "No governor takes me out in his suite."

48] As if I were maimed, a mere useless corpse with the right hand gone.

54 **Tanti tibi non sit &c.**] "Do not rate all the sand which thickens

Tagus, and the gold he rolls to the sea, so high as to lose your sleep for them, and take to your sorrow the fee you will have to pay again, and pass for the friend of one, who must always fear you, and can destroy you when he will, and therefore leave Rome where perilous baseness is necessary." For a similar use of *tanti esse*, cf. x. 97; for an opposite, xiii. 96, note.—*Opaci—aurum* is not exactly a hendiadys, as the second clause is an afterthought added to explain the first.

59 **Et fugiam**] And whom therefore I have most reason to avoid.

60 **Nec pudor obstabit**] It is disgraceful to be ousted by Greeks,

Graecam urbem; quamvis quota portio faecis Achaei?
Jam pridem Syrus in Tiberim defluxit Orontes,
Et linguam et mores et cum tibicine chordas
Obliquas, nec non gentilia tympana secum
Vexit, et ad Circum jussas prostare puellas.   65
Ite quibus grata est picta lupa barbara mitra!
Rusticus ille tuus sumit trechedipna, Quirine,
Et ceromatico fert niceteria collo.
Hic alta Sicyone, ast hic Amydone relicta,
Hic Andro, ille Samo, hic Trallibus aut Alabandis,   70
Esquilias dictumque petunt a vimine collem,
Viscera magnarum domuum dominique futuri.
Ingenium velox, audacia perdita, sermo
Promtus et Isaeo torrentior. Ede, quid illum
Esse putes? quem vis hominem, secum attulit ad nos: 75
Grammaticus, rhetor, geometres, pictor, aliptes,
Augur, schoenobates, medicus, magus : omnia novit.

and therefore shame might be expected to keep the speaker from owning that they have ousted him.

61 **quamvis**] "And yet," καίτοι; or, if there be any difference between *quamvis* and *quamquam*, "However, what proportion of the scoundrels are Greeks?"

64 **Obliquas**] sc. 'sambucae.'

66 **Ite**] To the circus.

67 **trechedipna**] "Vestimenta parasitica vel galliculas currentium ad coenam" (Schol.).

68] The Romans now took Greek exercises in private or public gymnasia. In Horace's time they took simpler exercises in the Campus Martius (*Carm.* I. viii. 4—12). Seneca and Pliny the elder thought wrestling an immoral exhibition.

71] The Esquiline (and probably the Viminal) was among the better quarters of Rome, as we might speak of foreign adventurers

making their way to Pimlico or Kensington.

72] Already the intimates of great houses, and soon to be their lords.

74 **Promtus et Isaeo torrentior**] In Greek and Latin, instead of comparing two similar things or persons, or two similar qualities, it is common to compare a quality with a person or thing. If we try in English, we can compare a person with a quality: "Isaeus was not so impetuously fluent as their ready talk." Isaeus is the Assyrian not the Athenian: he came to Rome 97 A.D. at the age of over sixty, and made a great impression by his skill as an extempore debater on the subjects of the rhetoric of the schools.

76 **aliptes**] Here in its earlier sense of trainer. At Rome it came to be sometimes used in a narrower etymological sense of the slave who attended his master in the gymnasium.

Graeculus esuriens in coelum, jusseris, ibit.

Ad summam, non Maurus erat neque Sarmata nec Thrax,

Qui sumsit pennas, mediis sed natus Athenis.   80

Horum ego non fugiam conchylia? me prior ille

Signabit? fultusque toro meliore recumbet

Advectus Romam, quo pruna et cottana vento?

Usque adeo nihil est, quod nostra infantia coelum

Hausit Aventini, bacca nutrita Sabina?   85

Quid? quod adulandi gens prudentissima laudat

Sermonem indocti, faciem deformis amici,

Et longum invalidi collum cervicibus aequat

Herculis, Antaeum procul a tellure tenentis,

Miratur vocem angustam, qua deterius nec   90

Ille sonat, quo mordetur gallina marito.

Haec eadem licet et nobis laudare: sed illis

Creditur. An melior, quum Thaida sustinet, aut quum

Uxorem comoedus agit vel Dorida nullo

78] 'Si' is omitted in these parenthetical conditions. Cf.:

"Tu quoque magnam
Partem opere in tanto, sineret dolor,
Icare, haberes." (*Aen.* vi. 30.)

"Par ad honesta, libeat, facultas."
(Sen. *ad Marc.* 16 § 1.)

"All sciences a fasting mounseer
    knows,
And bid him go to hell, to hell he
    goes."
             Jonson.

79, 80] "To sum up all, out of all possible nations, Daedalus was an Athenian."

81, 82] Instead of the *toga* the Greek *factotum* wears a gay outlandish mantle, *conchylia*: the patron asks him to witness his will, *signabit*, before the old client, and gives him a better place at his table.

84, 85] "Is it so mere a nothing that my childhood breathed the air of Aventine" (which is the proper place for an honest Plebeian to be

born), "and was reared" (not on the choice fruits of the East, but) "on the good old Sabine olive?"

86 **Laudat**] finds a way to praise.

88, 89] They are ingenious, as well as bold. The patron is not a strong man, he has a long throat, he tries to carry his head well up. This reminds them of Hercules' bull neck—when it was stretched upwards and backwards.

90 **qua—marito**] "So bad that the cock, when he feathers his hen, cannot make a worse." *Ille=vox illius*, Mayor; perhaps rather=*qua deteriorem non edit sonum ille.—Nec*=οὐδέ, not even; it gains the sense somehow as follows [nothing makes a worse noise], "nor the cock either," i.e. not even the cock; after which it is easy to omit the clause in brackets.

92 **lioot**] "We may if we please;" that privilege is left us.

94 **Dorida nullo cultam palliolo**] Cf. Eur. *Hec.* 933: μονόπεπλος

Cultam palliolo? Mulier nempe ipsa videtur,   95
Non persona loqui: vacua et plana omnia dicas
Infra ventriculum et tenui distantia rima.
Nec tamen Antiochus, nec erit mirabilis illic
Aut Stratocles aut cum molli Demetrius Haemo:
Natio comoeda est. Rides, majore cachinno   100
Concutitur; flet, si lacrimas conspexit amici,
Nec dolet; igniculum brumae si tempore poscas,
Accipit endromiden; si dixeris, "Aestuo," sudat.
Non sumus ergo pares: melior, qui semper et omni
Nocte dieque potest aliena sumere vultum   105
A facie, jactare manus, laudare paratus,
Si bene ructavit, si rectum minxit amicus,
Si trulla inverso crepitum dedit aurea fundo.
Praeterea sanctum nihil est et ab inguine tutum;
Non matrona laris, non filia virgo, neque ipse   10
Sponsus levis adhuc, non filius ante pudicus.
Horum si nihil est, aviam resupinat amici.
Scire volunt secreta domus atque inde timeri.
  Et quoniam coepit Graecorum mentio, transi

Δωρίς ὡς κόρα. As waiting women were not allowed shawls, and so were obliged to follow the Dorian fashion, Doris would be a natural name for them.

95 nempe] To be sure they act well; still they would be nothing among Greeks.

99 molli Haemo] An actor famous for his assumption of womanish delicacy.

100 Natio] This word is used in the purest prose writers of what we call tribes, while *gentes* are what we call nations. It would be easy and irrelevant to translate "it is a tribe of actors."

102 igniculum] "A bit of fire."

103 Accipit] Not merely *capit* or

induit, he is glad to get his cue from you.

105 aliena] So P.; all the rest *alienum*, which Juvenal *ought* to have written.

108] Almost certainly we are to think of a 'cottabus,' probably in this context of an indecent one, suitable to a man, "Qui Lacedaemonium pytismate lubricat orbem" (xi. 173).

114 transi] Leave the boyish rudiments of sin, and listen to the crimes of manhood. Some think *transi gymnasia = transi ad gymnasia*, to the philosophic schools; but it is not certain that *gymnasia* can mean schools; or *majoris abollae*, a bigger philosopher's cloak, without more help from the context than they get here.

Gymnasia atque audi facinus majoris abollae.   115
Stoicus occidit Baream, delator amicum,
Discipulamque senex, ripa nutritus in illa,
Ad quam Gorgonei delapsa est pinna caballi.
Non est Romano cuiquam locus hic, ubi regnat
Protogenes aliquis vel Diphilus aut Hermarchus,   120
Qui gentis vitio nunquam partitur amicum,
Solus habet. Nam quum facilem stillavit in aurem
Exiguum de naturae patriaeque veneno,
Limine summoveor; perierunt tempora longi
Servitii. Nusquam minor est jactura clientis.   125
    Quod porro officium, ne nobis blandiar, aut quod
Pauperis hic meritum, si curet nocte togatus
Currere, quum Praetor lictorem impellat et ire
Praecipitem jubeat, dudum vigilantibus orbis,

116 **Stoicus**] Publius Egnatius Celer, a client of Soranus Barea, denounced him and his daughter for magic and treason under Nero; they had to commit suicide. After the fall of Vitellius, Egnatius was banished.

117 **Discipulam**] So Ritter, for *discipulum*, to give force to *senex*, as the client could not be much older than the patron, while the copyists might easily forget Barea's daughter.

118] Though a native of Berytus, he might be educated at Tarsus, which Juvenal probably derived from Pegasus' hoof.—*Caballi*, slang, like nag. Cf. "pigri *sarraca* Bootae" (v. 23), "immeritis franguntur crura *caballis*" (x. 60).

125] He is sold cheap for another false smile from a Greek.

127 **hic**] At Rome. Contrast the following passage where Cicero is defending Muraena against Cato from the charge of hiring attendants to follow him in his canvass:—"Quid opus est, inquit, sectatoribus? A me tu id quaeris, quid opus sit eo, quo semper usi sumus? Homi-

nes tenues unum habent in nostrum ordinem aut promerendi aut referendi beneficii locum, hanc in nostris petitionibus operam atque adsectationem. Neque enim fieri potest neque postulandum est a nobis aut ab equitibus Romanis, ut suos necessarios candidatos adsectentur totos dies: a quibus si domus nostra celebratur, si *interdum* ad forum deducimur, si *uno basilicae spatio* [one turn through a basilica] honestamur, diligenter observari videmur et coli: tenuiorum et non occupatorum amicorum est ista adsiduitas: quorum copia bonis viris et beneficis deesse non solet" (*Pro. L. Mur.* c. xxxiv. § 70). I underline the words which mark how closely such homage was measured in the last age of the Republic.

129 **dudum vigilantibus orbis**] A scholiast who was puzzled by *dudum* says: "Quamvis contemnat, festinat tamen." The words give the reason not for *impellat* and *jubeat*, but for *ire praecipitem*, and give the praetor's view, even if not spoken in his person; he tells the lictor to

Ne prior Albinam et·Modiam collega salutet? 130
Divitis hic servi claudit latus ingenuorum
Filius : alter enim, quantum in legione tribuni
Accipiunt, donat Calvinae vel Catienae,
Ut semel atque iterum super illam palpitet : at tu,
Quum tibi vestiti facies scorti placet, haeres 135
Et dubitas alta Chionen deducere sella.
Da testem Romae tam sanctum, quam fuit hospes
Numinis Idaei ; procedat vel Numa vel qui
Servavit trepidam flagranti ex aede Minervam :
Protinus ad censum, de moribus ultima fiet 140
Quaestio : "quot pascit servos? quot possidet agri
Jugera? quam multa magnaque paropside coenat?"
Quantum quisque sua nummorum servat ·in arca,
Tantum habet et fidei. Jures licet et Samothracum
Et nostrorum aras ; contemnere fulmina pauper 145
Creditur atque Deos, Dis ignoscentibus ipsis.
Quid? quod materiam praebet causasque jocorum
Omnibus hic idem, si foeda et scissa lacerna,
Si toga sordidula est et rupta calceus alter
Pelle patet : vel si, consuto vulnere, crassum 150

hurry, because the dowagers must have been up this long time. Cf. for a somewhat similar use of the subjunctive xv. 60 n.

132, 133] Spends a tribune's pay in presents to wealthy matrons.

137 hospes] P. Scipio Nasica.

139] Lucius Caecilius Metellus saved the Palladium from the temple of Vesta, B.C. 241.

140 Protinus] "Straight to the point of his fortune." It is a curious coincidence that the standing epithet of a good witness is 'locuples.'

142 paropside] "Dish." The Roman, not the Attic sense.

144 Samothracum] The gods of Samothrace were called Cabiri : as Samothrace was a great centre of traffic in the beginning of Greek civilisation, its gods were widely known ; as the race which originally occupied the island was clearly distinct from the historical Greeks, and naturally made a secret to strangers of the precise nature and object of their worship, these gods exercised the attraction of mystery upon the religious consciousness of Greece, while it was impressible and fresh, and still continued in an age of scepticism to inspire a certain degree of superstitious awe.

150 crassum atque recens] He is always having his shoes mended, so there is always a glaring new patch to shew.

Atque recens linum ostendit non una cicatrix.

Nil habet infelix paupertas durius in se,

Quam quod ridiculos homines facit. "Exeat," inquit,

"Si pudor est de se, pulvino surgat equestri

Cujus res legi non sufficit, et sedeant hic   155

Lenonum pueri quocumque in fornice nati

Hic plaudat nitidi praeconis filius inter

Pinnirapi cultos juvenes juvenesque lanistae.

Sic libitum vano, qui nos distinxit, Othoni."

Quis gener hic placuit censu minor atque puellae   160

Sarcinulis impar? quis pauper scribitur heres?

Quando in consilio est Aedilibus? Agmine facto

Debuerant olim tenues migrasse Quirites.

Haud facile emergunt, quorum virtutibus obstat

Res angusta domi: sed Romae durior illis   165

---

154 Si pudor est de se] So the Scholiast, and probably Pithou's MS., the corrector whereof and the other MSS. have *Si pudor est, et de*, which is neater, and less vigorous.

157 nitidi] Like *cultos* in the next line: the auctioneer has commenced gentleman. The Scholiast has a curious note on *cultos* :—"Divitis degener gladiatoris," as if it was unmanly of them not to be gladiators too.

158 Pinnirapi] The gladiator matched with the Samnite. The *pinna* was a trophy: "Cum septem incolumis pinnis redit ac recipit se," Lucilius.

161 Sarcinulis] 'Collige sarcinulas' was a form of divorce. It would be convenient if it could be made a general term for a wife's fortune; but Achaintre, who makes it equal to *trousseau*, is nearer right than the Scholiast, who makes it *dos*. If so, instead of saying, "He gives her less than she brings him," he says, "He is not equal to giving her a house to put her things in."

162 Quando—Aedilibus] Cf. sup. 47: Nulli comes exeo, n. Here he complains of the difficulty of getting, not an appointment on a governor's staff, but a berth as assessor to the aediles, who were mere police magistrates. Such a position would add to the respectability of a thriving *bourgeois*, and perhaps had some of the practical conveniences of being on the vestry and the board of guardians. *Umbricius* means that the poor gentleman cannot make his way either at court, where he is ousted by Greeks, or in business, where he is cut out by freedmen.

163 Debuerant olim migrasse] 'Olim' carries the mind back to a past time, at which it had long been their duty to have emigrated, if the tenses can be tabulated in order of succession, except in direct narrative. In idiomatic English we might say, "they had ought," which is exactly like 'debuerant,' and means, not that the duty had been long incumbent, but that it was unperformed. Cf. inf. 315, note.

Conatus; magno hospitium miserabile, magno
Servorum ventres et frugi coenula magno.
Fictilibus coenare pudet, quod turpe negavit
Translatus subito ad Marsos mensamque Sabellam,
Contentusque illic veneto duroque cucullo.   170
    Pars magna Italiae est, si verum admittimus, in qua
Nemo togam sumit nisi mortuus. Ipsa dierum
Festorum herboso colitur si quando theatro
Majestas, tandemque redit ad pulpita notum
Exodium, quum personae pallentis hiatum   175
In gremio matris formidat rusticus infans,
Aequales habitus illic similemque videbis
Orchestram et populum : clari velamen honoris
Sufficiunt tunicae summis Aedilibus albae.
Hic ultra vires habitus nitor; hic aliquid plus   180
Quam satis est interdum aliena sumitur arca.

166, 167 **magno servorum ventres**] Slaves are expensive to buy and expensive to keep.

168 **negavit**] So the MSS. "When a man is transported, he is sure to deny," the aorist is unnecessary; but it is not worth while to alter it to *negabit*. The paraphrase of the Scholiast supports another conjecture, *negabis;* and it is more like Latin that the nominative to a verb shall be an unexpressed and indefinite 'you,' than an unexpressed and indefinite 'he.'

170 **cucullo**] Cf. "Tempora Santonico veles adoperta cucullo" (inf. viii. 145). The 'capote' does not seem to have been a purely Italian garment, as its dye in this passage suggests a foreign origin, as does also the epithet in the quotation above. The variant *culullo* is condemned by 'que' and all the MSS.

171 **si verum admittimus**] "If we can bear to realise the truth." Cf. i. 21: "Si vacat et placidi rationem admittitis, edam."

172 **togam**] Martial (I. l. 31) boasts that in Spain he never meets a senator, and never has to put on a toga: "Lunata nusquam pellis et nusquam toga."

nisi mortuus] When his dignity can give *him* no trouble.

173 **si quando**] Because the performances occur at rare intervals.— *Tandem*, because they are eagerly expected. Both are points of contrast with the constant shows of Rome. So 'in gremio matris,' she has no one with whom to leave her baby; but she will not stay at home, when the whole population is at the theatre.

177—179] "Everybody dresses alike there. There is no difference between the people at large and the Senate in the orchestra." The aediles think something is due to *their* dignity, so they wear white; but even they do not go beyond the tunic.

180] Cf. vii. 129—145.

Commune id vitium est: hic vivimus ambitiosa
Paupertate omnes. Quid te moror? Omnia Romae
Cum pretio. Quid das, ut Cossum aliquando salutes?
Ut te respiciat clauso Veiento labello?   185
Ille metit barbam, crinem hic deponit amati;
Plena domus libis venalibus. Accipe et istud
Fermentum tibi habe: praestare tributa clientes
Cogimur et cultis augere peculia servis.

Quis timet aut timuit gelida Praeneste ruinam   190
Aut positis nemorosa inter juga Volsiniis, aut
Simplicibus Gabiis, aut proni Tiburis arce?
Nos urbem colimus tenui tibicine fultam
Magna parte sui. Nam sic labentibus obstat
Villicus et, veteris rimae quum texit hiatum,   195
Securos pendente jubet dormire ruina.
Vivendum est illic, ubi nulla incendia, nulli
Nocte metus. Jam poscit aquam, jam frivola transfert
Ucalegon; tabulata tibi jam tertia fumant;

184 **aliquando**] After he has been repeatedly denied to you.

185 **Veiento**] iv. 113. His praenomen and nomen were *Aulus Fabricius*. He was banished by Nero, favoured, but scarcely powerful, under Nerva: so that this line would be written under Domitian.

187 **venalibus**] Probably everybody who helped himself had to give something to the *amatus:* they may have had to pay for getting in at all. Cf. sup. 184.

188 **Fermentum**] The cakes were unleavened.

190—192] Note the attractions, the climate of Praeneste, the wooded hills of Volsinii, the *sans façon* of Gabii, the picturesque situation of Tibur *proni;* cf. Tibur supinum. Hor. *Od.* iii, iv. 27. In one the town is conceived as running down the slope, in the other as running up it: only there is a sort of personification in

each. Horace hints at a beauty throwing herself on her back, in Juvenal she is flung forward on her face.

194—196] "That's the way your bailiff keeps the occupants from falling" (he puts up a 'tibicen'), "plasters up the crack, and tells them to sleep at ease, though ruin is hanging over them." Festus guesses that the *tibicen* was so called from supporting the house, as the piper supported the singers; it seems to have been a buttress if we suppose it bevelled away to a point at top, this might suggest the double pipes as viewed in front, or if it was simply sloped away to the wall this would suggest the single pipe when viewed in profile.—*Quum texit;* so P. Most MSS. *contexit,* which would be a harsh asyndeton.

199] Cf. "Jam proximus ardet Ucalegon" (*Aen.* ii. 311). If the

Tu nescis: nam si gradibus trepidatur ab imis,   200
Ultimus ardebit, quem tegula sola tuetur
A pluvia, molles ubi reddunt ova columbae.
Lectus erat Codro Procula minor, urceoli sex,
Ornamentum abaci; nec non et parvulus infra
Cantharus, et recubans sub eodem marmore Chiron;   205
Jamque vetus Graecos servabat cista libellos.
Et divina Opici rodebant carmina mures.
Nil habuit Codrus: quis enim negat? et tamen illud
Perdidit infelix totum nihil: ultimus autem
Aerumnae cumulus, quod nudum et frusta rogantem   210
Nemo cibo, nemo hospitio tectoque juvabit.
Si magna Asturici cecidit domus, horrida mater,
Pullati proceres, differt vadimonia praetor;
Tunc gemimus casus urbis, tunc odimus ignem.
Ardet adhuc, et jam accurrit qui marmora donet,   215
Conferat impensas: hic nuda et candida signa,
Hic aliquid praeclarum Euphranoris et Polycleti,

house is only three stories, trans.,
"The smoke has got to you in the
third story;" if more, "For your
information, the smoke has got past
him into the third story;" any way,
'tu' lives in the garret.
   203 **Procula minor**] "Too small
for Procula:" "Minor igne rogi"
(xv. 140); "Privatis majora focis"
(iv. 66). *Procula* was the proverbial
small woman, as *Codrus* is the proverbial poor man. It is better not
to marry them: it is far-fetched to
make Juvenal say his bed was too
small to leave room for the smallest
wife beside him.
   205 **Chiron**] A dog's name. Probably the representative of the dog
in mosaic, which adorns the thresh-
old of more prosperous houses. In
the same way the poor pleader,
when successful, puts up the palm-
branches on the landing, which a
more fortunate brother would put

up at the front door. Cf. inf., vii.
117, 118:

   "Rumpe miser tensum jecur,
      ut tibi lasso
   Figantur virides, *scalarum gloria*,
      palmae."

   206] "He had a box too, to
hold his books; but it was too
old to keep the mice of Italy from
gnawing the inspired poems of
Greece."
   209 **Perdidit**] Perf. not aor. as is
shewn by *juvabit*.
   212 **Asturici**] At Rome a great
mansion always kept the name of
its founder: the present owner is
Persicus. Inf. 221, note.
   215 **marmora**] For panels and
bosses, perhaps for pavement.
   216 **nuda et candida signa**]
Nude figures in white marble.
Euphranor and Polycletus worked
in bronze.

Phaecasianorum vetera ornamenta deorum,
Hic libros dabit et forulos mediamque Minervam,
Hic modium argenti: meliora et plura reponit   220
Persicus, orborum lautissimus et merito jam
Suspectus, tanquam ipse suas incenderit aedes.
Si potes avelli Circensibus, optima Sorae
Aut Fabrateriae domus aut Frusinone paratur,
Quanti nunc tenebras unum conducis in annum.   225
Hortulus hic puteusque brevis nec reste movendus
In tenues plantas facili diffunditur haustu.
Vive bidentis amans et culti villicus horti,
Unde epulum possis centum dare Pythagoreis.
Est aliquid, quocumque loco, quocumque recessu,   230
Unius sese dominum fecisse lacertae.
   Plurimus hic aeger moritur vigilando: sed ipsum

218] 'Phaecasianorum' is the reading of most MSS. 'Haec Asianorum,' which looks like a correction of the text, is found in P. and the Scholiast. If it is right, the women join the collection as well as the mourning; but their solitary representative looks forlorn among so many men. Hence Jahn reads *hic*, which would be quite unobjectionable, if Juvenal had written it; and others try to make *haec* neuter. It is very difficult to guess what gods could be characterized by the white woollen shoes of Athenian or Alexandrine priests; but "potior est lectio difficillima."

219] As other friends, 216—218, have furnished the gymnasium, this one furnishes the library.

220 **modium argenti**] About two gallons of small change worth eight hundred or a thousand pounds. Cf. Hor. *S.* I. i. 96, dives Ut metiretur nummos. After *Conferat impensas* (sup. 216), symmetry requires a contribution in money in addition to those in kind.

221 **orborum lautissimus**] So

that he lives in better style than any other *orbus*.

222 **Suspectus, tanquam &c.**] This use of *tanquam*, which is frequent in the Silver Age, does not imply the injustice of the suspicion, accusation, &c., as a clause with *tanquam* may either state the reason of an unjust charge or the nature of a just.

224 **paratur**] "Is bought." Contrast i. 105, 106:
   " Quinque tabernae
   Quadringenta parant."

225 **tenebras**] A dark smoky garret.

226—229] "Every thing is on a diminutive scale,—the garden, the young plants, that want all the water they get from the shallow well, that needs no rope to the bucket; still, if you stick to it you can get a dinner out of it that would be an event to a hundred Pythagoreans." The water is drawn with a swipe instead of a windlass; as it is turned out of the bucket it runs down along the little trenches between the little beds.

232—234] "Invalids die for

Languorem peperit cibus imperfectus et haerens
Ardenti stomacho. Nam quae meritoria somnum
Admittunt? Magnis opibus dormitur in Urbe: 235
Inde caput morbi. Redarum transitus arcto
Vicorum in flexu et stantis convicia mandrae
Eripient somnum Druso vitulisque marinis.
Si vocat officium, turba cedente vehetur
Dives et ingenti curret super ora Liburno,   240
Atque obiter leget aut scribet vel dormiet intus.
Namque facit somnum clausa lectica fenestra.
Ante tamen veniet: nobis properantibus obstat
Unda prior, magno populus premit agmine lumbos
Qui sequitur; ferit hic cubito, ferit assere duro   245
Alter: at hic tignum capiti incutit, ille metretam.
Pinguia crura luto, planta mox undique magna
Calcor, et in digito clavus mihi militis haeret.
   Nonne vides quanto celebretur sportula fumo?
Centum convivae; sequitur sua quemque culina.   250
Corbulo vix ferret tot vasa ingentia, tot res

want of sleep; and they lose their health because want of sleep disturbs their digestion."—*Sed* introduces the additional fact as a correction of the inadequacy of the previous statement. Cf. iv. 27 n. *Meritoria*, "lodgings." *Coenacula* seem to have been let by a more permanent tenure.

236] **Redarum transitus arcto &c.**] The streets are narrow and crooked, and so carriages make more noise in passing; while they pass, a drove of cattle is brought to a stand-still, and the drover abuses the drivers.

238] Tib. Claudius Drusus succeeded Caligula. He had a passion for hearing causes, and used to go to sleep on the bench; his intimates ventured to slip flesh gloves and combs over his hands that they might see his amazement when he came to wake and rub his eyes. *Vitulis marinis*, seals had a high reputation as sound sleepers, probably because they were generally seen when asleep on the shore.

242] "A litter with the windows shut does bring on sleep."

243 **nobis ... obstat**] Contrast (sup. 239) *turba cedente*.

245 **assere**] "A litter pole" (vii. 132): "Perque forum juvenes longo premit assere Medos."

246 **tignum**] The builder carries a piece of timber projecting upwards and forwards from his shoulder. *Metretam*, a large pot, this too is carried on the shoulder, and projects enough to strike another man's head.

250 **culina**] An apparatus to keep the cooked provisions hot, like that in which dinners are sent from restaurants abroad.

Impositas capiti, quot recto vertice portat
Servulus infelix et cursu ventilat ignem.
Scinduntur tunicae sartae modo : longa coruscat
Sarraco veniente abies, atque altera pinum   255
Plaustra vehunt; nutant alte populoque minantur:
Nam si procubuit qui saxa Ligustica portat
Axis, et eversum fudit super agmina montem,
Quid superest de corporibus? quis membra, quis ossa
Invenit? Obtritum vulgi perit omne cadaver   260
More animae. Domus interea secura patellas
Jam lavat et bucca foculum excitat, et sonat unctis
Striglibus, et pleno componit lintea gutto.
Haec inter pueros varie properantur : at ille
Jam sedet in ripa tetrumque novicius horret   265
Porthmea, nec sperat coenosi gurgitis alnum,
Infelix, nec habet quem porrigat ore trientem.
    Respice nunc alia ac diversa pericula noctis :
Quod spatium tectis sublimibus, unde cerebrum
Testa ferit, quoties rimosa et curta fenestris   270
Vasa cadant; quanto percussum pondere signent
Et laedant silicem. Possis ignavus haberi
Et subiti casus improvidus, ad coenam si
Intestatus eas. Adeo tot fata, quot illa
Nocte patent vigiles, te praetereunte, fenestrae.   275

254 **tunicae**] Must be the servants'; the masters wear the *toga*, and do not join so actively in the scramble.

257 **Nam**] As the people have no remedy they are alarmed at the waggons which can afford to be unsafe.

Ligustica] From Luna, near the modern Carrara.

258] Note the exaggeration; there are armies of people moving in a narrow street; the pile of marble blocks is a mountain.

262 **Jam**] Though they do not expect him for an hour or two.

265 **Jam**] So long before he could have sat down in his own house.

270 **rimosa et curta**] Cracked or chipped.

The praetor gave full damages for such accidents, except in case of the death of a freeman, where the amount was fifty 'aurei.'

272] "You may be fairly thought negligent, &c., so far have we got in providing death at every open window."

Ergo optes votumque feras miserabile tecum,
Ut sint contentae patulas defundere pelves.
   Ebrius ac petulans, qui nullum forte cecidit,
Dat poenas, noctem patitur lugentis amicum
Pelidae, cubat in faciem, mox deinde supinus.   280
Ergo non aliter poterit dormire? Quibusdam
Somnum rixa facit: sed, quamvis improbus annis
Atque mero fervens, cavet hunc, quem coccina laena
Vitari jubet et comitum longissimus ordo,
Multum praeterea flammarum et ahenea lampas: 285
Me, quem Luna solet deducere vel breve lumen
Candelae, cujus dispenso et tempero filum,
Contemnit. Miserae cognosce prooemia rixae,
Si rixa est, ubi tu pulsas, ego vapulo tantum.
Stat contra starique jubet; parere necesse est.   290
Nam quid agas, quum te furiosus cogat et idem
Fortior? Unde venis? exclamat: cujus aceto,
Cujus conche tumes? quis tecum sectile porrum
Sutor et elixi vervecis labra comedit?
Nil mihi respondes? Aut dic, aut accipe calcem.   295

---

276 **miserabile**] Pitiful.
   277 **defundere**] 'To empty' their bedroom ware instead of throwing it out of window bodily.
   278 **qui nullum forte cecidit**] "Ὅς οὐδένα πεπληγὼς τυγχάνει, 'Who, as it happens, has beaten nobody,' we might almost translate 'Who has given nobody a thrashing *that evening.*'
   283 **coccina laena**] These gay dresses do not appear in Horace; they are notorious in Persius: "Hic aliquis cui circum humeros hyacinthina laena est" (Pers. i. 32).
   284—287] The rich man has many humble friends who wait upon him home (probably he has taken some out to dinner with him as umbrae Hor. *Ep.* I. v. 28), he has several

slaves, one with an ornamental bronze lamp, the rest with blazing torches. The speaker has no escort to light him home but the moon or the little torch he carries himself and trims to make it last. *Candela* made of rope dipped in wax or tar, always a cheap light, probably we are to suppose it was carried in the hand without a holder of any kind.
   293 **sectile porrum**] 'Chives' haye a strong smell, which the roisterer pretends to recognise in the man's breath; they probably differed from *capitatum*, as sprouts from cabbages. Cf. xiv. 133 n.
   294 **elixi**] So Bailie Nicol Jarvie says, (*Rob Roy* Chap. XXVI.) "A sheep's head muckle owerboiled is rank poison," cf. xiii. 85 n.

Ede, ubi consistâs, in qua te quaero proseucha.
Dicere si tentes aliquid tacitusve recedas,
Tantundem est; feriunt pariter; vadimonia deinde
Irati faciunt. Libertas pauperis haec est:
Pulsatus rogat et pugnis concisus adorat,   300
Ut liceat paucis cum dentibus inde reverti.

     Nec tamen haec tantum metuas: nam qui spoliet te
Non deerit, clausis domibus, postquam omnis ubique
Fixa catenatae siluit compago tabernae.
Interdum et ferro subitus grassator agit rem,   305
Armato quoties tutae custode tenentur
Et Pomtina palus et Gallinaria pinus.
Sic inde huc omnes tanquam ad vivaria currunt.
Qua fornace graves, qua non incude, catenae?
Maximus in vinclis ferri modus, ut timeas, ne   310
Vomer deficiat, ne marrae et sarcula desint.
Felices proavorum atavos, felicia dicas

---

296 **quaero**] According to Madvig (*Opusc.* ii. 40), in Latin, German, and Danish, the pres. ind. is used in questions addressed to oneself, as "*Stantes* plaudebant in re ficta : quid arbitramur in vera facturos fuisse?" (Cic. *Lael.* § 24), or others, as inf. iv. 130; Cic. *ad Att.* xii. 40: "Quid mihi auctor es? advolone an maneo?" when the answer is altogether independent of the speaker's opinion, being either obvious or dependent upon the person questioned. Our only equivalent for this idiom, and the conjunctivus deliberativus, is the periphrasis, "Am I to," &c. He began by treating the poor gentleman as a snob; who therefore is embarrassed, since he cannot answer without contradicting a man who regards a contradiction as an insult.

300] Note the climax: "At the first push he *begs*, when he is beaten black and blue he *supplicates*."

302—308] "You have to fear not only the amateur bully, but the professional thief. He'll be upon you as soon as the streets are still, with the houses shut and shops barred" (this last point is mentioned, because a thief would find these more interesting than the streets by day, or because his victim might take refuge there); "or perhaps a highwayman does the business quicker with the sword. Whenever the Pomptine marshes and the fir-woods above Cumae" (where to be sure Umbricius was going, but though they attacked travellers they hardly cared about the plunder of a small town whose inhabitants came there for economy) "are made safe, thereupon they leave them, and run to Rome, as if it was their preserve."

Secula, quae quondam sub regibus atque tribunis
Viderunt uno contentam carcere Romam.

His alias poteram et plures subnectere causas :   315
Sed jumenta vocant, et sol inclinat ; eundum est.
Nam mihi commota jam dudum mulio virga
Innuit. Ergo vale nostri memor, et quoties te
Roma tuo refici properantem reddet Aquino,
Me quoque ad Helvinam Cererem vestramque Dianam 320
Converte a Cumis. Satirarum ego, ni pudet illas,
Adjutor gelidos veniam caligatus in agros."

313 **tribunis**] Sc. *plebis.* Juvenal had probably a not quite unfounded notion that they were the only officers of the free state who had the legal and effective power to send a citizen to prison ; of course the kings had this power : Juvenal speaks as if they never delegated it : under the empire it was in the hands of the city prefect. The second prison of Rome was built under the decemvirate just outside the city.

315 **poteram**] "I am able, [but do not.]" If he had wished to say, "I was able, [but did not,]" either 'potui' or 'potueram' would be used. (Vide sup. 163.)

319 **refici**] Goes with 'properantem,' not with 'reddet.'

322] "I'll come up to your cool farm to reinforce your satires, if they're not ashamed of my hobnailed boots." If we suppose that the festivals of Ceres Helvina and Diana at Aquinum corresponded roughly to those of Ceres and Cybele at Rome at the beginning of April, we shall get an explanation of *gelidos* and *caligatus.* Juvenal's farm would be cool then to a person coming up from the bay of Naples, and the tracks about the fields would still be muddy. It may be added that Juvenal was likely to choose that time to be out of town, "Nostra bibat vernum contracta cuticula solem Effugiatque togam" xi. 203, 204. Though the primary sense of *caligatus* is that given above, the word helps to turn *adjutor* into the hint of a military metaphor.

SATIRA IV.

Ecce iterum Crispinus, et est mihi saepe'vocandus
Ad partes, monstrum nulla virtute redemtum
A vitiis; aegrae solaque libidine fortes
Deliciae, viduas tantum aspernatur adulter.
Quid refert igitur, quantis jumenta fatiget   5
Porticibus,. quanta nemorum vectetur in umbra,
Jugera quot vicina foro, quas emerit aedes?
Nemo malus felix, minime corruptor et idem
Incestus, cum quo nuper vittata jacebat
Sanguine adhuc vivo terram subitura sacerdos.   10
Sed nunc de fáctis levioribus : et tamen alter
Si fecisset idem,. caderet sub judice morum.

---

3 **aegrae deliciae**] So P. and Schol. ; *deliciae* is at once rake and beau. Cf. Mart. VIII. xlviii. 5, 6 :

"Non quicunque capit saturatas
    murice vestes,
Nec nisi deliciis convenit iste
    color."

Most MSS. have 'aeger, fortis' and 'delicias' and even 'viduae,' all palpable and stupid corrections.

4 **viduas**] "Viduam non solum eam quae aliquando nupta fuisset, sed eam quoque mulierem quae virum non· habuisset' appellari ait Labeo" (*Dig.* xvi. 242).

5 **fatiget**] serves to emphasize *quantis*. Of course the arcades for his drives, and the shady walks where he takes an airing in his litter, are all within the limits of his city palace. ·

7] The construction is, "Quot

jugera vicina foro quas aedes (vicinis foro) emerit."

9 **Incestus**] *Incestum* could only be committed with a person with whom it was morally as well as legally impossible to contract a virtuous marriage. According to Roman notions there was the same moral impossibility of a valid marriage between any man and a Vestal who had not served out her thirty years, as between a brother and sister.

10] Domitian had revived this punishment in an arbitrary way, so Juvenal says, "to what a risk Crispinus exposed his Vestal!" in a serious poet we should have to infer her death. The Scholiast reads 'vitiata ;' if so, a Vestal under sentence seemed piquant to Crispinus.

12 **fecisset**] *Videtur fecisse* answered to our verdict, *feci* to our

Nam quod turpe bonis Titio Seioque, decebat
Crispinum. Quid agas, quum dira et foedior omni
Crimine persona est? Mullum sex millibus emit,   15
Aequantem sane paribus sestertia libris,
Ut perhibent qui de magnis majora loquuntur.
Consilium laudo artificis, si munere tanto
Praecipuam in tabulis ceram senis abstulit orbi.
Est ratio ulterior, magnae si misit amicae,   20
Quae vehitur clauso latis specularibus antro.
Nil tale exspectes: emit sibi. Multa videmus,
Quae miser et frugi non fecit Apicius. Hoc tu,
Succinctus patria quondam, Crispine, papyro!
Hoc pretium squamae! Potuit fortasse minoris   25
Piscator, quam piscis, emi. Provincia tanti
Vendit agros: sed majores Appulia vendit.
Quales tunc epulas ipsum glutisse putemus
Induperatorem, quum tot sestertia, partem
Exiguam et modicae sumtam de margine coenae,   30

plea, of "guilty."—*Sub judice morum*,
Domitian assumed the censorship at
the commencement of his reign; but
according to Juvenal he never exercised his authority against his favourites.

13 **Titio Seioque**] John Doe and
Richard Roe, Hunz und Kunz.

16, 17] "To be sure, they say it
weighed a pound for every sester-
tium; but that's an exaggeration."

19 **Praecipuam**] "Primam in
qua haeredes primi scribuntur"
(Schol.). "Prima cera secundo
versu haeredis continet nomen"
(Acron. *ad Hor. S.* ii. v. 53). *Abs-*
tulit must mean that there is nothing left for others; that the old
man bequeathed everything to him;
if so, *ulterior* cannot mean a still
stronger reason, though the sense is
found in Quint. (*Dec.* ix. 15).

21 **latis specularibus**] Measure
the size, and emphasize *antro;* they

were not quite equal to windows,
being translucent, not transparent.
Also *clauso antro* denotes her stately
seclusion, *latis specularibus* its freedom from austerity.

24 **Succinctus**] 'Alte cinctus,' as
a slave; if so, he wore a reed apron
instead of dealing in papyrus, as the
Scholiast infers.

26, 27] "In the provinces you
can get an estate at the price, to be
sure; aye, and a still larger in Apulia." (Cf. v. 147.) "A mushroom,
aye, a mushroom like that Claudius
ate." Cf. iii. 232 n. The land in
Apulia was depreciated by the hot
wind which swept its vast plains.

29 **Induperatorem**] With a sneer
at Domitian's antiquarianism; so inf.
46 *Pontifici summo*, with a sneer at
his ostentation of piety.

30, 31] Crispinus thought it a
modest dinner, though he gave
nearly 50*l*. for a small side-dish.

Purpureus magni ructarit scurra Palati,
Jam princeps equitum, magna qui voce solebat
Vendere municipes fracta de merce siluros!
Incipe, Calliope, licet et considere: non est
Cantandum, res vera agitur: narrate, puellae   35
Pierides: prosit mihi vos dixisse puellas!
    Quum jam semianimum laceraret Flavius orbem
Ultimus, et calvo serviret Roma Neroni,
Incidit Adriaci spatium admirabile rhombi
Ante domum Veneris, quam Dorica sustinet Ancon,   40
Implevitque sinus: neque enim minor haeserat illis,
Quos operit glacies Maeotica, ruptaque tandem
Solibus effundit torrentis ad ostia Ponti,

---

31 **Purpureus scurra**] This is the most definite indication which Juvenal gives anywhere of the foundation on which the influence of the person he calls Crispinus rested. Domitian was gloomy: it seems a person whom he allowed to amuse him could establish an ascendancy over him.

32, 33] "He used to buy the shads of his country out of a damaged cargo, and hawk them at the top of his voice."

32 **princeps equitum**] This almost makes one suspect that the lolling like Mæcenas (I. 66) was originally intended for Crispinus, though Juvenal eventually decided to father it upon an anonymous *signator*. Flatterers of Domitian would naturally compliment him on the resemblance of his easy-going useful favourite to the Minister of Augustus: the title may imply that he was *praefectus praetorio*.

34 **Calliope**] Muse of epics—that is, of hexameters.

licet et considere] "You need not even stand up to sing."

36 **puellas**] Opposed to both *anus* and *mulieres*.

37, 38] The Scholiast says that Juvenal wrote these lines to revenge his banishment. This nickname of Domitian seems to have passed into a proverb, at least Ausonius quotes it as such (*Monost.* 6; *XII. Imp.* 11, 12).

37 **jam**] probably goes with *semianimum*, not with *ultimus*, though that is possible. Nero had knocked half the life out of the world, and Domitian was mangling the remainder. It is worth noticing that on neither view does the writer make any allowance for Vespasian or Titus, though the one retained respect and the other roused enthusiasm.

40 **Dorica**] Founded by Syracusan refugees in the reign of Dionysius.

41, 42] The turbots of the Black Sea were supposed to get fat and big by hybernating.

43 **torrentis**] (so the Scholiast: the MSS. have *torpentis*) probably of the strong current of the Bosporus, so Pliny (*H. N.* ix. 20 [15] speaks of the fish caught in Euripo Threicii Bospori. There are other passages which speak of the fish *streaming* through the straits.

Desidia tardos et longo frigore pingues.
Destinat hoc monstrum cymbae linique magister   45
Pontifici summo. Quis enim proponere talem
Aût emere auderet, quum plena et litora multo
Delatore forent? Dispersi protinus algae
Inquisitores agerent cum remige nudo,
Non dubitaturi fugitivum dicere piscem,   50
Depastumque diu vivaria Caesaris ; inde
Elapsum veterem ad dominum debere reverti,
Si quid Palfurio, si credimus Armillato,
Quicquid conspicuum pulchrumque est aequore toto,
Res fisci est, ubicumque natat. Donabitur ergo,   55
Ne pereat. Jam letifero cedente pruinis
Autumno, jam quartanam sperantibus aegris,
Stridebat deformis hiems praedamque recentem
Servabat : tamen hic properat, velut urgeat Auster :

45 **monstrum**] As the fish is a prodigy, the Supreme Pontiff is the proper person to settle what ought to be done about it. Cf. sup. 29 n.

47 **et litora**] Where there was so little of value.

48 **algae inquisitores**] "Vexatos frutices pulsatas imputat algas" (Rutil. *It.* i. 366. 6), which tempts one to conjecture *dispersae;* at the same time it is to be observed that the *delator* in this line is a person who gives the treasury information of waifs and strays, and claims to casual profits; rather than an informer, who gives notice of crimes. It was in this sense that Domitian especially encouraged the *delatores;* for instance, if any one gave information that he had heard a man say when alive that Caesar would be his heir, Domitian annulled the will, ousted the heir, and took the property.

50—52] "Spatia maris sibi vindicant jure mancipii, pisciumque jura sicut vernaculorum conditione sibi servitii subjecta commemorant" (Am-

bros. *Hexaem.* v. 10 § 27). Domitian encroached on the *vivaria* of his subjects, as we learn from Pliny's encomium on Trajan's moderation (*Pan.* 50 § 1).

53] "Palfurius Sura, consularis filius, sub Nerone luctatus est, post inde a Vespasiano senatu motus transivit ad Stoicam sectam, in qua quum praevaleret et eloquentia et artis poeticae gloria, abusus familiaritate Domitiani, acerbissime partes delationis exercuit; quo interfecto, senatu accusante, damnatus est, quum fuissent inter delatores potentes apud Domitianum hi, Armillatus Demosthenes et Latinus archimimus, sicut Marius Maximus scribit" (Schol.); here, however, they appear as jurists.

57] They hope their fevers will subside into quartans.
"Saeva nocens febris saltem quartana fuisses." (Mart. x. lxxvii. 3.)

58, 59.] The winter made it hard to travel, and kept the fish fresh, and yet the man hurries.

Utque lacus suberant, ubi, quanquam diruta, servat   60
Ignem Trojánum et Vestam colit Alba minorem,
Obstitit intranti miratrix turba parumper.
Ut cessit, facili patuerunt cardine valvae;
Exclusi spectant admissa opsonia Patres.
Itur ad Atriden. Tum Picens, "Accipe," dixit,   65
"Privatis majora focis : genialis agatur
Iste dies : propera stomachum laxare saginae,
Et tua servatum consume in secula rhombum.
Ipse capi voluit." Quid apertius? et tamen illi
Surgebant cristae. Nihil est, quod credere de se   70
Non possit, quum laudatur Dis aequa potestas.
Sed deerat pisci patinae mensura. Vocantur
Ergo in consilium proceres, quos' oderat ille;
In quorum facie miserae magnaeque sedebat
Pallor amicitiae. Primus, clamante Liburno,   75
"Currite, jam sedit !" rapta properabat abolla
Pegasus, attonitae positus modo villicus urbi.

60, 61] The Vestals of Alba are mentioned in Orelli's inscriptions, 1393, 2240, and in the letters of Symmachus, a contemporary of St Ambrose. It is not improbable that Rome took the sacred fire from Alba, which, of course, would explain the reason why the Romans left the temples when they destroyed the town; Livy (i. 29) attributes this forbearance to prodigies.

66 majora] "Too great for" (iii. 203 n.).

67 Iste] "This day by *you*."— *Saginae,* dat.

68 servatum] As the fish is so large, he is presumably very old.

69, 70] "What could be more barefaced? and yet he was elated." It would be tempting to make the fisherman's speech go down to *apertius,* so that the sense would be, "He wished to be caught; what can be clearer?" But it was not clear to the fish; he set up his spines to keep their hands off, and would have floundered away if he could. This would suit *Erectas in terga sudes* (inf. 128), but what follows here seems to tell the other way; and *ille* ought to refer to Domitian, like *ille* (inf. 73).

73 proceres] Distinguished by Mayor from 'patres' (v. 64), as favourites from senators; if they *are* senators, they are called in for that reason only, having been compelled to dance attendance before.

75 amicitiae] Domitian made a point of being intimate with those he feared or hated ; it was the best way of keeping them harmless till he was ready to despatch them.

77—81] "Pegasus hurries in first, who had just been made bailiff to astonish a city of slaves"—(*attonitae,* perhaps because his father was a mere trierarch, who named his

Anne aliud tunc praefecti? quorum optimus atque
Interpres legum sanctissimus; omnia quanquam
Temporibus diris tractanda putabat inermi   80
Justitia. Venit et Crispi jucunda senectus,
Cujus erant mores, qualis facundia, mite
Ingenium. Maria ac terras populosque regenti
Quis comes utilior, si clade et peste sub illa
Saevitiam damnare et honestum afferre liceret   85
Consilium? Sed quid violentius aure tyranni,
Cum quo de pluviis aut aestibus aut nimboso
Vere loquuturi fatum pendebat amici?
Ille igitur nunquam direxit brachia contra
Torrentem, nec civis erat, qui libera posset   90
Verba animi proferre et vitam impendere vero.
Sic multas hiemes atque octogesima vidit
Solstitia, his armis illa quoque tutus in aula.
Proximus ejusdem properabat Acilius aevi
Cum juvene indigno, quem mors tam saeva maneret   95
Et domini gladiis tam festinata: sed olim
Prodigio par est cum nobilitate senectus:

son after his figure-head). " Prefects
were mere head slaves then" (possibly Juvenal means also that the
principal business of the city prefect
was to look after the revenues of
Domitian, who chose to call himself
owner (*dominus*) of the Roman Empire); "he was the best of them,
and a most conscientious lawyer"
(and author of the *S. C. Pegasi-
anum*), "though he thought he did
his duty in practising justice himself, without doing battle to with-
stand Domitian and chastise his
favourites."

81 **Crispi**] Tacitus places Vibius
Crispus "inter claros magis quam
inter bonos" (*Hist.* ii. 10), and represents him as a temptation to the
old (iv. 42). Quintilian is content
to praise his regular and harmonious

eloquence. Probus and the Scholiast
also give him a good character. Jahn
thinks they got their information
from Suetonius' lost work, *De Viris
Illustribus*; they confuse him with
Crispus Passienus.

85 **Saevitiam damnare**] The
proper use of *mite ingenium*.

86—88] "You had to talk of
the weather, and felt your life was
at stake all the time."

90] "He was not a citizen to be
capable of such a sacrifice."

95 **tam saeva, &c.**] This seems
to point to a somewhat different
story of his death to that generally
received. According to the latter,
he was condemned to the arena,
came off victorious, was exiled, and
put to death in banishment.

Unde fit, ut malim fraterculus esse Gigantis.
Profuit ergo nihil misero, quod cominus ursos
Figebat Numidas, Albana nudus arena   100
Venator. Quis enim jam non intelligat artes
Patricias? Quis priscum illud miratur acumen,
Brute, tuum? Facile est barbato imponere regi.
Nec melior vultu, quamvis ignobilis, ibat
Rubrius, offensae veteris reus atque tacendae,   105
Et tamen improbior satiram scribente cinaedo.
Montani quoque venter adest, abdomine tardus,
Et matutino sudans Crispinus amomo,
Quantum vix redolent duo funera; saevior illo
Pompeius tenui jugulos aperire susurro,   110
Et qui vulturibus servabat viscera Dacis
Fuscus, marmorea meditatus proelia villa,
Et cum mortifero prudens Veiento Catullo,
Qui nunquam visae flagrabat amore puellae,
Grande et conspicuum nostro quoque tempore monstrum, 115

98] And so I'd rather be a mere *terrae filius*, without the strength of a giant.

99, 100] On the contrary, it seems to have provoked Domitian, who hoped, by this taste of his, to have got rid of him. *Albana* shews that he only took part in *quasi* private performances; in viii. 185—210, Juvenal describes the nobility as becoming professional performers.

103 **barbato**] here, as at xvi. 31, connotes manliness and something like honesty: cruel as Tarquin was, he was too much of a man to be as cunning as the effeminate tyrants of Imperial Rome.

104 **quamvis ignobilis**] "However low-born," nearly equals "although low-born."

105 **Rubrius**] "Aliquando Juliam (Domitian's niece and mistress) in pueritia corruperat" (Schol.); if so, *tacendae* means which the of-

fended party had to pass in silence.

107 **Montani**] Generally, though conjecturally, identified with the accuser of the delator Regulus.

108] He scents himself in the morning (instead of waiting for dinner-time); he has come in a hurry, and is "in a perfumed perspiration." Cf. i. 28 n.

109 **Quantum...funera**] The comparison refers to the natural as well as to the artificial smell of a funeral.

saevior illo] Juvenal hated Crispinus chiefly as a dissolute foreign upstart; he is not mentioned by Tacitus.

111, 112] "Fuscus, whose heart was on war, though he had no better school for fighting than his villa; he might as well have died of braving Domitian as of blundering in Dacia."

114 **nunquam visae**] Though he had no eyes to see her.

115 **monstrum**] The prodigy is,

Caecus adulator, dirusque a ponte satelles,
Dignus Aricinos qui mendicaret ad axes,
Blandaque devexae jactaret basia. redae.
Nemo magis rhombum stupuit : nam plurima dixit
In laevum conversus : at illi dextra jacebat   120
Bellua. Sic pugnas Cilicis laudabat et ictus,
Et pegma et pueros inde ad velaria raptos.
Non cedit Veiento, sed ut fanaticus, oestro
Percussus, Bellona, tuo, divinat et, "Ingens
Omen habes," inquit, "magni clarique triumphi :   125
Regem aliquem capies, aut de temone Britanno
Excidet Arviragus : peregrina est bellua : cernis
Erectas in terga sudes ?" Hoc defuit unum
Fabricio, patriam ut rhombi memoraret et annos.
"Quidnam igitur censes ? conciditur ?" "Absit ab illo   130
Dedecus hoc," Montanus ait. "Testa alta paretur,
Quae tenui muro spatiosum colligat orbem.
Debetur magnus patinae subitusque Prometheus.
Argillam atque rotam citius properate : sed ex hoc
Tempore jam, Caesar, figuli tua castra sequantur."   135

that with the qualification of a beggar, he is the terror of a court.

118] **devexae**] As it comes down the Clivus Virbius.

119 **Nemo**] His wonder is ironically made to account for the mistakes of his blindness.

122] The pegma was a machine composed of two jointed sticks, supporting a platform; if the joints were allowed to bend the platform fell, while if they were suddenly stiffened by dropping the weights attached to the lower ends of the sticks, the platform rose; it would be useful to lift a stage Ganymede, who could hardly be raised by the claws of a stage-eagle without hurting him.

123 **fanaticus**] There is an inscription (*Grut.* 343. 1), "Caecilio

Apollinari fanatico de aede Bellonae."

126 **temone**] "Curru falcato" (Schol.).—*Arviragus*, not mentioned elsewhere except in the legend of St Joseph of Arimathea. A plausible Celtic etymology has been found for the word, which might be formed from *Ardriagh*, High King; it is also supposed that Arthur is another form of the same title.

128 **Erectas**] For resistance which has proved vain; hence the omen.

•130 **censes**] The regular word for a vote in the Senate : so inf. 136, *vicit*. **conciditur**] "Do we cut it up?" (iii. 276 n.)

131 **alta**] That the fish and sauce may stew together.

135 **tua castra**] As Domitian ac-

Vicit digna viro sententia: noverat ille
Luxuriam imperii veterem noctesque Neronis
Jam medias aliamque famem, quum pulmo Falerno
Arderet. Nulli major fuit usus edendi
Tempestate mea. Circeis nata forent, an   140
Lucrinum ad saxum Rutupinove edita fundo
Ostrea, callebat primo deprendere morsu ;
Et semel aspecti litus dicebat echini.
Surgitur, et misso proceres exire jubentur
Concilio, quos Albanam dux magnus in arcem   145
Traxerat attonitos et festinare coactos,
Tanquam de Cattis aliquid torvisque Sicambris
Dicturus, tanquam diversis partibus orbis
Anxia praecipiti venisset epistola pinna.

    Atque utinam his potius nugis tota illa dedisset   150
Tempora saevitiae, claras quibus abstulit urbi
Illustresque animas impune et vindice nullo !

---

tually took the command in Dacia, the flattery is appropriate enough for irony.

138 aliam famem] "A new appetite," due here to wine; not emetics, whereby Vitellius prepared himself for the *comissatio* after *coena* (Suet. *Vit.* 13).

140—143] The oysters of Circeis had black flesh and shells, but were *dulciora* than those imported from *Rutupiae* (Richborough) in Britain. Note the climax in *morsu* and *aspecti*.

145, 146] One would fancy they had been fetched from Rome, instead of having been waiting outside, the inference from 73.—*Arcem* implies a tyrant (x. 30). Domitian had established a fortified-camp at the Alban Villa to which he removed a portion of the praetorians.

147] Juvenal had heard of the Catti, under Domitian, and read of the Sicambri in Horace.

149 pinna] Gronovius quotes πτεροφόροι, from Hesychius, as a military office, and translates it *tabellarii*. According to the Scholiast alarming news came in 'pinnatae litterae,' good in 'laureatae;' and so Serv. *ad Æn.* ix. 473. It is clear from the following lines of Statius, *Silv.* v. i. 92, 93:

"Omnia nam laetas pila attollentia frondes,
Nullaque famosa signatur lancea pinna,"

that such a custom really existed; and it would be natural and piquant to allude to it here. (They came in haste as if Domitian had allowed his lieutenants to confess a defeat.) Mayor, after Casaubon, translates 'on hurried wing,' 'with great despatch;' which is of course an adequate rendering of the words as they stand.

Sed periit, postquam cerdonibus esse timendus
Coeperat: hoc nocuit Lamiarum caede madenti.

153 **cerdonibus**] The meaning is clear from the etymology; but some have imagined an eponymous hero. Bezonian is sometimes printed as a proper name; but most likely it is derived from 'bisogno,' as 'cerdo' from κέρδος.

154] A member of this highly respectable family had to give up his wife to Domitian, under Vespasian, and made some mild jokes on the subject, for which Domitian put him to death long after. His family is selected as the type of nobility, owing to Horace's quizzical ode (iii. 17).

SATIRA V.

Sɪ te propositi nondum pudet atque eadem est mens,
Ut bona summa putes aliena vivere quadra;
Si potes illa pati, quae nec Sarmentus iniquas
Caesaris ·ad mensas, nec vilis Gabba tulisset,
Quamvis jurato metuam tibi credere testi.   5
Ventre nihil novi frugalius. ᴧHoc tamen ipsum
Defecisse puta, quod inani sufficit alvo:
Nulla crepido vacat? nusquam pons et tegetis pars
Dimidia brevior? tantine injuria coenae?

---

2 **aliena vivere quadra**] "Et mihi dividuo findetur munere quadra" (Hor. *Ep.* I. xvii. 49). The sense of table sometimes assigned to *quadra* is an ancient inference from this passage and one in Vergil (*Æn.* vii. 114):
"Et violare manu malisque audacibus orbem,
Fatalis crusti, patulis neque parcere quadris."
3 **Sarmentus**] "seu P. Blessus, Junium, hominem nigrum et macrum et pandum, fibulam ferream dixit." Weichert and Orelli distinguish this man, the antagonist of Cicirrus, in Horace (*Sat.* I. v. 52), from a young favourite of Augustus, at the time of the battle of Actium. The Scholiast knew of a Sarmentus, once dependent on Marcus Favonius, whose wit and good looks made his fortune, whereupon he insulted the public by appearing in the theatre as a Roman knight. The spectators called out:

"Aliud scriptum habet Sarmentus, aliud populus voluerat
Digna dignis, sic Sarmentus habeat crassas compedes.
Rustici, ne nihil agatis, aliquis Sarmentum alliget."
He was brought to trial for usurping the dignity, but, being powerfully protected, found it enough to prove that Maecenas, who disposed of Favonius's estate, had allowed this liberty. He got through his property, but retained his wit, which he displayed as an auctioneer.
4 **Gabba**] A corruption of Galba, found in P., the Weimar MS., and the Scholiast; Quintilian mentions some jokes of Aulus Galba. The Scholiast calls this man Apicius, and places him under Tiberius.
5 **Quamvis jurato**] "Sworn with any oaths."
7 **alvo**] Cf. inf. 98 n.
8 **tegetis**] A beggar's mat, on which he sat, in which he slept.

Tam jejuna fames, quum possit honestius illic   10
Et tremere et sordes farris mordere canini?
Primo fige loco, quod tu, discumbere jussus,
Mercedem solidam veterum capis officiorum.
Fructus amicitiae magnae cibus : imputat hunc rex,
Et, quamvis rarum, tamen imputat. Ergo duos post   15
Si libuit menses neglectum adhibere clientem,
Tertia ne vacuo cessaret culcita lecto,
" Una simus," ait. Votorum summa : quid ultra
Quaeris? Habet Trebius, propter quod rumpere somnum
Debeat et ligulas dimittere, sollicitus, ne   20
Tota salutatrix jam turba peregerit orbem,
Sideribus dubiis, aut illo tempore, quo se
Frigida circumagunt pigri sarraca Bootae.

10] "Is hunger so very starved as to consent to this, when it might find dog's meat, which is so much more creditable to munch there?" All sorts of different readings have been tried. One, *cum possis*, has got into most MSS. Of course this cannot be right as *possis* is a spondee. *Possis cum* is so ugly that it might easily have been altered, and may be defended by 'cocto num adest honor idem' (Hor. *Sat.* II. ii. 28).

14 cibus] Not money or interest, or even small presents in kind.

17] The last couch the host would fill up would be the lowest, on which he lay himself; consequently the discourtesy of his eating a good dinner himself and giving the parasite at his elbow a bad one would be all the more glaring. Three was the regular number to a couch. We find as many as seven in one bas-relief; but the regular device was to have more 'triclinia.' Plutarch speaks of οἰκίαι τριακοντάκλινοι, 'which would accommodate ten 'triclinia,' and ninety guests as not uncommon. There was a tendency to supersede them by semi-circular couches:—

"Stella, Nepos, Cani, Cerealis, Flacce, venitis ?
Septem sigma capit, sex sumus, adde Lupum." (Martial, x. xlviii. 5,6.)

20 ligulas dimittere] "Never mind his buckles." The original notion was ' tongues,'—γλώσσας τῶν ὑποδημάτων; and the grammarians kept up the pronunciation; but it dwindled in common speech to 'ligula:' and the Scholiast gives an etymology to match.

22, 23] "When the stars are still fading, or if all the rest are gone, while the Bear is in sight turning round the Pole." The above is the received interpretation; but the distinction seems hardly sufficient to warrant *aut*. It may mean 'while the stars are still fading [in summer], or when winter is just setting in.' This would give more point to *illo tempore* and *frigida*; besides, it is hard to believe that the stars had begun to fade in winter at the hour at which clients chose to think themselves bound to be in attendance. If it should seem that the distinction between the grievance of having to rise early in summer, and having to face the cold in

Qualis co⌐na tamen? Vinum, quod succida nolit
Lana pati: de conviva Corybanta videbis.   25
Jurgia proludunt: sed mox et pocula torques
Saucius et rubra deterges vulnera mappa.
Inter vos quoties libertorumque cohortem
Pugna Saguntina fervet commissa lagena:
Ipse capillato diffusum Consule potat,   30
Calcatamque tenet bellis socialibus uvam,
Cardiaco nunquam cyathum missurus amico;
Cras bibet Albanis aliquid de montibus aut de
Setinis, cujus patriam titulumque senectus
Delevit multa veteris fuligine testae: 35
Quale coronati Thrasea Helvidiusque bibebant
Brutorum et Cassi natalibus. Ipse capaces

winter, is imperfectly made out in the text; it is to be remembered that where a habit exists—such as certainly existed among the poets of Juvenal's day, who were unhappily very numerous—of thinking and speaking in a series of allusions to a system of conventional imagery, such faults of style are likely to occur. Bootes sets on the 27th of October: *pigri* will any way refer to his slow apparent motion.—*Sarraca*, cf. iii. 225. 118 n.

24 succida—Lana pati] "Wool with the sweat in it," used with oil, vinegar, or wine, for fomentations.

27 rubra—mappa] "Till the napkin is red."

29 Saguntina—lagena] *i. q.* Catalonian port. The Saguntine earthenware was famous; but the contrast here is of the wines: that of the cups is 38—48; and there we see the guests drink from glass not earthenware, perhaps the subject of the fight is that Trebius thinks the freedmen don't 'drink fair.' Cf. 47: *nasorum quattuor*, n.

30] According to this line the wine is older than the importation of barbers in 300 B.C.

31] Is most likely an unfortunate imitation of Hor. *Od.* III. xiv. 18, as the wine would be no better for being a hundred years older. According to Pliny (*H. N.* xiv. 16), the Opimian wine, *diffusum* B.C. 120, was absolutely undrinkable, though valued for mixing.

32 Cardiaco] Does not mean "with heart disease."

cyathum] "To a glass," but it only held a twelfth of a pint.

33 Cras] Even when he has no party.

35 fuligine] From the 'fumarium,' where wine was sometimes stored, that the smoke might ripen it faster.

37—40] "The patron grasps a large cup, cased in amber, or studded with beryl. You are not trusted with gold, or else are watched." Martial (*Xen.* 108), says :—

"Quae non sollicitus teneat ser-
    vetque minister
Sume Saguntino pocula ficta
    luto."

There was a story that T. Vinius, the minister of Galba, stole a cup from Claudius' table.

Heliadum crustas et inequales beryllo
Virro tenet phialas: tibi non committitur aurum;
Vel, si quando datur, custos affixus ibidem, 40
Qui numeret gemmas, unguesque observet acutos.
Da veniam: praeclara illic laudatur iaspis.
Nam Virro, ut multi, gemmas ad pocula transfert
A digitis, quas in vaginae fronte solebat
Ponere zelotypo juvenis praelatus Iarbae. 45
Tu Beneventani sutoris nomen habentem
Siccabis calicem nasorum quatuor ac jam
Quassatum, et rupto poscentem sulfura vitro.
Si stomachus domini fervet vinoque ciboque,
Frigidior Geticis petitur decocta pruinis: 50
   Non eadem vobis poni modo vina querebar:
Vos aliam potatis aquam. Tibi pocula cursor
Gaetulus dabit, aut nigri manus ossea Mauri,
Et cui per mediam nolis occurrere noctem,
Clivosae veheris dum per monumenta Latinae. 55

42—45] Gems, with a mythical pedigree, eked out from Virgil (*Aen.* iv. 260), are transferred from the scabbard to the fingers, and at last to a goblet.

45 **juvenis**] As an English satirist might say, 'the swain;' he does not mean that Æneas was young, but that he was Dido's 'young man.'

47] "A cup, with four lips or spouts, modelled on the long nose of Vatinius, a favourite of Nero, the cracked glass of which calls out for sulphur." Cf. Martial, I. xlii. 3, 4 sqq.:
   "Transtiberinus ambulator
   Qui pallentia sulfurata fractis
   Permutat vitreis."
Instead of simply cementing broken glass, they made a new ware, with a pale yellow surface, and changed this as required for the raw material.

nasorum quatuor] This is an aggravation: the cup has four spouts that one guest may drink from each.

Perhaps it is hardly going too far to infer from *siccabis* that Trebius has to be content with the heel-taps; in order that each guest should have a cup or goblet of his own, it was necessary that they all should sit up to table.

50 **decocta**] Water boiled and cooled in snow was convenient, even in winter, to hard drinkers, who suffered from internal heat.

51] Would be better away, and though it would mend matters a little to put it after 48, this is not what Juvenal intended. *Non eadem ...aquam* is a perfectly appropriate and spirited introduction to a new contract between host and guest; the fault is, that instead of following it up, the writer has foisted in two lines just before, also excellent in themselves, which complete the sense but destroy the connexion.

55 **Clivosae**] Where you have to go slowly.—*Monumenta*, which may

Flos Asiae ante ipsum, pretio majore paratus,
Quam fuit et Tulli census pugnacis et Anci,
Et, ne te teneam, Romanorum omnia regum
Frivola.   Quod quum ita sit, tu Gaetulum Ganymedem
Respice, quum sities.   Nescit tot millibus emtus   60
Pauperibus miscere puer : sed forma, sed aetas
Digna supercilio.   Quando ad te pervenit ille ?
Quando vocatus adest calidae gelidaeque minister ?
Quippe indignatur veteri parere clienti,
Quodque aliquid poscas et quod se stante recumbas.   65
Maxima quaeque domus servis est plena superbis.

    Ecce, alius quanto porrexit murmure panem
Vix fractum, solidae jam mucida frusta farinae,
Quae genuinum agitent, non admittentia morsum !
Sed tener et niveus mollique siligine factus   70

hide his accomplices. Or perhaps the meaning is, that you would take him for a bogy stealing from behind a tomb if you caught sight of him before you saw his master's equipage : this view gives more point to *cursor* and to *monumenta;* the only meaning for *clivosae* would be that the uneven ground makes the darkness more 'eerie,' which seems forced, though possible.

56 ante ipsum] The Romans lay on sofas, to judge from bas-reliefs, higher than the tables, and certainly too high for the attendants to be able to hand things over the shoulder, as is done at a modern dinner; besides, it would be almost impossible for a guest lying on his elbow to take things so handed from behind.

57] Cf. Hor. *Od.* IV. vii. 14, 15 : "Nos ubi decidimus, | Quo pius Æneas, quo dives Tullus et Ancus."

62 Digna supercilio] Lit. 'deserve the privilege of disdain.' Give him a right to be insolent.

63 calidae gelidaeque] To suit the warmth to the taste of the host and the more favoured guests.

65 quod—poscas, &c.] The verbs give *his* two reasons for *indignatur.* Juvenal's would have been in the indicative. Cf. xv. 60 n.   Mayor seems to think that *poscas* and *recumbas* are co-ordinate to *parere.* If so, there is a sort of zeugma, "He is too indignant to attend to you, and indignant that you are a guest, with a claim on attention," which is neither necessary nor impossible.

67 alius] "Another" of these proud slaves. Why not the black runner? because bread was handed round once for all and every guest is always calling for wine, all through the dinner?

68 solidae] Proves that *vix fractum* means "coarsely ground" not 'too hard to cut and hard enough to break.'

69 Quae genuinum agitent] "Stuff to work your cheek-teeth." It does not appear clear whether they are wise-teeth or grinders.

Servatur domino. Dextram cohibere memento.

Salva sit artoplae reverentia: finge tamen te

Improbulum, superest illic, qui ponere cogat.

"Vis' tu consuetis, audax cònviva, canistris

Impleri, panisque tui novisse colorem?"   75

"Scilicet hoc fuerat, propter quod saepe, relicta

Conjuge, per montem adversum gelidasque cucurri

Esquilias, fremeret saeva quum grandine vernus

Jupiter et multo stillaret paenula nimbo!"

Aspice, quam longo distendat pectore lancem,   80

Quae fertur domino, squilla, et quibus undique septa

Asparagis, qua despiciat convivia cauda,

Quum venit excelsi manibus sublata ministri.

Sed tibi dimidiò constrictus cammarus ovo

Ponitur exigua, feralis coena, patella.   85

Ipse Venafrano piscem perfundit: at hic, qui

---

72 **artoptae**] Here a baker, but a bread-pan in Greek and Plaut. (*Aul.* ii. 9. 4); the genuineness of which is disputed by Pliny (xviii. 28), on the ground that professional bakers were not then known at Rome. Juvenal is not likely to have known better than Pliny. Some one who did, to preserve the sense, introduced *artocopi*, which became almost universal.

74 **Vis tu**] "Won't you," assumes that you will; "Will you," does not. Sometimes this assumption is suppressed, to avoid a show of presumption (inf. 135). Here it heightens the insult: the slave cannot trust the visitor to behave himself.

77 **gelidasque**] Cf. xi. 50 n.

80—106] It is to be remembered in justice to Vino that Trebius did not want a claw of his lobster, or a slice of his fish, he wanted a whole lobster to himself, a whole mullet worth £50, and if he had been Vino's equal, he would have had

them; but to say nothing of the expense, there were not mullets enough in the market to make it possible to treat everybody alike at a large party of Romans.

84 **dimidio constrictus cammarus ovo**] "Pinched up between the pieces of a split egg."

86—91] "He is served with the best oil for his fish at discretion. You have greens reeking with lamp oil. What comes up the Tiber from Africa is good enough for you, though it makes everybody avoid Boccar, at Rome, and in fact makes serpents afraid of Africans." As P. omits 91, though it will construe, I doubt if Juvenal wrote it. *Caulis* as well as *ovo* answers to *asparagis: alveolis,* 'pitiful paunches;' *venter* has scarcely any of the contemptuous significance that 'belly' has in literary English. *Micipsarum.* He talks of the Micipsas, as we might talk of the Pharaohs, or as Mr Lowell makes Birdofredum Sawin talk of "the halls of Monte-

Pallidus affertur misero tibi caulis, olebit
Laternam : illud enim vestris datur alveolis, quod
Canna Micipsarum prora subvexit acuta ;
Propter quod Romae cum Bocchare nemo lavatur,   90
Quod tutos etiam facit a serpentibus Afros.
Mullus erit domini, quem misit Corsica, vel quem
Tauromenitanae rupes, quando omne peractum est
Et jam defecit nostrum mare, dum gula saevit,
Retibus assiduis penitus scrutante macello   95
Proxima, nec patimur Tyrrhenum crescere piscem.
Instruit ergo focum provincia : sumitur illinc
Quod captator emat Laenas, Aurelia vendat.
Virroni muraena datur, quae maxima venit
Gurgite de Siculo : nam, dum se continet Auster,   100
Dum sedet et siccat madidas in carcere pennas,
Contemnunt mediam temeraria lina Charybdim.
Vos anguilla manet longae cognata colubrae,
Aut glacie aspersus maculis Tiberinus et ipse
Vernula riparum, pinguis torrente cloaca,   105
Et solitus mediae cryptam penetrare Suburae.
    Ipsi pauca velim, facilem si praebeat aurem.
Nemo petit, modicis quae mittebantur amicis
A Seneca, quae Piso bonus, quae Cotta solebat

zumy " at the time of the Mexican campaign. Micipsa was the uncle of Jugurtha.

94 **dum**] Cf. iii. 10, note.

98] There you get something for a fortune-hunter to buy, and a rich old woman to sell. Tiberius once sent a fine mullet to market, which he had received as a present.

100, 102 **Auster**] Is real, Charybdis is fabulous. The foundation for the fable is, that when there is a strong South Wind the current at one point makes a dangerous eddy.

103 **longae**] To emphasize the contrast with the plump lamprey.

104 **et ipse vernula riparum**] A home-born slave like you.

108—113] As the nobility lost their independence, they had less need to attract devoted retainers by munificence.

108—113] *Seneca* the philosopher, who was to have taken the place of Nero if the conspiracy had succeeded. *Cotta* may be Aurelius, pensioned by Nero in the same year as Corvinus i. 108 n., who got through his fortune (Tac. *Ann.* xiii. 34) by luxury, which it seems was not unsocial.

Largiri: namque et titulis et fascibus olim 110
Major habebatur donandi gloria: solum
Poscimus, ut coenes civiliter. Hoc face et esto,
Esto, ut nunc multi, dives tibi, pauper amicis.

    Anseris ante ipsum magni jecur, anseribus par
Altilis et flavi dignus ferro Meleagri 115
Fumat aper:'post hunc tradentur tubera, si ver
Tunc erit et facient optata tonitrua coenas
Majores. "Tibi habe frumentum," Allidius inquit,
"O Libye: disjunge boves, dum tubera mittas."

    Structorem interea, ne qua indignatio desit, 120
Saltantem spectas et chironomunta volanti
Cultello, donec peragat dictata magistri
Omnia. Nec minimo sane discrimine refert,
Quo gestu lepores et quo gallina secetur.

    Duceris planta, velut ictus ab Hercule Cacus, 125
Et ponere foris, si quid tentaveris unquam
Hiscere, tanquam habeas tria nomina. Quando propinat
Virro tibi sumitque tuis contacta labellis
Pocula? quis vestrum temerarius usque adeo, quis
Perditus, ut dicat regi, "bibe?" Plurima sunt, quae 130
Non audent homines pertusa dicere laena.

---

117 **optata**] Though they will damage the harvest. According to Pliny *H. N.* xix. 13, mushrooms are best in spring after an autumn in which there have been heavy thunderstorms: it is clear from *facient* instead of *fecerint*, and from the speech of Allidius, that this is the point of *optata*, and that Juvenal had not heard or did not remember that the thunder ought to have been in autumn. Mushrooms are said to be particularly plentiful in fairy-rings, now generally attributed to electricity.

120 **Structorem**] The same ser- vant was disher-up and carver; in the latter capacity he was called *carptor, diribitor*.

123 **Nec, &c.**] "And, to be sure, it makes the utmost difference."

127 **tanquam habeas tria nomina**] "As if you were free" (which you are). *Tanquam haberes* would be, "as if you were free" (which you are not). We cannot mark the distinction in idiomatic English. See *Dict. Ant.*, art. Nomen.

127—130] When does Virro pass his cup to you, or hold out his hand for yours? Who dares pass the cup to him, 'motu proprio'?

131 **pertusa laena**] A cloak in holes; τρίβων is one threadbare.

Quadringenta tibi si quis Deus aut similis Dis
Et melior fatis donaret homuncio : quantus
Ex nihilo fieres, quantus Virronis amicus !
"Da Trebio ! pone ad Trebium ! Vis, frater, ab ipsis   135
Ilibus ?"   O nummi, vobis hunc praestat honorem,
Vos estis fratres.   Dominus tamen et domini rex
Si vis tu fieri, nullus tibi parvulus aula
Luserit Aeneas, nec filia dulcior illo :
Jucundum et carum sterilis facit uxor amicum.   140
Sed tua nunc Migale pariat licet, et pueros tres
In gremium patris fundat simul : ipse loquaci
Gaudebit nido ; viridem thoraca jubebit
Afferri, minimasque nuces assemque rogatum,
Ad mensam quoties parasitus venerit infans.   145
Vilibus ancipites fungi ponentur amicis,
Boletus domino ; sed quales Claudius edit
Ante illum uxoris, post quem nil amplius edit.
    Virro sibi et reliquis Virronibus illa jubebit
Poma dari, quorum solo pascaris odore :   150
Qualia perpetuus Phaeacum autumnus habebat,

---

132 Quadringenta] If the man had only a knight's fortune, the patron would look forward to a legacy and treat him civilly; if the man were without children, he would do a great deal to be his heir.

134 Ex nihilo] After being nothing.

135 ipsis] So P. and most MSS. Al. *istis*, "There, won't you have a cut of the loin?" which is less ungentlemanly than *ipsis;* but Virro, and, I fear, Juvenal, were capable of the vulgarity.

137 Dominus—fieri] If you wish to have dependants of your own, and count your old master among them.

138, 139] "Vergilium ridet," says the Scholiast. Did he mean that Vergil, being unmarried, could and did leave his patrons something considerable, and was well treated during his life in consequence? if so, was he wrong?

Cf. Verg. *Aen.* iv. 328.   *illo* = 'domino.'

141—145] As it is, he likes you to have children; it is a cheap way of patronizing you (cf. *minimas nuces, assem rogatum*), and multiplies his flatterers (cf. *parasitus infans, assem rogatum*).

143] **viridem thoraca**] Armilausiam prasinam ut simiae. Schol. Probably "a green spencer;" as Augustus always wore a woollen *thorax* in winter.

147 sed quales C. edit] "Ay, and like those Claudius ate " (iv. 272).

150 quorum—odore] "The smell is enough to feast you; and that is all the feast you are to get."

Credere quae possis surrepta sororibus Afris :
Tu scabie frueris mali, quod in aggere rodit,
Qui tegitur parma et galea, metuensque flagelli
Discit ab hirsuta jaculum torquere capella.   155
    Forsitan impensae Virronem parcere credas.
Hoc agit, ut doleas : nam quae comoedia, mimus
Quis melior plorante gula ? Ergo omnia fiunt,
Si nescis, ut per lacrimas effundere bilem
Cogaris, pressoque diu stridere molari.   160
Tu tibi liber homo et regis conviva videris :
Captum te nidore suae putat ille culinae :
Nec male conjectat. Quis enim tam nudus, ut illum
Bis ferat, Etruscum puero si contigit aurum,
Vel nodus tantum et signum de paupere loro ?   165
Spes bene coenandi vos decipit. "Ecce, dabit jam
Semesum leporem atque aliquid de clunibus apri :
Ad nos jam veniet minor altilis." Inde parato

151] Hom. *Od.* vii. 114 sq. The fruit ripens summer and winter. In less primitive times a serious poet infers perpetual spring from perpetual flowers, a satirist unending autumn from unfailing fruit.

153—155] There are two theories of these lines both as old as the Scholiast. According to one the apple is munched by a monkey dressed in uniform and whipped into going through cavalry drill on the back of a she-goat : if so the *agger* will be the mound of Servius Tullius, a well-known lounge, and a good place to shew a performing monkey. According to the other, we have a barbarian recruit (liable to the *flagellum*, not merely the *vitis*) learning cavalry drill (*parma* not *scuto;* Horace had a *parma* as a mounted officer; the cavalry was generally recruited from half-dependent tribes on the frontier) from a shaggy old she-goat of a drill-master. The ob-

jection to the first, which is the most amusing, is that there is no authority for *ab equo*, or *ab capella*, in the sense of ἀφ' ἵππου. The objection to the second is that *capella* for a dirty old woman cannot be proved to be older than Ammianus Marcellinus.

160 **pressoque — molari**] After keeping your teeth close set a long time (to keep your countenance) you are obliged to gnash them a little at last.

161—163] " He is quite right in thinking you are enslaved by gluttony, not poverty; for no freeman would stand it, however poor."

164 **aurum**] In theory due to the sons of senators or knights; in practice worn by all respectable children.

166 **vos decipit**] "Cheats you into a false belief of your liberty" (sup. 161).

168 **minor altilis**] "A capon too

Intactoque omnes et stricto pane tacetis.
Ille sapit, qui te sic utitur. Omnia ferre   170
Si potes, et debes. Pulsandum vertice raso
Praebebis quandoque caput, nec dura timebis
Flagra pati, his epulis et tali dignus amico.

small for my lord," or "the capon when it is smaller" say by the liver wing? There is nothing to make one suppose Virro had two capons or more served to him.

168, 169 **Inde—tacetis**] "So you hold your tongues, get your bread ready, and arrange it like a drawn sword, and never touch it," or perhaps more probably, though the sense of *stringo* seems insufficiently supported, we are to understand that they have been using the hunks of bread as forks for the first two courses during which they have got something to eat, though it has been only a shabby imitation of the delicacies served to their betters; accordingly they get their bread ready for the third course by scraping it so as not to interfere with the flavour of the meat, and don't attempt to while away the time by nibbling at it; but they get nothing at all. Any way it is noticeable that it is only the third course which they actually do expect their master to share with them.

171—173] "You will one day act the 'morio,' with a shaven crown; you'll not be afraid of having your ears boxed, or a smart cut with the slave's whip, so you may be worthy of such a feast and such a friend."

SATIRA VII.

Et spes et ratio studiorum in Caesare tantum:
Solus enim tristes hac tempestate Camenas
Respexit, quum jam celebres notique poetae
Balneolum Gabiis, Romae conducere furnos
Tentarent, nec foedum alii, nec turpe putarent   5
Praecones fieri; quum, desertis Aganippes
Vallibus, esuriens migraret in Atria Clio.
Nam si Pieria quadrans tibi nullus in umbra
Ostendatur, ames nomen victumque Machaerae
Et vendas potius, commissa quod auctio vendit   10
Stantibus, oenophorum, tripodes, armaria, cistas,
Alcithoen Pacci, Thebas et Terea Fausti.

1 **Caesare**] I think that Domitian is meant. His prizes at the Capitoline and Alban games were the only encouragement general literature got after the time of Horace. Mayor's quotation, from Martial, xii. 6. 12, only means that Nerva had written as loose verse as Martial, who therefore felt freer under him than under a debauched Pharisee, like Domitian. His quotation from Pliny (*Pan.* 47) proves that Trajan encouraged teachers, as a part of the revival of public spirit, which is not quite the same as patronizing literature.

3 **jam**] Bad poets had always had to despair of their profession, and now even poets of reputation were beginning to despair.

4—8] "Poets try to take a little bath at Gabii; they have to be content with a bake-house at Rome. Others turn auctioneers." Cf. "ab *atriis* Licinii atque a praeconum concessu" (Cic. *p. Quint.* § 12).

9 **Machaerae**] Does the auctioneer get his name from the most invidious kind of auction (*sectio*)?

10 **commissa**] "Ubi licitantes utrinque pretio pugnant: translate a gladiatoribus qui proprie committi dicuntur." Grangaeus. Macleane wishes it to be "auctio bonorum commissorum;" but the phrase must be later than *commissum*, in the sense of a forfeit, and that is to the full as late as Juvenal.

12] The poems of his brethren, who stick to their trade. Their fur-

Hoc satius, quam si dicas sub judice, "Vidi,"
Quod non vidisti. Faciant equites Asiani
Quanquam, et Cappadoces faciant equitesque Bithyni,   15
Altera quos nudo traducit Gallia talo.
Nemo tamen studiis indignum ferre laborem
Cogetur posthac, nectit quicunque canoris
Eloquium vocale modis, laurumque momordit.
Hoc agite, O juvenes : circumspicit et stimulat vos   20
Materiamque sibi Ducis indulgentia quaerit.
Si qua aliunde putas rerum exspectanda tuarum
Praesidia, atque ideo croceae membrana tabellae
Impletur : lignorum aliquid posce ocius et, quae
Componis, dona Veneris, Telesine, marito,   25
Aut clude et positos tinea pertunde libellos.
Frange miser calamos vigilataque proelia dele,
Qui facis in parva sublimia carmina cella,
Ut dignus venias hederis et imagine macra.
Spes nulla ulterior : didicit jam dives avarus   30
Tantum admirari, tantum laudare disertos,
Ut pueri Junonis avem. Sed defluit aetas

niture, shabby as it is, is worth more.

15] Is in all the MSS.; and the proconsular Asia included neither Cappadocia nor Bithynia, through which last Galatian slaves (inf. 16) would naturally be imported; and, considering the laxity of Roman poets in proper names, it is not decisive against the line that the first syllable of Bithynia is long elsewhere, *e.g.* inf. x. 162.

19 laurum] Given to the Pythia, to promote ἐνθουσιασμός.

21] Cf. xiv. 106 n., xvi. 57—60 n. *Ducis*, cf. Mart. IV. ii. 3, 4 Quum plebs et minor ordo maximusque *Sancto cum Duce* candidus sederet.

23 croceae membrana tabellae] The Scholiast thinks of a book with saffron pages; Mayor, better, of a note-book with saffron covers, made of parchment, over boards.

25 Telesine] Another Telesinus, wealthy and miserly, is addressed by Martial.

29 hederis] Probably natural ivy, as Ovid, *Trist.* I. vii. 1, asks his friends to take the wreaths of Bacchic ivy off his busts. *Macra.* He is worn away by hunger as well as literary labours.

30—34] Rich misers have learned to feed genius, as boys feed peacocks, with praise, and only praise; meanwhile you are getting too old for the only respectable and lucrative professions, maritime commerce, war and husbandry.

Et pelagi patiens et cassidis atque ligonis.
Taedia tunc subeunt animos, tunc seque suamque
Terpsichoren odit facunda et nuda senectus. 35
    Accipe nunc artes; ne quid tibi conferat iste,
Quem colis, et Musarum et Apollinis aede relicta,
Ipse facit versus atque uni cedit Homero
Propter mille annos: et, si dulcedine famae
Succensus recites, maculosas commodat aedes; 40
Haec longe ferrata domus servire jubetur,
In qua sollicitas imitatur janua portas.
Scit dare libertos extrema in parte sedentes
Ordinis et magnas comitum disponere voces.
Nemo dabit regum, quanti subsellia constent 45
Et quae conducto pendent anabathra tigillo,
Quaeque reportandis posita est orchestra cathedris.
Nos tamen hoc agimus tenuesque in pulvere sulcos
Ducimus et litus sterili versamus aratro.
Nam si discedas, laqueo tenet ambitiosi 50
Consuetudo mali; tenet insanabile multos
Scribendi cacoethes, et aegro in corde senescit.

---

35 **Terpsichoren**] An allusion to the fable of the 'Ant and Grass-hopper.'
36 sqq.] "In order to reserve his poems for his patron's ear, he ceases to recite in the temples; but the patron pays him in kind (as Augustus once paid an importunate 'poetaster,' who rewarded him as liberally as he could with a few 'denarii,' and got a hundred 'sestertia' by his generosity). Then he tells you, if you really care about fame [though he cannot get anybody he tells you to appreciate him; nobody does do justice to modern poets], you can have his fly-blown house to recite in. It is a house barred up, ever so far off, must serve you, with its doors shut up as fast as the gates of a besieged town. Besides, he can give you his freedmen, to give the cue at the end of the rows, and post loud-voiced retainers up and down the room. None will give you enough to hire the benches, or the raised seats, with the framework to support them, or the easy chairs in the front, that you will have to pay for carrying back."
48 **tenuesque**] P. seems to have had 'tenuisque,' which got altered into 'tenuique.' The meaning is both that we take pains to draw our furrow fine, and that it does not go deep into the sand.
50] Jahn, "ambitiosum scripsi, ambitiosi P. S. ω, quod a correctore illatum est, postquam 51, quem spurium judico, additus est."

Sed vatem egregium, cui non sit publica vena,
Qui nihil expositum soleat deducere, nec qui
Communi feriat carmen triviale moneta,   55
Hunc, qualem nequeo monstrare et sentio tantum,
Anxietate carens animus facit, omnis acerbi
Impatiens, cupidus silvarum aptusque bibendis
Fontibus Aonidum. Neque enim cantare sub antro
Pierio thyrsumve potest contingere sana   60
Paupertas atque aeris inops, quo nocte dieque
Corpus eget : satur est, quum dicit Horatius, Euoe !
Quis locus ingenio, nisi quum se carmine solo
Vexant, et dominis Cirrhae Nysaeque feruntur
Pectora nostra, duas non admittentia curas ?   65
Magnae mentis opus nec de lodice paranda
Attonitae, currus et equos faciesque Deorum
Aspicere, et qualis Rutulum confundat Erinnys.
Nam si Vergilio puer et tolerabile deesset

53 **cui—vena**] Who works a mine that everybody cannot dig in.

54 **expositum—deducere**] "Spin out old thrums," is the natural sense, like "tenui deducta poemata filo" (Hor. *Ep.* ii. 6. 225). Here, however, between two metallic metaphors it would not be violent to think of wiredrawing a bald commonplace.

58 **aptus**] The Scholiast, who writes *Pierio* in 60, writes *avidus* here.

60 **sana**] So most MSS. The Scholiast says, "Insanire non potest pauper." The other MSS., including Pithous, read *saeva*, or *moesta*, both wanton corrections : poverty must be sane and sordid.

62 **satur—Euoe**] Juvenal thinks Horace was 'fou' when he wrote the 19th ode of the second book.

67 **Attonitae**] The poet ought to be *attonitus*, dazzled by the grandeur of his own creations, not dazed by

poverty which makes it a difficult and depressing question how to get a blanket.

68 **qualis—Erinnys**] Juvenal is thinking both of Allecto in the Seventh Book of the Aeneid, and of the Dira, *ib.* xii. 845. *Confundat* points to the latter, *hydri*, inf. 70, to the former, though the Dira has snakes like Megaera.

69] "If Vergil were now alive, and in want of attendance and lodging, we should see all the snakes drop from her hair." Cf. "Cur igitur Camillus doleret, si putaret, cur ego doleam si putem?" (Cic. *Tusc.* i. 37.) "Why was Camillus to grieve, if he thought? Why am I to grieve, if I think?" "Num tu igitur Opimium si tum esses temerarium civem aut crudelem putes?" (Id. *Phil.* viii. 4.) "Suppose you were a man of that day, should you think Opimius a violent politician?" "Non tam facile opes Car-

Hospitium, caderent omnes a crinibus hydri;   70
Surda nihil gemeret grave buccina. Poscimus, ut sit
Non minor antiquo Rubrenus Lappa cothurno,
Cujus et alveolos et laenam pignerat Atreus.
Non habet infelix Numitor, quod mittat amico:
Quintillae quod donet, habet; nec defuit illi,   75
Unde emeret multa pascendum carne leonem
Jam domitum: constat leviori bellua sumtu
Nimirum, et capiunt plus intestina poetae.
Contentus fama jaceat Lucanus in hortis
Marmoreis: at Serrano tenuique Saleio   80
Gloria quantalibet quid erit, si gloria tantum est?
Curritur ad vocem jucundam et carmen amicae
Thebaidos, laetam fecit quum Statius Urbem
Promisitque diem. Tanta dulcedine captos

thaginis concidissent nisi illud receptaculum classibus nostris pateret" (Id. *Verr.* ii. 1). "Carthage would not have fallen so easily, if we had not Sicily open to our fleets" (as we have now). "Persas Indos aliasque si Alexander adjunxisset gentes impedimentum majus quam auxilium traheret" (Liv. ix. 19). "Supposing Alexander had enrolled these tribes, he would have more burden to drag than help." "Haec si reipublicae causa faceres in vendendis decumis essent pronuntiata" (Cic. *Verr.* iii. 20). "This would have been laid down when you put up the tithes, if you were acting at the time in the public interest." I translate Madvig's instances (§ 347, b. 2); for it is difficult to grasp a rule. Almost all the MSS. have *desit.*

72 **Rubrenus Lappa**] An unknown tragedian, who has to live on his pots and solitary cloak while writing his Atreus.

74 **Numitor**] Cf. Piratae Cilicum (viii. 93).

74, 75 **mittat—donet**] The present-

sents to the mistress he takes himself, the presents to the friend would be sent by a slave; their amount would be small. In English and Latin alike a large gift is referred direct to the giver; if both came by post, a pair of mother-of-pearl sleevelinks might be either 'given' or 'sent,' a set of diamonds could only be 'given.'

77 **Jam domitum**] And so more expensive; there would not be even the economy of keeping it without food till it was tame.

80] Saleius Bassus was a good rough Epic poet, a contemporary of Statius. People have imagined a Calpurnius Serranus, who should write the Bucolics (they are a creditable imitation of Vergil), and be a friend of Persius; but the evidence breaks down. Martial is bored by one Afer, who dins into his ears how much Serranus and others owe him (iv. 37).

83] It is not quite clear that this brings the satire down to A.D. 94, when the Thebaid was finished, as Statius may have recited instalments,

Afficit ille animos tantaque libidine vulgi   85
Auditur : sed, quum fregit subsellia versu,
Esurit, intactam Paridi nisi vendat Agaven,
Ille et militiae multis largitur honorem,
Semestri vatum digitos circumligat auro.
Quod non dant proceres, dabit histrio : tu Camerinos   90
Et Bareas, tu nobilium magna atria curas?
Praefectos Pelopea facit, Philomela tribunos.
Haud tamen invideas vati, quem pulpita pascunt.
Quis tibi Maecenas? quis nunc erit aut Proculeius
Aut Fabius? quis Cotta iterum? quis Lentulus alter?   95
Tunc par ingenio pretium; tunc utile multis
Pallere et vinum toto nescire Decembri.

Vester porro labor fecundior, historiarum
Scriptores? petit hic plus temporis atque olei plus :
Namque oblita modi millesima pagina surgit   100
Omnibus et multa crescit damnosa papyro.
Sic ingens rerum numerus jubet atque operum lex.
Quae tamen, inde seges? terrae quis fructus apertae?
Quis dabit historico, quantum daret acta legenti?

87] Not a tragedy, as there would be no condescension in selling it (unless indeed Paris was to pass for the author), but a libretto for a pantomime; so also *Pelopea, Philomela,* inf. 92.

88] He not only pays money, he also handsomely throws in military rank (*honorem* the office of military tribune).

89] They wore a gold ring, as of equestrian rank, while their office lasted.

90 **Camerinos**] A distinguished old family of the early republic, which, from viii. 38, seems to have been ill represented in Juvenal's time.

94 **Proculeius**] A Roman Knight intimate with Augustus, chiefly known as bountiful to his own family (Hor. *Carm.* ii. 2).

95 **Fabius—Cotta**] Patrons of Ovid; the latter, a son of Messalla adopted into the Gens Aurelia: under Tiberius he was as conspicuous as a politician could be, for bitterness, which had the effect of servility. *Lentulus,* uncertain; perhaps the consul who restored Cicero.

97 **toto—Decembri**] Winter was the best season for lucubrations, here prolonged even through the universal holiday of the Saturnalia.

104 **acta legenti**] There were actuarii who kept the 'acta' of the city; and rich men sometimes kept actuarii of their own, to amuse them with an account of what happened on their property.

Sed genus ignavum, quod lecto gaudet et umbra !   105
　Dic igitur, quid causidicis civilia praestent
Officia, et magno comites in fasce libelli?
Ipsi magna sonant, sed tunc, quum creditor audit,
Praecipue, vel si tetigit latus acrior illo,
Qui venit ad dubium grandi cum codice nomen   110
Tunc immensa cavi spirant mendacia folles
Conspuiturque sinus.　Veram deprendere messem
Si libet: hinc centum patrimonia causidicorum,
Parte alia solum russati pone Lacernae.
Consedere Duces : surgis tu pallidus Ajax   115
Dicturus dubia pro libertate, Bubulco
Judice.　Rumpe miser tensum jecur, ut tibi lasso
Figantur virides, scalarum gloria, palmae.
Quod vocis pretium? siccus petasunculus et vas
Pelamydum, aut veteres, Maurorum epimenia, bulbi,   120

---

105 lecto] The Romans only used tables at meals, and so would write and read on sofas.

106 civilia] The reverse of *umbratilis*.

108—110] " They talk big to keep up their credit, still more to secure a large fee from a rich client."— *Dubium nomen*, " a doubtful debt."

112 Conspuitur] For fear their fictitious prosperity should provoke Nemesis.

114 russati] The rivalry between blue and green, the new colours, was much keener from the first than any rivalry between the old colours red and white, or between the old and new. Caligula and Nero favoured green, Vitellius blue: green was on the whole the popular colour, cf. xi. 196, "eventum viridis quo colligo panni," and the blues seem for some reason to have been in the position of butts, at least they had Martial against them, Mart. vi. 46; but we are not to infer that the red colour fell into disgrace. Hirpinus

and Aquilo (viii. 63 n.) ran under it. *Lacernae* must be a proper name, as otherwise it would be feminine.

115] "Consedere duces et vulgi stante corona, Surgit ad hos clypei dominus septemplicis Ajax." (Ov, *Met*. xiii. 1, 2.)

116 dubia pro libertate] "In defence of one who is claimed as a slave." Considering the nature of the case, it is as well to remember that Bubulcus occurs twice as a cognomen of the Junii Bruti.

118 scalarum] They would adorn his front door if he had a house instead of a garret.

119 siccus petasunculus] "A rusty little hind-quarter of bacon." The *perna* was a part of the *petaso*, which was fresh, while the *perna* was smoked.

120] The worst sort of *bulbi* but one is African; they get worse by keeping. Here 'Maurorum' may mark their origin, or the inferior class of slaves who used them.

Aut vinum Tiberi devectum, quinque lagenae,
Si quater egisti. Si contigit aureus unus,
Inde cadunt partes, ex foedere, pragmaticorum.
"Aemilio dabitur, quantum licet, et melius nos
Egimus: hujus enim stat currus aeneus, alti   125
Quadrijuges in vestibulis, atque ipse feroci
Bellatore sedens curvatum hastile minatur
Eminus, et statua meditatur proelia lusca."
Sic Pedo conturbat, Matho deficit; exitus hic est
Tongilli, magno cum rhinocerote lavari   130
Qui solet et vexat lutulenta balnea turba
Perque forum juvenes longo premit assere Medos,
Emturus pueros, argentum, murrhina, villas:
Spondet enim Tyrio stlataria purpura filo.

121 **vinum—devectum**] *i. e.* Veientine or Sabine wine. Foreign and Campanian wines would come up the river to Rome.

123] In the age of Cicero advocates were trained by intercourse with advocates who had already risen and possessed great practical knowledge. Accordingly Cicero could afford to deride the Greek speakers for their dependence for technicalities on prompters. *De Oratore*, §§ 198, 253. The pleaders of Juvenal's day had no training except in rhetoric, and a rhetorician who, like Quintilian, attempted to enforce legal studies was practically helpless.

124 **quantum licet**] Ten sestertia, a hundred times the fee of the 'causidicus,' even when exceptionally lucky.

126—128] He has statues of ancestors in chariots (which were erected in honour either of those who had triumphed, or even those who had driven in state through the circus as praetors), and a blinking equestrian statue of himself, as he brandished a javelin, which quivers and bends with the weight of the point.

128 **lusca**] The man is a civilian, he tries to look like a soldier; the result is a grimace which gives the impression that he has only one eye, because he has taken it into his head that to aim steadily he must close the other.

130 **rhinocerote**] Fashionable, because outlandish.

131 **lutulenta**] His counterfeit clients have had to tramp all the way from his house to the forum, and from the forum to the baths.

132 **Medos**] Another affectation: the bearers generally preferred came from the sturdy tribes between the Adriatic and the Danube.

133] Pliny speaks of *murrhina* being dug up (*H. N.* xxxiii. 2, § 5; xxxvii. 8, § 21); and of imitations in glass (*H. N.* xxxvi. 67, § 198), which would explain Propertius (IV. v. 26), "Murrheaque in Parthis pocula cocta focis;" but several of the ancients thought that silk was made of mulberry leaves instead of silk-worms; so it is still uncertain whether 'murrhea' were porcelain or fluor spar.

134 **stlataria**]. There are two explanations of this; one based on an

Et tamen est illis hoc utile: purpura vendit   135
Causidicum, vendunt amethystina: convenit illis
Et strepitu et facie majoris vivere census.
Sed finem impensae non servat prodiga Roma.
Fidimus eloquio? Ciceroni nemo ducentos
Nunc dederit nummos, nisi fulserit annulus ingens.   140
Respicit haec primum, qui litigat, an tibi servi
Octo, decem comites, an post te sella, togati
Ante pedes. Ideo conducta Paullus agebat
Sardonyche, atque ideo pluris, quam Cossus agebat,
Quam Basilus. Rara in tenui facundia panno.   145
Quando licet Basilo flentem producere matrem?
Quis bene dicentem Basilum ferat? Accipiat te
Gallia, vel potius nutricula causidicorum
Africa, si placuit mercedem imponere linguae.
    Declamare doces? O ferrea pectora Vetti,   150
Quum perimit saevos classis numerosa tyrannos!

etymology from *stlata* = *lata*, like *stlocus*, *stlis* = *locus*, *lis*, which looks conjectural. The explanation generally given with this etymology is "imported from foreign parts in a broad or piratical ship," which seems forced. The other explanation, "spurious," "deceptive," seems to rest on an independent tradition.

135—138] " *Their* wretched profession does require display beyond their means, but at Rome this is ruinous; they had better be 'cheap swells' in Africa or Gaul." Roman advocates of course found their most valuable openings in the Romanised provinces of the empire: in Africa, though the Punic language held its ground, Roman commerce was more active than elsewhere, and litigation was more active too. Gaul was more thoroughly Romanised than Spain, to say nothing of Britain.

139 **eloquio**] As contrasted with display.—*Ducentos*, one-fifth of the legal fee. Cicero was paid by legacies; the presents in kind to pleaders at the Saturnalia were a continuation of the old system.

141—143] " The first point with the client is, Do you enter the court with ten citizens before you, and leave a litter with eight bearers at the door?"

143 **Paullus**] Probably Aemilius.

145 **Basilus**] We have a fraudulent partner of the same name (x. 222).

145—147] " He does not speak well, he never gets an exciting case; if he were to try to be eloquent, it would be incongruous."

149] " If you *have* made up your mind to speak for a living."

151] " When a large [the sense is 'post-Augustan'] class is spouting themes in honour of tyrannicide." The master gave heads for a theme on both sides of a subject, sometimes hinting which side he

Nam quaecunque sedens modo legerat, haec eadem stans
Perferet atque eadem cantabit versibus isdem.
Occidit miseros crambe repetita magistros.
Quis color et quod sit causae genus, atque ubi summa   155
Quaestio, quae veniant diversa parte sagittae,
Nosse velint omnes, mercedem solvere nemo.
"Mercedem appellas?·quid enim scio?" "Culpa docentis
Scilicet arguitur, quod laeva in parte mamillae
Nil salit Arcadico juveni, cujus mihi sexta   160
Quaque die miserum dirus caput Hannibal implet;
Quidquid id est, de quo deliberat, an petat Urbem
A Cannis, an post nimbos et fulmina cautus
Circumagat madidas a tempestate cohortes.
Quantum vis stipulare, et protinus accipe quid do,   165
Ut toties illum pater audiat." Haec alii sex
Vel plures uno conclamant ore sophistae,
Et veras agitant lites, raptore relicto;

thought the class had better take; the boys the master thought cleverest were put on first when Quintilian was at school. He complains himself of the anxiety of parents to hear their sons declaim on many subjects, instead of grappling with the difficulties of one (cf. 160, "sexta quaque die").

152, 153] "They repeat the same notes in the same sing-song, with the same pauses and cadences."

155 **color**] As we say, "what colour can be given to his conduct;" it means a colourable excuse, an excuse only useful to give a colour to what is really unjustifiable. — *Causae genus.* As *demonstrativum*, like the funeral oration of Pericles; *deliberativum*, where the speaker has to advise or dissuade, and *judiciale* in civil and criminal trials.

156 **sagittae**] As we say, "points."

158] "What, call for pay! Why, what have I learnt?"—*Quid enim, τί γάρ;*

162 **an petat Urbem—an circumagat**] Branches of two distinct alternatives, not two branches of one; this is made probable by the double 'an;' certain as five years after Cannae a tempest made Hannibal withdraw from Rome.

165] The teacher says, "Make your bargain (with the formula *quid das?*) as high as you please, and I'll pay at once to get his father to hear him as often as I do." *Quid do* is awkward; but if Juvenal wished to recall the formula while changing the person, it is hard to see what else he could have said. Most MSS. have *quod*.

168 **raptore**] The cases which might arise from the right of the *rapta* to choose either the hand and property of the *raptor*, or his life, were frequent subjects of declamation, rather because they were ex-

Fusa venena silent, malus ingratusque maritus,
'Et quae jam veteres sanant mortaria caecos.   170
Ergo sibi dabit ipse rudem, si nostra movebunt
Consilia, et vitae diversum iter ingredietur,
Ad pugnam qui rhetorica descendit ab umbra,
Summula ne pereat, qua vilis tessera venit
Frumenti: quippe haec merces lautissima. Tenta,   175
Chrysogonus quanti doceat, vel Pollio quanti
Lautorum pueros, artem scindens Theodori.
Balnea sexcentis et pluris porticus, in qua
Gestetur dominus, quoties pluit. Anne serenum
Exspectet spargatque luto jumenta recenti?   180
Hic potius: namque hic mundae nitet ungula mulae.

citing than because they were actually common, as Tacitus (*Dial.*
32) mentions *vitiatarum electiones*
as one of the unreal and useless subjects which were harped on for ever
in the schools.

169 **Fusa venena**] Where a suspected poisoner is challenged to
drink, and manages to spill the
poison.

malus ingratusque maritus]
"Torta a tyranno uxor numquid
de tyrannicidio sciret perseveravit
negare, postea maritus ejus tyran-
num occidit: illam sterilitatis nomine dimisit intra quinquennium non
parientem. Agit illa ingrati." (Sen.
ii. *Contr.* 13). This excludes Medea,
who might otherwise explain all
three subjects.

170] One would think of Medea
here, but Grangaeus guesses plausibly that a son is disinherited on
his stepmother's accusation that he
is preparing poison instead of eye-
salve for his blind father.

174 **qua vilis tessera venit**] At
which some citizen would sell his
monthly ticket to the foreign, though
possibly naturalized, rhetor. The
list was limited, and the praetor

filled up vacancies. Augustus wanted
to have three distributions, instead
of twelve, a year; but precedent
was too strong for him.

177 **scindens**] So the MSS.
Though he knows no rhetoric, and
tears the art of Theodorus to tatters;
as we say, "Makes a mess of his
Lindley Murray." Jahn *scindes*,
which is much easier and better,
and might be adopted if it had any
MS. authority; but unless we suppose that all our MSS. are derived
ultimately from a single archetype,
it is difficult to see how *scindes* with
a blot over the *e* could have been
universally taken for *scindes*, *i. q.*
scindens. The sense of the future
will be "you will tear your text-
books of rhetoric to pieces." If the
sense of *scindo* were better established, it would be tempting to
translate 'you will,' or 'Chrysogonus does,' according as we have
the verb or participle, 'make fun
of,' 'cut up,' 'Theodorus and his
art of rhetoric.'

178 **sexcentis**] Nearly 5000*l.*
180] "Is he to wait for fine
weather, and splash his cattle with
fresh mud when it comes?"

Parte alia longis Numidarum fulta columnis
Surgat, et algentem rapiat coenatio solem.
Quanticunque domus, veniet qui fercula docte
Componat; veniet qui pulmentaria condat.   185
Hos inter sumtus sestertia Quintiliano,
Ut multum, duo sufficient: res nulla minoris
Constabit patri, quam filius. "Unde igitur tot
Quintilianus habet saltus?" Exempla novorum
Fatorum transi. Felix et pulcher et acer;   190
Felix et sapiens et nobilis et generosus,
Appositam nigrae lunam subtexit alutae;
Felix, orator quoque maximus et jaculator:
Et si perfrixit, cantat bene. Distat enim, quae
Sidera te excipiant modo primos incipientem   195
Edere vagitus et adhuc a matre rubentem.
Si Fortuna volet, fies de rhetore Consul:

182, 3 Parte alia] His corridor is put, no doubt, to catch the morning sun: he will not have his dining-room over it; he gets a fresh set of tall columns of yellow marble and builds it over them. *Algentem—solem,* "the chilly winter sun," "the sun that is too weak to scorch." —*Rapiat,* for it only falls there for a few hours.

184] As much again will be spent on slaves.

187 duo] About 17*l.*, a high fee for a rhetorician: the average grammarian's fee was about 4*l.* (inf. 243).

189] Quintilian could be asked (on the ground that such a sum was too small to be refused) to accept a present of rather more than 400*l.* on his daughter's marriage, though he had bought a good deal of cheap forest pasture to let again.

190 sqq.] Juvenal transfers to the *felix* all the accumulated attributes of the Stoic *sapiens.*

193, 194] "He is unrivalled in the sports of the Campus Martius, as well as the pleadings of the Forum, and is most praised for his singing, when he has a cold, and needs praise most."

196 vagitus] Coined from the first utterance of babies, 'wah;' which is one of the arguments for the alarming conclusion that the Roman *v* not merely corresponded to, but coincided with, our *w.*

197 Consul] Quintilian only received the consular ornaments. Does the next line mean that Cicero was reduced after his consulship to give lessons in rhetoric to Hirtius and Pansa (*ad Att.* xiv. 12, 22)? Plin. *Ep.* iv. 11 has a story of a praetorian senator who was banished by Domitian on his own confession, true or false, that he had been among the paramours of Cornelia. Under Trajan he was reduced to lecture on rhetoric in Sicily, and began his fourth lecture by complaining almost in these very words of his reverse of fortune.

Si volet haec eadem, fies de Consule rhetor.
Ventidius quid enim? quid Tullius? anne aliud, quam
Sidus et occulti miranda potentia fati?   200
Servis regna dabunt, captivis fata triumphos.
Felix ille tamen corvo quoque rarior albo.
Poenituit multos vanae sterilisque cathedrae,
Sicut Thrasymachi probat exitus atque Secundi
Carrinatis: et hunc inopem vidistis, Athenae,   205
Nil praeter gelidas ausae conferre cicutas.
Di, majorum umbris tenuem et sine pondere terram
Spirantesque crocos et in urna perpetuum ver,
Qui praeceptorem sancti voluere parentis
Esse loco! Metuens virgae jam grandis Achilles   210
Cantabat patriis in montibus, et cuï non tunc
Eliceret risum citharoedi cauda magistri;
Sed Rufum atque alios caedit sua quemque juventus,
Rufum, qui toties Ciceronem Allobroga dixit.

199, 200] What is Ventidius?
What is Tullius? What are they
but the children of their star and
the wonder-working power of mys-
terious fate? *Ventidius,* a *captive* of
the Social War, who triumphed
fifty-one years after, as a legatus of
Antonius, over the Parthians. *Tullius.* Servius Tullius, a *slave.*
202] " Though any caprice may
be expected from fortune, *his* luck
is remarkable."
204 **Thrasymachi**] " Rhetoris a-
pud Athenas qui suspendio periit."
Probably later than the interlocutor
of the *Republic.*
205, 206] "You beheld his
poverty (that of Secundus Carrinas,
banished by Caligula, perhaps employed by Nero to plunder Greece;
like that of Socrates; and hemlock
was all you contributed to the relief
of either." I do not feel sure
whether *ausae* means that they were
afraid to do anything for an exile,

or whether it is like the Greek
τλῆναι or τολμᾶν.
210 **jam grandis**] Though quite
a big boy.
211 **tunc**] In such an age of obe-
dience. The whole clause *cui—
magistri* is equivalent to another
epithet coupled by *et* to *grandis.*
214] It was a favourite joke on
the return of Pompeius from the
East to call him Sampsiceramus,
after the Emir of Emesa, because
he was fond of giving lists of such
potentates as a measure of the value
of his victories (Cic. *ad Att.* ii. 14,
16, 17, 23). As Cicero was fond of
explaining that he had saved Rome
from the Allobroges, whenever his
authority was quoted against a rule
of Rufus, he always replied that
Cicero was no better than his favourite barbarians. If this seems
forced we must read *quem* with P.,
and suppose that his class expressed
their sense of his vanity by calling

Quis gremio Enceladi .doctique Palaemonis affert   215
Quantum grammaticus meruit 'labor? et tamen ex hoc
Quodcunque est (minus est autem, quam rhetoris aera)
Discipuli custos praemordet Acoenonetus
Et, qui dispensat, frangit sibi. Cede, Palaemon,
Et patere inde aliquid decrescere, non aliter, quam   220
Institor hibernae tegetis niveique cadurci;
Dummodo non pereat, mediae quod noctis ab hora
Sedisti, qua nemo .faber, qua nemo sederet,
Qui docet obliquo lanam deducere ferro;
Dummodo non pereat totidem olfecisse lucernas,   225
Quot stabant pueri, quum totus decolor esset
Flaccus et haereret nigro fuligo Maroni.
Rara tamen merces, quae cognitione tribuni
Non egeat. Sed vos saevas imponite leges,
Ut praeceptori verborum regula constet,   230
Ut legat historias, auctores noverit omnes,
Tanquam ungues digitosque suos : ut forte rogatus,

him the Cicero of Gaul. According to Tacitus, *De Oratoribus*, c. 26 fin., nearly every spouter of the day felt that he had got beyond Cicero at any rate, though of course he came short of the great Gabinianus, a famous rhetorician of Gaul.

215 gremio] Most likely they were paid in silver, told into the lap.

— Palaemonis] The teacher of Quintilian and Persius, who made about 3300*l.* a year by his school, as much more by well-managed estates, and spent more than he made.

215—219] All are underpaid, all have to endure the extortion of the pedagogus,—who thinks yours is mine, and mine is my own,—and the nibblings of the steward.

221 Institor] A stationary or travelling salesman who puffs his winter rugs and snowy quilts. *Cadurci*, from a people of Gaul, whose name survives in the town of Cahors and the district of Querci.

222—224] Children were made to go to school before day, and their lamps made the air worse than any smithy or carding school.

228 tribuni] Under the empire the *tribuni plebis* had the "vocatio in jus" in the city, for they had to be restrained from usurping it in the country.

229 sqq. imponite—exigite—exigite] In English we should either say in the imperative "Impose your own severe terms (if you like), but then you ought to pay in proportion," or else say in the indicative, "You impose these onerous terms and yet you will not pay."

230, 231] He is required never to be at fault in his syntax, and to read history, in order to meet the questions which minute familiarity with all classical writers might suggest.

Dum petit aut thermas aut Phoebi balnea, dicat
Nutricem Anchisae, nomen. patriamque novercae
Archemori; dicat, quot Acestes vixerit annos,   235
Quot Siculus Phrygibus vini donaverit urnas.
Exigite, ut mores teneros ceu pollice ducat,
Ut si quis cera vultum facit; exigite, ut sit
Et pater ipsius coetus, ne turpia ludant,
Ne faciant vicibus. "Non est leve tot puerorum   240
Observare manus oculosque in fine trementes."
"Haec," inquit, "cura; sed quum se verterit annus,
Accipe, victori populus quod postulat, aurum."

---

233 **thermas aut Phoebi balnea**]
Public or private baths.

234—236] All these difficulties
are suggested by Vergil, *Aen.* vii.
1—4, who speaks of the nurse of
Æneas, which of course raises the
question who was the nurse of
Anchises. The Scholiast says she
was Tisiphone. From Sen. *Ep.*
88, § 32, it appears that the question
went deeper and became, Who was
the mother of Æneas in the sense
in which Amphitryon was the father
of Hercules? We know from Verg.
Aen. x. 388, 389 that Archemorus
or Anchemolus had a stepmother
the wife of Rhoetus, and that he
fought under Turnus. Servius adds
that the stepmother was Casperia a
Greek, and that Archemorus was
received by Daunus the father of

Turnus. We learn, *Aen.* v. 73, that
Acestes was old, *ib.* i. 195, that he
gave the Trojans wine. The questions how old he was, and how many
casks he gave, follow of course.
Tiberius had a great taste for annoy-
ing grammarians with these puzzles.
One set of grammarians actually
made it their business to start these
questions, and of course there was
another set to solve them.

239] "Be like their own father
to the whole tribe."

241, 242.] The yearly fee of the
grammarians is no more than the
five 'aurei' which a jockey gets for
winning one race.—*Quum se verterit
annus*, is a change for the worse.
Horace's neighbours paid monthly
(*S.* I. vi. 75).

SATIRA VIII.

STEMMATA quid faciunt? quid prodest, Pontice, longo
Sanguine censeri, pictosque ostendere vultus
Majorum et stantes in curribus Aemilianos,
Et Curios jam dimidios, humerosque minorem
Corvinum, et Galbam auriculis nasoque carentem?   5
Quis fructus, generis tabula jactare capaci
Corvinum, posthac multa contingere virga

1 **Stemmata**] The Romans had two ways of proclaiming their descent : one was to have painted waxen masks of the face and bust in niches in the 'atrium.' To this 1—5 mainly allude; so *pictos vultus*, mutilated Curii, and Corvinus with the shoulders gone, triumphal statues of the younger Africanus : the other, to have a great chart, with enwreathed medallions connected by lines, on which the titles of the portraits were written. 6—8 allude to this; hence Hermann cannot be allowed to omit 5, 6, to make way for 7. The representative of an old family which had maintained its state would have both the 'images' and the chart, the second to serve as a key to the first; but a man who had made his own position, though his ancient pedigree might be genuine, would have no 'images:' he would have a chart of the kind described above, and perhaps statues of the most distinguished of those whom he claimed as his ancestors. Plin. xxxv. 2 § 6 speaks of statues *in atria* as an innovation. As late as the time of Polybius, vi. 53, the 'images' of a man's deceased ancestors were worn at funerals by attendants who personated them.

5 **Galbam, &c.**] Juvenal was reminded of this family, which he knew to be noble, by the fact that a Galba had lately been emperor; but *his* private images would be still entire.

7] would be better away, as we have just had Corvinus before. Many MSS. omit it, perhaps by the authority of Juvenal's literary executors, but it is not like a gloss; and *capaci* is no objection, as a pedigree, which went so far back, would have to be wide enough to include many collateral lines of descent; and *posthac multa contingere virga* is very nearly equivalent in sense to *multa contingendos virga*. It is translated, "to have affinity through many ancestors, who bare the fasces." So the Scholiast, and Forcellini. Ruperti : "To have affinity through many a branch of the genealogical tree." So Pers. iii. 28 : "Stemmate quod Tusco ramum millesime ducis," which is a neat, and not a violent guess. Heinrich : "To dust with a great deal of broom." Hermann : "To

Fumosos equitum cum dictatore magistros,
Si coram Lepidis male vivitur? effigies quo
Tot bellatorum, si luditur alea pernox   10
Ante Numantinos; si dormire incipis ortu
Luciferi, quo signa duces et castra movebant?
Cur Allobrogicis et magna gaudeat ara
Natus in Herculeo Fabius Lare, si cupidus, si
Vanus et Euganea quantumvis mollior agna;   15
Si tenerum attritus Catinensi pumice lumbum
Squalentes traducit avos emtorque veneni
Frangenda miseram funestat imagine gentem?
Tota licet veteres exornent undique cerae
Atria, nobilitas sola est atque unica virtus.   20

touch with a great deal of wand."
Both the last give *multa* an unpleasant sense.

8 **cum dictatore**] "With a dictator here and there."

9 **coram Lepidis**] The best known
of this branch of the Æmilii were
the Consul of B.C. 79, only remarkable for his premature and disloyal
attempt to undo Sulla's work, and
the Triumvir. One is tempted to ask
why the ghostly presence of the
Lepidi should be an aid to self-
control. The answer is that they
were one of the few great families
of the republic that retained their
greatness under the early empire,
that a son of the triumvir held a
very high position and bore a very
high character in the reigns of
Augustus and Tiberius, and lastly
that it is safe to assume, that when
Juvenal wrote, a scapegrace of the
name was or had lately been notorious.

11 **Numantinos**] = *Aemilianos*
(sup. 3).

13, 14] "What good does Fabius
get from the fact that his family
earned a name from the Allobroges"
(whose submission his ancestor received, after conquering Bituitus

king of the Arverni, B.C. 121), "or
from the 'ara maxima' of Hercules"
(of which the Fabii claimed the
priesthood)? There may be two
reasons why the conqueror of
Bituitus is referred to rather than
the greater Fabii of the Samnite
and Punic wars. In the first place,
their line seems to have died out;
Allobrogicus was the son of an
Æmilius adopted into the Fabian
house. In the second place, *his* son
was forbidden by the prætor to ad-
minister to his father's property on
account of his notorious vices. Cic.
Tusc. i. 33.

15 **Euganea**] The Euganei, ex-
pelled by the Heneti, have given
their names to the hills nine miles
south - west of Padua. Martial
preferred the breeds of Apulia and
Parma (xiv. 155).

16 **Catinensi**] "Such as Catina
produces and employs." Cf. "Osce
senex Catinaeque puer Cumana
meretrix" Bibaculus (ap. Schol.).

18.] The 'gens' is already in
possession of his image. On his
conviction it has to be broken: it
would compromise them to keep
it.

Paullus vel Cossus vel Drusus moribus esto;
Hos ante effigies majorum pone tuorum;
Praecedant ipsas illi te Consule virgas.
Prima mihi debes animi bona : sanctus haberi
Justitiaeque tenax factis dictisque mereris,   25
Agnosco procerem. Salve, Gaetulice; seu tu
Silanus, quocunque alio de sanguine, rarus
Civis et egregius patriae contingis ovanti;
Exclamare libet, populus quod clamat, Osiri
Invento. Quis enim generosum dixerit hunc, qui   30
Indignus genere et praeclaro nomine tantum
Insignis? Nanum cujusdam Atlanta vocamus,
Aethiopem Cygnum, parvum extortamque puellam
Europen; canibus pigris scabieque vetusta
Levibus et siccae lambentibus ora lucernae   35
Nomen erit Pardus, Tigris, Leo, si quid adhuc est,

21 **Paullus,** sqq.] Be a Paullus or a Cossus or a Drusus in your character. Juvenal is thinking of the conquerors of Perseus, and of Lar Tolumnius (cf. however inf. 26 n.) and of the stepson of Augustus the brother of Tiberius.

22 **Hos**] sc. *mores.*

24 **animi**] opposed to *fortunae.*

26 **Gaetulice**] Cossus Cornelius Lentulus won this title and the triumphal ornaments by defeating the Gaetuli, who had invaded the dominions of Juba. The construction is not clear, Jahn and Mayor put a full stop or colon after *Silanus,* understanding *es.* This seems bald: the punctuation of the text may perhaps without too much forcing mean : Hail, Gaetulicus, you are a Gaetulicus indeed, or if you are granted as a Silanus or a scion of whatever race to a country ex-ulting to find a worthy citizen at last we are inclined to cry, &c. It is also possible to put a full stop at *ovanti,* and translate : Then [only

then] hail, Gaetulicus, or if you are Silanus, of whatever other race you are there are few like you; your country may exult at possessing such a citizen. The presumption that *seu—ovanti,* or *quocunque—ovanti,* ought to be the protasis to *Exclamare libet* is weakened by *Hic gaudere libet,* xv. 84.

27 **Silanus**] Ennobled by inter-marriage with the Caesars.

29 **quod clamat**] i. e. εὑρήκαμεν, συγχαίρομεν.

30 **generosum**] implies the noble nature of a noble race.

— **qui, &c.**] The omission of 'est' here is a shade beyond Horace (*Ep.* II. ii. 139), "*Cui sic extorta voluptas,*" where we have a participle instead of an adjective.

32—36] There are people who give their male and female dwarfs fine names which you have to call them by. You often find mangy starveling dogs called after the fiercest beasts of prey.

Quod fremat in terris violentius. Ergo cavebis
Et metues, ne tu sic Creticus aut Camerinus.
His ego quem monui? tecum est mihi sermo, Rubelli
Blande. Tumes alto Drusorum stemmate, tamquam   40
Feceris ipse aliquid, propter quod nobilis esses,
Ut te conciperet quae sanguine fulget Iuli,
Non quae ventoso conducta sub aggere texit.
"Vos humiles," inquis, "vulgi pars ultima nostri,
Quorum nemo queat patriam monstrare parentis: 45
Ast ego Cecropides!" Vivas et originis hujus
Gaudia longa feras: tamen ima plebe Quiritem
Facundum invenies; solet hic defendere causas
Nobilis indocti; veniet de plebe togata,
Qui juris nodos et legum aenigmata solvat.   50
Hic petit Euphraten juvenis domitique Batavi
Custodes Aquilas, armis industrius; at tu
Nil nisi Cecropides truncoque simillimus Hermae

---

38 **Creticus**] A. Caecilius Metellus reduced Crete in 68, 67 B.C., was deprived of his command, under the Gabinian law, by Pompeius, and kept waiting for his triumph till 62.—*Camerinus*, an old family of the Sulpicii, who revived under the empire.—*Sic*, P. has *si*, the other MSS. *sis*.

39 **Rubelli Blande**] Rubellius Plautus, son of Julia and Rubellius Blandus, was a man of high character slain by Nero. His son may have been empty-headed, and resumed his grandfather's cognomen; and Juvenal may have confounded him with his father; but I suspect the passage was written on Rubellius Plautus, as he is treated as a contemporary of Nero, and that *Blande* is an after-thought, like *Marius* (inf. 120), as the greater part of the satire would have much more point when the memory of Nero was fresh.

43] "A woman hired to weave under the mound of Servius;" there was no room for a loom in her lodgings.

47 **Quiritem facundum**] "With the eloquence of a Roman."

49 **Nobilis indocti**] "Of a noble, because he is unlearned."

— **plebe togata**] Cf. "Romanos rerum dominos gentemque togatam." After all, the commons are citizens.

50] Contrast with *armis industrius*, inf. 52.

— **solvat**] Students of law in their fourth year were called Lytae, in their fifth Prolytae.

51 **domiti**] After the war of Civilis, A.D. 69, 70.

53] The *Hermae* are revered in Attica; hence Juvenal gives *Cecropides* as a title of *Attic* nobility.
— *Trunco*, the man is a mere block, without hands or feet, he can go nowhere and do nothing.

Nullo quippe alio vincis discrimine, quam quod
Illi marmoreum caput est, tua vivit imago.   55
Dic mihi, Teucrorum proles, animalia muta
Quis generosa putet, nisi fortia? nempe volucrem
Sic laudamus equum, facili cui plurima palma
Fervet et exsultat rauco victoria Circo.
Nobilis hic, quocunque venit de gramine, cujus   60
Clara fuga ante alios et primus in aequore pulvis:
Sed venale pecus Corythae posteritas et
Hirpini, si rara jugo victoria sedit.
Nil ibi majorum respectus, gratia nulla
Umbrarum: dominis pretiis mutare jubentur   65
Exiguis, trito ducunt epirhedia collo
Segnipedes, dignique molam versare Nepotis.
Ergo ut miremur te, non tua, primum aliquid da,
Quod possim titulis incidere, praeter honores,
Quos illis damus et dedimus, quibus omnia debes.   70
    Haec satis ad juvenem, quem nobis fama superbum
Tradit et inflatum plenumque Nerone propinquo:

---

55 **tua vivit imago**] Almost "your
'frontispiece' is alive for the present."
Juvenal means that there is no more
in the man than in the waxen mask
of him that will be put up in due
course with the others in the hall of
the family mansion.

56 **Teucrorum proles**] Cf. "Ipsos
Trojugenas" (i. 100).

62 **Corythae**] It is not certain
whether the Scholiast read 'Coryphaei,' or whether he meant that
Corytha was of the best Greek, and
Hirpinus of a Sabine stock.   A
Paris MS., of the tenth century,
and a Roman read 'Coryphaei;' it
would be a natural guess if the
copyist read the Scholiast.

63 **Hirpini**] Grandson of Aquilo,
who won 130 races to Hirpinus'
113. Cf. vii. 114, n.

66 **epirhedia**] Quintilian notices

that neither Gauls nor Greeks use
this compound.   The Scholiast from
the etymology infers that it means
ornaments of the *rheda*, but it must
mean harness. With us broken-
down bloodhorses would pass to the
cabstand and the knacker's yard, not
to the stage coach (to which *rheda*
answers) or the mill.

68 **primum**] So the MSS. Sal-
maise conjecturally *privum*.

70 **Quos dedimus**] The offices
are granted on their account to you
as they were granted to them.

71 **fama**] 'Report.' Juvenal had
never come in contact with him. He
lived alone "casta et secreta domo,"
Tac. *Ann.* xiv. 22.

72 **Nerone propinquo**] Nero was
a discreditable relation to be proud
of, and Rubellius had nothing else.

Rarus enim ferme sensus communis in illa
Fortuna. Sed te censeri laude tuorum,
Pontice, noluerim sic, ut nihil ipse futurae 75
Laudis agas. Miserum est aliorum incumbere famae,
Ne collapsa ruant subductis tecta columnis.
Stratus humi palmes viduas desiderat ulmos.
Esto bonus miles, tutor bonus, arbiter idem
Integer; ambiguae si quando citabere testis 80
Incertaeque rei, Phalaris licet imperet, ut sis
Falsus, et admoto dictet perjuria tauro :
Summum crede nefas animam praeferre pudori
Et propter vitam vivendi perdere causas.
Dignus morte perit, coenet licet ostrea centum 85
Gaurana et Cosmi toto mergatur aheno.
Exspectata diu tandem provincia quum te
Rectorem accipiet, pone irae fraena modumque,
Pone et avaritiae : miserere inopum sociorum ;
Ossa vides regum vacuis exsucta medullis. 90
Respice, quid moneant leges, quid curia mandet,
Praemia quanta bonos maneant, quam fulmine justo
Et Capito et Numitor ruerint, damnante Senatu,
Piratae Cilicum. Sed quid damnatio confert?
Praeconem, Chaerippe tuis circumspice pannis, 95

73] "As a general rule, fellow-feeling is rare in that rank."

75 **Pontice**] Probably some definite person, perhaps Creticus, sup. 38: other proper names disguised on the same principle are Lesbia for Clodia in Catullus; Cynthia for Hostia in Propertius; probably Licymnia for Terentia in Horace *Od.* II. xii. 13.

76, 77] "It is miserable to rest on the fame of others; for then you have to fear, lest the building should collapse and come down when the columns are withdrawn."

78] The elm is the bride which the vine embraces with effusion.

85 **perit**] "Is already dead."

87 **Exspectata diu**] The noble has been counting on it from the cradle.

91 **curia**] must refer to some standing rule of the senate (see inf. 127, n.), as even the senatorial governors got their orders from the emperor.

93 **Capito**] was condemned by Thrasea's influence in 57, and accused Thrasea with fatal effect in 66.

94 **Piratae Cilicum**] "Spoliatores latronum" (Schol.). The allusion is to the piracy suppressed by Pompeius, which had its head-quarters in Cilicia.

Quum Pansa eripiat, quidquid tibi Natta reliquit,
Jamque tace : furor est post omnia perdere naulum.
Non idem gemitus olim, neque vulnus erat par
Damnorum, sociis florentibus et modo victis.
Plena domus tunc omnis, et ingens stabat acervus   100
Nummorum, Spartana chlamys, conchylia Coa,
Et cum Parrhasii tabulis signisque Myronis
Phidiacum vivebat ebur ; nec non Polycleti
Multus ubique labor ; rarae sine Mentore mensae.
Inde Dolabellae atque hinc Antonius, inde   105
Sacrilegus Verres : referebant navibus altis
Occulta spolia et plures de pace triumphos.

95, 96 **Pansa**] A Marian family, raised by Caesar.—*Natta*, an old cognomen of an obscure family of the gens Pinaria. Juvenal would know it from the snob in Horace. Probably, "When the noble governor robs you of what the plebeian left, relieve yourself by putting up your rags to auction, to get the money for a voyage to Rome. When you've got it, don't be such a fool as go." I give the MS. order: some ed. transpose 95, 96. The Scholiast thinks the object of the sale is simply to live on the proceeds.

101 **Spartana**] For the dye.—*Coa* for the material. The discovery of unravelling silk stuffs and weaving them up more loosely, was made in Ceos, according to Pliny, who adds, that there are silk-worms in Cos (*H. N.* xi. 20).

105 **Dolabellae**] A conjecture founded on the fact that P. has 'Dolabella est,' and most MSS. omit *est*. If so, the sense will be, "The Dolabellas on this side, and Antonius on that." The Dolabellas are Cneius, consul B.C. 81, prosecuted by Caesar B.C. 77 for extortion in Macedonia, and acquitted; Cneius, praetor 81, prosecuted B.C. 78 for extortion in Cilicia and condemned. Publius, Cicero's son-in-

law, consul B.C. 44, shewed great rapacity on his route to Syria. *Antonius*, the brother of the orator and uncle of the triumvir, consul B.C. 63: condemned after his return from the government of Macedonia.

106 **Verres**] A retainer of Sulla, who governed Sicily during the revolt of Spartacus: it was convenient to the government that he should raise as large a revenue from the province as possible: he did raise a large revenue ; but his administration was so cynically reckless that his was selected as the test case to support the measure of transferring the *judicia* from the exclusive possession of the Senate. Cf. *Verr.* Act. ii. iv. 25, where Cicero winds up a story of L. Piso Frugi with the remark,—"Nimirum ut hic [Verres] nomen suum comprobavit, sic ille [Piso] cognomen," which proves that Verres had no gentile name ; for if he had, Verres would not have ceased to be his primary cognomen, because Frugi was the secondary cognomen of Piso.—*Altis*, "loaded with high piles of plunder"?

107 **spolia**] "Spolium est quicquid de hostibus tollitur" (Serv. *ad Aen.* viii. 202).—*De pace*, 'de pacatis.'

Nunc sociis juga pauca boum, grex parvus equarum,
Et pater armenti capto eripietur agello ;
Ipsi deinde Lares, si quod spectabile signum,   110
Si quis in aedicula Deus unicus. Haec etenim sunt
Pro summis : nam sunt haec maxima. Despicias tu
Forsitan imbelles Rhodios unctamque Corinthum :
Despicias merito. Quid resinata juventus,
Cruraque totius facient tibi levia gentis ?   115
Horrida vitanda est Hispania, Gallicus axis
Illyricumque latus : parce et messoribus illis
Qui saturant urbem, Circo scenaeque vacantem.
Quanta autem inde feres tam dirae praemia culpae,
Quum tenues nuper Marius discinxerit Afros !   120
Curandum imprimis, ne magna injuria fiat
Fortibus et miseris : tollas licet omne, quod usquam est

108, sqq.] According to Finlay, continental Greece was never so depressed as under the Flavian dynasty; any considerable native there, or in the flourishing cities of Asia, bought or begged the franchise, so that there were no new rich Greek families to gild the decay of old ones.

109 capto agello] From the patch of land, and that is presently taken too.

110 Lares] The Greeks had nothing quite like the Lares.

111 Si quis in aedicula Deus unicus] A natural and spirited continuation of Lares, eked out with metrical stopgaps; hence some treat 111, 112 as spurious.

113 Rhodios] They presented the same combination of political prudence and dignity with social laxity as Venice in the latter part of her independence.

115] "A whole nation of smooth legs."

116 Horrida] Contr. resinata.

— Gallicus axis] As we might say 'the air of Gaul,' though the metaphor is a little different ; axis is properly any diameter of the earth and the concentric firmament, then the point of the firmament at which such diameter terminates, and so generally the sky above any place or country.

119 dirae] Because by plundering Africa you starve Rome.

120 discinxerit] A sort of apron would be their only covering.

122—124] "Though you take away all their gold and silver, and leave only shield, and sword, and helm, and dart, yet they are not destitute, — spoliatis arma supersunt," which is the phrase Juvenal was working up to, and afraid of having set down as a 'sententia,' i.e. a rhetorical commonplace. It is clear from Tacitus, Dial. de Oratoribus, that in the age of Juvenal and indeed earlier, oratory at Rome had degenerated into a knack of bandying such epigrammatic aphorisms. The courts had grown impatient of anything like an exposition of the facts of the case. They preferred that a

Auri atque argenti, scutum gladiumque relinquas
Et jacula et galeam, spoliatis arma supersunt.

Quod modo proposui, non est sententia : verum   125
Credite me vobis folium recitare Sibyllae.
Si tibi sancta cohors comitum, si nemo tribunal
Vendit Acersecomes, si nullum in conjuge crimen,
Nec per conventus et cuncta per oppida curvis
Unguibus ire parat nummos raptura Celaeno :   130
Tunc licet a Pico numeres genus, altaque si te
Nomina delectant, omnem Titanida pugnam
Inter majores ipsumque Promethea ponas :
De quocunque voles proavum tibi sumito libro.
Quod si praecipitem rapit ambitio atque libido,   135
Si frangis virgas sociorum in sanguine, si te
Delectant hebetes lasso lictore secures :

speaker should assume their knowledge of these or leave them to glean what knowledge they wanted from the evidence. What they liked was to have a series of plausible presumptions laid before them on which they could make up their minds. I give the Scholiast's reading, which, from its difficulty, has disappeared from all but one MS. of the ninth century. P. and several others have *relinquens*, the majority *relinques*, which gives an opportunity to whoever likes to improve Juvenal by omitting 124. I suspect P. originally had *tollat* with *injuria* as nom., as the corrector had to erase a letter to make room for *s*. Of course, if so, 124 must be as old as both P.'s variants.

126 folium] It seems that the Sibylline books consisted of packets of loose leaves, and that the way of consulting them was to take a leaf at random from the packet, and infer or invent the application of its contents to the emergency of the moment.

127 cohors comitum] Both words

are technical, as we might speak of a *suite* of *attachés*.

128] "Severus Caecina censuit (A.D. 21) ne quem magistratum cui provincia obvenisset uxor comitaretur...cogitarent ipsi quoties repetundarum aliqui arguerentur plura uxoribus objectari" (Tac. *Ann.* iii. § 33. Cf. 91 n.).

129 Nec...oppida] Note the climax. She is not content with the pickings she can make in the few towns in which her husband holds courts and transacts business; she goes the rounds of all.

131 a Pico] A pedigree ending in Picus might be a genuine tradition; one that included all the Titans, and all the first generation of Olympians, must be a concession to vanity. —*Numeres*, 'Αμφότεροι δ' ἀριθμεῦνται ἐς ἔσχατον 'Ηρακλῆα (Theoc. *Id.* xvii. 27).

133 ipsumque Promethea] is ironical. All mankind were made of clay, so this would be a genuine ancestor.

137 hebetes lasso lictore] Cf. "assiduo ruptae lectore," i. 13 n.

Incipit ipsorum contra te stare parentum
Nobilitas, claramque facem praeferre pudendis.
Omne animi vitium tanto conspectius in se   140
Crimen habet, quanto major qui peccat habetur.
Quo mihi, te solitum falsas signare tabellas
In templis, quae fecit avus, statuamque parentis
Ante triumphalem? quo, si nocturnus adulter
Tempora Santonico velas adoperta cucullo?   145
Praeter majorum cineres atque ossa volucri
Carpento rapitur pinguis Lateranus, et ipse,
Ipse rotam adstringit multo sufflamine Consul;
Nocte quidem: sed luna videt, sed sidera testes
Intendunt oculos.   Finitum tempus honoris   150
Quum fuerit, clara Lateranus luce flagellum
Sumet, et occursum nusquam trepidabit amici
Jam senis, ac virga prior annuet, atque maniplos
Solvet, et infundet jumentis hordea lassis.
Interea dum lanatas robumque juvencum   155

142] "What do I care that you had an ancestor who built temples for you to seal forged wills in, after abstracting the true?" Hor. *Ep.* I. v. 12, Quo mihi fortunam, si non conceditur uti? Cf. Ov. *Am.* III. iv. 41, Quo tibi formosam si non nisi casta placebat? In this construction the accusative comes to be practically the same as the nominative; it is the subject of one verb generally imaginary in the infinitive, which, with its subject, depends on the third person present indicative of another imaginary verb. Nor can we say that the Romans *understood* either the verb in the infinitive or the verb in the indicative in the sense that it was potentially present to their thoughts as a known element, fixed though latent.

147 **Carpento**] His low tastes do not prevent his being effeminate.

148 **sufflamine**] "Vinculum ferreum quod inter radios mittitur."

149 **testes**] may be either nom. or acc.

152 **nusquam**] "Not even in the most public place."

153 **Jam senis**] "Though quite an old man."   Once he kept Lateranus in countenance and shared his folly.

154 **hordea**] A plural condemned by Quintilian (i. 5, § 15), used by Verg. (*G.* i. 210), whereon Bavius and Maevius: "Hordea qui dixit superest ut tritica dicat."

155—157] "While in office he goes through the archaic forms with archaic victims (so *robumque juvencum*).   Even then he swears by his horsy goddess." *Robum* is from the Scholiast.   Three MSS. retain traces of it: other readings are 'rursus' and 'torvum.'

More Numae caedit Jovis ante altaria, jurat
Solam Eponam et facies olida ad praesepia pictas.
Sed quum pervigiles placet instaurare popinas,
Obvius assiduo Syrophoenix udus amomo
Currit, Idumaeae Syrophoenix incola portae,   160
Hospitis affectu dominum regemque salutat,
Et cum venali Cyane succincta lagena.

   Defensor culpae dicet mihi, "Fecimus et nos
Haec juvenes." Esto. Desisti nempe, nec ultra
Fovisti errorem. Breve sit, quod turpiter audes;   165
Quaedam cum prima resecentur crimina barba;
Indulge veniam pueris: Lateranus ad illos
Thermarum calices inscriptaque lintea vadit,
Maturus bello, Armeniae Syriaeque tuendis

157 **facies**] This is the only way in which Juvenal can identify the other objects of Lateranus' worship; he has not cared to remember their names, but he knows their images are painted up over the mangers.

158 **popinas**] They may have had hot baths attached, as Mayor infers from Thermae (inf. 168); but they would not be called after the great Thermae, more likely Thermarum = Thermopoliorum.

160 **Idumaeae — portae**] Some suppose a pass in Phoenicia: so "Albana porta" (Val. Flacc. iii. 497); others the arch of Titus.

162 **succincta**] "Ready both to wait and dance."

163, 164] "I may be told we did the same too when we were young. Be it so; you have given it up now, you mean to say." So Mayor.

167 **Lateranus**] A noble, who perished in the conspiracy of Piso, bore this name: he had had an intrigue with Messalina.

168 **Thermarum**] It would be luxurious, but not low, to drink at the baths; hence *lintea* is not likely to mean 'towel.' Cf. sup. 158 n.—

Inscriptaque lintea: "Hoc est pictis velis popinae accedit aut linteis capsariciis tergitur" (Schol.). According to the first view, Lateranus, as he was lounging aimlessly along, saw the awning with its advertisement of the accommodation within, and he goes up to profit by it. Orelli, *Corpus Inscript.* N. 4329, gives one of these advertisements from Lyons. Mercurius hic lucrum promittit Apollo salutem: Septumanus hospitium cum prandio. Qui venerit melius utetur. Post, hospes ubi maneas, prospice. This tavern offered facilities for play, kept an *iatralipta.* After arriving there the traveller could spend the evening, and sleep (for one night only) and get his breakfast before looking out for permanent quarters. According to the second view, instead of eating his dinner like a gentleman with a clean napkin of his own, or his host's, Lateranus uses napkins out of a greasy *capsa*, marked with the eating-house mark to prevent them from being stolen by discreditable customers.

169 **Armeniae Syriaeque**] The scene of Corbulo's campaigns.

Amnibus et Rheno atque Istro. Praestare Neronem   170
Securum valet haec aetas. Mitte Ostia, Caesar,
Mitte: sed in magna legatum quaere popina;
Invenies aliquo cum percussore jacentem,
Permixtum nautis et furibus ac fugitivis,
Inter carnifices et fabros sandapilarum   175
Et resupinati cessantia tympana Galli.
Aequa ibi libertas, communia pocula, lectus
Non alius cuiquam, nec mensa remotior ulli.
Quid facias talem sortitus, Pontice, servum?
Nempe in Lucanos aut Tusca ergastula mittas.   180
At vos, Trojugenae, vobis ignoscitis, et quae
Turpia cerdoni, Volesos Brutumque decebunt.
Quid, si nunquam adeo foedis adeoque pudendis
Utimur exemplis, ut non pejora supersint?
Consumtis opibus vocem, Damasippe, locasti   185
Sipario, clamosum ageres ut Phasma Catulli.
Laureolum velox etiam bene Lentulus egit,
Judice me dignus vera cruce. Nec tamen ipsi
Ignoscas populo: populi frons durior hujus,
Qui sedet et spectat triscurria patriciorum,   190
Planipedes audit Fabios, ridere potest qui

171 **Ostia**] "The mouths of the rivers to be defended."

176 **resupinati**] He is drunk, and in an indecent attitude, but without an indecent purpose. — *Cessantia,* simply "idle."

180 **Lucanos**] sc. campos. Etruria was the first part of Italy to adopt the system of cultivating estates by large gangs of slaves; the same system took firm root in Lucania, where the Sabellian aristocracy threw themselves into the arms of Rome rather than loosen their hold on their serfs. In the central parts of Italy slaves were still to a certain extent regarded as members of the household.

182 **Volesus**] Ancestor of the Valerii or Volesii.

185 **Damasippe**] Merely a name for a ruined noble.

187 **etiam bene**] He does not merely act like Damasippus, he ever acts well.

— **Lentulus**] This is not Lentulus, who wrote mimes, as Tertullian says that Laureolus was by Catullus too. Laureolus, according to Josephus, was a robber chief, crucified on the stage.

189 **populi frons durior hujus**] Cf. N.T., *Rom.* i. 32 ad finem.

190 **triscurria**] "The triple buffooneries."

191 **Planipedes**] Barefoot, like

Mamercorum alapas. Quanti sua funera vendant,
Quid refert? Vendunt nullo cogente Nerone,
Nec dubitant celsi praetoris vendere ludis.
Finge tamen gladios inde, atque hinc pulpita pone: 195
Quid satius? Mortem sic quisquam exhorruit, ut sit
Zelotypus Thymeles, stupidi collega Corinthi?
Res haud mira tamen, citharoedo Principe, mimus
Nobilis. Haec ultra quid erit, nisi ludus? Et illud
Dedecus urbis habes: nec mirmillonis in armis,   200
Nec clypeo Gracchum pugnantem aut falce supina.
(Damnat enim tales habitus; et damnat et odit)
Nec galea faciem abscondit; movet ecce tridentem,
Postquam librata pendentia retia dextra

the actors in mimes, while in comedy the slipper was worn, in tragedy the buskin.—*Fabios*, "*a* Fabius," not the Fabii.

192—195] Perhaps the least objectionable explanation of 'funera' is one suggested to me by the late Mr Robinson, of Queen's College, Oxford—"these stage executions," referring to 188, sup., which would be certain, but that we have had *triscurria patriciorum, planipedes Fabios*, and *Mamercorum alapas* between. Madvig thinks it means, "They sell not themselves, they are dead to honour, but the corpse of the patriciate," which is very difficult; other possible guesses are, "their right to honourable burial," or "their death on the arena;" but he is or ought to be speaking of the circus, which, by-the-bye, is not the place for mimes; the climax seems to be, if anything can be made out certainly, the theatre, the circus, the arena.

194 celsi] "His eminence," like *honorati*, "his honour;" at least, *celsitudo* is a title in the Theodosian code, but Madvig compares

"curribus altis
Exstantem, et medio sublimem in
   pulvere Circi." (x. 36, 37.)

196 **Quid**] For *utrum;* the substitution is the exception in Latin, the rule in modern English.

197] "To pretend jealousy of a profligate actress in the same play as a rascally buffoon"—*stupidus* was frequently a husband, it is the lover who was jealous. *Corinthi* must be the name of the husband in the play. *Thymele* was the wife or mistress of *Latinus* (cf. i. 36).

199 ludus] 'Gladiatorius;' though people who wish to think of the arena in 192, try here to make what is plain uncertain.

200 **mirmillo**] The Gallic name of the fish on the helmet of the opponent of the 'retiarius,' who sang, "Non te peto, piscem peto, quid me fugis, Galle?"

201—203] "He does not fight as Gallus, or as Thrax; he objects to their dress and won't hide his face; the trident is his weapon."

202 **damnat et odit**] The point is "he always speaks against that dress and he is quite sincere."

Nequidquam effudit, nudum ad spectacula vultum 205
Erigit et tota fugit agnoscendus arena.
Credamus tunicae; de faucibus aurea quum se
Porrigat et longo jactetur spira galero.
Ergo ignominiam graviorem pertulit omni
Vulnere cum Graccho jussus pugnare sequutor. 210
   Libera si dentur populo suffragia, quis tam
Perditus, ut dubitet Senecam praeferre Neroni;
Cujus supplicio non debuit una parari
Simia, nec serpens unus, nec culeus unus?
Par Agamemnonidae crimen; sed causa facit rem 215
Dissimilem. Quippe ille Deis auctoribus ultor
Patris erat caesi media inter pocula: sed nec
Electrae jugulo se polluit aut Spartani
Sanguine conjugii; nullis aconita propinquis
Miscuit, in scena nunquam cantavit Orestes, 220
Troica non scripsit. Quid enim Verginius armis
Debuit ulcisci magis, aut cum Vindice Galba?

205 **spectacula**] Literally here, "seeing places;" i. e., the benches of the amphitheatre.

207, 208] "We are to believe that we see one of the Salii, when we recognize the golden strings of the bonnet;" a 'retiarius' *might* wear a rich tunic, hence the embroidery on that, though evidence of rank, needs support.

209, 210] It is degrading to be known to fight an amateur, since amateurs must be degraded to fight.

211, 212] "Suppose the people free to choose, is any abandoned enough to hesitate about preferring the Spaniard to the descendant of Julius?"

213 **una**] He was guilty of double parricide by conniving at the death of his adoptive father, and by procuring that of his mother, not

to count wives, aunts, or stepbrother.

217 **media inter pocula**] The Homeric, not the Aeschylean story. The former has the advantage of suiting the death of Claudius, which it might be imagined Nero had to avenge on Agrippina, but for the differences in favour of Orestes which Juvenal proceeds to point out; he did not kill Electra or Hermione, as Nero did Octavia and Antonia, his sisters, and Octavia and Poppaea, his wives.

221] Verginius directed that his epitaph should run—

"Hic situs est Rufus pulso qui
   Vindice quondam
Imperium asseruit non sibi sed
   patriae."

Ten years after his death it was still neglected.

Quid Nero tam saeva crudaque tyrannide fecit?
Haec opera atque hae sunt generosi Principis artes,
Gaudentis foedo peregrina ad pulpita cantu   225
Prostitui, Graiaeque apium meruisse coronae.
Majorum effigies habeant insignia vocis :
Ante pedes Domiti longum tu pone Thyestae
Syrma vel Antigones, seu personam Menalippes,
Et de marmoreo citharam suspende colosso.   230
Quid, Catilina, tuis natalibus atque Cethegi
Inveniet quisquam sublimius? Arma tamen vos
Nocturna et flammas domibus templisque parastis,
Ut Braccatorum pueri Senonumque minores,

223 **Quid**] So all the MSS. Madvig conjectures *quod*, which gives a completer sense; *quid* may have caught Juvenal's ear, or the copyist's. "What called more for armed vengeance, what deed of Nero in that savage and brutal tyranny?"

226 **apium**] He selects the Nemean games, not as most characteristic of Nero, but as having the paltriest prize. Nero did not feel that he was a sovereign playing the buffoon to his subjects; in theory he was the first citizen who might claim to prove himself first in grace as in power, or else a god superior to human prejudices. No existing religion was popular or more sincere than Caesarism, and nobody was better qualified than Caesar to judge of its truth.

227 **insignia vocis**] The trophies of a vocalist.

228 **pedes Domiti**] The feet of a Domitius, so *marmoreo colosso* (inf. 230). Nero's own Colossus on the vestibule of the golden house was, of brass and 120 feet high; so a lyre would have looked ridiculous on it, even to Nero.

229 **Antigones**] On whom he wrote a tragedy.—*Personam*, gene-

rally copied from his own features, or those of his reigning mistress.

231 **Catilina**] L. Sergius Catilina, a fascinating and bountiful profligate, had profited by the licence of Sulla's proscription, after which he became the leader of the *populares;* and after being twice rejected as a candidate for the consulship, was driven into formal rebellion by the persevering exertions of Cicero (who had left the *populares* and wanted a bugbear to consolidate a party of order out of the senate and knights), while he (Catilina) was busy with preparations (probably alternative) for a third canvass and for a night riot on a grand scale in which the means once so effective against the Gracchi might be employed to avenge them. When Catilina had left Rome, his partisans compromised their cause still further by an intrigue with the Allobroges, whose ambassadors were at Rome, and easily gained by Cicero. The whole narrative illustrates the desperate condition from which the popular party was raised by Clodius and Caesar. *Cethegus* was a Cornelius.

234 **Braccatorum**] Opp. *togatorum.* It was the first Roman name for the inhabitants of the Narbonese.

Ausi, quod liceat tunica punire molesta. 235
Sed vigilat consul vexillaque vestra coercet.
Hic novus Arpinas, ignobilis et modo Romae
Municipalis eques, galeatum ponit ubique
Praesidium attonitis, et in omni monte laborat.
Tantum igitur muros intra toga contulit illi 240
Nominis et tituli, quantum non Leucade, quantum
Thessaliae campis Octavius abstulit udo
Caedibus assiduis gladio. Sed Roma parentem,
Roma Patrem Patriae Ciceronem libera dixit.
Arpinas alius Volscorum in monte solebat 245
Poscere mercedes, alieno lassus aratro;
Nodosam post haec frangebat vertice vitem,
Si lentus pigra muniret castra dolabra:
Hic tamen et Cimbros et summa pericula rerum
Excipit, et solus trepidantem protegit urbem; 250

Their conduct, unworthy of Roman patricians, became their barbarian allies and the descendants of those who sacked Rome.

235 tunica—molesta] The pitched shirt in which Nero burnt the Christians, and criminals were burnt to represent Hercules on Oeta.

239 omni monte] All the hills of Rome.

240—244 non Leucade] So the majority of MSS. including the corrector of P. The scholiast and P. and some others read *in*. Jahn conjectures *sibi*, which suits sense, grammar and metre; *in* suits the sense, but presents visible metrical and undeniable grammatical difficulties; if we read *non* we must suppose that Juvenal made a not wholly successful attempt to say that Octavian owed the high title of *pater patriae* not, as his flatterers pretended, to his victory over the apostate Roman who had leagued himself

with Cleopatra, but to his success in destroying the last republican army at Philippi.

Both Octavian and Cicero were hailed *pater patriae;* but in Cicero's case it was the voice of Rome, not of a distant battle-field; of peace, not of war; of liberty, not of slavery.—*Thessaliae campis.* The Romans believed that the battles of Philippi were fought on the same ground as Pharsalia, from the ambiguity of *bis* and *iterum*, and the inaccurate use of Aemathia (Verg. *Geor.* i. 489, 491).

247, 248] When the verb which expresses the condition is in the subjunctive, and the principal verb is the indicative, the principal clause is really independent. The conditional clause is added as a correction, and implies a suppressed apodosis also in the subjunctive: *dolabra* would be used to point the stakes for the *vallum*.

Atque ideo, postquam ad Cimbros stragemque volabant
Qui nunquam attigerant majora cadavera corvi,
Nobilis ornatur lauro collega secunda.
Plebeiae Deciorum animae, plebeia fuerunt
Nomina: pro totis legionibus hi tamen et pro   255
Omnibus auxiliis atque omni pube Latina
Sufficiunt Dis infernis Terraeque parenti:
Pluris enim Decii, quae quae servantur ab illis.
Ancilla natus trabeam et diadema Quirini
Et fasces meruit, regum ultimus ille bonorum.   260
Prodita laxabant portarum claustra tyrannis
Exsulibus juvenes ipsius Consulis et quos
Magnum aliquid dubia pro libertate deceret,
Quod miraretur cum Coclite Mucius et quae
Imperii fines, Tiberinum, virgo natavit.   265
Occulta ad Patres produxit crimina servus,
Matronis lugendus: at illos verbera justis
Afficiunt poenis et legum prima securis.
    Malo pater tibi sit Thersites, dummodo tu sis
Aeacidae similis Vulcaniaque arma capessas,   270
Quam te Thersitae similem producat Achilles.

253] This is an instance of Juvenal's unreality. The soldiers insisted that Catulus should share the triumph.

256 omni pube Latina] One does not know whether this is a zeugma or a blunder. The devotion of the elder Decius was to secure the *destruction* of the Latins. *Pubes* is related to chivalry, as *ingenuus* to gentleman.

259 trabeam] The striped mantle is always attributed to Romulus; the toga, with trimmings or embroidery, to Tullus or the Tarquins.

261 laxabant] "Were for opening."

265 Imperii fines] Juvenal does not mean that the dominion of Rome had fallen back from the Ciminian hills (or whatever was the frontier under the last king) to the Tiber, the contrast is between the Tiber and the Rhine.—*Tiberinum natavit,* as we say 'swam the Tiber.'

267, 268] He deserved the honours paid to Brutus, whose sons deserved death and servile stripes.—*Legum prima securis.* Cf. Liv. ii. 1: "Imperia legum potentiora quam hominum."

Et tamen, ut longe repetas longeque revolvas
Nomen, ab infami gentem deducis asylo.
Majorum primus quisquis fuit ille tuorum,
Aut pastor fuit aut illud, quod dicere nolo.   275

272 **tamen**] Although nobility is worth so little, no Roman nobility can be considered genuine.
275 **pastor**] And therefore had helped Romulus to found the asylum, if he did not actually use it.

SATIRA X.

OMNIBUS in terris, quae sunt a Gadibus usque
Auroram et Gangen, pauci dignoscere possunt
Vera bona atque illis multum diversa, remota
Erroris nebula. Quid enim ratione timemus
Aut cupimus? quid tam dextro pede concipis, ut te   5
Conatus non poeniteat votique peracti?
Evertere domos totas optantibus ipsis
Di faciles; nocitura toga, nocitura petuntur
Militia; torrens dicendi copia multis
Et sua mortifera est facundia; viribus ille   10
Confisus periit admirandusque lacertis.
Sed plures nimia congesta pecunia cura
Strangulat, et cuncta exsuperans patrimonia census,
Quanto delphinis balaena Britannica major.
    Temporibus diris igitur jussuque Neronis   15
Longinum et magnos Senecae praedivitis hortos

---

4 **ratione**] *Cum* is generally prefixed to the ablative of manner,
except when, as here, it borders on
the ablative of instrument, or when,
as in the next line, being accompanied by an adjective or pronoun,
it approximates to the so-called
ablative absolute.

8—11] *Toga* and *militia* are general: we have an instance corresponding to each, many perish by their
eloquence, another (Milo of Croton)
by trusting in his strength.—*Admirandusque* if wrong is a simple blunder retained by the perverse predi-

lection of some copyists: most MSS.
have *admirandisque*, which, if a
conjecture, is not too obvious to be
plausible.

12 **nimia—cura**] Closely connected both with *congesta* and
strangulat.

14 **Britannica**] Note that whales
were once common in our seas.

15 **igitur**] Introduces instances of
what might be expected under the
general rule laid down above.

16 **Longinum**] C. Cassius, the
jurist, banished by Nero to Sardinia,
because he was a man of high stand-

Clausit, et egregias Lateranorum obsidet aedes
Tota cohors : rarus venit in coenacula miles.
Pauca licet portes argenti vascula puri,
Nocte iter ingressus gladium contumque timebis   20
Et motae ad lunam trepidabis arundinis umbram :
Cantabit vacuus coram latrone viator.
Prima fere vota et cunctis notissima templis
Divitiae, crescant ut opes, ut maxima toto
Nostra sit arca foro. Sed nulla aconita bibuntur   25
Fictilibus : tunc illa time, quum pocula sumes
Gemmata et lato Setinum ardebit in auro.
Jamne igitur laudas, quod de sapientibus alter
Ridebat, quoties de limine moverat unum
Protuleratque pedem ; flebat contrarius auctor?   30
Sed facilis cuivis rigidi censura cachinni :
Mirandum est, unde ille oculis suffecerit humor.
Perpetuo risu pulmonem agitare solebat
Democritus, quanquam non esset urbibus illis

ing in open opposition : he kept in his house a bust of Cassius the Conspirator inscribed Dux Partium, as if that were the highest title of a man whom Caesar had made praetor; he was recalled by Vespasian.

17 **Lateranorum**] Cf. viii. 147.

18 **Tota cohors**] To measure their size.—*Coenacula*, contr. "egregias aedes—magnos hortos."

19] "Though you have not much plate, and that worth very little."

20 **contum**] Is generally taken as 'pike,' which seems a curious unhandy weapon for a robber. It might mean you are afraid of the robber's sword and the ferry-man's pole (lest he should turn robber for the nonce and knock you down with it), and look for the sword that casts the shadow when it was only a reed moving in the moonlight.

24 **Divitiae—opes**] Distinguished by Cic. *Lael.* § 22, Divitiae ut utare ;

opes ut colare; but *divitiae* includes *opes.*

27 **ardebit**] "Will glow," certainly used of fiery wine; possibly of sparkling wine, as the Scholiast thought here.

28 **Jamne**] Well after this do you still praise [the common sense of the world] which one of the wise men was always laughing at as soon as he had stirred a step to go outside his door, while it made the authority on the other side cry?

30 **auctor**] So P., and two other MSS.: the rest *alter.* "There is Heraclitus' authority for crying at mankind : where is your authority for admiring their taste?"

31 **rigidi cachinni**] "A grim chuckle," "a dry chuckle."

34 **esset**] In the subjunctive because there is still a reference to what Juvenal's contemporaries might be supposed to think of Democritus.

Praetexta et trabeae, fasces, lectica, tribunal,   35
Quid, si vidisset praetorem curribus altis
Exstantem et medio sublimem in pulvere Circi,
In tunica Jovis, et pictae Sarrana ferentem
Ex humeris aulaea togae, magnaeque coronae
Tantum orbem, quanto cervix non sufficit ulla?   40
Quippe tenet sudans hanc publicus, et, sibi Consul
Ne placeat, curru servus portatur eodem.
Da nunc et volucrem, sceptro quae surgit eburno,
Illinc cornicines, hinc praecedentia longi
Agminis officia et niveos ad fraena Quirites,   45
Defossa in loculis quos sportula fecit amicos.
Tum quoque materiam risus invenit ad omnes
Occursus hominum, cujus prudentia monstrat
Summos posse viros et magna exempla daturos
Vervecum in patria crassoque sub aere nasci.   50

35] These details are mentioned not as more ridiculous in themselves than anything Democritus had seen in Greece, but because Democritus regarded all human life as a farce, and at Rome the farce was more elaborate. *Lectica* refers to the procession of clients who accompanied it; *tribunal* to the display of empty eloquence before it.

36, sqq.] "What would he have said of the praetor's triumphal procession from the Capitol to the Circus?" The triumphal dress suggests the idea of triumph, and this *consul* (inf. 41).

38 **tunica Jovis**] Whom he personated, hence the eagle on his sceptre. The tunic was so costly that it was not till the third century that a private person possessed one of his own, even the emperors when they triumphed supplied themselves from the treasury of the Capitol or of the Palace.

— **Sarrana**] From the unhellenized form of Tyrus.

39 **aulaea**] A whole stage-curtain of a toga.

41 **Quippe**] "No head could support it: why it makes the slave sweat to hold it up."

44 **longi agminis officia**] There is no more difference between this and longa agmina officiosorum, than between 'a high-spirited nobleman on a long-tailed horse,' and 'a long-tailed nobleman on a high-spirited horse.'

45 **niveos**] In bran new togas probably given for the occasion.

46 **Defossa**] To make sure that they've got it: also to make sure that they will not lose it, cf. Fallacem circum, Hor. *Sat.* I. vi. 113.

47 **Tum**] Even between B.C. 460—357.

50] An Abderite would have hung himself. The cord giving way, he fell, and broke his head. He first went to the surgeon, and had his wound plastered, and then again hung himself.

Ridebat curas, nec non et gaudia vulgi,
Interdum et lacrimas, quum Fortunae ipse minaci
Mandaret laqueum, mediumque ostenderet unguem.
Ergo supervacua aut perniciosa petuntur,
Propter quae fas est genua incerare deorum.   55
Quosdam praecipitat subjecta potentia magnae
Invidiae; mergit longa atque insignis honorum
Pagina; descendunt statuae restemque sequuntur.
Ipsas deinde rotas bigarum impacta securis
Caedit, et immeritis franguntur crura caballis.   60
Jam stridunt ignes, jam follibus atque caminis
Ardet adoratum populo caput, et crepat ingens

51 **nec non et**] iii. 204, n.

52, 53] "While he bade fortune go hang, and stuck out his middle finger at her." Cf. Pers. i. 58: "O Jane, a tergo quem nulla ciconia pinsit."

53 **quum—unguem**] Gives the reason why he laughed at what naturally seems the reverse of laughable.

54] The metre and reading of this line are uncertain. Most MSS. have *aut*, one *vel;* whence Döderlein *aut vel*, which is a clumsy expression, and, if genuine, so far as I know, a ἅπαξ λεγόμενον. I could sooner believe a short syllable was left to count as long "in arsi et hiatu." Juvenal seems not to have accomplished a final revision; if so, then *vel* would be a creditable, though mistaken conjecture, instead of the ghost of the genuine reading. The vulgate *haec aut* is merely an old conjecture, left in the text for want of better. Lachmann reads

"Ergo, supervacua aut ne perniciosa petantur,
Propter quae fas est genua incerate Deorum."—

an alteration which is probably an improvement, and not too violent to be credible.

55 **incerare**] So MSS. Madvig, to avoid the difficulty of *fas*, suggested *incerate*, which is hopelessly abrupt. The line was meant to be ironical. It is no sin to plaster the knees of every god with prayers for these. *Fas* was a perfectly concrete traditional code enjoining some things, allowing some, forbidding others: of everything not forbidden it might be said *Fas est;* with the object either of accrediting the thing, or, as here, of discrediting *Fas*.

57 **mergit**] Stronger than *praecipitat; praecipitat* means that they topple over, under the stress of their invidious power; *mergit* that under the weight of their rank they sink to rise no more.

59, 60] "Then the very wheels of the biga are hacked away, and the poor nags have their innocent legs broken."— *Caballis:* cf. iii. 118; v. 60.

62 **adoratum populo**] The legions of Syria received special privileges, as it happened they had never joined this cultus. Sejanus offered sacrifices to himself (or, let us hope, his genius), to avert a portent, which befell his statue (Dio. L. viii. 7). Savage tribes think, some their heads, some their shadows sacred.

Sejanus : deinde ex facie toto orbe secunda
Fiunt urceoli, pelves, sartago, patellae.
"Pone domi lauros, duc in Capitolia magnum   65
Cretatumque bovem : Sejanus ducitur unco
Spectandus! gaudent omnes. Quae labra? quis illi
Vultus erat? nunquam, si quid mihi credis, amavi
Hunc hominem." "Sed quo cecidit sub crimine? quisnam
Delator? quibus indicibus, quo teste probavit?"   70
"Nil horum : verbosa et grandis epistola venit
A Capreis." "Bene habet; nil plus interrogo. Sed quid
Turba Remi?" "Sequitur fortunam, ut semper, et odit
Damnatos. Idem populus, si Nurtia Tusco
Favisset, si oppressa foret secura senectus   75
Principis, hac ipsa Sejanum diceret hora
Augustum. Jam pridem, ex quo suffragia nulli
Vendimus, effudit curas. Nam qui dabat olim
Imperium, fasces, legiones,· omnia, nunc se

---

65 **Pone domi lauros**] These words seem to mark the beginning of what is strictly dramatic, though the line between the dramatic and the picturesque was not as sharply drawn by Juvenal as it would be by a modern writer: this makes the division ·of the dialogue between the different speakers somewhat arbitrary. It would be tempting to make *nunquam—probavit* into a single speech, a sort of protest against popular caprice, but *Bene habet* shews that nothing of this kind is intended, and it seems livelier to suppose ·a new speaker breaking in with *Sed* both at 69 and 87.

66 **Cretatum**] To conceal any dark spots.

67 **Spectandus**] Which increases the popular joy.

70 **quibus indicibus**] "Who among his accomplices turned king's evidence?"

— **quo teste**] The informer could not give 'evidence' properly so called : this was ·a right of the citizen who came into court with clean hands.

— **probavit**] *Delator* is the nom.

74 **Nurtia**] Worshipped at Volsinii.

75] "If the aged emperor had been taken off his guard."

77] The speaker dates from the entire suppression of the comitia for electoral purposes by Tiberius which took place two years after his accession. Though the emperor nominated to all important offices, the elections kept up a kind of excitement; the nominal rights of the comitia were transferred to the senate, which could always be influenced more certainly and more easily; at the same time it soothed the pride of individual members of the order to be promoted by their colleagues and their prince without having to canvass their inferiors.

79 **Imperium**] Any curule office,

Continet, atque duas tantum res anxius optat,   80
Panem et Circenses." "Perituros audio multos."
"Nil dubium: magna est fornacula: pallidulus mi
Brutidius meus ad Martis fuit obvius aram.
Quam timeo, victus ne poenas exigat Ajax,
Ut male defensus!" "Curramus praecipites et,   85
Dum jacet in ripa, calcemus Caesaris hostem."
"Sed videant servi, ne quis neget et pavidum in jus
Cervice astricta dominum trahat." Hi sermones
Tunc de Sejano, secreta haec murmura vulgi.
Visne salutari sicut Sejanus? habere   90
Tantundem atque illi summas donare curules,
Illum exercitibus praeponere? tutor haberi
Principis augusta Caprearum in rupe sedentis
Cum grege Chaldaeo? Vis certe pila, cohortes,
Egregios equites et castra domestica. Quidni   95
Haec cupias? et qui nolunt occidere quenquam,

especially one which led to the command of an army; *fasces* the consulate, *legiones* the offices of military
tribune and *legatus*.

83 **Brutidius**] Niger, an orator
under Tiberius, who may well have
spoken on the arms of Achilles.
If so, Ajax is supposed to avenge
a half-hearted defence, by involving
his advocate in the fate of Sejanus.
Tiberius cannot be intended, as he
was not 'victus,' even if he thought
himself ill-defended.

— **Martis aram**] Outside the
Porta Fontinalis, near the polling-
booths.

87, 88] The slave arresting his
master is of course a satirical exaggeration: it was already an extreme
innovation, when Tiberius ordered
that in a case of treason the prose-
cutor should be authorized to pur-
chase the slaves of the accused and
take their evidence.

91, 92 **illi — Illum**] For the

double *ille*, cf. "Ille gradu pro-
prior sanguinis ille comes" (Ov.
Her. iii. 28).

93 **augusta**] Most MSS. *angusta*, which is easier, and worse.

94 **certe**] Even if you have no
ambition you would like the personal power that a military force of
your own would give; think of the
pleasure of knowing that you can
have your enemies assassinated if
you have any.

95 **Egregios equites**] The *equites
egregii* were a distinct order; they
too were at the disposal of Sejanus,
who had a body-guard quartered in
his house (*castra domestica*). If Macleane's notion of successive promo-
tions from *primipilus* to *praefectus
praetorio* is to be maintained, we
must suppose that *equites egregios*
and *castra domestica* both indicate
the same rank. The theory suits
pila fairly, and *cohortes* well.

Posse volunt. Sed quae praeclara et prospera tanti
Ut rebus laetis par sit mensura malorum?
Hujus, qui trahitur, praetextam sumere mavis,
An Fidenarum Gabiorumque esse potestas,   100
Et de mensura jus dicere, vasa minora
Frangere, pannosus vacuis Aedilis Ulubris?
Ergo quid optandum foret, ignorasse fateris
Sejanum: nam qui nimios optabat honores
Et nimias poscebat opes, numerosa parabat   105
Excelsae turris tabulata, unde altior esset
Casus, et impulsae praeceps immane ruinae.
Quid Crassos, quid Pompeios evertit? et illum,
Ad sua qui domitos deduxit flagra Quirites?
Summus nempe locus nulla non arte petitus,   110
Magnaque· numinibus vota exaudita malignis.
Ad generum Cereris sine caede et vulnere pauci
Descendunt reges et sicca morte tyranni.
    Eloquium ac famam Demosthenis aut Ciceronis
Incipit optare et totis Quinquatribus optat,   115

---

97 **tanti**] i. q. "Tantum habent
pretium ut propter ea parem quis
esse velit mensuram malorum"
(Mal. *Op.* ii. 189).

100 **potestas**]=podestà.

102 **Aedilis**] A common title of
the contemptible municipal *duum-
viri.*

107 **praeceps**] Subst.: "Subiti
praeceps juvenile pericli" (Stat.
S. I. iv. 51). The construction is,
"et unde praeceps" (the crash)
"impulsae ruinae" (gen.) "immane esset" (Mayor).

108 **Quid Crassos, quid Pompeios**] A Crassus and a Pompeius
(viii. 3, 11).

109] He does not venture to name
Caesar as a tyrant, and it could not
have been proved that he did not
mean Marius.

111] Cf. *Aen.* vi. 624 "Ausi omnes immane nefas ausoque potiti."

113 **sicca**] Bloodless.

115 sqq.] He begins praying his
first holidays, and wastes them all
on the folly. After his second half-
year he will be wiser. He is at a
thrifty school for thrifty parents,
and has a little slave to look after
his few books; his own morals are
in no danger yet. *Parcam* is preserved by P. only: the other MSS.
have *partam.* This is just one of
the characteristic readings for which
a careless copy of a careful original
may be trusted.

— **Quinquatribus**] A festival of
Minerva kept March 19—23; it was
a holiday for school-boys, who paid
up to the end of February before
they went home. Masters some-

Quisquis adhuc uno parcam colit asse 'Minervam,
Quem sequitur custos angustae vernula capsae.
Eloquio sed uterque perit orator; utrumque
Largus et exundans leto dedit ingenii fons.
Ingenio manus est et cervix caesa; nec unquam   120
Sanguine causidici maduerunt rostra pusilli.
" O fortunatam natam me Consule Romam !" •
Antoni gladios potuit contemnere, si sic
Omnia dixisset. Ridenda poemata malo,
Quam te conspicuae, divina Philippica, famae,   125
Volveris a prima quae proxima. Saevus et illum
Exitus eripuit, quem mirabantur Athenae
Torrentem et pleni moderantem fraena theatri.
Dis ille adversis genitus fatoque sinistro,
Quem pater, ardentis massae fuligine lippus,   130
A carbone et forcipibus gladiosque parante
Incude et luteo Vulcano ad rhetora misit.
    Bellorum exuviae, truncis affixa tropaeis
Lorica, et fracta de casside buccula pendens,
Et curtum temone jugum, victaeque triremis   135

times dedicated the first-fruits of their wages to Minerva.

117 **vernula**] Cf. xiv. 168, 169 "infantes ludebant quatuor, unus vernula tres domini;" here too the slave is one of the family.

118 **perit**] The crasis is post-Augustan.

121 **causidici**] Cf. i. 32 n.

123 **potuit contemnere**] May be regarded as equivalent to *jure contempsisset*, the radical meaning of ' potuit' corresponding to the formal meaning of the subjunctive termination, or this principle may be facilitated by the application of that stated on viii. 247. Cf. for the sentiment, Cic. *Phil.* 2. xlvi. 118.

129] Cf. Pers. iv. 27 "Hunc Dis iratis genioque sinistro."

130] Demosthenes' father was in the first place a man of substance ; in the second, did not live to send him to school. He was not a smith, but master of a sword-cutlery.

132 **luteo Vulcano**] He was sent, not from the smith, but from the smithy, which last is impersonated in Vulcan, though (iv. 138) Prometheus is the impersonation of the potter, not of the pottery.

133 **truncis**] A depreciatory circumstance, the mutilated armour is heaped on mutilated trees ; so too the chariot without the pole, the crest torn from the stern.

134 **buccula**] The cheek-piece : later, a buckle, so called from the resemblance of shape.

Aplustre, et summo tristis captivus in arcu,
Humanis majora bonis creduntur: ad hoc se
Romanus Graiusque ac barbarus induperator
Erexit: causas discriminis atque laboris
Inde habuit. Tanto major famae sitis est, quam   140
Virtutis. Quis enim virtutem amplectitur ipsam,
Praemia si tollas? Patriam tamen obruit olim
Gloria paucorum et laudis titulique cupido
Haesuri saxis cinerum custodibus, ad quae
Discutienda valent sterilis mala robora ficus: 145
Quandoquidem data sunt ipsis quoque fata sepulcris.
Expende Hannibalem; quot libras in duce summo
Invenies? hic est quem non capit Africa Mauro
Percussa Oceano Niloque admota tepenti,
Rursus ad Aethiopum populos aliosque elephantos.   150
Additur imperiis Hispania: Pyrenaeum
Transilit. Opposuit natura Alpemque nivemque:
Diducit scopulos et montem rumpit aceto.

---

138 **induperator**] Mock solemnity. Cf. iv. 29 n.
141] Cf. xiii. 144:
  "Rem pateris modicam et mediocri bile ferendam
  Si flectas oculos majora ad crimina,"
where "ferendam" = "quam feras," the apodosis to *si flectas*. Here the apodosis to "praemia si tollas" is some clause added *in epexegesi* to *ipsam*, e.g. "qualis futura sit si tollas praemia." Mayor, however, "who embraces virtue for her own sake" (or would embrace her at all), "supposing the rewards away?"
142] Though their motive is fame, not virtue, yet they have been known before now to sacrifice their country to it.
144, 145] Three circumstances

depreciatory of glory:—*a*. It only takes root on stones; *b*. These have nothing better to guard than ashes; *c*. These stones are split by useless trees. Contr. Thuc. ii. 43:
κοινῇ γὰρ τὰ σώματα διδόντες ἰδίᾳ τὸν ἀγήρων ἔπαινον ἐλάμβανον καὶ τὸν τάφον ἐπισημότατον, οὐκ ἐν ᾧ κεῖνται μᾶλλον, ἀλλ' ἐν ᾧ ἡ δόξα αὐτῶν παρὰ τῷ ἐντυχόντι ἀεὶ καὶ λόγου καὶ ἔργου καιρῷ ἀείμνηστος καταλείπεται. ἀνδρῶν γὰρ ἐπιφανῶν πᾶσα γῆ τάφος, καὶ οὐ στηλῶν μόνον ἐν τῇ οἰκείᾳ σημαίνει ἐπιγραφή, ἀλλὰ καὶ ἐν τῇ μὴ προσηκούσῃ ἄγραφος μνήμη παρ' ἑκάστῳ τῆς γνώμης μᾶλλον ἢ τοῦ ἔργου ἐνδιαιτᾶται.
150 **Rursus**] In another direction.
—*Aliosque*. So Priscian and most MSS.; it is much more pointed than *altos*.
153] The Scholiast, on Luc. iv. 658, quotes as from Juvenal—

Jam tenet Italiam: tamen ultra pergere tendit:
"Actum," inquit, "nihil est, nisi Poeno milite portas   155
Frangimus et media vexillum pono Suburra."
(O qualis facies et quali digna tabella,
Quum Gaetula ducem portaret bellua luscum!)
Exitus ergo quis est? O gloria! vincitur idem
Nempe et in exsilium praeceps fugit, atque ibi magnus   160
Mirandusque cliens sedet ad praetoria regis,
Donec Bithyno libeat vigilare tyranno,
Finem animae, quae res humanas miscuit olim,
Non gladii, non saxa dabunt, nec tela; sed ille
Cannarum vindex et tanti sanguinis ultor,   165
Annulus. I, demens, et saevas curre per Alpes,
Ut pueris placeas et declamatio fias!
Unus Pellaeo juveni non sufficit orbis:
Aestuat infelix angusto limite mundi,
Ut Gyari clausus scopulis parvaque Seripho: 170

"Deductisque viam scopulis sibi fecit aceto."
Probably the variation is due to a lapse of memory. Livy tells the story of the vinegar, xxi. 37.

156 **Suburra**] Not *Capitolio:* as if a satirist should describe Napoleon at Boulogne vowing to plant the tricolor in the heart of Houndsditch.

157, 158] "What a grotesque sight it must have been, a general with one eye gone, in state on his elephant, what a picture it would have made!" Hannibal rode the elephant to save his eyes, and it seems doubtful whether he was permanently *disfigured* by his attack of ophthalmia, which came on through exposure to fluctuations of temperature in the marshes of the Arno.

159 **vincitur**] Near Croton, B.C. 204, according to Livy, xxix. 36; near Zama, B.C. 202, for the first time, according to Polybius, xv. 5, sq.

160 **Nempe**] "Why." Cf. sup. 110.—*Praeceps.* Nine years after Zama, during the greater part of which he had been almost despot at Carthage.

161 **praetoria**] The place where the king transacted business in person; the centre of administration like the *praetorium* of a Roman governor, cf. i. 75 n.

162] "Till his Bithynian majesty be pleased to wake;" as a client he has to attend early in the morning.

165 **Cannarum vindex**] One ring avenged all the knights, whose spoils filled two or three modii at Cannae.

167] Cf. vii. 160, 161.

169 **Aestuat**] "The world is too close for him, he cannot breathe in it."

Quum tamen a figulis munitam intraverit urbem,
Sarcophago contentus erit. Mors sola fatetur,
Quantula sint hominum corpuscula. Creditur olim
Velificatus Athos, et quidquid Graecia mendax
Audet in historia : constratum classibus isdem   175
Suppositumque rotis solidum mare : credimus altos
Defecisse amnes epotaque flumina, Medo
Prandente, et madidis cantat' quae Sostratus alis.
Ille tamen qualis rediit Salamine relicta,
In Corum atque Eurum solitus saevire flagellis   180
Barbarus, Aeolio nunquam hoc in carcere passos,
Ipsum compedibus qui vinxerat Ennosigaeum ?
(Mitius id sane, quod non et stigmate dignum
Credidit. Huic quisquam vellet servire Deorum !)
Sed qualis rediit ? nempe una nave cruentis   185

171] "Dicitur altam fictilibus muris cinxisse Semiramis urbem" (Ov. *Met.* iv. 57, 58).

173 **Creditur**] And quite correctly; but history (except in certain circles the history of Roman institutions and the achievements of Roman families) formed no part of the ordinary Roman education ; it was as exceptional for a Roman gentleman to be well acquainted with Greek and Oriental historians, as for an English gentleman twenty years ago to be acquainted with writers on natural science.

175 **isdem**] "Quibus Athos velificatus."

177 **epota flumina**] Scamander, Melas, Lissus, Onochonos, Epidanus would be intermittent torrents with little water, except in exhaustible pools.

178 **Prandente**] And none was left for dinner. The story does not suit Herodotus (vii. 120), whence it appears that the army took no meal except after the evening halt.

—**madidis alis**] *a.* "Dank, drooping wings;". *b.* = 'uvidi,' contr. 'sicci;' *c.* "perspiring shoulders" (Schol.),

183] A Persian trained to minister dutifully to running streams of sweet water, would be peculiarly liable to this reaction against "the bitter river" of the Hellespont (Her. vii. 25). To suit Herodotus, Weber conjectures "Quid ? non et stigmate dignum Credidit ?" which Juvenal had some reason to write, the copyists no reason to change. The fact is Juvenal had read Sostratus and Sostratus had read Herodotus, from whom he repeated positively the story of the chaining and scourging and expressed Pindaric disbelief of the branding which Herodotus mentioned doubtfully. It is possible of course that the story of the chaining arose from inflated language about the bridge over the Hellespont. Cf. Aesch. *Pers.* 87 sqq. δόκιμος οὗτις ὑποστὰς μεγάλῳ ῥεύματι φωτῶν ἐχυροῖς ἔρκεσιν εἴργειν ἄμαχον κῦμα θαλάσσας. It should be added that up to the present time all our knowledge of Sostratus is derived from the present passage. He probably competed with success for a Greek Prize at Domitian's Agon Capitolinus.

Fluctibus, ac tarda per densa cadavera prora.

Has toties optata exegit gloria poenas !

"Da spatium vitae, multos da, Jupiter, annos !"

Hoc recto vultu, solum hoc et pallidus optas.

Sed quam continuis et quantis longa senectus   190

Plena malis ! Deformem et tetrum ante omnia vultum

Dissimilemque sui, deformem pro cute pellem,

Pendentesque genas et tales aspice rugas,

Quales, umbriferos ubi pandit Thabraca saltus,

In vetula scalpit jam mater simia bucca.   195

Plurima sunt juvenum discrimina : pulcrior ille

Hoc, atque ille alio ; multum hic robustior illo :

Una senum facies, cum voce trementia membra,

Et jam leve 'caput madidiqué infantia nasi.

Frangendus misero gingiva panis inermi :   200

Usque adeo gravis uxori natisque sibique,

Ut captatori moveat fastidia Cosso.

Non eadem vini atque cibi, torpente palato,

Gaudia : nam coitus jam longa oblivio ; vel si

Coneris, jacet exiguus cum ramice nervus   205

Et, quamvis tota palpetur nocte, jacebit.

Anne aliquid sperare potest haec inguinis aegri

Canities? quid? quod merito suspecta libido est,

Quae Venerem affectat sine viribus. Aspice partis

187] Cf. 97, 98, 243—245, though there the subject is continued again after the general reflection which sums it up.

189, 190] "This is your prayer in health, when you can face the world; this is your only prayer in sickness also." Cf. on the desire for life Maecenas' verses—

"Debilem facito manu,
  Debilem pede, coxa.
Tuber adstrue gibberum,
  Lubricos quate dentes.
Vita dum superest, bene est,

Hanc mihi, vel acuta
Si sedeam cruce, sustine."

194 **Thabraca**] Is on the eastern borders of Numidia.

195] A monkey looks like a wrinkled old woman as soon as she gets children.

196, 197 **Ille hoc—hic illo**] Each has his own advantages, so that none are badly off.

198] Cf. 227, which gives the variety in disease.

201, 202] "He is such a degraded nuisance to his family and

Nunc damnum alterius: nam quae cantante voluptas,   210
Sit licet eximius citharoedus sitye Seleucus,
Et quibus aurata mos est fulgere lacerna?
Quid refert, magni sedeat qua parte theatri,
Qui vix cornicines exaudiet atque tubarum
Concentus? clamore opus est; ut sentiat auris,   215
Quem dicat venisse puer, quot nunciet horas.
Praeterea minimus gelido jam in corpore sanguis
Febre calet sola; circumsilit agmine facto
Morborum omne genus: quorum si nomina quaeras,
Promtius expediam, quot amaverit Hippia moechos,   220
Quot Themison aegros autumno occiderit uno,
Quot Basilus socios, quot circumscripserit Hirrus
Pupillos, quot longa viros exsorbeat uno
Maura die, quot discipulos inclinet Hamillus;
Percurram citius, quot villas possideat nunc,   225
Quo tondente gravis juveni mihi barba sonabat.
Ille humero, hic lumbis, hic coxa debilis; ambos
Perdidit ille oculos et luscis invidet; hujus
Pallida labra cibum accipiunt digitis alienis.
Ipse ad conspectum coenae diducere rictum   230

himself, that even his toadeater is disgusted."

211, 212] Even though he is Seleucus, or some one else at the head of his profession, who can afford to perform in cloth of gold.

One is inclined to think the passage incomplete. Another line is wanted to give another name, and some quality common to successful singers to which their wearing mantles of cloth of gold can be appended.

213] Whether he is a senator or a knight.

221 Themison] The Scholiast thought Juvenal was speaking of a contemporary. A Themison of Laodicea founded the medical school of Methodici in the first century B. C.

222 Basilus] Perhaps the pleader (cf. vii. 145) had changed his trade. Cf. Cic. *pro Rosc. Com.* § 16 : "Si qua enim sunt privata judicia summae existimationis et paene dicam capitis tria haec sunt, fiduciae, tutelae, societatis. Aeque enim perfidiosum et nefarium est, fidem frangere quae continet vitam, et pupillum fraudare qui in tutelam pervenit, et socium fallere qui se in negotio conjunxit."

228 luscis invidet] "Au royaume des aveugles, les borgnes sont rois."

229] "Cheragra est debilis qui ab alio cibatur" (Schol.). To gape at dinner-time is all he can do for *himself,* '*ipse.*'

Suetus, hiat tantum, ceu pullus hirundinis, ad quem
Ore volat pleno mater jejuna. Sed omni
Membrorum damno major dementia, quae nec
Nomina servorum, nec vultum agnoscit amici,
Cum quo praeterita coenavit nocte nec illos,   235
Quos genuit, quos eduxit. Nam codice saevo
Heredes vetat esse suos; bona tota feruntur
Ad Phialen: tantum artificis valet halitus oris,
Quod steterat multis in carcere fornicis annis.
Ut vigeant sensus animi, ducenda tamen sunt   240
Funera natorum, rogus aspiciendus amatae
Conjugis et fratris plenaeque sororibus urnae.
Haec data poena diu viventibus, ut renovata
Semper clade domus, multis in luctibus inque
Perpetuo moerore et nigra veste senescant.   245
Rex Pylius, magno si quidquam credis Homero,
Exemplum vitae fuit a cornice secundae.
"Felix nimirum, qui tot per secula mortem
Distulit atque suos jam dextra computat annos,
Quique novum toties mustum bibit." Oro, parumper   250
Attendas, quantum de legibus ipse queratur
Fatorum et nimio de stamine, quum videt acris
Antilochi barbam ardentem; quum quaerit ab omni,
Quisquis adest socius, cur haec in tempora duret,

231, 232] Homer makes Achilles
(*Il.* IX. 322 sqq.) compare himself to
the careful mother. Juvenal compares the dotard to the gaping
chick.

236 **eduxit**] "Quod nos *educare*
dicimus, antiqui educere dixerunt"
(Calp. *ad Heaut.* ii. 1—14).

237 **bona tota feruntur**] She
takes possession — in theory the
heredes sui would have a remedy,
especially against a *persona turpis.*

239 **multis annis**] As if he might
have left her there; so Livy, i. 29 fin.,

speaks of the centuries which Alba
had stood, as if it might have stood
for ever.

249 **jam dextra**] As they exceed
a hundred.

250 **Quique...bibit**] "To whom
the month of vintage came round
so often." This is the sense, but
it is purposely put in a way to vul-
garise it.

252, 253] He lived to see his
son a man, and a brave man, and
to lose him when he would feel it
most.

Quod facinus dignum tam longo admiserit aevo?   255
Haec eadem Peleus, raptum quum luget Achillem,
Atque alius, cui fas Ithacum lugere natantem.
Incolumi Troja Priamus venisset ad umbras
Assaraci, magnis solemnibus, Hectore funus
Portante ac reliquis fratrum cervicibus, inter   260
Iliadum lacrimas, ut primos edere planctus
Cassandra inciperet scissaque Polyxena palla,
Si foret exstinctus diverso tempore, quo non
Coeperat audaces Paris aedificare carinas.
Longa dies igitur quid contulit? omnia vidit   265
Eversa et flammis Asiam ferroque cadentem.
Tunc miles tremulus posita tulit arma tiara
Et ruit ante aram summi Jovis, ut vetulus bos,
Qui domini cultris tenue et miserabile collum
Praebet, ab ingrato jam fastiditus aratro.   270
Exitus ille utcunque hominis : sed torva canino

256, 257] "Peleus says the same when he is mourning the early death of Achilles; and so does another, who had a right to mourn Ulysses as dead, he was at sea so long."

260 reliquis] All the fifty would have been left to bury him.

261, 262] Cassandra and Polyxena are mentioned, because both were slain in consequence of the capture of Troy. If it were not for the Homeric formula, ἦρχε γόοιο, of which *primos edere planctus* is a possible, though unsatisfactory translation, the sense would be pretty clear; *scissa palla* would apply to both (as it must any way), and *primos edere planctus* to Cassandra alone, meaning that she was only just beginning to be a trouble to her friends. *Ut* would be preceded by *ita*, or some equivalent word or words in prose.

263 non] So P. uncorrected, the others *jam*, which is better, per se.

267] Cf. Verg. *Aen.* ii. 509, 557.

270 ab] It would be perfectly possible to translate *ab*, 'from,' 'dismissed with scorn from the unthankful plough;' but it is safer to explain the passage on the general principle that when the ablative after a passive verb could be turned into the nominative to an active verb, *ab* is used, as here; when another subject would be supplied to the active verb, the ablative is used alone. Cic. *de Off.* i. 29: "Ita generati a naturâ sumus," i. q. ita natura nos generavit. *Id.* v. 2; "Omnis enim quae a ratione suscipitur de aliquâ re institutio debet a definitione profiscisci." Here we might convert either "quam ratio suscipit," or better, "quam ratione suscipimus." Hence some plausibly propose to omit *a;* though, as "ita nos natura generavit" is less classical than its equivalent, the cor-

Latravit rictu, quae post hunc vixerat, uxor.
Festino ad nostros, et regem transeo Ponti,
Et Croesum, quem vox justi facunda Solonis
Respicere ad longae jussit spatia ultima vitae.   275
Exsilium et carcer, Minturnarumque paludes,
Et mendicatus victa Carthagine panis
Hinc causas habuere. Quid illo cive tulisset
Natura in terris, quid Roma beatius unquam,
Si, circumducto captivorum agmine et omni   280
Bellorum pompa, animam exhalasset opimam,
Quum de Teutonico vellet descendere curru?
Provida Pompeio dederat Campania febres
Optandas: sed multae urbes et publica vota
Vicerunt. Igitur Fortuna ipsius et urbis   285
Servatum victo caput abstulit. Hoc cruciatu
Lentulus, hac poena caruit ceciditque Cethegus
Integer, et jacuit Catilina cadavere toto.

rection is not certain. Ov. *A. A.* i.
509 :
    " Minoida Theseus
Abstulit a nulla tempora comtus
    acu."
i. q. Cujus tempora nulla acus
compserit.
" Nil moveor lacrimis; ista sum
    captus ab arte."
i.q. Nihil lacrimis me moves,
ista ars me cepit, where the variation is capricious, as Hand says
(*Turs.* i. 27).
  272 **vixerat**] "His wife, who
had survived him, lived to bark;"
we should observe this distinction
of tenses in telling a new story, not
in alluding to an old one.
  274 **Solonis**] Solon's legislation
is placed B.C. 594, the usurpation
of Peisistratus, which he survived,
560. Croesus' accession is dated
560 by Grote, 568 by Rawlinson.
The story would not present any

grave chronological difficulty unless
we were sure that Herodotus was
quite accurate in implying that Solon
was only away from Athens ten
years, and that he left almost immediately after carrying his reforms.
Grote objects to the story on internal evidence. Duplicate stories are
always suspicious, and we have certainly a duplicate of this story referred to Gyges, xiv. 120, n.
  275 **spatia ultima**] Probably the
last rounds in the race, a metaphor
from the circus.
  277 **victa**] "Which he had subdued." Juvenal did not distinguish
between Numidia and Africa.
  281 **opimam**] The *spolia opima*
are the choice spoils; his soul would
have been choice incense.
  287 **Lentulus**] Being praetor, was
left to manage the conspiracy, which
he ruined by his intrigue with the
Gauls.
  288] Catilina's head was cut off

Formam optat modico pueris, majore puellis
Murmure, quum Veneris fanum videt anxia mater,   290
Usque ad delicias votorum. "Cur tamen," inquit,
"Corripias? Pulcra gaudet Latona Diana."
Sed vetat optari faciem Lucretia, qualem
Ipsa habuit: cuperet Rutilae Virginia gibbum
Accipere atque suam Rutilae dare. Filius autem   295
Corporis egregii miseros trepidosque parentes
Semper habet. Rara est adeo concordia formae
Atque pudicitiae. Sanctos licet horrida mores
Tradiderit domus, ac veteres imitata Sabinos,
Praeterea castum ingenium vultumque modesto   300
Sanguine ferventem tribuat natura benigna
Larga manu: (quid enim puero conferre potest plus
Custode et cura natura potentior omni?)
Non licet esse viro: nam prodiga corruptoris
Improbitas ipsos audet tentare parentes.   305
Tanta in muneribus fiducia! Nullus ephebum
Deformem saeva castravit in arce tyrannus:
Nec praetextatum rapuit Nero loripedem, nec
Strumosum atque utero pariter gibboque tumentem.
I nunc et juvenis specie laetare tui, quem   310
Majora exspectant discrimina! fiet adulter

as a trophy, according to Dio (xxxvii. 40).

289, sqq.] *Majore puellis murmure*. Then she is not afraid of being *over*heard — "she goes into all sorts of dainty details," *delicias votorum*.

292, sq.] Cf. "Latonae tacitum pertentant gaudia pectus" (*Aen.* i. 502. Cf. *Od.* vi. 102 sq.). The speaker foresees the objection to her prayer and tries to meet it by the example of Diana. The satirist replies, "beauty may be a blessing to a goddess, not to the chastest of women."

295 suam] 'Faciem.'

300, 301, **vultumque modesto Sanguine ferventem**] A face with modest blood enough for a blush in it.

304 viro] The MSS. have 'viros' or 'viris;' the uncertainty and the singular (302, 295) favour Jahn's conjecture.

306] "So bold are they in the matter of gifts."

307 arce] Cf. iv. 145.

310 juvenis] When he has reached manhood without misfortune or disgrace.

311 Majora] Greater than these I have described.

Publicus, et poenas metuet, quascunque maritis
Iratis debet: nec erit felicior astro
Martis, ut in laqueos nunquam incidat. Exigit autem
Interdum ille dolor plus, quam lex ulla dolori   315
Concessit. Necat hic ferro, secat ille cruentis
Verberibus, quosdam moechos et mugilis intrat.
Sed tuus Endymion dilectae fiet adulter
Matronae: mox quum dederit Servilia nummos,
Fiet et illius, quam non amat; exuet omnem   320
Corporis ornatum. Quid enim ulla negaverit udis
Inguinibus, sive est haec Oppia, sive Catulla?
Deterior totos habet illic femina mores.
"Sed casto quid forma nocet?" Quid profuit immo
Hippolyto grave propositum? quid Bellerophonti?   325
Erubuit nempe haec, ceu fastidita, repulso
Nec Stheneboea minus, quam Cressa, excanduit, et se
Concussere ambae. Mulier saevissima tunc est,
Quum stimulos odio pudor admovet. Elige, quidnam
Suadendum esse putes, cui nubere Caesaris uxor   330

313 **debet**] A detention of twenty hours, and relegation with the loss of half his property, and in some cases death.

317 **mugilis**] More commonly *mugil* (Phocas ii. 5, p. 326, Lind.).

318 **Sed...matronae**] At least you think that if he is not spotless, he will keep to one, and then the risk will be less.

320 **exuet**] "He will strip her."

323 **Deterior**] "When corrupted." Hor. *Od.* III. v. 30: "Curat reponi deterioribus."

326 **haec**] refers to Phaedra, daughter of Minos, hence Cressa inf. 327; because the writer beginning with the case of Hippolytus has her before his eyes as the principal, and therefore the nearest subject. Of course also *Stheneboea* the wife of

Proetus instead of *illa* softens the unusual sense of *haec*.

— **repulso**] So P. and the Scholiast; most others *repulsa;* the text is the ablative absolute. Cf. 'certato' (Tac. *Ann.* xi. 16).

327 **excanduit**] Like *erubuit* is purely subjective: *se concussere* 'shook themselves up' marks the transition to active resentment; the next sentence gives the reason why their resentment was so dangerous.

330, sq.] According to Tacitus, Messalina made Silius divorce his wife, and openly constituted herself his mistress; but after a year *he* proposed the marriage; while she, though attracted by the scandal, shrank a little from the risk of losing her lover. Suetonius tells a story that Claudius had heard some pro-

Destinat. Optimus hic et formosissimus idem
Gentis patriciae rapitur miser exstinguendus
Messalinae oculis: dudum sedet illa parato
Flammeolo, Tyriusque palam genialis in hortis
Sternitur, et ritu decies centena dabuntur   335
Antiquo: veniet cum signatoribus auspex.
Haec tu secreta et paucis commissa putabas?
Non nisi legitime vult nubere. Quid placeat, dic:
Ni parere velis, pereundum erit ante lucernas:
Si scelus admittas, dabitur mora parvula, dum res   340
Nota urbi et populo contingat principis aures.
Dedecus ille domus sciet ultimus: interea tu
Obsequere imperio: sit tanti vita dierum
Paucorum. Quidquid melius leviusque putaris,
Praebenda est gladio pulcra haec et candida cervix.   345
   "Nil ergo optabunt homines?" Si consilium vis,
Permittes ipsis expendere numinibus, quid
Conveniat nobis, rebusque sit utile nostris.
Nam pro jucundis aptissima quaeque dabunt Di.
Carior est illis homo quam sibi. Nos animorum   350

phecy of evil to Messalina's husband, and himself assisted at her marriage. According to Merivale, we have fragmentary accounts of an intelligible transaction, instead of complete accounts of an unintelligible.

331 **Optimus**] Not *sanctissimus*.

332 **patriciae**] Simply noble.

333 **dudum**] Notice her impatience; she is ready first, at most weddings it would be necessary to wait for the bride.

336 **veniet cum signatoribus auspex**] Cf. Cic. *Div.* i. § 28: "Nuptiarum auspices qui re omissa nomen tantum tenent." The Romans never thought indignation misplaced at the profanation of an understood conventionality.

337] Did you think the matter was to be a secret? of course she will only marry in proper style.

339] **ante lucernas**] περὶ λύχνων ἁφάς (Herod. vii. 215).

350, sq.] **Nos—uxor**] A common sophistry, as if no one ever had sense to pray for a *happy* marriage; it is stated with more refinement and effect in Mrs. Browning's "Nun with the brown rosarie." It may be doubted whether earthly happiness is valuable; but we do not prove that it is not, by pointing to individuals or classes who act as if it were identical with some of its external conditions. In vv. 356—366 the thought becomes distinctly Stoical; vv. 346—353 are simply Socratic. It is likely however that Juvenal only knew the Socratic tradition through the Stoics, though such

Impulsu et caeca magnaque cupidine ducti
Conjugium petimus partumque uxoris : at illis
Notum, qui pueri qualisque futura sit uxor.
Ut tamen et poscas aliquid, voveasque sacellis
Exta, et candiduli divina tomacula porci :   355
Orandum est, ut sit mens sana in corpore sano.
Fortem posce animum, mortis terrore carentem,
Qui spatium vitae extremum inter munera ponat
Naturae, qui ferre queat quoscunque labores,
Nesciat irasci, cupiat nihil et potiores   360
Herculis aerumnas credat saevosque labores
Et Venere et coenis et pluma Sardanapali.
Monstro quod ipse tibi possis dare : semita certe
Tranquillae per virtutem patet unica vitae.
Nullum numen abest, 'si sit Prudentia : nos te,   365
Nos facimus, Fortuna, Deam coeloque locamus.

---

a phrase as *carior est illis homo quam sibi* is hardly in harmony with the spirit of Stoicism ; the characteristic Stoical view of disappointed wishes is rather that the parts must consent to be sacrificed to the order of the whole.

351 caeca magnaque] Blind and therefore great. Of course *impulsu* corresponds to *ducti* and is not governed by it.

354 et poscas] Go on to petition. *Sacellis* not *templis;* the man is addicted to exotic or highly localised devotions.

355 divina] Of course ironical : "a dish for gods.'

361 aerumnas] A harsh and obsolescent word.

362 pluma] "Tam vigilabit [Maecenas] in pluma quam ille [Regulus] in cruce" (Sen. *Prov.* iii. § 9).—*Sardanapali.* Chaerilus, from

what purported to be an inscription on his tomb, or on the cities of Tarsus and Anchialus which he was held to have built in a day, wrote

ταῦτ' ἔχω ὅσσ' ἔφαγον καὶ ἐφύβρισα
καὶ μετ' "Ερωτος
τέρπν' ἔπαθον· τὰ δὲ πολλὰ καὶ
ὄλβια κεῖνα λέλειπται.

Whereupon Crates, an ugly and fascinating cynic with whom a rich and handsome girl ran away,

ταῦτ' ἔχω ὅσσ' ἔμαθον καὶ ἐφρόν-
τισα καὶ μετὰ Μούσων
σέμν' ἐδάην· τὰ δὲ πολλὰ καὶ ὄλβια
τῦφος ἔμαρψεν.

363 semita] A narrow track. "Ego illius pro semita feci viam" (Phaed. iii. Prol. 38).

365] Repeated with the variation, in the best MSS., of *habes* for *abest* (xiv. 315, 316).

SATIRA XI.

ATTICUS eximie si coenat, lautus habetur:
Si Rutilus, demens. Quid enim majore cachinno
Excipitur vulgi, quam pauper Apicius? Omnis
Convictus, thermae, stationes, omne theatrum
De Rutilo. Nam dum valida ac juvenilia membra 5
Sufficiunt galeae, dumque ardens sanguine, fertur,
(Non cogente quidem, sed nec prohibente tribuno,)
Scripturus leges et regia verba lanistae.
Multos porro vides, quos saepe elusus ad ipsum
Creditor introitum solet exspectare macelli, 10
Et quibus in solo vivendi causa palato est.
Egregius coenat meliusque miserrimus horum,
Et cito casurus jam perlucente ruina.
Interea gustus elementa per omnia quaerunt,

---

4 Omnis convictus, &c.] Every place where people spend their time together, the baths, where they lounge, the corners, where they stand and talk, &c. Every lounge, the baths, the corners.

6 fertur] He has not put down his litter.

7 tribuno] Macleane refers this to the tribunitian power of the emperors; and for him it is a very plausible guess. If not, we must take a weaker sense of *cogente*, "compelling him indirectly, by assigning his estate to his creditors."

8 leges] It seems simpler to take *leges et regia verba* as the terms of the contract ; but cf. "Vitandi atque

inferendi ictus subtiliorem rationem legibus ingeneravit" (Val. Max. ii. 3), where *legibus* is of course the rules of the art of fencing. *Regia verba*, because the *lanista* is the king in whose service he enlists.

12 Egregius] Cf. Prisc. *Lex.* iii. 2. 6, for this old comparative. The sense is, "quo quisque est inter miserrimos miserior eo melius coenat."

13 jam perlucente ruina] As the ruin begins to let light through, i. e. as his desperate condition comes to be known.

14 gustus] Either simply a taste of food, and so luncheon, or as here something to give a taste, whet the

Nunquam animo pretiis obstantibus : interius si   15
Attendas, magis illa juvant, quae pluris emuntur.
Ergo haud difficile est perituram arcessere summam,
Lancibus oppositis vel matris imagine fracta,
Et quadringentis nummis condire gulosum
Fictile. Sic veniunt ad miscellanea ludi.   20
Refert ergo, quis haec eadem paret : in Rutilo nam
Luxuria est, in Ventidio laudabile nomen
Sumit et a censu famam trahit. Illum ego jure
Despiciam, qui scit, quanto sublimior Atlas
Omnibus in Libya sit montibus, hic tamen idem   25
Ignoret, quantum ferrata distet ab arca
Sacculus. E coelo descendit γνῶθι σεαυτόν,
Figendum et memori tractandum pectore, sive
Conjugium quaeras vel sacri in parte Senatus
Esse velis, (nec enim loricam poscit Achillis   30
Thersites, in qua se traducebat Ulixes
Ancipitem); seu tu magno discrimine causam
Protegere affectas, te consule, dic tibi, quis sis,

appetite, and so a technical name for the first course.

18] "Pawning their plate, or breaking up their mother's bust for old silver." Cf.:

"Furi villula nostra non ad Austri
Flatus opposita est neque ad Favoni ;
Verum ad millia quindecim et ducentos.
O ventum horribilem atque pestilentum." (Cat. xxvi.)

20 Fictile] For the plate is gone. —*Ad miscellanea ludi*, to the gladiator's mess, where all ingredients and guests are confounded.

21 Rutilo] A poor man, as *Rutilae* (sup. x. 294) is a poor woman.

22 laudabile nomen] e. g. elegantia.

25] Hic and idem emphasize *tamen*, and leave *qui* as nom. to *ignoret ;* hence the change of mood. The first relative clause is adjectival, the second causal.

28—34] The construction is less symmetrical than is usual in Latin, each branch of the protasis has a separate apodosis, sive...velis in Figendum...pectore, seu...affectas in te...buccae. As *figendum*, &c. is a secondary predicate, its protasis is in the subjunctive.

31 Thersites] Juvenal ought to have remembered that Achilles, and all the poets after Arctinus, except Sophocles, had killed Thersites, to avenge an insult to the memory of Penthesilea.—*Traducebat—ancipitem*, "exhibited himself with doubtful effect."

Orator vehemens, an Curtius et Matho buccae.
Noscenda est mensura sui spectandaque rebus   35
In summis minimisque, etiam quum piscis emetur,
Ne mullum cupias, quum sit tibi gobio tantum
In loculis. Quis enim te, deficiente crumena,
Et crescente gula, manet exitus, aere paterno
Ac rebus mersis in ventrem, fenoris atque   40
Argenti gravis et pecorum agrorumque capacem?
Talibus a dominis post cuncta novissimus exit
Annulus, et digito mendicat Pollio nudo.
Non praematuri cineres, nec funus acerbum
Luxuriae, sed morte magis metuenda senectus.   45
Hi plerumque gradus: conducta pecunia Romae
Et coram dominis consumitur: inde ubi paullum
Nescio quid superest et pallet fenoris auctor,
Qui vertere solum, Baias et ad ostrea currunt.
Cedere namque foro·jam non est deterius, quam   50
Esquilias a ferventi migrare Suburra.
Ille dolor solus patriam fugientibus, illa

---

34 **Matho**] Cf. vii. 129.—*Buccae*, "mere wind-bags."

37 **Ne cupias**] depends on "noscenda est, &c."—*Gobio*, a gudgeon, i. e. the price of one.

38 **crumena**] Two MSS. have *culina;* and P. seems to have had it.

40, 41 **fenoris...capacem**] First he calls in his spare cash that was lying at interest and spends it, then he sells his plate [it was old fashioned]. Cf. "Argentum grave rustici patris, sine ullo opere et nomine artificis" (Sen. *de Tranq. An.* i. § 4). Then his cattle go, and then his land.

42, 43] These lines are the answer to the question, "quis te manet exitus." People like you have to pawn their rings and take to begging. The last thing to go is the ring, which proves he has been a gentle-man, and would have helped him to beg with a grace.

44 **acerbum**] "Untimely;" a metaphor from unripe fruit. A spendthrift need not be afraid of dying before his time; he has to fear old age more than death.

48 **auctor**] i.e. the lender.

49] "People who have really decided on bankruptcy, tell you they are oft to Baiae."

51] The Esquiliae were cool (v. 77) and healthy (Hor. *Sat.* I. viii. 14); the Suburra crowded and busy, which is implied in 'ferventi,' more than physical heat.

52 **Ille—illa**] In English both would be in the neuter. In Latin they take the gender of the predicate; and the same rule holds in Greek. It would not surprise us if the predicate took the gender of

Moestitia est caruisse anno Circensibus uno.
Sanguinis in facie non haeret gutta : morantur
Pauci ridiculum fugientem ex urbe Pudorem.　　　55
　Experiere hodie, numquid pulcherrima dictu,
Persice, non praestem vita nec moribus et re ;
Si laudem siliquas occultus ganeo; pultes
Coram aliis dictem puero, sed in aure placentas.
Nam quum sis conviva mihi promissus, habebis　　　60
Evandrum, venies Tirynthius aut minor illo
Hospes et ipse tamen contingens sanguine coelum :
Alter aquis, alter flammis ad sidera missus.
Fercula nunc audi nullis ornata macellis.
De Tiburtino veniet pinguissimus agro　　　65
Haedulus et toto grege mollior, inscius herbae,
Necdum ausus virgas humilis mordere salicti,
Qui plus lactis habet, quam sanguinis; et montani
Asparagi, posito quos legit villica fuso. ,
Grandia praeterea tortoque calentia foeno　　　70

the subject. Cf. Verg. *Aen.* vi.
128, 9:

"Sed revocare gradum, superas-
　que evadere ad auras,
Hoc opus, hic labor est."

54] There is not the ghost of a
blush : every drop of blood keeps
its course.

59 **dictem puero**] The master
goes out marketing with his slave,
and sends him back with orders for
dinner.

61] "Excipieris . . . a me hospitio paupere ut scilicet Hercules
ab Evandro aut Aeneas" (Schol.).

62 **contingens sanguine**] Whose
blood comes down from heaven: the
words would bear another sense,
reaching heaven by a bloody death,
and the ambiguity may be inten-
tional.

63 **aquis**] So the Sibyl to Aeneas :—

"Illic sanctus eris quum te ve-
　neranda Numici
Unda deum coelo miserit in-
　digetem."
　　　　(Tibull. II. v. 43.)

64 **nullis ornata macellis**] Which
is not furnished forth by any mar-
kets.

67 **humilis**] So that he could
stand and browse quite comfortably
without having to put up his forefeet
or scramble into uncomfortable po-
sitions.

69 **posito—fuso**] In his household everybody is profitably employed : gathering savoury herbs is a
holiday for the bailiff's wife.

70 **tortoque calentia foeno**]
"Wrapt up in hay, and therefore
still warm."

Ova adsunt ipsis cum matribus, et servatae
Parte anni, quales fuerant in vitibus, uvae :
Signinum Syriumque pirum, de corbibus isdem
Aemula Picenis et odoris mala recentis,
Nec metuenda tibi, siccatum frigore postquam   75
Autumnum et crudi posuere pericula succi.
Haec olim nostri jam luxuriosa Senatus
Coena fuit. Curius, parvo quae legerat horto,
Ipse focis brevibus ponebat oluscula, quae nunc
Squalidus in magna fastidit compede fossor,   80
Qui meminit, calidae sapiat quid vulva popinae.
Sicci terga suis, rara pendentia crate,
Moris erat quondam festis servare diebus
Et natalicium cognatis ponere lardum,
Accedente nova, si quam dabat hostia, carne.   85
Cognatorum aliquis titulo ter consulis atque

---

72 **Parte anni**] "By the season;"
"By the cold of late autumn and
early winter." It is as well to keep
to the common instrumental sense
of the ablative; as the abl. is seldom
used of duration, though instances
are found, as Cic. *N. D.* ii. § 130.
—*Quales fuerant in vitibus*, i.e.
not as raisins. Grapes were preserved in air-tight casks, or sawdust,
or hung up, and sometimes smoked
(Plin. *H. N.* xv. 18; Varro, *R. R.*
i. 54). The last process would give
raisins.

73 **de corbibus isdem**] "The
fruit is brought up in baskets. Of
these there are no more than necessary" (Mayor).

74, 75] "The fruit is fresh, as
having been carefully packed; whole-
some, as having been kept so long."

78, 79] One learns of Curius:
that he had neither cook nor gardener
(*ipse* and *legerat*): that he dined off
vegetables (*oluscula*): that he had
only a scanty supply of these (*parvo
horto focis brevibus*).

80 **Squalidus**] Because he is out
of reach of baths.

81] "Who can remember the taste
of a sow's paunch in a steaming cook-
shop," which he used to frequent before he was banished from the city
establishment: very likely he was
banished partly for frequenting it.
Probably 80, 81 are reminiscences of
Hor. *Sat.* II. vii. 118, *Ep.* I. xiv.
15—25.

82 **rara**] Constructed to hold
few flitches.

84 **natalicium**] "For a birthday
feast," in honour of the genius;
hence 'hostia.' The sacrificial
notion of a feast is very clearly
given in *Aen.* iii. 221, 222 :—

"Divosque ipsumque voca-
mus
In partem praedamque Jovem."

Men were afraid to feed themselves
before the gods. The inadequacy
of this view is exposed in the Psalms
and Prophets.

Castrorum imperiis et dictatoris honore
Functus, ad has epulas solito maturius ibat,
Erectum domito referens a monte ligonem.
Quum tremerent autem Fabios durumque Catonem   90
Et Scauros et Fabricios, postremo severos
Censoris mores etiam collega timeret :
Nemo inter curas et seria duxit habendum,
Qualis in Oceano fluctu testudo nataret,
Clarum Trojugenis factura ac nobile fulcrum :   95
Sed nudo latere et parvis frons aerea lectis
Vile coronati caput ostendebat aselli,

87 **Castrorum imperiis**] If this mean anything more than military commands, it will be a sneer on Domitian and the other *Imperatores* who owed the title to anything but their victories.

90 **autem**] seems to refer to 77, 78. If so, *Curius—ligonem* is an overgrown parenthesis; and the connexion will be: "This was the way our senate supped when luxury was coming in (to be sure, Curius lived on pot-herbs, with bacon for a treat on birthdays, and his distinguished friends were glad to join him). On the other hand, when a Fabius, a Scaurus, and the rest were left to keep the world in awe, no one thought seriously of tortoise-shell couches."

— **Fabios**] The Scholiast has a story that Q. Fabius Maximus when censor told P. Decius his colleague either to reform the state himself or leave him to do so. The story is hardly invented from this passage and is quite in the style of the lovers' quarrels in Livy x. 24, though he with finer artistic sense keeps them for the close of their career. It is even possible that Juvenal may have been thinking of it, and the plural (a Fabius) is no objection.

91 **Scauros**] refers to M. Aemilius, consul B.C. 115 (when he passed a sumptuary law against eating dormice), censor B.C. 109. His diligence, tact, and decorum, gave him immense influence in his life, and his posthumous reputation was the higher, because he was the last statesman who proved capable of administering affairs in the interest of the nobility.

92] Juvenal sees the discreditable quarrel of M. Livius Salinator and C. Claudius Nero, B.C. 204, through an antiquarian halo.

94 **Oceano fluctu**] Ocean-wave. *Oceanum mare* is frequent.

95] They think this silly ostentation due to their imaginary dignity.

96] The meaning is, "Lectus parvus nudo latere et fronte aerea;" but the sentence is so turned, as to throw *aerea* into the nom., and bring out the contrast with *testudo*. *Nudo latere* means not without a side-rail, but the side plain. *Frons aerea* is the head, which had a cheap design of satyrs playing round an ass's head, unless we are to understand country children playing about the feasters like satyrs.

97 **coronati**] With vine-leaves, as sacred to Bacchus; for the ass either discovered the sweetness of the vine, or the benefit of pruning vineyards by nibbling the leaves. One wonders why the goat got such

Ad quod lascivi ludebant ruris alumni.

Tales ergo cibi, qualis domus atque supellex.

Tunc rudis et Graias mirari nescius artes,   100

Urbibus eversis, praedarum in parte reperta

Magnorum artificum frangebat pocula miles,

Ut·phaleris gauderet equus, caelataque cassis

Romuleae simulacra ferae mansuescere jussae

Imperii fato, geminos sub rupe Quirinos,   105

Ac nudam effigiem clypeo venientis et hasta

Pendentisque Dei, perituro ostenderet hosti.

Argenti quod erat, solis fulgebat in armis.

Ponebant igitur Tusco farrata catino ;

Omnia tunc quibus invideas, si lividulus sis.   110

Templorum quoque majestas praesentior, et vox

Nocte fere media, mediamque audita per urbem,

Litore ab Oceani Gallis venientibus et Dîs

Officium vatis peragentibus, his monuit nos.

hard measure for the same beha-viour; but asses are a worse substitute for veal, than goats for venison.

99] In all the MSS. Would be better away.

100 *mirari*] Almost 'appreciate.'

101 **praedarum in parte reperta**] Almost as if they shared the booty into heaps of about the same size, and then when each man had appropriated a heap they began to look what was in them.

105 **fato**] Dative after *mansuescere*. *Geminos—Quirinos;* so "geminus Pollux" (Hor. *Od.* III. xxix. 64).

106] There actually were representations of Mars hanging over Ilia in his armour, which explains *pendentis* better than to think of him as fighting, though even as a lover he looks terrible to the falling enemy.

— **nudam**] He is represented Greek fashion without the breast-plate or the kilt which completed it.

108] A group of MSS., which

Jahn thinks interpolated, and mostly late, shew their taste by omitting this line, though it makes 'igitur' come in more naturally.

109] Is a more pointed repetition of 99: one suspects that the author wrote them as alternatives, and then he or an editor unwilling to sacrifice either found a place for both. *Tusco catino* is just the opposite of *gulosum fictile,* sup. 19: it is the old-fashioned cheap ware to match the old-fashioned cheap food.

113, 114] **Gallis venientibus—Dis peragentibus**] Two parallel prodigies.

114 **his monuit nos**] These words are awkward in themselves and it is a choice of evils whether we are to take them with what goes before or what follows. The punctuation of the text is Heinrich's and has the advantage of making *audita* a participle instead of a verb : *his* of course will be an ablative absolute, things being in this state. If we put the

Hanc rebus Latiis curam praestare solebat   115
Fictilis et nullo violatus Jupiter auro.
Illa domi natas nostraque ex arbore mensas
Tempora viderunt: hoc lignum stabat ad usus,
Annosam si forte nucem dejecerat Eurus.
At nunc divitibus coenandi nulla voluptas;   120
Nil rhombus, nil dama sapit, putere videntur
Unguenta atque rosae, latos nisi sustinet orbes
Grande.ebur, et magno sublimis pardus hiatu,
Dentibus ex illis, quos mittit porta Syenes
Et Mauri celeres et Mauro obsourior Indus,   125
Et quos deposuit Nabathaeo bellua saltu,
Jam nimios capitique graves. Hinc surgit orexis,
Hinc stomacho vires: nam pes argenteus illis,

full stop at *peragentibus*, which is favoured by *hanc* at the beginning of the next line, *his* will mean *hujusmodi signis*.

116—118] " They had tables of home-grown wood. Then they did not even cut down a tree on purpose. If the wind blew down an old nut, there was their wood; they put it up to stand till wanted." *Hoc* and *ad* are from P.: nearly all the rest have *hos* and *in*, which are easier. *Hos* seems an improvement, but if this were intended, we ought to have *hunc—usum*. *Ad usus* means for use of any kind.

123] A large leopard rampant, in the attitude which would require the largest amount of ivory.

125] According to Pliny (*H. N.* viii.), there were elephants in Africa, and south of the Sahara (Syrticas solitudines); but the largest came from India.

126 **deposuit**] Has shed. The elephant changes its tusks once in its life, as children change their teeth for larger ones; hence *nimios* is a blunder. Perhaps Juvenal was thinking of the horns of deer, which after a certain age get smaller every

year.—*Nabathaeo saltu*. A blunder like that involved in the name of turkey. The bird was introduced from the Indies, i. e. America; as what came from India had till lately come through Turkey, the Indies and Turkey were confused in the popular mind: so as Indian ivory came with Indian spices by way of Petra, poets who had not travelled (of course this is an argument against Juvenal's visit to Egypt), and had not read immense treatises on geography, confounded Arabia with India as our ancestors confounded Turkey: they had the additional excuse that some spices came from Arabia, others through Arabia. Of course there is no such thing as a glade in the territory of the Nabathaei.—*Nabathaeo*, the Nabathaeans bordered on Petra. The Roman poets used the word ignorantly for the whole East.

128] **vires**] So P. Most others *bilis*, which one might translate, "This rouses their appetite; this gives a stimulus to their digestion." *Vires* looks like a correction. The rich men think a silver stand as vulgar as an iron ring.

Annulus in digito quod ferreus. Ergo superbum
Convivam caveo, qui me sibi comparat, et res   130
Despicit exiguas. Adeo nulla uncia nobis
Est eboris, nec tessellae, nec calculus ex hac
Materia : quin ipsa manubria cultellorum
Ossea : non tamen' his ulla unquam opsonia fiunt
Rancidula, aut ideo pejor gallina secatur.   135
Sed nec structor erit, cui cedere debeat omnis
Pergula, discipulus Trypheri doctoris, apud quem
Sumine cum magno lepus, atque aper, et pygargus,
Et Scythicae volucres, et phoenicopterus ingens,
Et Gaetulus oryx hebeti lautissima ferro   140
Caeditur et tota sonat ulmea coena Suburra.
Nec frustum capreae subducere, nec latus Afrae
Novit avis noster tirunculus, ac rudis omni
Tempore, et exiguae furtis imbutus ofellae.
Plebeios calices et paucis assibus emtos   145
Porriget incultus puer atque a frigore tutus ;

131 **Adeo**] "So absolutely destitute am I of so much as an ounce of ivory."

135, 136] "The bone handles carve as well as ivory, and the meat tastes just as nice; but you won't get a professional carver either" (any more than an ornamental knife).

137 **Trypheri**] τρυφέρου, delicate.

139 **Scythicae volucres**] Generally taken for pheasants, which Pertinax never served at private feasts; and Alex. Severus only "Jovis epulo et Saturnalibus et hujusmodi festis diebus."

— **phoenicopterus ingens**] "The tongue and brain of the *flamingo* were most esteemed." Mayor.

140] The wooden dinner represents the greatest dainties; but they are taught to carve it with blunt knives, as good workmen should never find fault with their tools.—*Lautissima* cannot refer to their present attainment, as they are so noisy. In another writer one would hardly venture to suspect, at the expense of the connection, that *hebeti lautissima ferro* refers exclusively to *Gaetulus oryx*, and translate "And the Gaetulian oryx is cut up with a blunt knife, which is the best way to keep the flavour of the meat."

142, sq.] "Not having been taught to carve dainty dishes, he does not know how to steal from them." The Roman servants seem to have stolen *at* table.—*Avis Afrae*, probably guinea fowl.

144 **ofellae**] "Et quae non egeant ferro structoris ofellae" (Mart. x. xlviii. 15). Diminutive of 'offa,' the first shortened, as 'mamilla,' from mamma.'

146 a **frigore tutus**] "Not half-naked." He needs to be decently

Non Phryx aut Lycius, non a mangone petitus
Quisquam erit; in magno quum posces, posce Latine.
Idem habitus cunctis, tonsi rectique capilli,
Atque hodie. tantum propter convivia pexi.   150
Pastoris duri est hic filius, ille bubulci:
Suspirat longo non visam tempore matrem
Et casulum, et notos tristis desiderat haedos,
Ingenui vultus puer ingenuique pudoris,
Quales esse decet, quos ardens purpyra vestit: 155
Nec pupillares defert in balnea raucus
Testiculos, nec vellendas jam praebuit alas,
Crassa nec opposito pavidus tegit inguina gutto.
Hic tibi vina dabit, diffusa in montibus illis,
A quibus ipse venit, quorum sub vertice lusit: 160
Namque una atque eadem est vini patria atque ministri.
Forsitan exspectes, ut Gaditana canoro
Incipiat prurire choro, plausuque probatae
Ad terram tremulo descendant clune puellae:
Spectant hoc nuptae juxta recubante marito,   165

clad, being used to live out of
doors.

148 in magno quum posces]
"When you call for a bumper."
Most MSS. give the obvious guess
et magno as an addition to what
goes before, bought from a dealer
and at a high price. Macleane defends it by asking, Why should he
not call for a small cup? Because
the slave would hand it as a matter
of course.

149 Idem habitus cunctis] I have
no special favourite.

153 notos] You will frighten him,
you are a stranger.

154, 155] My slave is an example of modesty to 'ingenui.'

156 pupillares] Probably simply
under age, though the Scholiast is
relevant: "Quales habent hi qui
patres non habent, scilicet tumentes
in licentia pueritiae."

157 vellendas jam praebuit alas]
As a debauched master might say
of a slave that was growing up too
fast.

159] The wine is not of the famous Greek kinds or of the choice
sorts of south Italy.

162 Gaditana] Dancing girls
seem to have been the principal and
absorbing luxury of this great tra-
ding station, which was founded by
orientals before the Greek and Roman forms of dissipation were invented, nor were these, if they ever
penetrated as far as Gades, so well
suited to elderly business men, who
must have given the tone, as the
dreamy contemplation of voluptuous
dances.

165, 166] are so hopelessly
without a place, that they are
omitted in the same sort of MSS.
as omit 108. Others place them

Quod pudeat narrasse aliquem praesentibus ipsis:
Irritamentum Veneris languentis et acres
Divitis urticae. Major tamen ista voluptas
Alterius sexus : magis ille extenditur, et mox
Auribus atque oculis concepta urina movetur.   170
Non capit has nugas humilis domus : audiat ille
Testarum crepitus cum verbis, nudum olido stans
Fornice mancipium quibus abstinet; ille fruatur
Vocibus obscoenis omnique libidinis arte,
Qui Lacedaemonium pytismate lubricat orbem.   175
Namque ibi fortunae veniam damus : alea turpis,
Turpe et adulterium mediocribus. Haec eadem illi
Omnia quum faciunt, hilares nitidique vocantur.
Nostra dabunt alios hodie convivia ludos :
Conditor Iliados cantabitur, atque Maronis   180
Altisoni dubiam facientia carmina palmam.
Quid refert, tales versus qua voce legantur?
     Sed nunc dilatis averte negotia curis
Et gratam requiem dona tibi, quando licebit
Per totam cessare diem : non fenoris ulla   185
Mentio, nec, prima si luce egressa reverti
Nocte solet, tacito bilem tibi contrahat uxor,
Humida suspectis referens multicia rugis,
Vexatasque comas, et vultum auremque calentem.

---

after 159, 160, 171, 172, 175, 202,
which looks as if they must have
been so old, as to impose the duty
of finding a place for them. If they
are not J.'s, they are a parallel
passage, not a mere gloss.

169 **Alterius sexūs**] Perhaps
women enjoy such an exhibition
more than men; perhaps dancing
boys are more enjoyable than
dancing girls.

175] "Who tries his wine till
his marble pavement is slip-
pery." The rich man tastes

many wines, instead of drinking
one.

182] Macleane thinks this line
is an apology for J.'s voice; but the
host seems never to have read any
poems but his own. Perhaps the
point may be, if I were going to read
you my own verses, you might ask
if I thought I had a voice to make
the infliction tolerable ; as it is, you
will not mind whom I have hired to
chant Homer.

187 **bilem**] Here P. and the
Scholiast have *vilem*.

Protinus ante meum, quidquid dolet, exue limen: 190
Pone domum et servos et quidquid frangitur illis
Aut perit: ingratos ante omnia pone sodales.
Interea Megalesiacae spectacula mappae,
Idaeum sollemne, colunt, similisque triumpho
Praeda caballorum praetor sedet ac, mihi pace 195
Immensae nimiaeque licet si dicere plebis,
Totam hodie Romam Circus capit et fragor aurem
Percutit, eventum viridis quo colligo panni.
Nam si deficeret, moestam attonitamque videres
Hanc urbem, veluti Cannarum in pulvere victis 200
Consulibus. Spectent juvenes, quos clamor et audax
Sponsio, quos cultae decet assedisse puellae:
Nostra bibat vernum contracta cuticula solem.
Effugiatque togam. Jam nunc in balnea, salva
Fronte, licet vadas, quanquam solida hora supersit 205
Ad sextam. Facere hoc non possis quinque diebus
Continuis, quia sunt talis quoque taedia vitae
Magna. Voluptates commendat rarior usus.

191 **illis**]? Dative: whatever they amuse themselves by breaking or losing: *perit* is exactly the passive of *perdo*.

193 **mappae**] By dropping which he gave the signal for the start.

195 **Praeda**] "Whose horses eat up his fortune." There is an allusion to Diomedes of Thrace.

197 **Totam Romam**] As we say, "All the world is out of town."

198 **eventum**] "The success."—*Viridis panni*, probably the parties of the circus were so passionate and powerful, because they were the only outlet for popular sympathies and antipathies under the empire. In the time of Mauricius we catch glimpses of regularly organized societies, like the confederacies against which the Statute of Maintenance was enacted, and which justified the Star Chamber. Cf. vii. 114 n.

199 **si deficeret**] "Si vinceretur Prassinos" (Schol.).

203 **contracta**] "In a corner." "Contractusque leget" (Hor. *Ep.* I. vii. 12).

204 **togam**] Ruperti connects this with *cultae puellae* (202) and refers it to the 'toga meretricis,' and is duly scolded by Macleane, who refers *quinque diebus* to the five remaining days of the Megalesiaca. Cf. note, iii. 172. The *toga* was worn in such an elaborate manner as to be uncomfortable and troublesome.—*Salva fronte*, "and still hold up your head."

208] So Milton:—
" He who of such delights can
judge and spare,
To interpose them oft is not
unwise."

SATIRA XII.

NATALI, Corvine, die mihi dulcior haec lux,
Qua festus promissa Deis animalia cespes
Exspectat, niveam Reginae ducimus agnam,
Par vellus dabitur pugnanti Gorgone Maura.
Sed procul extensum petulans quatit hostia funem,   5
Tarpeio servata Jovi, frontemque coruscat:
Quippe ferox vitulus, templis maturus et arae
Spargendusque mero, quem jam pudet ubera matris
Ducere, qui vexat nascenti robora cornu.
Si res ampla domi similisque affectibus esset,   10
Pinguior Hispulla traheretur taurus, et ipsa
Mole piger, nec finitima nutritus in herba,
Laeta sed ostendens Clitumni pascua sanguis
Iret, et a grandi cervix ferienda ministro
Ob reditum trepidantis adhuc horrendaque passi   15
Nuper et incolumem sese mirantis amici.

---

1 **Natali die**] So Cicero; but Horace uses either Natalis (*Od.* IV. xi. 18) or Natales (*Ep.* II. ii. 210).

3 **Reginae**] Juno.

4 **pugnanti Gorgone Maura**] "To her whose weapon is the Moorish Gorgon."— *Maura*, because the Gorgons are placed in the west, or because Herodotus assigns a Libyan origin to the Aegis.

5 **sed**] 'Introduces the contrast between *ducimus* and *procul extensum quatit hostia funem*.

8 **spargendus mero**] Apparently this was not done with sucklings.

— **mero**] Ablative. The usual dat. of the agent could easily be supplied.

11 **Hispulla**] = Hisponilla, from Hispo; so Marulla, from Maro.

12 **finitima in herba**] The hill pastures round Arpinum contrasted with the rich water meadows of the Clitumnus.

13, 14] "You should say his blood did credit to the pastures of Clitumnus, and that it would take a tall sacrificer to give the blow, as he went along."

15] "Still trembling at the horrors he endured but now."

Nam praeter pelagi casus et fulminis ictus
Evasit. Densae coelum abscondere tenebrae
Nube una, subitusque antennas impulit ignis,
Quum se quisque illo percussum crederet, et mox   20
Attonitus nullum conferri posse putaret
Naufragium velis ardentibus. Omnia fiunt
Talia, tam graviter, si quando poetica surgit
Tempestas. Genus ecce aliud discriminis : audi
Et miserere iterum : quanquam sint cetera sortis   25
Ejusdem pars dira quidem, sed cognita multis,
Et quam votiva testantur fana tabella
Plurima. Pictores quis nescit ab Iside pasci ?
Accidit et nostro similis fortuna Catullo.
Quum plenus fluctu medius foret alveus, et jam,   30
Alternum puppis latus evertentibus undis
Arboris incertae nullam prudentia cani

---

20 Quum—crederet] "'Twas a time to make every one believe."

21, 23] "In a poetical tempest things are as bad" (they cannot be worse).

24 aliud] The loss of goods.

25 miserere iterum, &c.] He makes a fresh appeal to pity on the ground that Catullus has suffered loss as well as exceptional peril, and immediately qualifies his appeal by the admission that everybody who is shipwrecked does lose his property.

28 Iside] A man ruined by a shipwreck begged by exhibiting before the temple of Isis the picture he was going to dedicate. Cf. 3—6. Was it usual to make vows to orgiastic foreign deities, calm thank-offerings to national gods? In the time of Horace, *Od.* 1. v. 13—16, the votive picture was still dedicated to Neptune.

31] 'When the ship was always on her beam-ends,' lit. 'as the waves heaved up each side of the vessel by turns.'

32 Arboris incertae] The passage is clumsy upon any hypothesis : if we retain the reading of P. it will be better to translate 'the experience of the gray steersman of the crazy log' instead of putting *arboris incertae* in apposition to *puppis:* there is a plausible MS. variant, *arboris incerto*, which may be taken either with the previous line or with what follows, meaning 'as the tottering mast made the ship roll' or 'when no skill could help the tottering mast.' Lachmann has a pretty and credible conjecture, *Arbori incertae.* One is tempted to suspect that the verses about the storm and about Catullus' property, were written in parallel columns, and that it was more or less an accident where the second should be inserted. If the mast had been cut away immediately after *decidere jactu,* there would be no doubt as to the meaning of *arbor,* which would unmistakably refer to the mast. *Taeda,* inf. 59, is the only colour for making *arboris* mean ship.

Rectoris conferret opem : decidere jactu
Coepit cum ventis, imitatus castora, qui se
Eunuchum ipse facit, cupiens evadere damno   35
Testiculi : adeo medicatum intelligit inguen.
"Fundite, quae mea sunt," dicebat, "cuncta," Catullus,
Praecipitare volens etiam pulcherrima, vestem
Purpuream, teneris quoque Maecenatibus aptam,
Atque alias, quarum generosi graminis ipsum   40
Infecit natura pecus, sed et egregius fons
Viribus occultis et Baeticus adjuvat aer.
Ille nec argentum dubitabat mittere, lances
Parthenio factas, urnae cratera capacem,
Et dignum sitiente Pholo vel conjuge Fusci ;   45
Adde et bascaudas et mille escaria, multum
Caelati, biberat quo callidus emtor Olynthi.
Sed quis nunc alius, qua mundi parte, quis audet
Argento praeferre caput rebusque salutem ?

33 **decidere**] means a bargain, especially a compromise with creditors; so Martial tells Domitian, that if the gods wished to square accounts with him, Heaven would be bankrupt, and Jove would not be able to offer a whole penny in the shilling (ix. 4).

37 **Fundite**] Most of Catullus' stores were too light to make the ship labour, and accordingly we hear that she was not eased by parting with them; he seems to have had a crazy fear of drowning, which was no better than a stupefying fear of poverty.

40 **quarum—pecus**] "The flocks whereof, the flocks that supply these." On the Guadalquivir the sheep have a sort of golden wool, or a deep brown. The passage looks an unsuccessful attempt at a sneer, as if Juvenal would have said "Which realises the apocalyptic promises of the *Pollio*, about sheep running about with their fleeces ready dyed,

only the air and the water have something to do with it too."

44 **Parthenio factas**] "Which Parthenius could claim as his work;" this is the force of the dative (cf. i. 54, n.).

— **urnae**] About 3 gallons : of course the crater held more, though it is not clear how much. Juvenal means to say either that it would hold 3 gallons of wine, and water in proportion, or more probably, as water was drawn in an urna, that it would hold 3 gallons of water, and wine in proportion, about 4 or 5 gallons in all.

45 **conjuge Fusci**] Of course a well-known character. Juvenal, unlike Martial, never proclaims his respect for the sanctity of private life ; and it may be doubted whether even Martial avoided butts too notorious to be hurt by a joke.

47 **callidus emtor Olynthi**] Philip, quoted as a rich drinker who could employ old Greek artists.

[Non propter vitam faciunt patrimonia quidam, 50
Sed vitio caeci propter patrimonia vivunt.]
Jactatur rerum utilium pars maxima : sed nec
Damna levant. Tunc, adversis urgentibus, illuc
Reccidit, ut malum ferro submitteret; ac se
Explicat angustum; discriminis ultima, quando 55
Praesidia afferimus navem factura minorem.
I nunc et ventis animam committe, dolato
Confisus ligno, digitis a morte remotus
Quatuor aut septem, si sit latissima taeda !
Mox cum reticulis et pane et ventre lagenae 60
Aspice sumendas in tempestate secures.
Sed postquam jacuit planum mare, tempora postquam
Prospera vectoris fatumque valentius Euro
Et pelago ; postquam Parcae meliora benigna
Pensa manu ducunt hilares, et staminis albi 65
Lanificae, modica nec multum fortior aura

50, 51] come in stupidly in all the MSS.

52] They throw away [not only Catullus' pretty things, but] the greater part of the stores and tackling. *Nec*=οὐδέ. There is little difference between "this had no effect either" and "even this had no effect."

54 **Reccidit**] Most MSS. through a weak fear of a false quantity give *Decidit.* Cf. " Reccidit in solidam longo post tempore terram." Ov. *Met.* x. 180. The nominative of course is *rector*, a strong confirmation of the suspicion expressed in the note on 32 sup.
— **ac se**] And so releases himself from his strait, lit. his straitened self. One MS. reads *hac re*, 'by this expedient he clears the strait,' which is a curious use of *angustum;* and it seems hard to do without *se ; hac se* might be a genuine reading, altered in opposite directions.

56, sq.] " It is bad enough to embark and think there is only a plank between you and drowning, worse to see hatchets for use in a tempest."—*Dolato*, probably in contrast to the refinements of upholstery on "terra firma."—*Taeda.* Did he remember what he had said about fire, as *pinus* would have been usual and scanned ?—*Latissima*, some MSS. read, and P. most likely read *lautissima*, as if it were a fine thing to have the inflammable timber thick enough to keep alight.

62—4] One looks in vain for a finite verb between *tempora* and *pelago.* As it would be a violence to the run of Latin to make *prospera* and *valentius* predicates instead of epithets, we have to choose between supposing that Juvenal intended to supply at least one verb to which *fatum* and *tempora* could be nominatives, and supplying two ourselves to suit our taste from the context.

Ventus adest: inopi miserabilis arte cucurrit
Vestibus extentis et, quod superaverat unum,
Velo prora suo. Jam deficientibus Austris,
Spes vitae cum sole redit: tum gratus Iulo,　　　　70
Atque novercali sedes praelata Lavino,
Conspicitur sublimis apex, cui candida nomen
Scrofa dedit, laetis Phrygibus mirabile sumen,
Et nunquam visis triginta clara mamillis.
Tandem intrat positas inclusa per aequora moles　　75
Tyrrhenamque Pharon porrectaque brachia rursum,
Quae pelago occurrunt medio longeque relinquunt
Italiam. Non sic igitur mirabere portus,
Quos natura dedit: sed trunca puppe magister
Interiora petit, Baianae pervia cymbae,　　　　80
Tuti stagna sinus, gaudent ubi vertice raso
Garrula securi narrare pericula nautae.
Ite igitur, pueri, linguis animisque faventes,
Sertaque delubris et farra imponite cultris,
Ac molles ornate focos glebamque virentem!　　85
Jam sequar et, sacro quod praestat rite peracto,

69 **Velo prora suo**] The jib, or dolon, is the one regular sail left in its regular place.

72 **sublimis apex**] As the town of Alba had been long destroyed, Iulus could be represented as settling on the Mons Albanus; of course the top only was visible, and the site of the town out of sight.

74 **nunquam visis**] The satirist had not to decide between "which nobody had ever seen," and "which nobody ever saw;" his translators are restricted to the first and worst.

76 **rursum**] Mayor, "stretched out and bending back;" perhaps it is sufficiently emphatic to be separated from *porrectaque brachia*, and carried back to *intrat.—Tyrrhenam Pharon*, the marvels of Egypt are reproduced in Italy.

79 **Quos natura dedit**] Does this mean that they are surpassed; that at Alexandria the isle of Pharos was ready to hand?

80 **Baianae**] Such as ply about Baiae. While you are admiring the grand port, the master makes for the snug inner basin.

81 **vertice raso**] They offered their hair in accordance with a vow.

83 **linguis animisque**] Because if a slave sulked, that would be as unlucky as ill-omened language.

84 **delubris**] Little chapels serving for all the country side. They held the images, in front of which anybody inclined to sacrifice made one or more turf altars, sup. 2 *cespes*, inf. 85 *molles focos*, 94 *altaria*.

86—88] "I will make my principal offering in public, and then go

Inde domum repetam, graciles ubi parva coronas
Accipiunt fragili simulacra nitentia cera.
Hic nostrum placabo Jovem, Laribusque paternis
Thura dabo, atque omnes violae jactabo colores.   90
Cuncta nitent; longos erexit janua ramos
Et matutinis operatur festa lucernis.

Nec suspecta tibi sint haec, Corvine: Catullus,
Pro cujus reditu tot pono altaria, parvos
Tres habet heredes. Libet exspectare, quis aegram   95
Et claudentem oculos gallinam impendat amico
Tam sterili. Verum haec nimia est impensa: coturnix
Nulla unquam pro patre cadet. Sentire calorem
Si coepit locuples Gallita et Paccius orbi,
Legitime fixis vestitur tota tabellis   100
Porticus; exsistunt qui promittant hecatomben,
Quatenus hic non sunt nec venales elephanti,
Nec Latio, aut usquam sub nostro sidere talis
Bellua concipitur: sed furva gente petita
Arboribus Rutulis et Turni pascitur agro,   105

home, and pay a small tribute to my private gods."

simulacra] Probably of marble.— *Fragilicera*, "a cheap varnish liable to crack;" or a constant epithet thrown in to complete the depreciation.

89 **nostrum Jovem**] "The Jupiter of the house," every householder had a Jove of his own, and every matron a Juno. Cf. "Et per Junonem domini jurante ministro," where the 'dominus' is effeminate, and Cicero's household goddess Minerva.

90 **violae**] includes gilliflowers and perhaps irides.

92 **operatur festa**] "Does festal service."

97 **coturnix**] As quails feed on poison, and are liable to epilepsy, they were not valued for food.

98 **patre**] Opposite to 'orbus.'

— **Sentire calorem**] Exactly as we say 'feel the heat,' probably by a touch of fever.

99] Observe the order which justifies the singular *coepit* and *locuples*, followed by the plural *orbi*. We might translate, "if fever attacks a rich man like Gallita and Paccius who have no children."

101, sq.] "There are people found to promise a hecatomb—of oxen, inasmuch as there are no elephants in the market, none to be caught in Italy, and those imported by Caesar are reserved (for his chariot and the circus), and no wonder, considering their ancient military importance."

105] We learn that the elephants were kept near Ardea, that they were allowed to range a forest as if at home, that the whole realm of

Caesaris armentum, nulli servire paratum
Privato : siquidem Tyrio parere solebant
Hannibali, et nostris ducibus, regique Molosso,
Horum majores, ac dorso ferre cohortes,
Partem aliquam belli, et euntem in proelia turrim.   110
Nulla igitur mora per Novium, mora nulla per Histrum
Pacuvium, quin illud ebur ducatur ad. aras,
Et cadat ante Lares Gallitae victima, sola
Tantis digna Deis et captatoribus horum.
Alter enim, si concedas mactare, vovebit   115
De grege servorum magna et pulcherrima quaeque
Corpora ;. vel pueris et frontibus ancillarum
Imponet vittas, et, si qua est nubilis illi
Iphigenia domi, dabit*hanc altaribus, etsi
Non sperat tragicae furtiva piacula cervae.   120
Laudo meum civem, nec comparo testamento
Mille rates : nam si Libitinam evaserit aeger,
Delebit tabulas, inclusus carcere nassae,
Post meritum sane mirandum, atque omnia soli ›
Forsan Pacuvio breviter dabit. Ille superbus   125
Incedet victis rivalibus. Ergo vides, quam
Grande operae pretium faciat jugulata Mycenis.

Turnus was only enough for an imperial preserve.

111 **Novium — Histrum]** Unknown.

112 **ebur]** The elephant. Cf. *vellus*, sup. 4 ; *sanguis*, 13.

113 **Lares Gallitae]** Together.

115 **Alter]** Pacuvius, inf. 125.
—*Si concedas*, " Supposing you allow ;" ten to one, we should say in English, "if you *were* to allow him."

116, 117] According to the punctuation of the text, which is Macleane's, the household wear the sacrificial fillets as ministers assisting at the sacrifice of the daughter ; Mayor, who like Jahn only puts a comma

at *corpora*, supposes that the household are themselves the victims : if so, there is an antithesis between the field hands and the house slaves. *Nubilis*, because Iphigenia was brought to Aulis under the pretence that she was to marry Achilles.

125 **breviter]** It would be enough to say, ": M. Pacuvius heres esto."

126 **Incedet]** "Will walk in state."—*Rivalibus*, always used of rivals in the affections of somebody, generally a woman, here a patron ; a man can be said to have no *rivalis* in his own affections.

127 **Mycenis]** Because Agamemnon reigned at Mycenae.

Vivat Pacuvíus, quaeso, vel Nestora totum;
Possideat, quantum rapuit Nero; montibus aurum
Exaequet; nec amet quenquam, nec ametur ab ullo! 130

129 **rapuit**] Both in Italy and Greece during his Olympian pilgrimage.

130] The curse is reasonable, since he sacrifices family ties to counterfeit friendship.

SATIRA XIII.

EXEMPLO quodcunque malo committitur, ipsi
Displicet auctori. Prima est haec ultio, quod se
Judice nemo nocens absolvitur, improba quamvis
Gratia fallaci Praetoris vicerit urna.
Quid sentire putas omnes, Calvine, recenti   5
De scelere et fidei violatae crimine? Sed nec
Tam tenuis census tibi contigit, ut mediocris
Jacturae te mergat onus: nec rara videmus,
Quae pateris. Casus multis hic cognitus, ac jam
Tritus, et e medio fortunae ductus acervo.   10
Ponamus nimios gemitus: flagrantior aequo
Non debet dolor esse viri; nec vulnere major.
Tu quamvis levium minimam exiguamque malorum
Particulam vix ferre potes, spumantibus ardens
Visceribus, sacrum tibi quod non reddat amicus   15

2 **auctori**] The man who sets a bad precedent is *auctor* to those who follow it for acting like him.

4 **urna**] The balloting urn, where the votes were put, not the lottery urn, for the preliminary *sortitio*, where *gratia* would have less weight than in the final decision.

5 **recenti**] Till they have got used to the sense of guilt.

6 **scelere**] *Scelus* is the internal stain, *crimen* the public liability; *probrum* the social disgrace, *flagitium* the public scandal; as we say, a "burning shame;" *facinus* wavers between our word 'feat,' and the Scotch quasi-legal term 'fact,' which is generally opprobrious.

— **Sed nec, &c**.] The connection is, A rogue is sufficiently punished by his conscience, but, apart from that, *you* have no excuse for fuming at such a common trifle.

13, 14 **quamvis levium**] "However light," "as light as you please." It might seem that persons whom the consciousness of very small injuries or misfortunes afflicts with a sense of intolerable misery were as reasonable as those whom the consciousness of very small faults afflicts with a sense of intolerable sin. But the majority of right-minded people proceed on the assumption that it is right to be as anxious as possible about perfection and as in-

Depositum? stupet haec, qui jam post terga reliquit
Sexaginta annos, Fonteio Consule natus?
An nihil in melius tot rerum proficit usu?
Magna quidem sacris quae dat praecepta libellis
Victrix fortunae sapientia: ducimus autem   20
Hos quoque felices, qui ferre incommoda vitae,
Nec jactare jugum, vita didicere magistra.
Quae tam festa dies, ut cesset prodere furem,
Perfidiam, fraudes atque omni ex crimine lucrum
Quaesitum, et partos gladio vel pyxide nummos?   25
Rari quippe boni: numero vix sunt totidem, quot
Thebarum portae vel divitis ostia Nili.
Nona aetas agitur pejoraque secula ferri

different as possible about comfort, or, to put it in another way, that it is foolish to idealise rights or interests and unworthy not to idealise duties. At the same time this is only a practical answer; to a speculative observer the world is just as incurably bad because it fails to produce a faultless happiness, as human nature because it fails to shew a faultless virtue.

17 Fonteio Consule] One Fonteius was consul A.D. 12, another A.D. 59, a third A.D. 67. See Introduction.

18 proficit usu] Most MSS. have *proficis*, all *usu;* the Scholiast and P. have *proficit; usus* is a possible inference from the Scholiast. The Stoics oddly distinguished 'proficientes' among the universal mass of madness. The teachers did not claim to have attained wisdom (or their lives would have condemned them), but only to be approaching it (or their profession would have been useless), while they were obliged to call the world mad, as preachers now call it wicked, lest they should give the world a dispensation from hearing them.

19] As a question of taste, I should take *magna* with *praecepta,*

not *sapientia.* Of course the compliment to theoretical stoicism is rather ambiguous. "No doubt it is very fine to conquer fortune with a book; after all though, a man is well off who can learn from life to bear with its ills."

22 jactare jugum] Does not mean to try to get rid of the yoke, but to toss about under it. Tr. "to kick against the pricks." •

23] What day is such a festival that it can take a holiday from producing a thief?

25 pyxide] sc. *veneni*, as liquid poisons were practically unknown.

26 numero vix sunt] So P. and most others; three MSS. have "numerus vix est." One of the two must be a correction. As to the number, the Scholiast thinks of the Seven Sages.

28 Nona aetas] *Nunc*, the reading of P., involves a real and clumsy hendiadys; *nona* would mean that we are all but at the end of the *magnus annus* of ten ages, in a period whose depravity cannot be measured by any metal in the Greek scale. One Paris MS. of the tenth century has *non alias*, a very pretty conjecture, "We are living at

Temporibus, quorum sceleri non invenit ipsa
Nomen, et a nullo posuit natura metallo.   30
Nos hominum Divumque fidem clamore ciemus,
Quanto Faesidium laudat vocalis agentem
Sportula. Dic, senior bulla dignissime, nescis,
Quas habeat Veneres aliena pecunia? nescis,
Quem tua simplicitas risum vulgo moveat, quum   35
Exigis a quoquam, ne pejeret et putet ullis
Esse aliquod numen templis araeque rubenti?
Quondam hoc indigenae vivebant more, priusquam
Sumeret agrestem posito diademate falcem
Saturnus fugiens, tunc, quum virguncula Juno,   40
Et privatus adhuc Idaeis Jupiter antris,
Nulla super nubes convivia coelicolarum,
Nec puer Iliacus, formosa nec Herculis uxor
Ad cyathos, et jam siccato nectare tergens

Rome, and nowhere else, the times are worse than the iron age."

29 **ipsa**] "From her own resources." We have to invent a name if we can, for there is no natural substance to suggest one.

30 **a nullo metallo**] "after no metal," *ab* after *nomen* is entirely independent of the verb which governs *nomen*. It is always easy and never right to understand a participle agreeing with, *nomen*, for the ablative and *ab* to depend upon.

31, sq.] Impotent outcries at unheard-of crimes are characteristic of our times.

32 **vocalis**] "Which cries from their pockets."

37 **rubenti**] Where he has just sacrificed.

41 **Idaeis**] There was an Ida in Crete and another in Phrygia; both mountains, for those who lived under them, were the throne of Zeus; the legend of his infancy is generally told of Crete; if we could trust Propertius, III. i. 27, it was told of the other Ida too.

43, 44 **Nec nec et**] Cf. xv. 124 n. The nearest approach to a general principle seems to be that *et* introduces an afterthought, which instead of forming a new alternative is tacked on to the last. Here we might explain "they had neither their new cupbearer Ganymede, not their old waitress Hebe with Vulcan as a supernumerary," *Il.* i. 596. Luc., *Dial. Deor.* 5, §§ 4, 5, makes the same mistake.—*Ad cyathos.* This phrase may be compared with some which are familiar in English, King-at-arms, Sergeant-at-law, &c. Here the local reference is more discernible; on the other hand, the admission of any immediate object of reference shews that the phrase is further from its origin. When Vulcan has done his duty to the nectar as cupbearer and guest, he thinks of making himself tidy. *Il.* xviii. 414, he does the

Brachia Vulcanus Liparaea nigra taberna. 45
Prandebat sibi quisque Deus, nec turba Deorum
Talis, ut est hodie, contentaque sidera paucis
Numinibus miserum urgebant Atlanta minori
Pondere. Nondum aliquis•sortitus triste profundi
Imperium, aut Sicula torvus cum conjuge Pluton; 50
Nec rota, nec Furiae, nec saxum aut vulturis atri
Poena; sed infernis hilares sine regibus umbrae.
Improbitas illo fuit admirabilis aevo.
Credebant hoc grande nefas et morte piandum,
Si juvenis vetulo non assurrexerat et si 55
Barbato cuicumque puer, licet ipse videret
Plura domi fraga et majores glandis acervos.
Tam venerabile erat praecedere quatuor annis,
Primaque par adeo sacrae lanugo senectae!
Nunc, si depositum non infitietur amicus, 60
Si reddat veterem cum tota aerugine follem,
Prodigiosa fides et Tuscis digna libellis,
Quaeque coronata lustrari debeat agna.
Egregium sanctumque virum si cerno, bimembri

same the "moment the arrival of a visitor makes him leave off work." He is made one of the standing cupbearers on the strength of the solitary passage, *Il.* i. 596. Luc. *Dial. Deor.* v. §§ 4, 5 makes the same mistake.

45 **Liparaea taberna**] "His *shop* at Lipara," a serious poet would have spoken of his *forge* or his *anvil*.

46 **Prandebat**] A simple solitary meal, contrasted with *convivia coelicolarum.—Turba*, swelled by the Caesars and outlandish gods, to say nothing of Juppiter's large family.

48 **Atlanta**] Juvenal might have remembered that he was not put on duty till the accession of Jove.

49, 50] "There was no one yet

whose lot was the empire of the deep, no Pluto frowning with his Sicilian queen."

51 **vulturis atri**] Refers to Tityus, not Prometheus.

52] Now they have a king who confines them to hell, where he reigns.

56 **cuicumque**] Of any age; perhaps too of any rank.

61 **veterem**] For the deposit was made long ago, *cum tota aerugine*, for it has never been touched: a grotesque and picturesque turn is given to a very simple transaction.

62 **Tuscis—libellis**] Which explain how to avert the evil portended by the prodigy.

64 **bimembri**] Parts of two kinds, or two sets of parts.

Hoc monstrum puero aut miranti sub aratro   65
Piscibus inventis et fetae comparo mulae,
Sollicitus, tanquam lapides effuderit imber,
Examenque apium longa consederit uva
Culmine delubri, tanquam in mare fluxerit amnis
Gurgitibus miris et lactis vortice torrens.   70
Intercepta decem quereris sestertia fraude
Sacrilega? Quid si bis centum perdidit alter
Hoc arcana modo? majorem tertius illa
Summam, quam patulae vix ceperat angulus arcae?
Tam facile et pronum est superos contemnere testes,   75
Si mortalis idem nemo sciat! Aspice, quanta
Voce neget, quae sit ficti constantia vultus.
Per solis radios Tarpeiaque fulmina jurat,
Et Martis frameam et Cirrhaei spicula vatis,
Per calamos venatricis pharetramque puellae   80
Perque tuum, pater Aegaei Neptune, tridentem:
Addit et Herculeos arcus hastamque Minervae,

---

65 **miranti sub aratro**] Some MSS. and editors, finding the astonishment of a plough too strong, read *mirandis* or *mirantis*, others get rid of the hiatus by altering *aut* into *vel* or by interpolating *jam* after *miranti*, which has the advantage of throwing *miranti* into the dative.

68 **longa uva**] βοτρυδόν, just as we speak of a cluster of bees.

70 **Gurgitibus miris**] Depends rather on *fluxerit* and is parallel to *lactis vortice torrens*.

71] "Apostropham facit ad illum cujus ob reditum sacrificavit." Schol. The writer confounds Catullus with Corvinus, to whom the description of Catullus' shipwreck is addressed: the mistake is worth noticing as it indicates that there were people to whom Calv and Corv were indistinguishable.

73 **arcana**] "Depositos sine ullis testibus." Britannicus.

74] The chest is large, and filled in every corner.

76 **Si mortalis idem nemo sciat**] Grangaeus says it was common for a man to talk of crimes he should like to commit, si je ne craignais autre que Dieu.

77 **neget**] Like *sit* depends upon *aspice;* we are not to compare such phrases as κτύπον δέδορκα. Juvenal tells the reader to look at the man and learn how loud his voice is and how steady his face.—*Ficti* "though feigned."

78 **Per solis radios** &c.] By the rays of the sun [which beheld him], by the thunder of Jove [which may crush him].

79 **frameam**] A German word.

82 **arcus**] Bequeathed to Philoctetes. Artists have popularised the

Quidquid habent telorum armamentaria coeli.
Si vero et pater est, "Comedam," inquit, "flebile nati
Sinciput elixi Pharioque madentis aceto." 85
    Sunt in Fortunae qui casibus omnia ponunt,
Et nullo credunt mundum rectore moveri,
Natura volvente vices et lucis et anni,
Atque ideo intrepidi quaecumque altaria tangunt.
Est alius metuens, ne crimen poena sequatur: 90
Hic putat esse Deos et pejerat, atque ita secum:
"Decernat, quodcumque volet, de corpore nostro
Isis, et irato feriat mea lumina sistro,
Dummodo vel caecus teneam, quos abnego, nummos.
Et phthisis et vomicae putres et dimidium crus 95
Sunt tanti. Pauper locupletem optare podagram
Nec dubitet Ladas, si non eget Anticyra nec
Archigene. Quid enim velocis gloria plantae

---

club in preference; but the bow and arrows (*arcus*) poisoned in the hydra's blood are of more importance in mythology and it seems in popular devotion.

84, 85] "May my son be murdered, and his poor head be served up to me at table, stewed with plenty of Egyptian vinegar." Cf. iii. 292—4, where it appears that a *sheep's* face with vinegar and beans was a treat to the lower classes; the man prays that in this familiar dish his *son's* face may be substituted. Egyptian vinegar was famous for its strength.

86 **Fortunae**] Plin. (*H. N.* ii. 5) notes a tendency to refer every thing to Fortune, as a middle term between Atheism and superstition.

88] Cf. "All things continue as they were from the beginning of the creation" (2 *Pet.* iii. 4). *Natura* like *fortuna* above is a 'metaphysical' conception.

93 **Isis**] It is worth noticing that the believer is afraid of an outlandish deity.

95 **dimidium**] Wasted by sores, or perhaps amputated in consequence; any way, one must think of disease in this context.

96 **Sunt tanti**] "Are not too much," "are of this value and no more;" i.e. are a sufficient and only a sufficient sacrifice to make for such a prize; the commoner use is, "are of this value and no less." Cf., however, "Aut si rescierit, sunt, o, sunt jurgia tanti" (Ov. *Met.* ii. 424). "Nunc et damna juvant, sunt ipsa pericula tanti" (Mart. I. xiii. 11). — *Locupletem podagram,* gout and the wealth it implies.

97 **Nec**] = οὐδέ. Let him do it, and not hesitate either. — *Ladas,* a proverb of speed, from a Spartan who won the δόλιχος at Olympia, and an Achaean who won the στάδιον. — *Anticyra,* one was on the Corinthian, one on the Melian gulf.

98 **Archigene**] Born at Apamaea, practised at Rome under Trajan, wrote on Hellebore.

Praestat, et esuriens Pisaeae ramus olivae?
Ut sit magna, tamen certe lenta ira Deorum est.   100
Si curant igitur cunctos punire nocentes,
Quando ad me venient? sed et exorabile numen
Fortasse experiar: solet his ignoscere. Multi
Committunt eadem diverso crimina fato:
Ille crucem sceleris pretium tulit, hic diadema."   105
Sic animum dirae trepidum formidine culpae
Confirmant. Tunc te sacra ad delubra vocantem
Praecedit, trahere immo ultro ac vexare paratus.
Nam quum magna malae superest audacia causae,
Creditur a multis fiducia. Mimum agit ille,   110
Urbani qualem fugitivus scurra Catulli:
Tu miser exclamas, ut Stentora vincere possis,
Vel potius, quantum Gradivus Homericus: "Audis,
Jupiter, haec, nec labra moves, quum mittere vocem
Debueras vel marmoreus vel aheneus? aut cur   115
In carbone tuo charta pia thura soluta
Ponimus, et sectum vituli jecur albaque porci
Omenta? Ut video, nullum discrimen habendum est

99 **esuriens**] Cf. "Parcam Minervam" (sup. x, 116).

100] Cf. ὀψὲ Θεῶν ἀλέουσι μύλοι, ἀλέουσι δὲ λεπτά, and "Because sentence against an evil work is not executed speedily, therefore the heart of the sons of men is fully set in them to do evil" (*Eccles.* viii. 11).

103 **his**] Such trifles (as perjury about a sum of money that the owner can bear to lose).

105 **diadema**] It is a common thought since Plato, *Gorg.* xxvi. p. 471 *a*, *b*, that dynasties begin with crime.

106 **dirae—culpae**] Trembling for fear of the terrible fault they are about to commit.

108] "To revile you for your charges, and worry you with his impatience to clear himself."

110 **fiducia**] "Conscious innocence."

111] It seems from the Scholiast, that in some play of Catullus a slave, when overtaken, arrested his master for having run away from *him*.

112 **Stentora**] *Il.* v. 785, 786.

113 **Homericus**] *Il.* v. 859.

115 **vel marmoreus vel aheneus**] The speaker doubts whether the idol be more than a dumb image; even so, it ought to be animated by such an outrage.

116 **soluta**] He does not stint his offering. Jove gets the whole paperful.

117 **alba**] On which the brown slices of liver would shew up well.

Effigies inter vestras statuamque Vagelli,"
Accipe quae contra valeat solatia ferre,   120
Et qui nec Cynicos, nec Stoica dogmata legit
A Cynicis tunica distantia, non Epicurum
Suspicit exigui laetum plantaribus horti.
Curentur dubii medicis majoribus aegri :
Tu venam vel discipulo committe Philippi.   125
Si nullum in terris tam detestabile factum
Ostendis, taceo ; nec pugnis caedere pectus
Te veto, nec plana faciem contundere palma
Quandoquidem accepto claudenda est janua damno,
Et majore domus gemitu, majore tumultu   130
Planguntur nummi, quam funera. Nemo dolorem
Fingit in hoc casu, vestem diducere summam
Contentus, vexare oculos humore coacto.
Ploratur lacrimis amissa pecunia veris.

119 **Vagelli**] " Declamatoris mulino corde Vagelli" (xvi. 23). Obviously there was a familiar joke about his statue : putting the two passages of Juvenal together, one may guess that as nothing could stop his speaking, people affected surprise that nothing could make his statue speak.

122 **A—distantia**] The Cynics made the emancipation of the individual the end of philosophy, and sought it simply by the rejection of superfluities : accordingly they wore the *pallium* double and dispensed with the tunic; the Stoics held that man should not live for himself alone; they felt that the decencies of society were a part of the order of the world, accordingly they resumed the tunic while they maintained the protest against superfluities by wearing a coarse cloak. It is worth noticing that the early Buddhist ascetics who regarded asceticism as a means for the salvation of the world were models of decorum, while the contemporary Brahmanical ascetics for whom asceticism was

either an instrument of personal salvation or perhaps more frequently a condition of preternatural power were cynically shameless in their obtrusive mortifications.

123 **exigui—horti**] As Epicurus was so easily pleased he would never have thrown himself into an excitement about a hundred pounds; his name is introduced to shew that *both* the sects in vogue were independent enough of circumstances to rebuke Calvinus.

125] "To Philip, or even his apprentice."

127 **pugnis**] To make a good noise.

128 **plana**] For you don't want to hurt yourself after all.

129 **claudenda est**] As we pull down blinds between a death and a funeral.

132 **vestem diducere summam**] "To part the upper edge of the tunic." N.B., 'diducere,' not 'discindere.' He just pulled out the seam.

Sed si cuncta vides simili fora plena querela,   135
Si, decies lectis diversa parte tabellis,
Vana supervacui dicunt chirographa ligni,
Arguit ipsorum quos litera gemmaque princeps
Sardonychum, loculis quae custoditur eburnis :
Ten', O delicias, extra communia censes   140
Ponendum? Qui tu gallinae filius albae,
Nos viles pulli nati infelicibus ovis?
Rem pateris modicam et mediocri bile ferendam,
Si flectas oculos majora ad crimina. Confer
Conductum latronem, incendia sulfure coepta   145
Atque dolo, primos quum janua colligit ignes :
Confer et hos, veteris qui tollunt grandia templi
Pocula adorandae robiginis et populorum
Dona vel antiquo positas a rege coronas.
Haec ibi si non sunt, minor exstat sacrilegus, qui   150

136 **diversa parte**] "On the other side."

137] Is repeated (xvi. 41).

138 **princeps**] Hence well known, and a proof of wealth.

140 **delicias**] "My dainty dear," not "what dainty airs," as Juvenal is always goodnatured to his friend.

141 **gallinae — albae**] A white hen's egg was rare, like a white elephant. A white hen carried off by an eagle, and dropt in Livia's lap, might account for a proverb about white hens, but not about their chickens, though that particular hen *had* a brood and a large one afterwards; in general silver-spangled hens refuse to sit.

143 **ferendam** = 'Quam feras' (see note x. 141), εὐφόρητον ἂν γινόμενην.

145 **Conductum**] Hired to fire and rob the house. It seems probable that here as 147, 154, inf. *confer* introduces a single class of crime; it would be an offence against symmetry to make *conductum latronem* a crime standing by itself; 144—146

deal with the guilt of incendiarism, which implies that of the suborner as well as of the criminal who actually applies the light. So 154, 155 we have the parricide, the person he sends to buy the poison and the habitual criminal who prepares it.

— **sulfure**] Not by charcoal.

146 **dolo**] Not by chance.— *Janua*, a point very convenient for the incendiary, where no chance fire could begin.

147 **templi**] It is not clear where the temple is supposed to be : probably Juvenal was thinking at once of the offerings by kings and subject states which would be dedicated in temples at Rome, and of the offerings, at Delphi and Olympia, some of which would be as old as Croesus and Midas.

148 **adorandae robiginis**] There is a little ambiguity here; the writer does not decide for himself or the reader whether the rust is a title to the veneration of the antiquary or of the devotee.

150, sq.] If there are no histori-

Radat inaurati femur Herculis et faciem ipsam
Neptuni; qui bracteolam de Castore ducat.
An dubitet, solitus totum conflare Tonantem?
Confer et artifices mercatoremque veneni
Et deducendum corio bovis in mare, cum quo   155
Clauditur adversis innoxia simia fatis.
Haec quota pars scelerum, quae Custos Gallicus urbis
Usque a Lucifero, donec lux occidat, audit?
Humani generis mores tibi nosse volenti
Sufficit una domus. Paucos consume dies, et   160
Dicere tè miserum, postquam illinc veneris, aude.
Quis tumidum guttur miratur in Alpibus? aut quis
In Meroe crasso majorem infante mamillam?
Caerula quis stupuit Germani lumina, flavam
Caesariem et madido torquentem cornua cirro?   165
Nempe quod haec illis natura est omnibus una.

---

cal offerings to be carried off whole, lesser thieves start up to scrape the thigh of Hercules, or even the face of Neptune, which they can do without blazoning their guilt; hence *minor*, for they would melt down whole statues, if there were any left.—*Solitus* is very puzzling: how can a man in the habit of melting down Juppiter be a *minor sacrilegus?* Gifford accuses Juvenal of negligence, Macleane suspects the text. Perhaps we are to think of an underling in Nero's wholesale perquisitions, who had helped to melt his plunder, and when that employment came to an end went into the same business in a small way on his own account.—*Conflare*, almost by way of retaliation, melt down the thunderer, as the thunderbolt, which sinners generally fear, melts the hills.

156] The monkey is clearly unlucky, since he suffers in his innocence.

157 **Gallicus**] A gentle praefec-

tus urbis under Domitian. It is difficult to make this agree with any Fonteius, as the first would place the satire soon after 72 A.D.: and Gallicus can hardly have been in office then.

160 **una**] That of Gallicus.

165 **madido cirro**] The reeking topknot into which the stiffened curly locks were twisted after being moistened with the soap used as a dye.

166] So far the connection with the subject is obvious; it is as absurd to be surprised at wickedness in Rome as at any other local peculiarity, but the next illustration confuses the sense. Calvinus does not think his loss a laughing matter; what is gained by telling him that the pygmies do not dream of laughing at their military misadventures? We need not answer the question if we suppose that vv. 162—173 were written without reference to Calvinus and shoved in from Juvenal's commonplace book.

Ad subitas Thracum volucres nubemque sonoram
Pygmaeus parvis currit bellator in armis :
Mox impar hosti raptusque per aera curvis
Unguibus a saeva fertur grue. Si videas hoc   170
Gentibus in nostris, risu quatiare : sed illic,
Quanquam eadem assidue spectentur proelia, ridet
Nemo, ubi tota cohors pede non est altior uno.
"Nullane perjuri capitis fraudisque nefandae
Poena erit?" Abreptum crede hunc graviore catena   175
Protinus, et nostro (quid plus velit ira?) necari
Arbitrio : manet illa tamen jactura, nec unquam
Depositum tibi sospes erit : sed corpore trunco
Invidiosa dabit minimus solatia sanguis :
"At vindicta bonum vita jucundius ipsa."   180
Nempe hoc indocti, quorum praecordia nullis
Interdum aut levibus videas flagrantia causis.
Quantulacunque adeo est occasio, sufficit irae :
Chrysippus non dicet idem nec mite Thaletis
Ingenium dulcique senex vicinus Hymetto,   185
Qui partem acceptae saeva inter vincla cicutae

167] The pygmies see something in the air like a cloud, and they hear a noise coming from it, and they know the cranes have come from Thrace to pounce upon them. Juvenal gives the result of their observation first, the grounds of it second; the order which is natural for the poet of the pygmies, is the reverse of that which is natural for them.

172] "Though it isn't for want of better opportunity than ours."

173] Certainly implies that what is sport to us is death to them.

177, sq.] "Still you don't get your money back; and when you behead him, you won't get much blood to console you, and you'll be hated for that." Mayor makes *minimus*

"though you only take a few drops," in spite of 'corpore trunco.'

181] After dilating from 120—173 on the sufficiency of a little common sense to subdue excessive irritation at a trifling loss, Juvenal here falls back on an appeal to philosophy; the subject is not congenial, and after a dozen lines on the folly of desiring vengeance, we have more than fifty on the certainty that in some form or other Calvinus will have his revenge.

184 **mite**] Thales was wise, *ergo* gentle.

185 **dulci**] From its honey, which it is hinted, made Socrates good-tempered.

186 **saeva inter vincla**] With the cruel accompaniment of chains.

Accusatori nollet dare. Plurima felix
Paullatim vitia atque errores exuit omnes,
Prima docet rectum Sapientia: quippe minuti
Semper et infirmi est animi exiguique voluptas   190
Ultio. Continuo sic collige, quod vindicta
Nemo magis gaudet, quam femina. Cur tamen hos tu
Evasisse putes, quos diri conscia facti
Mens habet attonitos et surdo verbere caedit
Occultum quatiente animo tortore flagellum?   195
Poena autem vehemens ac multo saevior illis,
Quas et Caedicius gravis invenit aut Rhadamanthus,
Nocte dieque suum gestare in pectore testem.
Spartano cuidam respondit Pythia vates:
Haud impunitum quondam fore, quod dubitaret   200
Depositum retinere et fraudem jure tueri
Jurando: quaerebat enim, quae numinis esset

Juvenal does not mean that he was in irons at the moment of his execution: from the *Phaedo* 60 *d*, we know that he was not.

187 **Accusatori**] Who, the Scholiast thinks, asked for it.

188, sq.] "Will certainly teach you that the wish for vengeance is foolish, and probably extinguish the wish."

189 **minuti**] "Dwarfed," never allowed to attain its proper stature, whereas *exigui* means naturally small.

194 **surdo**] Incorporeal, and therefore inaudible.

197 **Caedicius**] According to the Scholiast, Juvenal wished to hold up the cruelty of this courtier of Nero to public reprobation; perhaps we may trust him for Caedicius having been a courtier; but the scholiasts have invented so many impossible references to Nero that it is impossible to be sure about this.

199 **Spartano**] Glaucus, son of Epicydes, was requested by a Mile-

sian to preserve the half of his fortune. The sons of the Milesian claimed the money. Glaucus consulted the oracle of Delphi on the results of perjury, and received this answer:—

Γλαῦκ' Ἐπικυδείδη, τὸ μὲν αὐτίκα
   κέρδιον οὕτω
ὅρκῳ νικῆσαι, καὶ χρήματα λητσ-
   σασθαι.
ὄμνυ'· ἐπεὶ θάνατός γε καὶ εὔορκον
   μένει ἄνδρα.
ἀλλ' Ὅρκου πάϊς ἐστὶν ἀνώνυμος,
   οὐδ' ἔπι χεῖρες,
οὐδὲ πόδες· κραιπνὸς δὲ μετέρχε-
   ται, εἰσόκε πᾶσαν
συμμάρψας ὀλέσει γενεήν, καὶ οἶκον
   ἄπαντα.
ἀνδρὸς δ' εὐόρκου γενεὴ μετόπισθεν
   ἀμείνων.

He repented, but was told it was too late, and his family had expired before the battle of Salamis. (Cf. Her. vi. 86.)

200 **dubitaret retinere**] Just the opposite sense of *dubito* to *dubitet optare*, sup. 97.

Mens et an hoc illi facinus suaderet Apollo?
Reddidit ergo, metu, non moribus; et tamen omnem
Vocem adyti dignam templo veramque probavit   205
Exstinctus tota pariter cum prole domoque
Et, quamvis longa deductis gente, propinquis.
Has patitur poenas peccandi sola voluntas.
Nam scelus intra se tacitum qui cogitat ullum,
Facti crimen habet. "Cedo, si conata peregit?"   210
Perpetua anxietas nec mensae tempore cessat,
Faucibus, ut morbo, siccis interque molares
Difficili crescente cibo: sed vina misellus
Exspuit; Albani veteris pretiosa senectus
Displicet; ostendas melius, densissima ruga   215
Cogitur in frontem, velut acri ducta Falerno.
Nocte brevem si forte indulsit cura soporem,
Et toto versata toro jam membra quiescunt:
Continuo templum et violati numinis aras
Et, quod praecipuis mentem sudoribus urget,   220
Te videt in somnis; tua sacra et major imago
Humana turbat pavidum cogitque fateri.
Hi sunt, qui trepidant et ad omnia fulgura pallent,

206 **pariter**] Sc. ac si juravisset.

207] "However far you had to go back to prove the connection," i. e., however remote it might be.

208—211] He seems to mean that providential punishment follows the resolve: execution has a further punishment in the fear of detection.

213 **Difficili crescente cibo**] The food is a difficulty which seems to grow because it does not vanish.—*Sed vina*, so all the MSS. *Setina* is a very pretty conjecture, which no copyist had any temptation to alter. *Sed* comes as near as it ever does to *tamen*—though his mouth is parched and his food sticks in his throat, he cannot wash it down with wine.

216 **acri**] Horace gives the im-

pression that Falernian was valued in his day, but this was only for its strength and when it was matured by keeping.

221, 222 **tua — humana**] This phantom is related to the person it represents as Peter's angel to Peter in the belief of the then Church; death is not presupposed in either case. Cf. Verg. *Aen.* iv. 465:

"Agit ipse furentem
In somnis ferus Aeneas."

—*Major humana*, cf. Verg. *Aen.* ii. 772, *nota major imago*, where also Creusa is as much wraith or double as ghost.

223] The ancients did not distinguish physical susceptibility to

Quum tonat, exanimes primo quoque murmure coeli;
Non quasi fortuitus, nec ventorum rabie, sed   225
Iratus cadat in terras et judicet ignis.
Illa nihil nocuit, cura graviore timetur
Proxima tempestas, velut hoc dilata sereno.
Praeterea, lateris vigili cum febre dolorem
Si coepere pati, missum ad sua corpora morbum   230
Infesto credunt a numine; saxa Deorum
Haec et tela putant. Pecudem spondere sacello
Balantem et laribus cristam promittere galli
Non audent: quid enim sperare nocentibus aegris
Concessum? vel quae non dignior hostia vita?   235
Mobilis et varia est ferme natura malorum.
Quum scelus admittunt, superest constantia: quid fas
Atque nefas, tandem incipiunt sentire peractis
Criminibus. Tamen ad mores natura recurrit
Damnatos, fixa et mutari nescia. Nam quis   240
Peccandi finem posuit sibi? quando recepit
Ejectum semel attrita de fronte ruborem?
Quisnam hominum est, quem tu contentum videris uno
Flagitio? Dabit in laqueum vestigia noster
Perfidus et nigri patietur carceris uncum,   245
Aut maris Aegaei rupem scopulosque frequentes

electricity from the awe of conscious guilt. Caligula was abjectly afraid of thunder; but perhaps this was no disparagement to the sincerity of his atheism.

225 **fortuitus**] For the crasis of the second and third syllables, cf. *pituita* (Hor. *Epist.* I. i. 108). Pliny (*H. N.* ii. 43, § 113) debates whether thunder is a natural or supernatural phenomenon. Seneca (*Qu.* vi. 3, § 1) thinks the former hypothesis most edifying.

236—240] Their wishes are always changing; their villainous nature is fixed. The connection is:

they are afraid to sacrifice, though when they committed the crime they trusted, sup. 102, to sacrifices to propitiate heaven.

240 **Damnatos**] Which on reflection they have condemned.

242 **attrita**] The notion is, smoothing the forehead, in preparation for a brazen stare.

245 **nigri patietur carceris uncum**] "Will be strangled in prison and dragged through the streets."

246 **frequentes**] If so the rocky islands of the Aegean must have had some of the alleviations of Boulogne.

Exsulibus magnis. Poena gaudebis amara
Nominis invisi tandemque fatebere laetus,
Nec surdum, nec Tiresiam quenquam esse Deorum.

247 **magnis**] Cf. sup. i. 73, when he is banished he will find plenty who have made their fortune by crimes like him; if he has made his, so much the better.

SATIRA XIV.

Plurima sunt, Fuscine, et fama digna sinistra
Et nitidis maculam haesuram figentia rebus,
Quae monstrant ipsi pueris traduntque parentes.
Si damnosa senem juvat alea, ludit et heres
Bullatus, parvoque eadem movet arma fritillo.
Nec melius de se cuiquam sperare propinquo
Concedet juvenis, qui radere tubera terrae,
Boletum condire et eodem jure natantes
Mergere ficedulas didicit, nebulone parente,
Et cana monstrante gula. Quum septimus annus   10
Transierit puero, nondum omni dente renato,
Barbatos licet admoveas mille inde magistros,
Hinc totidem, cupiet lauto coenare paratu
Semper, et a magna non degenerare culina.
Mitem animum et mores modicis erroribus aequos   15

---

2 **nitidis—rebus**] As we say, "a tidy property."
— **haesuram**] So P. and S. The other MSS. have et (ac) rugam from the Vulgate of *Eph.* v. 27.
3 **monstrant—traduntque**] Cause and effect.
4 **senem**] Lusimus γεροντικῶς (Suet. *Aug.* 71).
5 **Bullatus**] He does not begin too late for mischief.
6 **melius**]? Quam de patre? quam de bullato herede.
8 **eodem**] As his father.
9 **didicit**] He has learnt to do it

himself, for he cannot trust the cook.—*Nebulone parente*, &c. Because his father is a spendthrift, and his hoar hairs guide the son to gluttony. *Nebulone parente* must be abl. abs., like *monstrante gula*.
10 **septimus annus**] Seven was the usual age for beginning regular education: *nondum omni dente renato* is added to shew what an early age this is, and yet it is too late.
12 **Barbatos**] Of course philosophers.
15 **erroribus**] Dat.

Praecipit, atque animas servorum et corpora nostra
Materia constare putat paribusque elementis,
An saevire docet Rutilus, qui gaudet acerbo
Plagarum strepitu et nullam Sirena flagellis
Comparat, Antiphates trepidi Laris ac Polyphemus,   20
Tum felix, quoties aliquis tortore vocato
Uritur ardenti duo propter lintea ferro?
Quid suadet juveni laetus stridore catenae,
Quem mire afficiunt inscripta ergastula, carcer?
Rusticus exspectas, ut non sit adultera Largae   25
Filia, quae nunquam maternos dicere moechos
Tam cito, nec tanto poterit contexere cursu,
Ut non ter decies respiret?   Conscia matri
Virgo fuit: ceras nunc hac dictante pusillas
Implet, et ad moechum dat eisdem ferre cinaedis.   30
Sic natura jubet: velocius et citius nos
Corrumpunt vitiorum exempla domestica, magnis
Quum subeunt animos auctoribus.   Unus et alter
Forsitan haec spernant juvenes, quibus arte benigna
Et meliore luto finxit praecordia Titan :   35
Sed reliquos fugienda patrum vestigia ducunt,

18 **Rutilus**] A Rutilus is mentioned xi. 2, 5, 21.
19 **Sirena**] Suggests the ogres of
the Odyssey; there may be an allusion to *Od.* ix. 114, 115 Θεμιστεύει
δὲ ἕκαστος παίδων ἠδ᾽ ἀλόχων, οὐδ᾽
ἀλλήλων ἀλέγουσιν.
22 **propter**] "On account of two
bath towels;" to find out where they
were.—*Ferro*, with a heated plate.
23 **laetus**] "His delight," Rutilus
is still the subject.
24 **inscripta ergastula**] Branded
gangs. He likes while going through
the country to notice the branded
gangs of slaves, and to see in the
distance the prison where they will
be locked up at night.
25] Cf. Hor. *Ep.* I. ii. 42, "Rusticus expectat dum defluat amnis,"
&c.   But for this line, it would be
almost certain that the stop ought
to be after *Rusticus*, not *carcer*.
29 **Virgo**] While still unmarried.
—*Pusillas*, she is still a girl, and
has every thing small; besides, she
is only beginning, and has not much
to say.
30 **ferre**] Cic. *ferendas;* but Hor.
(*Od.* I. xxvi. 2), "tradam . . . por-
tare."
32 **magnis—auctoribus**] "Under
high authority," parents are *magni
auctores* to their children if to no
one else.
36 **vestigia**] "Foot-prints," not
simply "steps."

Et monstrata diu veteris trahit orbita culpae.
Abstineas igitur damnandis : hujus enim vel
Una potens ratio est, ne crimina nostra sequantur
Ex nobis geniti : quoniam dociles imitandis   40
Turpibus ac pravis omnes sumus, et Catilinam
Quocunque in populo videas, quocunque sub axe :
Sed nec Brutus erit, Bruti nec avunculus usquam.
Nil dictum foedum visuque haec limina tangat,
Intra quae pater est. Procul hinc, procul inde puellae   45
Lenonum et cantus pernoctantis parasiti.
Maxima debetur puero reverentia. Si quid
Turpe paras, ne tu pueri contemseris annos :
Sed peccaturo obstet tibi filius infans.
Nam si quid dignum Censoris fecerit ira   50
Quandoque, et similem tibi se non corpore tantum
Nec vultu dederit, morum quoque filius, et qui
Omnia deterius tua per vestigia peccet :
Corripies nimirum et castigabis acerbo
Clamore ac post haec tabulas mutare parabis !   55
Unde tibi frontem libertatemque parentis,

37] "The example was long before them; they imitated it from the first; hence their fault also is old, and the evil habit,—their parents' and their own,—is a rut which carries them on, they cannot get out."

38—42] *Home* should be pure ; for none is proof against temptation, and the *world* is full of it.—*Damnandis*, what you will have to condemn in him.—*Hujus* depends on *potens*, the single consideration of preventing our children from imitating our crimes is enough for this.

43 **Bruti——avunculus**] The younger Cato, a truly admirable character, whose political Quixotism was the result of a hopeless situation quite as much as of his own unreasonableness.

45 **hinc—inde**] They are to go off on every side ; P. reads *hac*, which looks more like an unsuccessful attempt to resolve an abbreviation *hc* than the relic of a genuine reading *ah*.

48 **annos**] As if he were too young to notice.

49 **obstet**] Most MSS. have *obsistat* to avoid the hiatus.

53] "And one to commit all your sins over again ; so much the worse, as he is treading in your steps."

56 **frontem**] Almost "the frown;" it does not mean how can you face your son? but how can you meet him with a face of fatherly reproof?— *Libertatem*, a father ought to be able to give his son his opinion not only freely but with authority, so this word is studiously mild, though not

Quum facias pejora senex vacuumque cerebro
Jam pridem caput hoc ventosa cucurbita quaerat?
  Hospite venturo, cessabit nemo tuorum.
"Verre pavimentum, nitidas ostende columnas,   60
Arida cum tota descendat aranea tela ;
Hic leve argentum, vasa aspera tergeat alter:"
Vox domini furit instantis virgamque tenentis.
Ergo miser trepidas, ne stercore foeda canino
Atria displiceant oculis venientis amici,   65
Nec perfusa luto sit porticus; (et tamen uno
Semodio scobis haec emendat servulus unus:)
Illud non agitas, ut sanctam filius omni
Aspiciat sine labe domum vitioque carentem?
Gratum est, quod patriae civem populoque dedisti,   70
Si facis, ut patriae sit idoneus, utilis agris,
Utilis et bellorum et pacis rebus agendis.
Plurimum enim intererit, quibus artibus et quibus hunc tu
Moribus instituas.   Serpente ciconia pullos
Nutrit et inventa per devia rura lacerta: 75
Illi eadem sumtis quaerunt animalia pinnis.

so mild as it would be with us, to whom *libertas filii* is not an inconceivable expression.

  57 cerebro] Here as in English the brain is a synonym for sense; in Horace *Sat.* I. ix. 11, O te Bolane cerebri Felicem, it means hot temper.

  58 cucurbita] A cupping-glass of horn or brass, so called from its shape.—*Ventosa*, from the draught of air escaping.

  62 aspera] Verg. *Aen.* v. 267, "Cymbiaque argento perfecta atque *aspera signis.*"

  65 Atria] Where the dog was chained.

  67 scobis] Laid down before a dinner, to prevent the scraps staining the pavement, and to facilitate a clean sweep afterwards, to make the room pleasant next day or next course; here, however, the floor has been neglected as long as the ceiling, and has to be cleaned before dinner. Tea-leaves are used for the purpose now.

  68, 69 omni sine labe] Without *any* stain, free from all stain. The comedians are said to use *omni,* Cicero, *ullo.* He doubtless set usage aside in favour of a form more obviously logical.

  71 Si facis] Is the condition of *gratum est,* not of *dedisti.*—*Patriae idoneus* a good citizen, *utilis agris* a capable husbandman, a useful housekeeper; or to put it generally, useful in public and private, which corresponds to the antithesis of the next line, useful both in peace and war.

Vultur, jumento et canibus crucibusque relictis,
Ad fetus properat, partemque cadaveris affert.
Hic est ergo cibus magni quoque vulturis et se
Pascentis, propria quum jam facit arbore nidos.   80
Sed leporem aut capream famulae Jovis et generosae
In saltu venantur aves : hic praeda cubili
Ponitur: inde autem, quum se matura levarit
Progenies stimulante fame, festinat ad illam,
Quam primum praedam rupto gustaverat ovo.   85
    Aedificator erat Cetronius et modo curvo
Litore Caietae, summa nunc Tiburis arce,
Nunc Praenestinis in montibus alta parabat
Culmina villarum, Graecis longeque petitis
Marmoribus, vincens Fortunae atque Herculis aedem: 90
Ut spado vincebat Capitolia nostra Posides.
Dum sic ergo habitat Cetronius, imminuit rem,
Fregit opes, nec parva tamen mensura relictae
Partis erat : totam hanc turbavit filius amens,
Dum meliore novas attollit marmore villas.   95

77 **Jumento—relictis**] She leaves the body on the gibbet, and the mule by the roadside to the dogs. "Appuleius, *de Asino*, L. 6 fin., speaks of 'patibuli cruciatum cum canes et vultures intima protrahunt viscera,'" Macleane. The feet of the victim cannot have been more than just clear of the ground.

77, 78] The vulture leaves her prey and rivals to teach her young the taste of carrion.

81 **famulae Jovis et generosae**] Closely together; "of noble race, and ministers of Jove."

82 **In saltu**] Non in crucibus neque in pulvere: ubi scilicet jumentum jacet.

86 **Aedificator**] "Took to building," "was a building man," as we say, "a racing man." So *amator*, distinguished from *amans*, Cic. *Tusc.*

iv. xii. 22. If Juvenal wrote under Hadrian, this passage is a reflection on him; his detractors doubtless said that he would exhaust the finances of the empire, and that it was bad taste to attempt to outshine national monuments by personal extravagance.

90 **Fortunae**] At Praeneste.—*Herculis*, at Tibur.

91 **Posides**] A freedman of Claudius, who presented him with a decoration in his British triumph; it would be easy for him to build something which would dwarf the Capitol, which in Claudius's reign was so low as to be mean. Perhaps his work was unfinished, or no longer standing, as the imperfect is used ; or perhaps Domitian's Capitol had no need to fear a comparison with Posides' work.

Quidam sortiti metuentem sabbata patrem,
Nil praeter nubes et coeli numen adorant,
Nec distare putant humana carne suillam,
Qua pater abstinuit; mox et praeputia ponunt:
Romanas autem soliti contemnere leges,   100
Judaicum ediscunt et servant ac metuunt jus,
Tradidit arcano quodcunque volumine Moses:
'Non monstrare vias, eadem nisi sacra colenti,
Quaesitum ad fontem solos deducere verpos.
Sed pater in causa, cui septima quaeque fuit lux   105
Ignava, et partem vitae non attigit ullam.
Sponte tamen juvenes imitantur cetera: solam
Inviti quoque avaritiam exercere jubentur.
Fallit enim vitium specie virtutis et umbra,
Quum sit triste habitu vultuque et veste severum.   110
Nec dubie tanquam frugi laudatur avarus,
Tanquam parcus homo, et rerum tutela suarum
Certa magis, quam si fortunas servet easdem

96] Seneca (ap. S. Aug. *Civ. Dei*, vi. 11,) speaks of the observance as a universal custom.

97] This would be a natural misrepresentation of the superstitions of a nation whose poets were taught of God to conceive of a thunderstorm as a Theophany (*Ps.* xviii. 7—15). Accordingly, we find this belief attributed to the Jews by Diodorus and Strabo. Tertullian alludes to the same mistake; and a law of Honorius (A.D. 409) mentions a sect of *coelicolae*, perverting Christians to Judaism. Varro, Tacitus, and Dio, simply say that the Jews conceive God as unseen or invisible.

98] Here cannibalism seems to be conceived principally as a pollution of the person eating; it is generally conceived rather as an outrage on the person eaten.

99 et] Which the father had not.

101] The three stages are guilty curiosity, criminal compliance, slavish degradation.

102 arcano] Juvenal may have heard of the Apocrypha, or the Rabbinical hypothesis of a secret tradition of Moses' oral teaching; or the proselyte may have been made to wait some time for a sight of the Pentateuch.

106 partem vitae ullam] Any of the functions of life.—*Attigit*, by a capricious brachylogy characteristic of the silver age, instead of saying that he touched nothing useful on that day Juvenal says that day touched nothing useful.

108 Inviti quoque] "Even if unwilling."

109] Plato treats the oligarchical man, the thrifty, stingy householder, as the popular ideal of virtue.

111 Nec dubie] "And that without hesitation."

Hesperidum serpens aut Ponticus. Adde quod hunc, de
Quo loquor, egregium populus putat acquirendi   115
Artificem: quippe his crescunt patrimonia fabris!
Sed crescunt quocunque modo majoraque fiunt
Incude assidua, semperque ardente camino.
Et pater ergo animi felices credit avaros,
Qui miratur opes, qui nulla exempla beati   120
Pauperis esse putat: juvenes hortatur, ut illam
Ire viam pergant, et eidem incumbere sectae.
Sunt quaedam vitiorum elementa: his protinus illos
Imbuit et cogit minimas ediscere sordes.
Mox acquirendi docet insatiabile votum.   125
Servorum ventres modio castigat iniquo,
Ipse quoque esuriens: neque enim omnia sustinet unquam
Mucida caerulei panis consumere frusta,
Hesternum solitus medio servare minutal
Septembri, nec non differre in tempora coenae   130
Alterius conchem aestivam cum parte lacerti

114] One dragon guarded the golden apples, another the golden fleece.

117, 118]. They grow by foul play and over-work. 118 looks like a reference to some such proverbial phrase as ours about "burning a candle at both ends."

119 Et pater ergo] "So you see the father like the rest."

120 beati] Ambiguous, like ὀλβίου, "who never heard of a poor man that was well off." The Scholiast has a story of one Aglaus of Arcadia who was pronounced by the Delphic oracle to be happier than Gyges king of Lydia. It may be presumed that he was collaterally related to the great great grandfather of Tellus the Athenian; Hdt. i. 30, and that the old man of Verona who owes his reputation to Claudian, c. 52, was a yet more distant offshoot of the same family. The

father thinks all such stories mythical.

126 modio iniquo] The Attic slave's allowance was a *choenix* a day, i.e. a modius every six; here one suspects that the short measure has to last a week.

127 neque enim] "For indeed he can never bear."

128 frusta] He saves the scraps of bread till they are mouldy, even then he is too thrifty to finish them at a meal.

129 minutal] Vegetables minced with fish or meat, and flavoured according to taste. The ingredients appear fresh one day, next day they appear as hash, even then they are not finished.—*Medio Septembri*, when the pestilential south winds prevailed.

131 aestivam] So P.: the Corrector and the rest *aestivi*. It is a pure question of taste whether P.'s

Signatam, vel dimidio putrique siluro,
Filaque sectivi numerata includere porri.
Invitatus ad haec aliquis de ponte negavit.
Sed quo divitias haec per tormenta coactas,   135
Quum furor haud dubius, quum sit manifesta phrenesis,
Ut locuples moriaris, egentis vivere fato?
Interea pleno quum turget sacculus ore,
Crescit amor nummi, quantum ipsa pecunia crevit;
Et minus hanc optat qui non habet. Ergo paratur   140
Altera villa tibi, quum rus non sufficit unum,
Et proferre libet fines, majorque videtur
Et melior vicina seges: mercaris et hanc et
Arbusta et densa montem qui canet oliva.
Quorum si pretio dominus non vincitur ullo,   145
Nocte boves macri lassoque famelica collo
Jumenta ad virides hujus mittentur aristas;
Nec prius inde domum, quam tota novalia saevos
In ventres abeant, ut credas falcibus actum.
Dicere vix possis, quam multi talia plorent,   150

archetype shall be said to have blundered, or the rest to have altered to avoid a double epithet of *conchem*.

132 siluro] The shad always appears as part of a cheap dinner.

133 sectivi] iii. 293, n.—*Capitatum*, was allowed to grow to a head; *sectivus*, sown thick, and cut like asparagus. Did the miser sow this to make the most of the ground?

134 aliquis de ponte] Any beggar.—*Negavit*. So P. uncorrected, and the Scholiast. Cf. iii. 168, where a similar aorist has been effaced by Jahn, though found in *all* the MSS.

137, 139 egentis—crevit] So P. and a few others: the rest, *egenti*, which is neater, and *crescit*, which is less accurate. *Crevit* is corrected in P.

140 sq.] There is a slight change of view here; instead of the mere miser,

who has no ambition beyond pinching, we have the enterprising covetousness of Massinger's Sir Giles Overreach. The man finds that a single farm hardly supplies his household.

143]—
"Fertilior seges est alienis semper
    in agris,
Vicinumque pecus grandius
    uber habet."
                (Ov. *A. A.* i. 349.)

144 Arbusta] For firewood and hurdles.

146] The cattle have the better appetites, that they are hardworked as well as starved.

147 mittentur] So P. The tense marks a subsequent stage in the process.

150] The Roman law provided no summary remedy for trespass before a local court: except perhaps

Et quot venales injuria fecerit agros.
Sed qui sermones! quam foedae buccina famae!—
"Quid nocet haec?" inquit. "Tunicam mihi malo lupini,
Quam si me toto laudet vicinia pago,
Exigui ruris paucissima farra secantem."   155
Scilicet et morbis et debilitate carebis,
Et luctum et curam effugies, et tempora vitae
Longa tibi post haec fato meliore dabuntur,
Si tantum culti solus possederis agri,
Quantum sub Tatio populus Romanus arabat.   160
Mox etiam fractis aetate ac Punica passis
Proelia, vel Pyrrhum immanem, gladiosque Molossos,
Tandem pro multis vix jugera bina dabantur
Vulneribus. Merces haec sanguinis atque laboris
Nullis visa unquam meritis minor, aut ingratae   165
Curta fides patriae. Saturabat glebula talis
Patrem ipsum turbamque casae, qua feta jacebat
Uxor, et infantes ludebant quatuor, unus
Vernula, tres domini: sed magnis fratribus horum
A scrobe vel sulco redeuntibus, altera coena   170
Amplior et grandes fumabant pultibus ollae.

the aedilician action for *pauperies;* one does not know whether the aedile of a petty town perhaps twenty miles off was either formidable to the rich or accessible to the poor.

153 **Tunicam**] A pod. The cynicism beats the French proverb : "J'aime mieux un raisin pour moi que deux figues pour toi."

158 **meliore**] Assigning you a longer life, better health, and better luck than you were originally entitled to.

163 **jugera bina**] Two plough-gates—a block 240 feet square—the antiquarian and senatorian standard for a homestead. Tribunes were more liberal, and allowed seven.

167 **turbamque casae**] A large family to a small farm. The father, wife, and children dine early. There is plenty for them; plenty too for the big brother's supper.

169 **Vernula**] Cf. x. 117 n.—*Horum,* i. q. *infantium,* not *dominorum.* At the same time we are to contrast the farmer's wife with the fine lady of Juvenal's time who would be proud of having three children *at all,* while the farmer's wife has three so to speak in the nursery now and has had ever so many before.

171 **pultibus**] The traditional spelt porridge ; *polenta* was the Greek equivalent.

Nunc modus hic agri nostro non sufficit horto.
Inde fere scelerum causae; nec plura venena
Miscuit, aut ferro grassatur saepius ullum
Humanae mentis vitium, quam saeva cupido   175
Immodici census: nam dives qui fieri vult,
Et cito vult fieri. Sed quae reverentia legum,
Quis metus aut pudor est unquam properantis avari?
"Vivite contenti casulis et collibus istis,
O pueri!" Marsus dicebat et Hernicus olim   180
Vestinusque senex; "panem quaeramus aratro,
Qui satis est mensis: laudant hoc numina ruris,
Quorum ope et auxilio gratae post munus aristae,
Contingunt homini veteris fastidia quercus.
Nil vetitum fecisse volet, quem non pudet alto   185
Per glaciem perone tegi; qui summovet Euros
Pellibus inversis. Peregrina ignotaque nobis
Ad scelus atque nefas, quaecunque est, purpura ducit."—
     Haec illi veteres praecepta minoribus: at nunc
Post finem autumni media de nocte supinum   190
Clamosus juvenem pater excitat: "Accipe ceras,.

176 **Immodici**] So the best MSS.
Most *indomiti;* perhaps because the
last syllable of *cupido* was still buz-
zing in the transcriber's head.

179 **istis**] 'These' which *you,*
see, *his* would be which *we* see;
in later Latin from the fourth century onwards this becomes the pre-
valent sense of *iste,* and *hic* is in
great measure superseded.

182 **Qui satis est**] They are to
want nothing better, to have enough
of that.

184 **fastidia**] "The right to disdain."

186 **glaciem**] Is probably mud
frozen at the top, through which the
man does not mind splashing in high
galligaskins.

187 **inversis**] "Turned inside
out." "The skinny side out and

the woolly side in," as the old song
says.

188 **quaecunque est**] "Whatever it be:" emphasizes *ignota.*

190 **Post finem autumni**] For
early rising in our sense was of no
use for purposes of study to busy
men. Cicero could only write considerable books in winter (*Parad.
Prooem.* § 5). The father comes
with the tablets (hence *accipe*) to the
boy's bedside, and makes him get
up at midnight in the cold. Dili-
gent people began to work by can-
dlelight at the Vulcanalia, Aug. 23,
with or without superstitious mo-
tives. Of course it would not be
such a great effort till winter set in;
but his father makes him go on then.

— **media de nocte**] Before the
night is well over.

Scribe, puer, vigila, causas age, perlege rubras
Majorum leges, aut vitem posce libello.
Sed caput intactum buxo naresque pilosas
Annotet, et grandes miretur Laelius alas.   195
Dirue Maurorum attegias, castella Brigantum,
Ut locupletem aquilam tibi sexagesimus annus
Afferat: aut, longos castrorum ferre labores
Si piget, et trepidum solvunt tibi cornua ventrem
Cum lituis audita, pares, quod vendere possis   200
Pluris dimidio, nec te fastidia mercis
Ullius subeant ablegandae Tiberim ultra,
Neu credas ponendum aliquid discriminis inter
Unguenta et corium. Lucri bonus est odor ex re
Qualibet. Illa tuo sententia semper in ore   205
Versetur Dís atque ipso Jove digna poetâ:
Unde habeas, quaerit nemo: sed oportet habere."—
Hoc monstrant vetulae pueris repentibus assae;
Hoc discunt omnes ante alpha et beta puellae.
Talibus instantem monitis quemcunque parentem   210

192 rubras] The first words of
the laws were written in vermilion.
193 libello] A memorial, probably addressed to the emperor.
194 buxo] Boxwood does not
split, and was therefore useful to
combmakers, and is now to wood-
engravers.
195 Laelius] The point is, mind
your commander admires you for
your vigour and ostentatious hardi-
hood as Laelius admired Marius.
The story is commonly told of Scipio.
196] The son will have to bear
heat and cold both among savages.
The Brigantes stretched from the
Mersey to the wall of Severus.
197 locupletem] Which brings
wealth for a peasant. Already in
the time of Horace, *Sat.* I. vi. 72,
centurions were tritons among min-
nows.

201 Pluris dimidio] For more
by one-half than the original price.
202 ablegandae] e. g. tanning.
204] Cf. the *Non olet*, extorted
from Titus, on being presented with
a piece of money raised by an inde-
licate tax.
206 poeta] So P. and the Schol.;
the rest 'poetae.' The line is not
quite like "Reliquias Danaum atque
immitis Achilli" (*Aen.* i. 30). What
is good enough for the gods is not
necessarily good enough for Jove.
208 assae] Dry nurses. So P.
and the Scholiast. Carrio proposes
reptantibus, which would account
for the old variant *repetentibus*,
which seems to have suggested
poscentibus, either of which would
lead by a plausible conjecture to
assem.

Sic possem affari: "Dic, o vanissime, quis te
Festinare jubet? meliorem praesto magistro
Discipulum. Securus abi: vinceris, ut Ajax
Praeteriit Telamonem, ut Pelea vicit Achilles.
Parcendum est teneris: nondum implevere medullas   215
Maturae mala nequitiae. Ast quum pectere barbam
Coeperit, et longi mucronem admittere cultri,
Falsus erit testis, vendet perjuria summa
Exigua, et Cereris tangens aramque pedemque.
Elatam jam crede nurum, si limina vestra   220
Mortifera cum dote subit. Quibus illa premetur
Per somnum digitis! nam quae terraque marique
Acquirenda putas, brevior via conferet illi.
Nullus enim magni sceleris labor." "Haec ego nunquam
Mandavi," dices olim, "nec talia suasi."   225
Mentis causa malae tamen est et origo penes te.
Nam quisquis magni census praecepit amorem
Et laevo monitu pueros producit avaros,
[Et qui per fraudes patrimonia conduplicare]
Dat libertatem, et totas effundit habenas   230

215] Your son does not equal you yet. Never mind, he has not yet attained the full vices of maturity.

216 **Ast—Coeperit**] Most MSS. omit *ast;* the particle is quite superfluous, the pleonasm is characteristic of *old* Latin. Juvenal is almost the last writer who can have used it if he used it spontaneously. He tells the father he will not have to wait long, the boy will be a finished rogue as soon as he fancies the down on his chin wants combing, as soon as he begins to shave. This last was a solemn ceremony, iii. 186 n.; until his friends decided to perform it, a boy had to assert his consciousness of his beard by combing it.

217 **longi**] His face is too small now for there to be room to apply the whole edge of a long rasor: *admittere*, however, rather means that there is use for the rasor on his cheeks than space.

219 **Cereris**] It is difficult to say whether Ceres comes in as the patroness of the Eleusinian mysteries, or as *legifera*, because law and order begin with agriculture.

220 **vestra**] Of your family.

221 **Mortifera**] Though by the Roman common law the dowry in such a case would go back to her family, yet in fact it was a matter of course for the husband to enrich himself by every wife he buried: cf. "Nerio jam tertia conditur uxor." Pers. ii. 14.

Curriculo: quem si revoces, subsistere nescit,
Et te contemto rapitur metisque relictis.
Nemo satis credit tantum delinquere, quantum
Permittas: adeo indulgent sibi latius ipsi.
Quum dicis juveni, stultum qui donet amico,   235
Qui paupertatem levet attollatque propinqui;
Et spoliare doces et circumscribere et omni
Crimine divitias acquirere, quarum amor in te,
Quantus erat patriae Deciorum in pectore, quantun
Dilexit Thebas, si Graecia vera, Menoeceus: 240
In quorum sulcis legiones dentibus anguis
Cum clypeis nascuntur, et horrida bella capessunt
Continuo, tanquam et tubicen surrexerit una.
Ergo ignem, cujus scintillas ipse dedisti,
Flagrantem late et rapientem cuncta videbis.   245
Nec tibi parcetur misero, trepidumque magistrum
In cavea magno fremitu leo tollet alumnus.
    Nota mathematicis genesis tua: sed grave tardas
Exspectare colus. Morieris stamine nondum
Abrupto. Jam nunc obstas et vota moraris,   250
Jam torquet juvenem longa et cervina senectus.
Ocius Archigenen quaere atque eme quod Mithridates
Composuit, si vis aliam decerpere ficum

229] Has no intelligible place. Is therefore omitted in several MSS., but is a fair line, not like a gloss.

233 **tantum**] So far, no further (cf. xiii. 96, n.).

234 **adeo**]. So certainly.

237 **circumscribere**] To cheat wards.

241, 242] Bear on the doubt, *si Graecia vera.—Quorum*, the antecedent is *Thebanorum*, from *Thebas*, or rather *Graecorum*, from *Graecia*, as *Graecia* is nearer, as otherwise such strange stories would discredit Thebes, not Greece; and as the imputation of a constant practice based

on one instance, is more suitable to a whole country than a single town.

242, tr. "where armies spring up in the furrows from a serpent's teeth," &c.

248 **Nota**] For your son has told them as a basis of calculation.— *Mathematicis*, lit. wise men, almost always used of astrologers; so a 'cunning man' or woman in Devonshire means a white witch.

251 **cervina**] 3456 years, according to Hesiod.

252 **Archigenen**] Cf. xiii. 98, n.

253, 254] "Lest you should be poisoned in these innocent things;"

Atque alias tractare rosas. Medicamen habendum est,
Sorbere ante cibum quod debeat et pater et rex.   255
   Monstro voluptatem egregiam, cui nulla theatra,
Nulla aequare queas praetoris pulpita lauti,
Si spectes, quanto capitis discrimine constent
Incrementa domus, aerata multus in arca
Fiscus, et ad vigilem ponendi Castora nummi,   260
Ex quo Mars Ultor galeam quoque perdidit, et res
Non potuit servare suas. Ergo omnia Florae
Et Cereris licet et Cybeles aulaea relinquas:
Tanto majores humana negotia ludi.
   An magis oblectant animum jactata petauro   265
Corpora, quique solet rectum descendere funem,
Quam tu, Corycia semper qui puppe moraris
Atque habitas, Coro semper tollendus et Austro,
Perditus ac vilis sacci mercator olentis:
Qui gaudes pingue antiquae de litore Cretae   270
Passum, et municipes Jovis advexisse lagenas?
Hic tamen ancipiti figens vestigia planta
Victum illa mercede parat brumamque famemque
Illa reste cavet: tu propter mille talenta
Et centum villas temerarius. Aspice portus   275

or, "if you wish to live another year, to pluck the roses of spring or the fruits of summer."

257 **lauti**] Though he caters for you like a gentleman.

259, 260] The Temple of Castor, built according to tradition in consequence of the vow of the Dictator at Lake Regillus; it was the strong room of the old Forum, and regularly patrolled (hence Castor is Vigil because there was a watch in his temple, as Concord twitters, because the storks in her temple do); the temple of Mars Ultor erected by Augustus, in accordance with a vow before the battle of Philippi, seems to have been in the same way the strong room of the new Forum of Augustus, until the robbery mentioned in the text, which made capitalists think the old place safest.

265 **petauro**] i. q. πέταυρον, Aeolic for μετέωρον, which is a hoop hung up, from which two tumblers tried to throw each other: the loser had to jump through blazing rings.

267 **Corycia**] From the saffron promontory in Cilicia ; hence *sacci olentis* (inf. 269).

274, 275] May mean that he is rich, and wants to be richer, to make up the 1000 talents, and the 100 villas. It would be enough to suppose he wants to be rich.

Et plenum magnis trabibus mare; plus hominum est jam
In pelago; veniet classis, quocunque vocarit
Spes lucri, nec Carpathium Gaetulaque tantum
Aequora transiliet, sed, longe Calpe relicta,
Audiet Herculeo stridentem gurgite solem.   280
Grande operae pretium est, ut tenso folle reverti
Inde domum possis, tumidaque superbus aluta,
Oceani monstra et juvenes vidisse marinos.
Non unus mentes agitat furor. Ille sororis
In manibus vultu Eumenidum terretur et igni,   285
Hic bove percusso mugire Agamemnona credit
Aut Ithacum. Parcat tunicis licet atque lacernis,
Curatoris eget qui navem mercibus implet
Ad summum latus, et tabula distinguitur unda,
Quum sit causa mali tanti et discriminis hujus   290
Concisum argentum in titulos faciesque minutas.
Occurrunt nubes et fulgura: "solvite funem,"
Frumenti dominus clamat piperisque coempti;
"Nil color hic coeli, nil fascia nigra minatur;
Aestivum tonat." Infelix hac forsitan' ipsa   295
Nocte cadet fractis trabibus, fluctuque premetur
Obrutus, et zonam laeva morsuque tenebit.
Sed cujus votis modo non suffecerat aurum,

279 **longe Calpe relicta**] Far
beyond the world's end.
280 **stridentem**] Hissing as he
goes under water.
282 **tumida aluta**] Full purse.
Aluta, softened with alum.
284 **Ille**] Orestes.
286 **Hic**] Ajax.
287 **Parcat—lacernis**] Destruc-
tive mania was one of the common-
est legal tests of insanity at Rome.
289 **tabula distinguitur unda**]
A consequence of overlading, bring-
ing the deck below the water-
line.

290, 291 **tanti**] Contrasts with
minutas.
293 **coempti**] He has made up a
large and early cargo.
294 **fascia**] Swathe of clouds.
295 **Aestivum tonat**] Juvenal is
speaking of the Mediterranean: in
England summer is the only time
when we expect a serious thunderstorm.
297 **zonam**] Out of all his wealth,
μάλιστα μέν, he will be drowned
clinging to his money; εἰ δὲ μή,
he will be a beggar.
298 **Sed**] Stay, the man, &c., i.e.

Quod Tagus et rutila volvit Pactolus arena,
Frigida sufficient velantes inguina panni   300
Exiguusque cibus, mersa rate naufragus assem
Dum rogat, et picta se tempestate tuetur.
    Tantis parta malis cura majore metuque
Servantur.   Misera est magni custodia census.
Dispositis praedives hamis vigilare cohortem   305
Servorum noctu Licinus jubet, attonitus pro
Electro signisque suis Phrygiaque columna,
Atque ebore et lata testudine.   Dolia nudi
Non ardent Cynici: si fregeris, altera fiet
Cras domus, atque eadem plumbo commissa manebit.   310
Sensit Alexander, testa quum vidit in illa
Magnum habitatorem, quanto felicior hic, qui
Nil cuperet, quam qui totum sibi posceret orbem,
Passurus gestis aequanda pericula rebus.
Nullum numen habes, si sit Prudentia: nos te,   315
Nos facimus, Fortuna, Deam.   Mensura tamen quae
Sufficiat census, si quis me consulat, edam:
In quantum sitis atque fames et frigora poscunt,
Quantum, Epicure, tibi parvis suffecit in hortis,
Quantum Socratici ceperunt ante penates.   320
Nunquam aliud Natura, aliud Sapientia dicit.

I told you he would cling to his money; but he will find he can get on as a beggar.

305 **hamis**] In case of fire.

cohortem] A detachment told off for the night.   He depends on his own slaves, not on the watch, of whom there were only seven cohorts for the whole city.

307 **suis**] "Because they are his own."

309, 310 **altera—manebit**] "He'll get another to-morrow, and the old one will mend, and last on." P. and some others have *atque*, the rest *aut*.

314 **aequanda**] That ought to count for as much as his achievements.

315 **habes**] So P. and some others; the rest, *abest*. At x. 365, it is just the reverse.   *Habes* must mean, you have no divine power of your own.

319 **Epicure**] Juvenal quotes Epicurus, to shew that his own philosophy was not sectarian.   Perhaps he disliked the Stoics, who were often hypocritical and turbulent.

320] Socrates, Plat. *Ap.* 38 b, values his whole property at a mina.

Acribus exemplis videor te claudere.   Misce
Ergo aliquid nostris de moribus: effice summam,
Bis septem ordinibus quam lex dignatur Othonis.
Haec quoque si rugam trahit extenditque labellum: 325
Sume duos Equites, fac tertia quadringenta.
Si nondum implevi gremium, si panditur ultra:
Nec Croesi fortuna unquam, nec Persica regna
Sufficient animo, nec divitiae Narcissi,
Indulsit Caesar cui Claudius omnia, cujus   330
Paruit imperiis, uxorem occidere jussus.

325]—
"If yet thou frown'st, yet hang'st
   the lip, then be
   As rich as two knights; if thou
   wilt, as three."—(Holyday.)

329 **Narcissi**] Who made between
800,000*l.* and 900,000*l.*
   331] He ordered the execution
of Messalina, after Claudius had
promised her an interview.

SATIRA XV.

Quis nescit, Volusi Bithynice, qualia demens
Aegyptus portenta colat? Crocodilon adorat
Pars haec; illa pavet saturam serpentibus ibin.
Effigies sacri nitet aurea cercopitheci,
Dimidio magicae resonant ubi Memnone chordae,   5
Atque vetus Thebe centum jacet obruta portis.
Illic aeluros, hic piscem fluminis, illic
Oppida tota canem venerantur, nemo Dianam.
Porrum et caepe nefas violare et frangere morsu.
O sanctas gentes, quibus haec nascuntur in hortis   10
Numina! Lanatis animalibus abstinet omnis
Mensa; nefas illac fetum jugulare capellae:
Carnibus humanis vesci licet. Attonito quum

1 **Bithynice**] A Bithynicus was a friend of Martial (Mart. vi. 50. 5).

3 **pavet**] A comic exaggeration of *veretur*.

5 **Dimidio**] Broken, probably by Cambyses, since restored, perhaps under Septimius Severus. The first writer who mentions the sound is Strabo, the last Pausanias.

6 **obruta**] It was in ruins when visited by Germanicus. It had been sacked by Cambyses—who doubtless got credit for much that Esarhaddon had done—and drained by Alexandria and its dependencies.

8 **Dianam**] Herodotus identifies Bubastis or Pasht with Artemis

(Herod. ii. 137). Her head was like a cat's.

9—12] There is a good deal of exaggeration here. Gellius, xx. 8, says that at Pelusium there was a superstition about leeks and garlic that they withered when the moon was waxing and only grew when she was waning: the Theban nome abstained from sheep, the Mendesian from goats.

13—16 **quum—narraret—Moverat**] "On occasion of Ulysses telling a story like this, he found he had roused anger, or may be laughter."—*Aretalogus*, a Stoic or Cynic parasite, who would hold

SATIRA XV.

Tale super coenam facinus narraret Ulixes
Alcinoo, bilem aut risum fortasse quibusdam   15
Moverat, ut mendax aretalogus. " In mare nemo
Hunc abicit, saeva dignum veraque Charybdi,
Fingentem immanes Laestrygonas atque Cyclopas?
Nam citius Scyllam vel concurrentia saxa
Cyaneis, plenos et tempestatibus utres   20
Crediderim, aut tenui percussum verbere Circes
Et cum remigibus grunnisse Elphenora porcis.
Tam vacui capitis populum Phaeaca putavit?"
Sic aliquis merito nondum ebrius et minimum qui
De Corcyraea temetum duxerat urna: 25
Solus enim hoc Ithacus nullo sub teste canebat.
Nos miranda quidem, sed nuper consule Junio
Gesta super calidae referemus moenia Copti,
Nos vulgi scelus et cunctis graviora cothurnis.
Nam scelus, a Pyrrha quamquam omnia syrmata volvas,   30
Nullus apud tragicos populus facit. Accipe, nostro

forth upon virtue for the entertainment of the company.

17 **abicit**] 'Abjicit.' Cf. 'adicit, Mart. x. 82. 1; 'reice,' Verg. Ecl. iii. 96.

19 **Scyllam**] She is mentioned rather as a hybrid monster, than as a cannibal. — *Concurrentia saxa.* One is not to blame Juvenal for not following the mythologists who localised the Cyanean rocks at the entrance of the Bosporus. Homer, *Od.* xii. 60—72, distinctly identifies the Planctae in Trinacrian waters with the rocks through which Argo passed, and these were certainly the Cyaneae : the fact is, at the earliest point at which we can trace the legend they are the mythical gates of a mythical sea ; it is a further question whether they represent anything in the experience of the first navigators or are absolutely mythical. The construction, ' the rocks

that meet at the Cyanean isles,' is curious, not to say clumsy.

21 **percussum**] The stroke is as fabulous, but less disgusting.

25 **temetum**] Connected with *temulentus, abstemius :* " Abstemias egisse hoc est, vino semper, quod temetum prisca lingua appellatur, abstinuisse " (Gell. x. 23).

27 **Junio**] Q. Junio Rustico, cons. A.D. 119, or App. Junio Sabino, cons. A.D. 84. *Junco* looks like a conjecture of P.'s archetype, though there was a consul suffect of that name, A.D. 127.

28 **super**] South of, as we say, up the country. He names Coptos because, being the point at which merchandise brought up the Red Sea was re-shifted for the Nile, it was better known at Rome than most other places in Egypt.

29] The crimes of tragedy are committed by (a) individuals (b)

Dira quod exemplum feritas produxerit aevo.
Inter finitimos vetus atque antiqua simultas,
Immortale odium et nunquam sanabile vulnus
Ardet adhuc, Ombos et Tentyra.   Summus utrinque   35
Inde furor vulgo, quod numina vicinorum
Odit uterque locus, quum solos credat habendos
Esse Deos, quos ipse colit.   Sed tempore festo
Alterius populi rapienda occasio cunctis
Visa inimicorum primoribus ac ducibus, ne   40
Laetum hilaremque diem, ne magnae gaudia coenae
Sentirent, positis ad templa et compita mensis
Pervigilique toro, quem nocte ac luce jacentem
Septimus interdum sol invenit.   Horrida sane
Aegyptus : sed luxuria, quantum ipse notavi,   45
Barbara famoso non cedit turba Canopo.
Adde, quod et facilis victoria de madidis et
Blaesis atque mero titubantibus.   Inde virorum
Saltatus nigro tibicine, qualiacunque

high in rank ; *vulgi* is contrasted with both.

33 **finitimos**] They were ninety miles apart, with Thebes between ; they are called Khoum Ombou and Denderah now.   One can hardly argue from the mistake against the tradition, supported by *quantum ipse notavi* inf. 45, that Juvenal himself had been in Egypt : it proves at most that he had not been up the country as far as Tentyra, and so supposed that they must be neighbours to fight.

· 36] The Egyptian religion consisted of a sacerdotal pantheism, superinduced on (or perhaps evolved from) a number of popular and local fetichisms.

39, 40 **Alterius**] "Ombitarum. —*Inimicorum*, Tentyritarum."

45 **luxuria**] The taste, rather than the talent for self-indulgence.

46 **Canopo**] The purely commercial settlement of Canopus is contrasted with the native Egyptians : one might infer from a note of the Scholiast that part of it was known as Ripa Latina, which in itself is possible ; but he implies also that Alexandria was *barbara :* and he is hardly authority enough for supposing that Alexandria ceased to be substantially a Greek city before the Arab conquest.

47 **et facilis**] As well as sweet.

48 sq. **Inde**] Among the Ombites ; *hinc,* among the Tentyrites.—*Virorum,* at Rome men would have been spectators, not actors.—*Tibicine* and *unguenta* emphasize *luxuriæ; nigro* and *qualiacunque, horrida.*   They wanted to enjoy themselves, and did not know how.

Unguenta et flores multaeque in fronte coronae : 50
Hinc jejunum odium. Sed jurgia prima sonare
Incipiunt animis ardentibus : haec tuba rixae.
Dein clamore pari concurritur, et vice teli
Saevit nuda manus : paucae sine vulnere malae ;
Vix cuiquam aut nulli toto certamine nasus 55
Integer. Aspiceres jam cuncta per agmina vul
Dimidios, alias facies et hiantia ruptis
Ossa genis, plenos oculorum sanguine pugnos.
Ludere se credunt ipsi tamen et pueriles
Exercere acies, quod nulla cadavera calcent : 60
Et sane quo tot rixantis millia turbae,
Si vivunt omnes? Ergo acrior impetus, et jam
Saxa inclinatis per humum quaesita lacertis
Incipiunt torquere, domestica seditioni
Tela ; nec hunc lapidem, quales et Turnus et Ajax, 65
Vel quo Tydides percussit pondere coxam
Aeneae ; sed quem valeant emittere dextrae
Illis dissimiles et nostro tempore natae.
Nam genus hoc vivo jam decrescebat Homero.
Terra malos homines nunc educat atque pusillos : 70
Ergo Deus, quicunque aspexit, ridet et odit.

---

52 haec tuba rixae] Scolding bears the same relation to a trumpet as a brawl to a fight.

56 Aspiceres] We say, "One might see," oftener than "You might see." In Latin almost always the last form prevails.

60 calcent] Egyptian reason for *ludere*. *Calcant* would be Juvenal's reason for *credunt*.

63 inclinatis — lacertis] This seems as if the stones were large enough to be sunken, so that to raise them it was necessary to stoop and heave them up, using the arms stretched straight as a lever ; unless we are to suppose that "inclinatis—

lacertis" is simply ironical as the stones are not of heroic size : for the stone of Turnus cf. Verg. *Aen.* xii. 896 sqq., for those of Ajax and Diomed, cf. *Il.* vii. 268, v. 304.

69 jam decrescebat] Which is the reason why the stone hurled by Turnus would have taken twelve of Vergil's contemporaries to lift, while that hurled by Diomed, a hero not less distinguished, could have been raised by two of Homer's.

70 malos—atque pusillos] Perhaps "evil and puny to match," hence :

71 ridet et odit] "Can laugh as well as tease."—*Ridet et*, cf. for simi·

A diverticulo repetatur fabula.   Postquam
Subsidiis aucti, pars altera promere ferrum
Audet, èt infestis pugnam instaurare sagittis :
Terga fuga celeri praestant instantibus Ombis   75
Qui vicina colunt umbrosae Tentyra palmae.
Labitur hinc quidam, nimia formidine cursum
Praecipitans, capiturque : ast illum in plurima sectum
Frusta et particulas, ut multis mortuus unus
Sufficeret, totum corrosis ossibus edit   80
Victrix turba : nec ardenti decoxit aeno
Aut verubus : longum usque adeo tardumque putavit
Exspectare focos, contenta cadavere crudo.
Hic gaudere libet, quod non violaverit ignem,
Quem summa coeli raptum, de parte Prometheus   85

lar inelegancies *audet et*, inf. 74,
licet et, iii. 92.

74 **instaurare**] This is more naturally said of the side which up to
a certain point were losing.

75, 76] Most MSS. read *praestantibus omnibus instant*. P.'s
corrector has effaced the original
reading for *praestantibus omnibus
instans;* and several others have the
same. The vulgate must mean
either that "the Tentyrites ran
after everybody who ran away," or,
"when everybody ran away, the
Tentyrites ran after." *Instans* does
make sense, but does not account
for the original reading of P., or
the reading found in two old MSS.
praestant instantibus omnes, whence
Mercerus restored the reading in
the text. One must suppose that
Ombis got altered into *omnes* by one
copyist, while another thought it
was a contraction of *omnibus*. It
may be added that the Ombites,
who were at home, would be more
easily reinforced than the Tentyrites. It is curious that this passage
where the reading is uncertain is
our only clue to determine which is
which in 39, 40, and 48—51.

77 **hinc**] Either "from among
the Tentyrites," or "hereupon," "at
this point."

78 **ast illum**] 'Ast' emphasizes
the change of subject. Cf. iii.
264 :—

"Haec inter pueros varie pro-
          perantur : at ille."

81 **decoxit**] Hence we must supply roasted with *verubus*. Cf. Val.
Flac. viii. 254 : "Pars verubus, pars
undanti despumat aeno."

83 **focos**] Almost "the comfort
of cooking it at their own fireside,"
an additional proof that the invaders
were the losing side, and the re-
vellers the winning.

84 **Hic gaudere libet**] Here one
fancies what a blessing it was that
they did not profane the stolen present of Prometheus. For the capricious piety (or impiety) of *libet*, cf.
Soph. *O. T.* 911, χώρας ἄνακτες,
δόξα μοι παρεστάθη ναοὺς ἱκέσθαι
δαιμόνων.

85 **summa coeli de parte**] "From
the empyrean heights." Juvenal
doubtless takes the notion of a fiery
sphere above the visible heavens
from the Stoics, who took it from

Donavit terris. Elemento gratulor et te
Exsultare reor. Sed qui mordere cadaver
Sustinuit, nil unquam hac carne libentius edit.
Nam scelere in tanto ne quaeras et dubites, an
Prima voluptatem gula senserit. Ultimus autem,   90
Qui stetit absumto jam toto corpore, ductis
Per terram digitis, aliquid de sanguine gustat.
Vascones, haec fama est, alimentis talibus olim
Produxere animas: sed res diversa, sed illic
Fortunae invidia est bellorumque ultima, casus   95
Extremi, longae dira obsidionis egestas.
Hujus enim, quod nunc agitur, miserabile debet
Exemplum esse cibi: sicut modo dicta mihi gens
Post omnes herbas, post cuncta animalia, quicquid
Cogebat vacui ventris furor, hostibus ipsis   100
Pallorem ac maciem et tenues miserantibus artus,
Membra aliena fame lacerabant, esse parati
Et sua. Quisnam hominum veniam dare, quisve Deorum

Heraclitus. It is hardly likely that Heraclitus invented it, for the quinta essentia of the Pythagoreans standing above and beside the visible elements seems like a parallel form of the same conception, though it is difficult to determine anything with respect to a school that lived on plagiarism.

89 Nam] Introduces a special fact, to illustrate and confirm the general proposition, "sed—edit," which is naturally thrown into the aorist. "We rejoice ... but he who is capable of tasting a corpse, thinks it the most delicious meal he ever tasted; for you mustn't think the first man might enjoy it perhaps, but no one else: rather, the man who stood waiting for his turn till the last, wiped his fingers along the ground, and sucked them to have a taste of the blood, though the body was gone."

93 Vascones] At Calagurris, now Calahorra, on the Ebro, the birth-place of Quintilian. The place stood two sieges: one under Sertorius, B.C. 75, against Metellus, the other, B.C. 72, after Sertorius' death against Pompeius. It was in the latter that they fed upon human flesh, salting it to make it last.

95 Fortunae invidia] A thing for mankind to bear Fortune a grudge for, cf. inf. 123 n., cf. also 2 Kings iii. 27, "There arose great indignation against Israel," when the king of Moab burnt the eldest son of the king of Edom.

97, 98] Pity is due to a case of cannibalism, like theirs which we are treating.—*Sicut*, as we ought to pity them; so they were in great distress when they did it.

99 herbas] Which could only be disagreeable, *animalia* which might be disgusting: *quicquid* supply *post*.

Viribus abnuerit dira atque immania passis,
Et quibus illorum poterant ignoscere manes,   105
Quorum corporibus vescebantur? Melius nos
Zenonis praecepta monent: nec enim omnia, quaedam
Pro vita facienda putat. Sed Cantaber unde
Stoicus, antiqui praesertim aetate Metelli?
Nunc totus Graias nostrasque habet orbis Athenas.   110
Gallia causidicos docuit facunda Britannos:
De conducendo loquitur jam rhetore Thule.
Nobilis ille tamen populus, quem diximus, et par
Virtute atque fide, sed major clade, Saguntus
Tale quid excusat. Maeotide saevior ara   115
Aegyptus: quippe illa nefandi Taurica sacri
Inventrix homines (ut jam, quae carmina tradunt,
Digna fide credas) tantum immolat, ulterius nil
Aut gravius cultro timet 'hostia. Quis modo casus

104] *Ventribus*, the conjecture of H. Valerius, is most like Juvenal; but all the MSS. have *viribus*, or *urbibus*.

106, 7] It is worth noticing that this tribute to stoicism is not balanced by any approach to a sneer in any part of the Satire.

108 **Cantaber**] J. had read of their resistance to Augustus; but they had nothing to do with Calagurris.

109 **antiqui**] It was at least 150 years ago; and Horace speaks of all poets a hundred years old as ancient.

110 **Athenas**] i.q. litteras, or perhaps litteraturam Atticam.

111] The implied assertions that Gaul is eloquent, and that there are pleaders in Britain, is more important than the express assertion that Britain is taught by Gaul.

113] "Still the people is a noble one; and the precedent of Saguntus may excuse such a deed;" or "and Saguntus has a deed of the

same kind which it has to excuse on the same grounds," or, "Saguntus has some such plea" (necessity) "to urge." The Romans generously forgot that there had been a strong Carthaginian party in Saguntum up to the last.

114 **fide**] The fidelity of Saguntus to the Roman alliance is compared with the fidelity of Calagurris to the remains of Sertorius, which were in the town. It seems that, after all, Calagurris must have capitulated, as the *clades* of Saguntus was simply the ordinary fate of towns taken by storm, unless Juvenal means that it was a peculiar *clades* that the heads of the Roman party burnt their property instead of leaving it to be plundered, and their families, instead of leaving them to be sold.

117 **Inventrix**] Sc. Diana.
— **jam**] After the ferocity of Egypt.
119 **modo**] Mayor, "What ca‑ lamity, if nothing more?" citing,

Impulit hos? quae tanta fames infestaque vallo   120
Arma coegerunt tam detestabile monstrum
Audere? Anne aliam, terra Memphitide sicca,
Invidiam facerent nolenti surgere Nilo?
Qua nec terribiles Cimbri, nec Britones unquam,
Sauromataeque truces aut immanes Agathyrsi,   125
Hac saevit rabie imbelle et inutile vulgus,
Parvula fictilibus solitum dare vela phaselis,
Et brevibus pictae remis incumbere testae.
Nec poenam sceleri invenies, nec digna parabis

"Nihil impedit quominus *certe* intelligas nam opponi potest quamvis" (Hand. *Turs.* iii. 634), who quotes no passages where *modo* must be taken closely with an interrogative pronoun or particle; hence I should paraphrase, "I should only like to know what calamity these had, to drive them to such a deed."

120 vallo] Is the ablative of the instrument after either *infesta* or *coegerunt*. Tr. "what famine had power to drive them to it, when their enemies were arrayed against them and had shut them in?"

122, 123] "What else could they do to put the Nile's conduct in not rising in an invidious light as having caused a famine?"

124, 125] The Britons practised human sacrifices, and had their wives in common; so had the Agathyrsi. The Sarmatians were a proverb of ferocity; it is possible that they may have owed their reputation in part to what Herodotus says iv. 116, 117 of the ferocity of their women, who never married till they had killed an enemy. Such irregularities as *que* and *aut*, instead of a succession of *necs*, are common both in English and Latin, and very little or no principle can be traced in their use or avoidance. Here one might fancy that Britons, and either

Sauromatae or Agathyrsi, are collectively opposed to Cimbri. It is disputed whether 'Brito' means a Briton or a Breton. Ausonius, who unfortunately wrote when the connexion between Britain and Brittany was growing closer, uses it as a synonym of Britannus (*Ep.* iii. 112):

"Sylvius iste bonus fertur, ferturque Britannus
Aut Brito hic non est Sylvius, aut malus est."

This passage is however nearly decisive, the inhabitants of Brittany had done nothing, by any peculiarly energetic resistance to Rome on this wise, to earn a poetical reputation as exceptionally fierce or terrible.

127, 128]—

"——— Pellaei gens fortunata Canopi . . .
. . . circum pictis vehitur sua rura phaselis."
Verg. *Georg.* iv. 287, 289.

As the dangers of the sea were a commonplace with Roman poets, they were especially struck by the easy navigation of the expanse of water during an inundation, where it was possible, in the absence of storms and rocks, to use gay boats of earthenware: Juvenal treats their easy pleasant sailing in toy-boats almost as a proof of childishness,

Supplicia his populis, in quorum mente pares sunt   130
Et similes ira atque fames. Mollissima corda
Humano generi dare se natura fatetur,
Quae lacrimas dedit: haec nostri pars optima sensus.
Plorare ergo jubet causam dicentis amici
'Squaloremque rei, pupillum ad jura vocantem   135
Circumscriptorem, cujus manantia fletu
Ora puellares faciunt incerta capilli.
Naturae imperio gemimus, quum funus adultae
Virginis occurrit, vel terra clauditur infans,
Et minor igne rogi. Quis enim bonus et face dignus   140
Arcana, qualem Cereris vult esse sacerdos,
Ulla aliena sibi credat mala? Separat hoc nos
A grege mutorum, atque ideo venerabile soli
Sortiti ingenium divinorumque capaces
Atque exercendis capiendisque artibus apti   145
Sensum a coelesti demissum traximus arce,
Cujus egent prona et terram spectantia. Mundi
Principio indulsit communis conditor illis

---

133 **Quae lacrimas dedit**] The
Nature who gave us tears.—"*Haec
qua mollissima corda habemus.*"

134 **causam dicentis amici**] If
we are to keep the reading of most
MSS., *casum lugentis* is only found
in suspicious MSS.; and several
which have *lugentis* keep *causam*.
One is almost inclined to translate,
"the cause of our friend as he pleads
it," "the cause he has to plead in
a civil action, or the mourning he
has to assume as a criminal." The
alternative is to suppose Juvenal intended *squalorem causam dicentis
reique*, which is very harsh.

137 **incerta**] As to the sex.—
The whole line is intended to mark
the tender age of the ward; he has
just taken the *toga virilis*, and when
he lets his hair grow again for the

trial you might take him for a
girl.

138 **adultae**] Who has lived long
enough to look forward to a happy
marriage and dies without enjoying it.

140 **minor**] "Too small to burn."
Children were not burnt till they
had cut their teeth.

140, 141 **face—arcana**] The torch
carried by the initiated on the fifth
day of the Eleusinian mysteries.

143 **venerabile**] "Capable of
veneration." Cf. "genitabilis aura
Favoni."

147] Ovid, *Met.* i. 86 sq., has a
similar commonplace:

" Pronaque cum spectant animalia
        cetera terram,
Os homini sublime dedit caelum-
        que tueri."

Tantum animas, nobis animum quoque, mutuus ut nos
Affectus petere auxilium et praestare juberet,   150
Dispersos trahere in populum, migrare vetusto
De nemore et proavis habitatas linquere silvas;
Aedificare domos, Laribus conjungere nostris
Tectum aliud, tutos vicino limite somnos
Ut collata daret fiducia; protegere armis   155
Lapsum, aut ingenti nutantem vulnere civem,
Communi dare signa tuba, defendier isdem
Turribus, atque una portarum clave teneri.
Sed jam serpentum major concordia: parcit
Cognatis maculis similis fera. Quando leoni   160
Fortior eripuit vitam leo? quo nemore unquam
Exspiravit aper majoris dentibus apri?
Indica tigris agit rabida cum tigride pacem
Perpetuam; saevis inter se convenit ursis.
Ast homini ferrum letale incude nefanda   165
Produxisse parum est; quum rastra et sarcula tantum
Assueti coquere, et marris ac vomere lassi
Nescierint primi gladios extendere fabri.
Aspicimus populos, quorum non sufficit irae

149] Animus est quo sapimus; anima qua vivimus.

151 trahere] Seems to be intransitive, as dispersos should to avoid zeugma agree with nos and depend directly on juberet.

154 limite] So P.: limine is easier, as a neighbour shutting your house in, though intelligible, is rather clumsy here.

160 fera] Θηρίον, probably the serpent, as a general proposition would be awkward. Lions like stags and many other animals fight for the possession of their females.

168 Nescierint] Here the Scholiast and several MSS. write nesci-erunt. Nescierint looks like a correction, but it seems to be necessary, as quum must mean 'whereas.'

— extendere] Because the only instruments made by the smiths of the gold and the silver age were short and thick compared to swords.

169, 171 quorum—cibi] "Quibus non sufficit occidisse hominem nisi et crediderint," would be regular; so would "Quibus non sufficit sed credunt," or "credant," which last would mean, "who are not satisfied in fact, but are of a character to think." The tense of 'crediderint' is probably due to the attraction of 'occidisse' (cf. xi. 23—26), "qui scit—hic tamen idem ignoret."

Occidisse aliquem; sed pectora, brachia, vultum   170
Crediderent genus esse cibi.   Quid diceret ergo,
Vel quo non fugeret, si nunc haec monstra videret
Pythagoras, cunctis animalibus abstinuit qui
Tanquam homine et ventri indulsit non omne legumen?

170 **pectora, brachia, vultum**]
The most distinctively human parts.
174 **non omne legumen**] Referring to the well-known, ill-establish-
ed, and inexplicable prohibition of
beans.

SATIRA XVI.

Quis numerare queat felicis praemia, Galle,
Militiae? Nam si subeuntur prospera castra,
Me pavidum excipiat tironem porta secundo
Sidere. Plus etenim fati valet hora benigni,
Quam si nos Veneris commendet epistola Marti   5
Et Samia genitrix quae delectatur arena.
    Commoda tractemus primum communia : quorum
Haud minimum illud erit, ne te pulsare togatus
Audeat; immo etsi pulsetur, dissimulet, nec
Audeat excussos praetori ostendere dentes   10
Et nigram in facie timidis livoribus offam
Atque oculum, medico nil promittente, relictum.
Bardaicus judex datur haec punire volenti
Calceus, et grandes magna ad subsellia surae,

2 **Nam**] "Lucky soldiers get on very well; for, in fact, with good fortune, I should not mind serving myself. If the camp is lucky in itself, may I be taken in as a shy recruit, and find luck there; luck, I say, for fate can do more for a man in the army than an introduction to Mars from his mistress or his mother."

6 **Samia**] Where Polycrates, to keep the people low, had built her the largest temple known to Herodotus.

8 **ne**] Is used because "subest notio impediendi vel prohibendi" (Hand, *Turs.* iv. 42), "'ubi cujus vis omnis haec semper fuit ne Clo-dius vi oppressam civitatem tene-ret ;" all his force had this purpose of preventing.

9 **dissimulet**] He is afraid to have it known that he has been in a brawl, however onesided, with a soldier.

12] He has lost one eye completely, he has one left to be sure, but the doctor cannot promise to save it.

13 **datur**] If you go to the praetor, he assigns a centurion as 'judex,' to keep the custom of Camillus (who established a standing army, so that the soldiers could not attend to their suits in the winter).

Legibus antiquis castrorum et more Camilli   15
Servato, miles ne vallum litiget extra
Et procul a signis. Justissima Centurionum
Cognitio est igitur de milite ; nec mihi deerit
Ultio, si justae defertur causa querelae.
Tota cohors tamen est inimica, omnesque manipli   20
Consensu magno efficiunt, curabilis ut sit
Vindicta et gravior, quam injuria. Dignum erit ergo
Declamatoris mulino corde Vagelli,
Quum duo crura habeas, offendere tot caligas, tot
Millia clavorum. Quis tam procul absit ab urbe ?   25
Praeterea quis tam Pylades, molem aggeris ultra
Ut veniat ? Lacrimae siccentur protinus, et se
Excusaturos non sollicitemus amicos,
Da testem, judex quum dixerit, audeat ille,
Nescio quis, pugnos qui vidit, dicere, Vidi ?   30
Et credam dignum barba, dignumque capillis
Majorum. Citius falsum producere testem
Contra paganum possis, quam vera loquentem

17 **Justissima,** sq.] The words of the imaginary litigant, "Well, the centurion has a right to judge the soldier, and he is sure to judge him justly,"&c.

21 **curabilis**] Such as need a remedy, perhaps more generally 'anxious,' 'an anxious business.'

24 **caligas**] The boots of the rank and file, who are certain to take the part of their comrade even if the centurions do not ; the latter wear the *calceus*, though it is presumably of the kind known as Bardaicus, which was adopted from the Bardaei, a people of Illyria.

25 **quis—urbe**] Juvenal anticipates the excuse that the civilian's friends are sure to make ; though the excuse is transparent, it is not unmeaning : the praetorian camp was a considerable distance from the former, and most of the pleasantest and busiest parts of Rome.

26] Here Juvenal suggests their real motive for putting forward the above excuse.

31] Barbers are said to have been introduced from Sicily, B.C. 300. The date was attested by public documents at Ardea (Varro, *R. R.* ii. 11, § 10).

33 **paganum**] "A civilian." Antonius Primus (Tac. *Hist.* iii. 24) taunts his soldiers by this word, as Caesar subdued a mutiny by calling his soldiers *Quirites*. The distinction is worth noticing. The Quirites points to the legal status of unarmed citizens, *paganus* it can scarcely be doubted is originally a piece of military slang.

Contra fortunam armati contraque pudorem.

Praemia nunc alia atque alia emolumenta notemus   35
Sacramentorum. Convallem ruris aviti
Improbus aut campum mihi si vicinus ademit
Et sacrum effodit medio de limite saxum,
Quod mea cum patulo coluit puls annua libo;
Debitor aut sumtos pergit non reddere nummos,   40
Vana supervacui dicens chirographa ligni:
Exspectandus erit, qui lites inchoet, annus
Totius populi: sed tunc quoque mille ferenda
Taedia, mille morae; toties subsellia tantum
Sternuntur; tum facundo ponentę lacernas   45
Caedicio, et Fusco jam micturiente, parati
Digredimur: lentaque fori pugnamus arena.
Ast illis, quos arma tegunt et balteus ambit,
Quod placitum est ipsis, praestatur tempus agendi,
Nec res atteritur longo sufflamine litis.   50
   Solis praeterea testandi militibus jus
Vivo patre datur: nam, quae sunt parta labore
Militiae, placuit non esse in corpore census,
Omne tenet cujus regimen pater. Ergo Coranum
Signorum comitem, castrorumque aera merentem,   55

---

34 pudorem] He will appeal to his honour, and face you down.

38 sacrum] An idol has been defined as a compromise between a symbol and a fetich. Hermae, Termini, Priapi, were probably nearer fetiches.

39 patulo] Flat. Originally, it was forbidden to offer bloody offerings to Terminus.

41] Repeated from xiii. 137.

42, 43] "I must wait to begin my cause for the year, whatever it is that begins everybody else's."

45] The advocates are almost ready, taking off their wrappers to shew the toga, when they find the bench cushioned, to be sure, but empty.

46 Fusco] Has a drunken wife (xii. 115), and drinks; hence, j. m., in order to start fair.

47] lenta—arena] "We find it is slow fighting in the lists of the law."

52] "Castrense peculium est quod a parentibus vel cognatis in militia donatum est, vel quod ipse filius familias in militia acquisiit quod, nisi militaret, acquisiturus non fuisset: nam quod erat et sine militia acquisiturus, id peculium ejus castrense non est" (Dig. xlix. 17).

54 Coranum] From Horace (Sat. II. v. 57).

Quamvis jam tremulus, captat pater. Hunc labor aequus
Provehit, et pulcro reddit sua dona labori,
Ipsius certe ducis hoc referre videtur,
Ut, qui fortis erit, sit felicissimus idem,
Ut laeti phaleris omnes et torquibus omnes.　　　　60

57—60] Coranus deserves it; at least, it is the general's own interest to promote the bravest, and be liberal to all. One might suspect that from this point onwards we should have had a satire on abuses in the army; the connexion being that commanders do *not* understand their own interest. The apparent change of subject would not be so great as in Sat. xiv., where the subject up to 106 is education by example, from thence to the end, avarice. Another parallel would be the seventh Satire, which begins with the advantages of imperial patronage, and after v. 21 dilates exclusively on public neglect.

CAMBRIDGE: PRINTED BY C. J. CLAY, M.A. AT THE UNIVERSITY PRESS.

LIST OF BOOKS

PUBLISHED

BY JOHN ALLYN,

30, FRANKLIN STREET, BOSTON.

Abbott, E. A., D.D. Latin Prose through English Idiom $0.90
Æschylus. Prometheus Bound. Edited by R. H. Mather . . 1.00
Æsop's Fables, with Notes and Vocabulary. Edited by Timayenis 1.30
American Institutions. By A. de Tocqueville 1.20
Aristophanes. Acharnians and Knights. Ed. by W. C. Green 1.20
    Birds. Edited by C. C. Felton 1.10
    Clouds. Edited by Felton 1.10
Bennett, G. L. Easy Latin Stories, with vocabulary and notes . . .70
    First Latin Writer, with accidence 90
    First Latin Exercises, without accidence 70
    Second Latin Writer 90
Bigg, Charles. Thucydides, Books I., II., with notes 1.60
Bowen, Francis. A Treatise on Logic 1.50
    Hamilton's Metaphysics 1.50
Cæsar. Edited, with vocab. and illustrations, by F. W. Kelsey . . 1.25
Champlin, J. T. Constitution of the United States 80
    Selections from Tacitus, with notes 1.10
Chardenal, C. A. First French Course 40
    Second French Course 60
    French Exercises for Advanced Pupils 90
Chase, R. H. Macleane's Horace, with notes 1.30
Chemical Philosophy. By Professor J. P. Cooke 3.50
Chemical Physics. By Professor J. P. Cooke 4.50

Chemical Tables. By S. P. Sharples, S.B. $2.00
Cicero de Senectute and de Amicitia. Edited by F. W. Kelsey . 1.20
    Each part separately 75
    Oratio pro Cluentio. Edited by A. Stickney 80
Comstock, D. Y. First Latin Book 1.00
Constitution of the United States. Champlin 80
Cooke, J. P. Elements of Chemical Physics 4.50
    Principles of Chemical Philosophy 3.50
Democracy in America. De Tocqueville. 2 vols. 5.00
Demosthenes. On the Crown. Edited by W. S. Tyler 1.20
    Olynthiacs and Philippics. Edited by Tyler 1.20
    Separately : The Olynthiacs, $0.70 ; Philippics 80
Felton, C. C. Selections from Modern Greek Writers 1.25
    See Aristophanes ; Isocrates.
Fernald, O. M. Selections from Greek Historians 1.50
French Course. *See* Chardenal.
Greece, History of. By R. F. Pennell 60
Greek Conditional Sentences. By J. B. Sewall 18
Greek Historians. Selections. By O. M. Fernald 1.50
Greek Reader, First. By C. M. Moss. 70
Green, W. C. Aristophanes, Acharnians and Knights 1.20
Hart, S. *See* Juvenal ; Persius.
Herodotus and Thucydides. Selections. Edited by R. H. Mather .90
Holbrooke, G. O. Selections from Pliny's Letters 1.00
Homer's Iliad. Edited by Robert P. Keep. Books I. to VI. . . . 1.50
    Books I. to III. 90
Horace. With Notes by Macleane and Chase 1.30
Isocrates, Panegyricus. Edited by Felton 80
Jebb, R. C. *See* Sophocles.
Juvenal. Edited by S. Hart and Macleane 1.10
    Edited by G. A. Simcox 1.20
Kampen. Fifteen Maps to Cæsar's Gallic War. In wrappers 75
Keep, R. P. *See* Homer's Iliad.
Kelsey, F. W. *See* Cæsar ; Cicero ; Lucretius.
Latin Book, First. *See* Comstock ; Nichols.
Latin Prose through English Idiom. By E. A. Abbott 90
Latin Selections. Edited by E. H. Smith 1.75
Latin Stories, Writers, and Exercises. *See* Bennett

Latin Subjunctive. By R. F. Pennell $0.25
Logic, Treatise on. By Francis Bowen 1.50
Lucian, Selections from. Edited by C. R. Williams 1.40
     Short Extracts. Edited by C. R. Williams 80
Lucretius. Edited by Francis W. Kelsey 1.75
Macleane, A. J. *See* Horace; Juvenal.
Mather, R. H. *See* Æschylus; Herodotus; Sophocles.
Metaphysics, Hamilton's. Edited by Francis Bowen 1.50
Morris, E. P. Mostellaria of Plautus 1.00
Moss, C. R. First Greek Reader. 70
Nichols, William. First Steps in Latin.
Pennell, R. F. History of Ancient Greece 60
     History of Ancient Rome 60
     The Latin Subjunctive 25
Persius, Satires of. Edited by Samuel Hart 75
Plato. The Apology and Crito. Edited by William Wagner . .90
     The Phædo. Edited by William Wagner 1.20
Plautus. The Mostellaria. Edited by E. P. Morris 1.00
Pliny. Selected Letters. Edited by George O. Holbrooke . . . 1.00
Rome, History of. By R. F. Pennell 60
Sewall, J. B. Greek Conditional Sentences 18
Sharples, S. P. Chemical Tables 2.00
Simcox, G. A. Thirteen Satires of Juvenal 1.20
Smith, E. H. Latin Selections 1.75
Sophocles. The Ajax. Edited by R. C. Jebb 1.10
     The Electra. Edited by R. C. Jebb and R. H. Mather . . . 1.10
Stickney, A. Cicero pro Cluentio 80
Tacitus, Selections from. Edited by J. T. Champlin 1.10
Thucydides, Books I., II. Edited by Charles Bigg 1.60
Tocqueville, A. de. Democracy in America. 2 vols. 5.00
     American Institutions 1.20
Tyler, W. S. *See* Demosthenes.
Wagner, William. *See* Plato.
Williams, Charles R. *See* Lucian.
Winans, S. R. *See* Xenophon.
Worthington, A. M. Physical Laboratory Practice 1.20
Xenophon. The Memorabilia. Edited by S. R. Winans . . . 1.20
     The Symposium. Edited by S. R. Winans 50

WEALE'S CLASSICAL SERIES.

16mo.   Uniformly bound in Flexible Cloth.   Any volume sold separately.

BIBLIOTHECA CLASSICA.

A series of Greek and Latin authors, with English commentaries; edited by various scholars under the direction of George Long and Rev. A. J. Macleane. 8vo. Cloth.

"A credit to the classical learning of England." — *London Athenæum*.

Reduced net Prices.

Aeschylus, by F. A. Paley, M.A. 4th edition $5.60
Cicero's Orations, by George Long, M.A. 4 vols. 20.00
    Separately, Vol. I., $5.25; Vol. II., $4.50; Vol. III., $5.25; Vol. IV., $5.75.
Demosthenes, by R. Whiston, M.A. 2 vols. .   10.00
    Either vol. separately 5.25
Euripides, by F. A. Paley, M.A. 3 vols. 15.00
    Any vol. separately 5.25
Herodotus, by Rev. J. W. Blakesley, B.D. 2 vols. 10.00
Hesiod, by F. A. Paley, M.A. 3.25
Homer's Iliad, by F. A. Paley, M.A. 2 vols. 8.00
    Separately, Vol. I., $4.00; Vol. II., $4.50.
Horace, by Rev. A. J. Macleane, M.A.; new edition, revised by George Long 5.60
Juvenal and Persius, by Rev. A. J. Macleane, M.A.; new edition, revised by George Long 3.75
Plato's Phædrus and Gorgias, by W. H. Thompson, D.D. 2 vols. . 4.75
    Either vol. separately 2.50
Sophocles, by Rev. F. H. Blaydes, M.A. Vol. I., Oed. Tyr., Oed. Col., Antig. 5.60
———— Vol. II., by F. A. Paley, M.A.; Philoct., Elect., Trach., Ajax. 3.75
Tacitus, The Annals, by Rev. P. Frost 4.75
Terence, by E. St. J. Parry, M.A. 5.60
Virgil, by J. Conington, M.A. 3 vols. 12.50
    Separately, Vol. I., Bucol. and Georg., $4.50; Vol. II., Æneid, Bks. 1–6, $4.50; Vol. III., Æneid, Bks. 7–12, $4.50.

☞ *Any volume sent post-paid on receipt of the price. Any 10 volumes, 10 per cent discount from above prices. Any 15 volumes, 15 per cent discount from above prices. A complete set, 26 volumes, for $93.00.*

JOHN ALLYN, Importer and Publisher, 30, Franklin Street, Boston.

GREEK TEXT BOOKS.

Æschylus, Prometheus Bound. Edited by Professor R. H. MATHER, Amherst College. With the lyric parts arranged according to the system of Schmidt. Second Edition. 16mo, cloth, 180 pages. $1.00.

Prof. N. L. Andrews, *Madison University, N.Y.* — I have examined with great care Professor Mather's edition of the Prometheus. The notes are well adapted to the literary appreciation of the play; and the Introduction, with its graphic and interesting sketch of the representation of Greek dramas, is a valuable feature. I shall adopt it for use with my classes.

Prof. T. L. Seip, *Muhlenberg College, Pa.* — The Introduction is very valuable to the student, and meets a want seldom supplied in similar works. The article·on the lyric parts, and the metrical scheme, furnish in concise form much-needed information. The text is very good; and the notes are a satisfactory aid for beginners in Greek Tragedy.

Aristophanes, Acharnians and Knights. Edited by W. C. GREEN, M.A., late Fellow of King's College, Cambridge. (*Catena Classicorum.*) 12mo, 210 pages. $1.20.

The text of this edition is mainly that of Dindorf. In the notes brevity has been studied, as short notes are more likely to be read, and, therefore, to be useful. Each play is preceded by an Introduction and an Argument.

Aristophanes, Birds. With Notes, by C. C. FELTON, LL.D., President of Harvard University. Third Edition, revised by W. W. GOODWIN, Eliot Professor of Greek Literature in Harvard University. 12mo, 250 pages. $1.10.

Aristophanes, Clouds. With Notes, by C. C. FELTON, LL.D. New Edition, revised. 12mo, 250 pages. $1.10.

President Felton, by his tastes and his studies, was especially fitted for the difficult task of editing Aristophanes, and the notes of these two books show with what skill and thoroughness the congenial labor has been performed. Great care has been taken to explain the judicial expressions and the frequent allusions to the political and social life of Athens. In the new editions the commentary has been enlarged by references to Goodwin's Moods and Tenses of the Greek Verb.

Demosthenes, on the Crown. Edited by Professor W. S. Tyler, Amherst College. Seventh Edition. 16mo, 304 pp. $1.20.

Prof. A. Harkness, *Brown University, Providence.* — I have already expressed to Professor Tyler my high appreciation of his De Corona of Demosthenes, and shall take pleasure in recommending it as the best edition for college use.

Prof. J. R. Boise, *University of Chicago, Ill.* — Professor Tyler, in his revision, has wisely omitted much that was entirely unnecessary, or out of place, in a work of this kind; and his additions are all of great value. The entire work, in its present form, seems to me excellent. I know of no handsomer or better school edition of the Oration on the Crown published in any country.

Demosthenes: the Olynthiacs and Philippics. Edited by Professor W. S. Tyler, Amherst College. Seventh Edition. 16mo, 256 pages. $1.20. Separately : The Olynthiacs, 70 cents; the Philippics, 80 cents.

Prof. W. W. Goodwin, *Harvard College.* — I have the greatest confidence in Professor Tyler's scholarship and good taste, and am glad to say that I find the book, as I expected, the best in the market.

Prof. M. L. D'Ooge, *University of Michigan.* — We have just finished reading Professor Tyler's Olynthiacs and Philippics, and find the book very serviceable. The annotations are clear and scholarly, and the text is very correct.

Fernald's Greek Historians. Edited by Professor O. M. Fernald, Williams College. With three maps. Fourth Edition, revised. 12mo, 412 pages. $1.50.

This book includes extracts from Diodorus Siculus, Book IV.; Herodotus, Books VI., VII., VIII., and IX.; Thucydides, Books I., II., VI., VII., and VIII. Xenophon, Hellen. Books I., II.

Prof. Jacob Cooper, *Rutgers College, New Brunswick, N. J.* — I am glad you have published a new edition of Felton's Selections. This book has been used by me for more than ten years with great satisfaction. The references and notes of Professor Fernald add greatly to its value, and will make it still more deservedly popular than before.

Prof. H. Z. McLain, *Wabash College, Crawfordsville, Ind.* — I am using Fernald's Selections from Greek Historians, and regard it as a most excellent text-book, its notes being always careful and accurate, and not so full or numerous as to make the students' work too easy.

Herodotus and Thucydides. Selections. Edited by Professor R. H. MATHER, Amherst College. Sixth Edition. 16mo, 150 pages. 90 cents.

Prof. **W. F. Swahlen,** *McKendree College, Ohio.* — I am pleased with the selections themselves, because of their exceedingly interesting nature; pleased with the amount selected, because it is just what will be read in a term; pleased with the notes, because of their brevity, pertinence, and comprehensiveness; and now, after having used it for the past two years, with college classes, I find myself liking it better still.

Prof. **N. L. Andrews,** *Madison University, New York.* — It is a most admirable text-book.

Homer's Iliad. Books I. to VI. With Fac-simile of the Venetian Manuscript of the Iliad. Edited, with an Introduction and Notes, by ROBERT P. KEEP, Ph.D., Principal Free Academy, Norwich, Ct. 12mo, 364 pages. $1.50.

—— —— **Books I. to III.** Without the Fac-simile of the Venetian Manuscript. With Introduction and Notes by ROBERT P. KEEP, Ph.D. 12mo, 216 pages. $0.90.

Prof. **J. H. Wright,** *Dartmouth College.* — It possesses many features that place it far beyond all its competitors.

Prof. **George H. White,** *Principal Preparatory Department, Oberlin College, Ohio.* — Keep's Iliad is evidently superior to any edition now in use, and we have voted to adopt it for our classes. The introductory matter is valuable, and includes a satisfactory outline of the Homeric forms; the notes are scholarly, graceful, and suggestive; and the whole work reveals the hand of the experienced and enthusiastic teacher.

Prof. **Charles F. Smith,** *Vanderbilt University, Nashville, Tenn.* — I have examined Keep's Iliad with the greatest care, and consider it by far the best American edition, and, indeed, one of the very best text-books we have.

Prof. **Alexander Kerr,** *State University, Madison, Wis.* — Keep's Iliad is incomparably the best edition which has appeared in this country.

Isocrates, the Panegyricus. With Notes by C. C. FELTON, LL.D. Third Edition, revised by Professor W. W. GOODWIN. 12mo, 155 pages. $0.80.

The Panegyricus has been selected for publication, partly because it is an excellent specimen of the best manner of Isocrates, and partly because by its plan, it presents a review of the history of Athens from the mythical ages down to the period following the treaty of Antalcidas, and is a convenient work to make the text-book for lessons in Greek history. The present edition has been revised by Professor Goodwin, who has added grammatical and other notes.

Lucian, Selections. With Introductions and Notes by Professor CHARLES R. WILLIAMS, Lake Forest University. Second Edition. 16mo, 340 pages. $1.40.

———— **Short Extracts.** Edited by Professor CHARLES R. WILLIAMS. 16mo, 180 pages. $0.80.

The SHORT EXTRACTS contain The Dream, Timon, and seventeen Dialogues. The SELECTIONS include the same matter, together with Charon, The Cock, and Icaromenippus.

Prof. J. E. Goodrich, *University of Vermont.* — These Dialogues of Lucian are just the thing for rapid reading or for reading at sight. Lucian is so alert, so keen, and withal so modern in feeling and temper, that the student is driven to read on and on, just to see how the witty debate will end. I am glad to see that Professor Williams has furnished an edition which will fully meet the demands of the class-room.

Prof. Henry M. Baird, *University of the City of New York.* — A convenient edition of Lucian has long been needed. The want has now been met by Professor Williams's industry and scholarship, and I have no doubt that the book will be duly appreciated. The editor has collected in his introduction all that is most essential for the student to know respecting the author of the dialogues and respecting the dialogues themselves ; while the notes show a most judicious choice between the extremes of too great fulness and barrenness of illustration. The typography and external appearance are unexceptionable.

Moss's First Greek Reader. With Introduction, Notes, and Vocabulary, by Professor CHARLES M. Moss, Wesleyan University, Illinois. 16mo, 151 pages. 70 cents.

It is the aim of the author to furnish a Greek book for beginners which shall be simple and interesting, and at the same time contain a large number of such words, phrases, and idioms as are of frequent occurrence in Attic Greek. There has for some time been a demand for such a book, to precede the Anabasis, which is of uneven difficulty, and which is quite apt, when read slowly by a beginner, to grow very tedious.

The book contains no disconnected sentences. It consists of a series of carefully graduated exercises for translation, beginning with the simplest stories, and ending with extracts from Xenophon, Herodotus, and Lucian, which have been changed and adapted to the knowledge of the beginner. The text is preceded by valuable hints on translation, and followed by notes and a complete vocabulary.

It is believed that the time spent in reading this book, before taking up any Greek author for consecutive study, will be more than saved in the subsequent rapid progress of the pupil.

Plato's Apology of Socrates and Crito. With Notes, criti-
cal and exegetical, and a logical Analysis of the Apology, by W.
WAGNER, Ph.D.   Revised Edition.   16mo, 145 pages. $0.90.

The text of this edition is based on that of the Bodleian MS., and is
claimed to be the most correct text extant. Throughout the work, the
editor's aim has been to be as brief and concise as possible, not attempting
originality, but carefully using and arranging the materials amassed by
preceding commentators. In the revised edition, some references to parallel
passages have been omitted, and extended references to American gram-
mars have been added.

Prof. F. D. Allen, *Harvard College.* — I am glad you have republished
the book, which, I think, will be useful in this country. The work, like
others of Wagner, abounds in original and sensible remarks; the notes are
to the point, and tersely expressed.

Prof. H. Whitehorne, *Union College, Schenectady.* — I confidently recommend it to the favorable consideration of all students. It is eminently scholarly without any parade of scholarship, and gives all the requisite information
without removing from the student the necessity for using his own brains.

Plato's Phædo. With Notes, critical and exegetical, and an
Analysis. By WILHELM WAGNER, Ph.D.   16mo, 206 pp. $1.20.

This edition enters especially into the critical and grammatical explanation
of the Phædo, and does not profess to exhaust the philosophical thought of
the work, least of all to collect the doctrines and tenets of later philosophers
and thinkers on the subjects treated by Plato.

Prof. Ch. Morris, *Randolph Macon College, Virginia.* — I have now in
use, with my higher classes, your edition of the Phædo of Plato, and find it
altogether satisfactory. It shows much greater care and scholarship than
are usually found in college text-books.

Prof. J. Cooper, *Rutgers College, New Jersey.* — The edition of Plato's
Phædo, by Wagner, is one of rare excellence. Seldom, if ever, has there
been so much of value in a text-book compressed in so small a space.

Sophocles, the Ajax. Edited by R. C. JEBB, M.A., Fellow
of Trinity College, Cambridge. (*Catena Classicorum.*) 12mo,
206 pages. $1.10.

Mr. Jebb has produced a work which will be read with interest and profit,
as it contains, in a compact form, not only a careful summary of the labors
of preceding editors, but also many acute and ingenious original remarks.
All questions of grammar, construction, and philology are handled, as they
arise, with a helpful and sufficient precision. An exhaustive introduction
precedes the play.

Sophocles, the Electra. With Notes by R. C. JEBB. Revised and edited, with additional Notes, by R. H. MATHER, Professor of Greek in Amherst College. 16mo, 232 pages. $1.10.

Prof. W. W. Goodwin, *Harvard College.* — It is rare to find an edition of a classic author so admirably adapted to the wants of students as Mr. Jebb's "Electra." I hope this new edition will aid in making it better known in our colleges.

Thucydides. The History of the War between the Peloponnesians and the Athenians. Books I. and II. Edited, with Notes and Introduction, by CHARLES BIGG, M.A., Christ Church, Oxford. (*Catena Classicorum.*) 12mo, 360 pages. $1.60.

Mr. Bigg prefixes an Analysis to each book, and an admirable introduction to the whole work, containing full information as to all that is known or related of Thucydides, and the date at which he wrote, followed by a very masterly critique on some of his characteristics as a writer. — *London Athenæum.*

Xenophon's Memorabilia. With Introduction and Notes, by Professor SAMUEL ROSS WINANS, College of New Jersey. 16mo, 289 pages. $1.20.

The text is separated into convenient divisions by English summaries, which take the place of the customary argument prefixed to the chapters, and put a logical analysis of the text where it cannot escape the attention of the student. The notes are designedly compact, yet are believed to contain all that is practically useful to the student. The editor has endeavored to supply brief sketches of everything of biographical, historical, or philosophical interest.

Prof. A. C. Merriam, *Columbia College, New York.* — It supplies a want long felt, and I have no doubt will be largely used, as it deserves. The introduction of the summaries into the text adds greatly to its value, while the notes are succinct, with good references and apt illustrations.

Prof. C. M. Moss, *Wesleyan University, Illinois.* — The notes are excellent, the paragraphing of the text is a great and valuable help to students, and the book itself is a model of neatness. It is one of the few unexceptionably well-edited school-books in my library. I shall use it in my classes exclusively when we read the "Memorabilia."

Xenophon's Symposium. Edited, with Notes, by Professor S. R. WINANS. 18mo, cloth, 96 pages. $0.50.

The "Symposium," according to its original design, makes a delightful afterpiece to the "Memorabilia." As a source of information on Attic morals and manners its value is not easily overestimated; and its lively conversational style enables the student to appreciate Greek idiom and enjoy the spirit of the language.

LATIN TEXT BOOKS.

Abbott's Latin Prose through English Idiom. Rules and Exercises on Latin Prose Composition. By the Rev. EDWIN A. ABBOTT, D.D., Head-Master of the City of London School. With Additions by E. R. HUMPHREYS, A.M., LL.D. 18mo, 205 pages, $0.90.

The author's object is to prepare students for the study and composition of Latin Prose, by calling their attention first to the peculiarities of English idiom, and then to the methods of representing the English in the corresponding Latin idiom. A good deal of space has been given to the Prepositions. The Exercises are purposely unarranged, as connected examples are useless to test a pupil's knowledge.

Prof. Geo. O. Holbrooke, *Trinity College, Hartford.* — Abbott's Latin Prose is the best book of the kind with which I am acquainted. It teaches the student to compose Latin, instead of translating stock sentences.

Prof. E. H. Griffin, *Williams College, Williamstown.* — Any book by the author of " English Lessons " and the " Shaksperian Grammar " I should expect to be good. This seems to me simply admirable, and is quite as valuable for the study of English as for the study of Latin

Prof. C. L. Smith, *Harvard College.* — I feel sure the book will be widely used, as it deals with Latin Composition in the only right way.

Bennett's Latin Books. By GEORGE L. BENNETT, M.A., Head-Master of Sutton Valence School.

I. Easy Latin Stories for Beginners. With Vocabulary and Notes. 16mo, 156 pages, $0.70.

II. First Latin Writer. Comprising Accidence, the easier Rules of Syntax, illustrated by copious examples and Progressive Exercises in Elementary Latin Prose, with Vocabularies. 16mo, 218 pages, $0.90.

III. First Latin Exercises. Containing all the Rules, Exercises, and Vocabularies of the FIRST LATIN WRITER, but omitting the Accidence. 16mo, 164 pages, $0.70.

IV. Second Latin Writer. Containing Hints on Writing Latin Prose, with graduated continuous Exercises. 16mo, 198 pages, $0.90.

Prof. A. P. Montague, *Columbian University, Washington, D. C.* — I am using all the books of the Bennett Series in my various classes, and am charmed with them. So far as my experience goes, they are by far the best books of the kind now before the public, and I heartily commend them.

Dr. A. C. Perkins, *Phillips-Exeter Academy.* — We take Bennett's "First Latin Writer" as the best Manual of Latin Composition for the first two years of our course. The "Easy Latin Stories," by the same author, is excellently fitted for pupils when they are beginning to read Latin.

Dr. H. T. Fuller, *St. Johnsbury Academy, Vt.* — We have used Bennett's "First Latin Writer" for the last two years, and find it eminently satisfactory. It involves a knowledge of all the principles of grammar and Latin idioms, and, by a skilful selection of review work, obliges the pupil to keep what he has once acquired. Its breadth of vocabulary is commendable in that it is not restricted to the words of any single author.

Prof. C. L. Smith, *Harvard College.* — The "Second Latin Writer" is quite a useful book, and contains a very valuable collection of exercises. The Introduction gives the student sound advice, and many excellent notes on idiom.

Cicero De Senectute and De Amicitia. With Notes by

JAMES S. REID, M.A., Cambridge, England. American edition, revised by Professor FRANCIS W. KELSEY, Lake Forest University. Second Edition. 16mo, 279 pages, $1.20. Each part separately, $0.75.

Prof. M. M. Fisher, *University of Missouri.* — The edition is in every respect the best I have seen, and I shall use it in my classes.

Prof. J. H. Chamberlin, *Marietta College, Ohio.* — It is certainly the best edition of these works of Cicero with which I am acquainted. I have used the edition by Reid, and consider it a work of high merit. Professor Kelsey's revision seems to me to retain all the desirable features of the original edition, while much has been added which is of especial value to the American student.

Prof. A. G. Hopkins, *Hamilton College, New York.* — It is a handsome piece of work in every respect, and will, I doubt not, meet with a cordial reception. The text is far better than that of any other edition, and the notes are very clear and scholarly. I know of nothing better for our use here.

Cicero Pro Cluentio. With Notes by Professor AUSTIN

STICKNEY. Fourth Edition. 16mo, 156 pages, $0.80.

This edition is intended for use as a college text-book, and the notes are designed to supply the student only with such information in respect to the facts of the case and the scope of the argument, as is necessary to the proper understanding of the Oration.

Comstock's First Latin Book. Designed as a Manual of Progressive Exercises and Systematic Drill in the Elements of Latin. By D. Y. Comstock, M.A., Phillips Academy, Andover, Mass. 12mo, cloth, 400 pages, $1.00.

John S. White, LL.D., *Head-Master Berkeley School, New York City.* — Comstock's Latin Book I find the best book for its purpose that I have ever used. The review of English Grammar at the beginning; the separation of the vocabularies from the exercises; judicious and progressive presentation of the various uses of the verb in the different moods; and the condensed exhibit of the grammar, — are such valuable features gathered within the covers of a text-book, that it has no rival.

Nathan Thompson, A.M., *Principal Lawrence Academy, Groton, Mass.* — It is altogether the best Latin book for beginners with which I am acquainted.

Geo. B. Turnbul, *Colgate Acad., Hamilton, N. Y.* — I am using Comstock's First Latin Book with the Junior Class, and find it even more satisfactory than I had hoped.

Prof. E. Alexander, *University of Tennessee, Knoxville.* — Comstock's Latin Book is in use in our preparatory department, and is perfectly satisfactory. A better text-book is not often seen.

Prof. H. C. Missimer, *High School, Erie, Pa.* — It is very easy to see that Comstock's First Latin Book is the work of a thorough teacher, who has had actual experience in the class-room with the difficulties which beginners in Latin usually meet. Its classification and methods are thorough and complete; its language is clear and simple. Mr. Comstock has hit the nail on the head. He knows just what and just how much grammar is needed for good, clean work. We have had Leighton and Jones, — both good, — but we like Comstock more, because it is better.

Horace. With English Notes, by the Rev. A. J. Macleane, M.A. Revised and edited by R. H. Chase, A.M. Thirteenth Edition. 12mo, 580 pages, $1.30.

Chas. P. Parker, *Harvard College.* — Chase's Macleane's Horace I have long known and used, and have found it thoroughly satisfactory both in study and in teaching.

Prof. Herbert W. Smyth, *Williams College, Mass.* — I am glad to express my commendation of Macleane's Horace as republished by you. Its scholarly character places it at the head of all editions used in schools, while its just discrimination in the selection of notes adds materially to its usefulness.

Prof. J. H. Chamberlin, *Marietta, Ohio.* — I recommend Macleane's Horace to my classes. It is a most excellent edition.

Juvenal. Thirteen Satires, with Notes by MACLEANE. Revised and Edited by Professor SAMUEL HART, Trinity College, Hartford. Fifth Edition. 16mo, 262 pages, $1.10.

Prof. E. P. Crowell, *Amherst College.* — The work of the American editor is done with excellent judgment, and his additions to the notes will greatly increase their value for our students.

Prof. L. Coleman, *Lafayette College, Easton, Pa.* —I am happy to say that I have in use Professor Hart's edition of Juvenal, and find it a very useful, judicious, and scholarly manual, admirably adapted to the wants of the class.

Juvenal. Thirteen Satires, with Notes and Introduction by G. A. SIMCOX, M.A., Fellow of Queen's College, Oxford. Second Edition, revised and enlarged. (*Catena Classicorum.*) 16mo, 225 pages, $1.20.

Prof. F. P. Nash, *Hobart College, New York.* — The charm of Mr. Simcox's work lies in the very scholarly character of his notes and their freshness. They are original, and are marked by a real desire to place in the hands of the learner all that is most effective to throw light upon the author. The introduction is calculated to give the student much insight into the writings of Juvenal and their relation to his age.

Latin Selections. Being Specimens of the Latin Language and Literature from the earliest times to the end of the Classical period. Edited by Professor EDMUND H. SMITH, Hobart College, N. Y. 12mo, 420 pages, $1.75.

Prof. Charles Chandler, *Denison University, Granville, Ohio.* — I consider the Selections to be an excellent and long-needed book. I shall use it more or less every term from the beginning of Freshman year. For reading at sight it is just the thing that I have wanted, and, in connection with the study of the development of Roman Literature, such a book will be highly interesting and profitable. I have always maintained that it is a flat, stale, and unprofitable task for the student to read *about* the productions of Latin authors, without at the same time studying the productions themselves.

Prof. J. H. Hewitt, *Williams College, Williamstown, Mass.* — The Selections have been made with discretion, not only in that they are interesting in themselves, but in that they are such as to show the peculiarities of the thought and style of the several writers. The book cannot fail to be useful as a manual of exercises for translation at sight, and also as a text-book in connection with instruction in the history of Latin literature.

Prof. Tracy Peck, *Yale College, New Haven, Conn.* — The plan seems to me to be carried out with excellent judgment and taste. This work certainly gives in succinct and attractive form a clear view of Roman literature throughout its best periods

Lucretius; De Rerum Natura Libri Sex. With an Introduction and Notes to Books I., III., and V., by FRANCIS W. KELSEY, M.A., Professor of Latin in Lake Forest University. 16mo, 444 pages, $1.75.

Prof. Saml. Hart, *Trinity College, Hartford.* — It is a most excellent edition, and, coming at a time when renewed interest is felt in the doctrines and writings of Lucretius, its publication meets a real want.

Prof. C. J. Harris, *Washington and Lee University, Va.* — It is an admirable edition, and will be thoroughly helpful in the difficult work of developing the school-boy into the scholar. The editor has caught much of the enthusiasm of his author, and the wide and varied reading which he has brought to bear upon his work, and his freshness and vigor of treatment, cannot but prove very stimulating to earnest and ambitious students.

Prof. L. S. Potwin, *Adelbert College, Cleveland, O.* — I like it much, and think it not only well annotated, but also prepared on the true theory, viz.: to give the whole text, and notes on a part. This gives a chance for independent study on a portion, and practice in reading at sight.

Persius. The Satires ; with Notes, based on those of Macleane and Conington, by the Rev. SAMUEL HART, M.A., Professor in Trinity College, Hartford. 16mo, 91 pages, $0.75.

The text of this edition agrees in most places with that of Jahn. In the arguments prefixed to each satire, the editor has endeavored to give a suggestive outline of the poet's thoughts, and in the notes, to point out as clearly as possible the connection of one idea, or one part of the poem, with another.

Plautus. The Mostellaria. Edited by Professor E. P. MORRIS, Williams College, Mass. Third Edition. 16mo, 180 pages, $1.00.

Prof. J. E. Goodrich, *University of Vermont.* — It is the best American edition of any play of Plautus.

Prof. A. G. Hopkins, *Hamilton College, New York.* — Your edition of the Mostellaria by Morris is elegant in appearance, and has a scholarly finish to it which no American edition of Plautus has hitherto shown. The Introduction is full and interesting; the text is a model of typographical beauty ; and the notes explain to the young student all the difficulties and peculiarities of the text.

Prof. John K. Lord, *Dartmouth College, N. H.* — I think the notes judicious, correct, and well digested, giving the right kind of information in the right way.

Pliny's Letters. Selections from the Letters of the Younger Pliny. Edited, with Notes and Index, by GEORGE O. HOLBROOKE, M.A., Professor of Latin in Trinity College, Hartford. 16mo, 218 pages, $1.00.

Prof. F. P. Nash, *Hobart College, Geneva, N. Y.* — It is evident on every page of this interesting volume that it is the work of a scholar, and that it belongs to that new school of American editions which has at last learned to stand on its own legs, and use its own brains to some better purpose than merely to decide from whom it is best to borrow.

Prof. Minton Warren, *Johns Hopkins University, Baltimore, Md.* — I find the text and notes very satisfactory, and shall make use of the book in our course here next year.

Tacitus. Selections, embracing the more striking portions of his different works. With Notes, Introduction, and a Collection of his Aphorisms. By J. T. CHAMPLIN. Fifth Edition. 16mo, 272 pages, $1.10.

The design of this book is to give a comprehensive view of the writings of Tacitus in a comparatively small space. For this purpose, portions have been taken from all his works, except the Germania, but not without due regard to unity in the main parts. All biographical and historical information which seemed to be required has been introduced into the notes. The introduction contains a translation of Dr. Draeger's excellent essay on the peculiarities of the language and style of Tacitus.

Thomas Chase, *President Haverford College, Pa.* — A very interesting and useful text-book has been made up by these admirable selections. The notes are able and judicious, and supply just the information needed by students. Dr. Draeger's exhaustive essay on the language and style of Tacitus is of the greatest value to scholars.

ENGLISH TEXT BOOKS.

BOWEN'S HAMILTON'S METAPHYSICS. The Metaphysics of Sir William Hamilton, collected, arranged, and abridged by FRANCIS BOWEN, Alford Professor of Moral Philosophy in Harvard College. 12mo, 570 pages. $1.50.

The editor has endeavored to prepare a text-book which should contain, in amilton's own language, the substance of all that he wrote upon the subject of metaphysics.

I cannot refrain from congratulating you on your success. You have given the Metaphysics of Sir Wm. Hamilton in his own words, and yet in a form admirably adapted to the recitation room, and also to private students. — *James Walker, D.D. LL.D., late President of Harvard University.*

The students of our colleges are to be congratulated that the labors of the great master of metaphysical science are now rendered much more availing for their benefit, than they were made, perhaps than they could have been made, by his own hand. — *North American Review.*

BOWEN'S LOGIC. A Treatise on Logic, or the Laws of Pure Thought; comprising both the Aristotelic and Hamiltonian Analyses of Logical Forms, and some chapters on Applied Logic. By Prof. F. BOWEN. 12mo, 476 pages. $1.50.

Throughout the work the author has kept constantly in view the wants of learners, much of it having been first suggested by the experience of his own class room.

I have found it the most thorough and systematic text-book on the subject with which I am acquainted. It fully supplies the purpose for which it was written, and, in the hands of a good teacher, it furnishes all the aid that he or his class will need. — *E. O. Haven, LL.D., late President of University of Michigan.*

As an English text-book in this department of philosophy, I have seen nothing to be compared with it. — *James Walker, D.D., LL.D., late President of Harvard University.*

COOKE'S CHEMICAL PHILOSOPHY. Principles of Chemical Philosophy, by JOSIAH P. COOKE, Jr., Erving Professor of Chemistry and Mineralogy in Harvard College. Fourth Edition, revised and corrected. 8vo, 600 pages. $3.50.

The object of this book is to present the philosophy of chemistry in such a form that it can be made with profit the subject of college recitations. The author has found, by long experience, that a recitation on mere descriptions of apparatus and experiments is all but worthless, while the study of the philosophy of chemistry may be made highly profitable both for instruction and discipline. Part I. of the book contains a statement of the general laws and theories of chemistry, together with so much of the principles of molecular physics as are constantly applied to chemical investigations. It might be called a Grammar of the science.

Part II. presents the scheme of the chemical elements, and should only be studied in connection with experimental lectures or laboratory work. In the new edition, the text has been altered wherever corrections have been made necessary by the recent progress of the science.

I consider it one of the very best works on the subject in the English language. It is concise, compact, philosophical, capital. — *Professor J. S. Schanck, College of New Jersey, Princeton.*

As far as our recollection goes, we do not think there exists in any language a book on so difficult a subject as this so carefully, clearly, and lucidly written. — *London Chemical News.*

COOKE'S CHEMICAL PHYSICS. Elements of Chemical Physics. By Professor JOSIAH P. COOKE, Jr. Third Edition. 8vo, 750 pages. $4.50

This volume is intended to furnish a full development of the principles involved in the investigation of chemical phenomena. In order to adapt it to the purposes of instruction, it has been prepared on a strictly inductive method throughout; and any student with an elementary knowledge of mathematics will be able to follow the course of reasoning without difficulty. Each chapter is followed by a large number of problems, which are calculated, not only to test the knowledge of the student, but also to extend and apply the principles discussed in the work.

PENNELL'S ANCIENT HISTORIES.

ANCIENT GREECE, from the Earliest Times down to 146 B. C. By R. F. PENNELL, Professor of Latin in Phillips Exeter Academy. With Map and Plans. 16mo, 130 pages. 60 cents.

ROME, from the Earliest Times down to 476 A.D. 16mo, 206 pages. 60 cents.

These books are compiled respectively from the works of Curtius and Rawlinson, and from Mommsen and Niebuhr. They contain amply sufficient matter to prepare a pupil for any of our colleges. All minor details are, however, omitted, thus avoiding a confused mass of matter so perplexing to every beginner. Important events, names, and dates are printed in **heavy type,** strongly impressing them upon the student's memory.

I knew of no other compend of Roman Geography and History so well fitted for students in the early stages of a classical education. In addition to its worth as a school book, it is of no little value as a reference book for the leading names, dates, and facts of Roman history. — *A. P. Peabody, D.D., Harvard University.*

It is a most judicious epitome of Greek history, containing just those salient points about which all the minor events naturally group themselves. Teachers and pupils will rejoice to be free from Smith's maze of petty names and events. — *Professor W. M. Jefferis, Delaware College.*

I am very much pleased with the Greek history, and believe it will meet the wants of classes fitting for college, better than any thing of the kind that has been published. — *Professor Charles Dole, Northfield, Vermont.*

PENNELL'S LATIN SUBJUNCTIVE. The Latin Subjunctive, a Manual for Preparatory Schools. By Professor R. F PENNELL 16mo, sewed, 56 pages. 25 cents.

CHARDENAL'S FRENCH SERIES.

By C. A. CHARDENAL,

Bachelier-ès-Lettres de l'Université de France.

First French Course, or Rules and Exercises for Beginners. 16mo, 230 pages. 40 cents.

Second French Course, or French Syntax and Reader. 16mo, 250 pages. 60 cents.

Exercises for Advanced Pupils, containing Rules of Syntax, Exercises on Rules and Idioms, and a Dictionary of nearly Four Thousand Idiomatical Verbs, Sentences, Familiar Phrases, and Proverbs. 16mo, 332 pages. 90 cents.

This Series has been adopted for use at : —

Harvard College,	Johns Hopkins University,
Yale College,	Columbia College, N. Y.,
Williams College,	Hamilton College, N. Y.,
Bowdoin College,	Washington and J. College, Pa.,
Wabash College, Ind.,	Adelbert College, Ohio,
State University, Ind.,	Marietta College, Ohio,
Norfolk College, Va.,	Wesleyan University, Ohio,
Washington University, Mo.,	Iowa State University,
University of Kansas,	Olivet College, Mich.;.

ıd in numerous High Schools and Academies throughout the country.

These books have been prepared for *all who wish to begin or continue* the study of French, and by the simplicity of the language, the careful progression of the exercises, and the thoroughness of the treatment are adapted to the wants of all pupils between the ages of twelve and seventeen. The First Course in itself supplies all the instruction necessary for reading intelligently easy French prose, and the subsequent volumes aim to develop a mastery of all the principles of syntax, as well as ease and fluency in French conversation.

The First and Second Courses contain carefully graded extracts from Jules Verne, Erckmann-Chatrian, E. About, Béranger, Louis Blanc, Alexandre Dumas, Balzac, Lamartine, Victor Hugo, and other modern writers, together with complete vocabularies; thus affording **interesting instruction in reading** in addition to the usual translation of exercises. The last book of the series contains a long list of French idioms and phrases, arranged in sections, with exercises for translation and retranslation on each section.

Prof. Schele De Vere, *University of Virginia.* — After a painstaking examination, I can endorse Chardenal's French Course as the work of an experienced, highly-gifted teacher. The Junior and the Advanced Courses are admirably arranged, and cannot fail to bring the student almost imperceptibly forward, till teacher and pupil alike feel that the task is accomplished. Among new features the carefully chosen vocabularies, and above all the collection of idioms deserve special commendation. I am sure the volumes need only to be well known to be very generally adopted.

Prof. Henry Johnson, *Bowdoin College, Me.* — They are excellent textbooks, and a teacher who would speak French to and with his class could not fail to use them with great advantage. I use them in our advanced class here.

Prof. A. M. Elliott, *Johns Hopkins University, Md.* — We have adopted both the Advanced and First Courses in our work in this University. I like them better than anything else I have seen in English.

Prof. S. B. Platner, *Adelbert College, Ohio.* — I am using Chardenal's Series with my classes, and am exceedingly well pleased with the books. They are by far the best that I know of for the purpose intended.

Prof. Alcée Fortier, *Tulane University, New Orleans.* — I find the books excellent, and well suited to give to the pupil a *practical,* as well as a theoretical, knowledge of the language.

Prof. Karcher, *Royal Military Academy, Woolwich.* — Le recueil d'exercices publié par M. Chardenal répond parfaitement, selon moi, au but que l'auteur se propose. . . . En un mot, ces exercices apprendront aux élèves à parler français, au lieu de se servir de phrases littéralement traduites de l'anglais.

Prof. Ch. Cassal, LL.D., *University College, London.* — Je puis vous dire en toute sincérité, que vous avez fait un travail bon et utile. Le recueil d'expressions idiomatiques est excellent et ferait à lui seul le succès de votre livre.

BENNETT'S LATIN BOOKS.

By GEORGE L. BENNETT, M.A.,

Head Master of the High School, Plymouth, Eng., formerly Assistant Master at Rugby School.

I. Easy Latin Stories for Beginners. With Vocabulary and Notes. 16mo. 70 cts.

The aim of this book is to supply easy stories illustrating the elementary principles of the Simple and Compound Sentence. It is intended to be used either as a First Reader, introductory to Cæsar, or for READING AT SIGHT, for both of which purposes it is admirably adapted. The stories are various and amusing, and it is hoped the notes will be found careful and judicious.

II. First Latin Writer. Comprising Accidence, the easier Rules of Syntax, illustrated by copious examples and Progressive Exercises in Elementary Latin Prose, with Vocabularies. 16mo. 90 cts.

"The book is a perfect model of what a Latin Writer should be, and is so graduated that from the beginning of a boy's classical course it will serve him throughout as a text-book for Latin Prose Composition."

III. First Latin Exercises. Containing all the Rules, Exercises, and Vocabularies of the FIRST LATIN WRITER, but omitting the Accidence. 16mo. 70 cts.

IV. Second Latin Writer. Containing Hints on Writing Latin Prose, with graduated continuous Exercises. 16mo. 90 cts.

Intended for those who have already mastered the elementary rules of Latin Prose, this book contains hints on the difference between English and Latin in idiom and in style, some notes on the commoner difficulties, and a table of differences of idiom. The Three Hundred Exercises are fresh and interesting, and give ample room for selection.

MOSS'S FIRST GREEK READER.

With Introduction, Notes, and Vocabulary, by Professor CHARLES M. Moss, Wesleyan University, Illinois. 16mo, 160 pages. Revised edition. 70 cents.

It is the aim of the author to furnish a Greek book for beginners which shall be simple and interesting, and at the same time contain a large number of such words, phrases, and idioms as are of frequent occurrence in Attic Greek. There has for some time been a demand for such a book, to precede the Anabasis, which is of uneven difficulty, and which is quite apt, when read slowly by a beginner, to grow very tedious.

The book contains no disconnected sentences. It consists of a series of carefully graduated exercises for translation, beginning with the simplest stories, and ending with extracts adapted from Xenophon, Herodotus, and Lucian. The text is preceded by valuable hints on translation, and followed by notes and a complete vocabulary.

It is believed that the time spent in reading this book, before taking up any Greek author for consecutive study, will be more than saved in the subsequent rapid progress of the pupil.

This book was on publication immediately adopted for use in : —

Phillips Exeter Academy ; St. Paul's School, Concord, N. H. Roxbury Latin School, Boston; Academy at Worcester, Mass. Lawrenceville School, N. J. ; Webb's Classical School, Tenn. ;

In the preparatory departments of: —
Muhlenberg, Geneva, and Swarthmore Colleges, Pa. Oberlin and Adelbert Colleges and Wooster University, Ohio., State University and Hanover College, Indiana. Lake Forest University and Ewing College, Illinois. State University and Ripon College, Wisconsin. ;

In the High Schools of : —
Bangor, Me. ; Portsmouth and Dover, N. H. Fall River, Mass. ; Binghamton, New York. Newark, N. J. ; Washington, D. C. ;

In the Normal Schools at : —
Cortland and Geneseo, N. Y. ; Normal, Ill. ;

and in many other seminaries of high standing.

PROFESSOR PENNELL'S TEXT-BOOKS.

Ancient Greece, from the Earliest Times down to 146 B.C. By R. F. PENNELL, Professor of Latin in Phillips-Exeter Academy. With Maps and Plans. 16mo. 130 pages. 60 cents.

Rome, from the Earliest Times down to 476 A.D. 16mo. 206 pages. 60 cents.

These books are compiled respectively from the works of Curtius and Rawlinson, and from Mommsen and Niebuhr. They contain amply sufficient matter to prepare a pupil for any of our colleges. All minor details are, however, omitted, thus avoiding a confused mass of matter so perplexing to every beginner. Important events, names, and dates are printed in **heavy type,** strongly impressing them upon the student's memory.

Professor GEORGE R. GEAR, *Marietta College, Ohio.* — I regard Professor Pennell's "Ancient Greece" and "Rome" as capital compendiums, preserving admirably, not merely the dry bones, but the juicy meat of larger works.

Professor O. HOWES, *Madison University, Hamilton, N. Y.* — It is an excellent summary of Roman history, — a difficult task well performed.

Rev. MARTIN E. CADY, *Poultney, Vt.* — It is by far the best compendium of Roman history that I have seen for classes in academies.

Professor W. M. JEFFERIS, *Delaware College.* — It is a most judicious epitome of Greek history, containing just those salient points about which all the minor events naturally group themselves. Teachers and pupils will rejoice to be free from Smith's maze of petty names and events.

A. P. PEABODY, D.D., *Harvard University.* — I know of no other compend of Roman Geography and History so well fitted for students in the early stages of a classical education. In addition to its worth as a school book, it is of no little value as a reference book for the leading names, dates, and facts of Roman history.

The Latin Subjunctive. A Manual for Preparatory Schools. By Professor R. F. PENNELL. 16mo. Sewed. 56 pages. 25 cents.

Professor W. L. THRELKELD, *Kentucky University, Lexington, Ky.* — It is the best elementary manual of the Latin Subjunctive that can be placed in the hands of a beginner.

T. B. MACKEY, *Gouverneur, N. Y.* — I believe it to be the best work on the subject for preparatory schools. The hand of the experienced teacher is discernible throughout. The classification of conditional sentences is especially to be commended.

www.ingramcontent.com/pod-product-compliance
Lightning Source LLC
Chambersburg PA
CBHW020102030726
47498CB00006B/1912